ROUGH DIAMONDS

GILLIAN GODDEN

Boldwood

First published in Great Britain in 2022 by Boldwood Books Ltd.

Copyright © Gillian Godden, 2022

Cover Photography: depositphotos

Every effort has been made to obtain the necessary permissions with reference to copyright material, both illustrative and quoted. We apologise for any omissions in this respect and will be pleased to make the appropriate acknowledgements in any future edition.

A CIP catalogue record for this book is available from the British Library.

Paperback ISBN 978-1-80280-076-0

Large Print ISBN 978-1-80280-077-7

Hardback ISBN 978-1-80280-075-3

Ebook ISBN 978-1-80280-079-1

Kindle ISBN 978-1-80280-078-4

Audio CD ISBN 978-1-80280-070-8

MP3 CD ISBN 978-1-80280-071-5

Digital audio download ISBN 978-1-80280-073-9

Boldwood Books Ltd
23 Bowerdean Street
London SW6 3TN
www.boldwoodbooks.com

Thanks to Sue for being there.

1

THE PROPOSAL

The peeling plastered walls, painted white to brighten them up, made Patsy Diamond shudder. Prison would be anyone's nightmare, she was sure of that. It made her skin crawl.

She heard the lock in the door and the jangle of keys, and the warder entered. A line of women followed behind. It was hard to find who she was looking for; they all looked the same in their prison uniforms. Patsy watched as small children ran towards some of them, shouting 'Mummy!' Some were holding painted pictures they had done specially for the day, but no one seemed particularly happy to be there. It was a sombre place and although the prisoners would look forward to this break in routine, the conversation would be minimal and heart-breaking for both parties.

Swallowing hard and glancing around, Patsy lit a cigarette. She felt nervous and checked herself in the mirror of her compact, brushing a wisp of her hair from her face.

At last, at the end of the queue, she saw who she was looking for and beckoned to her, trying to catch her eye. The young, sullen woman with her swollen stomach walked towards her and folded her arms. She had a stubborn, bored look on her face. Very much like a teenager who had been grounded for a week.

'What do you want Patsy? You've written to me for weeks wanting this visiting order. Have you come for a good laugh at my expense? Well don't bother – I feel shit enough as it is!'

'Sit down Natasha, take the weight off your feet, and don't cause a scene because that lot will send you back to your cell. I got you a cup of tea.' Patsy pushed forward the cup in front of her. 'I got you some chocolate as well – you need to keep your strength up.'

Although Natasha's stance was defensive, Patsy could see straight through the façade. Natasha was putting on a brave face, not only for herself but for the other prisoners staring at her expensively-dressed visitor, who clearly wasn't from social services.

Looking down at the tea and chocolate bar, Natasha pursed her lips and glanced at the prison warder standing in the corner.

'Sit down Natasha and stop being so prickly. At least drink your tea.' Rolling her eyes at the ceiling, Patsy took a drag on her cigarette and stubbed it out in the ashtray.

'You know, you should smoke it all. The women in here would sell their souls for that half cigarette you're wasting.' Dragging the chair from underneath the table, Natasha sat down, picked up the now cool tea and took a sip. 'Why are you here Patsy? Why would you even *want* to come here? I was having an affair with your husband, so I know you hate me and want me to suffer and believe me, you've got your wish!' Looking down, she reached for the chocolate bar and quickly ripped it open and took a bite, half closing her eyes as she savoured the chocolate taste.

Patsy looked the young woman in front of her up and down. She could understand why Nick Diamond, Patsy's late husband, had found Natasha attractive, but seeing her now, with a black eye that was turning yellow and her unkempt and unwashed natural blonde hair pulled back into a pony tail, concerned Patsy. She hadn't come here today to scold Natasha or humiliate her. She wanted her help and maybe she could help Natasha in return.

'You look like you enjoyed that; do you want another?' A faint smile crossed Patsy's face. She felt like an older sister or mother figure to this poor young mite. 'When is your court case up? You've been in custody for quite a few months now, have they set a date yet?' Tentatively enquiring, Patsy was building up to her next proposal. She knew it wouldn't go down well, but it was worth mentioning.

'Two weeks,' Natasha said, licking the chocolate off her fingers. 'I've been here for four months Patsy, you know that. I wasn't even allowed to go to Nicky's funeral because I'm not a family member. How can I not be a family member when I'm carrying his baby?' She glared and pouted once more.

'No one asked me about that. But maybe it was for the best.' Patsy's voice was low and level. She showed no emotion at Natasha's words, although they made her wince inside. The truth was, they hurt like hell. After fifteen years of marriage to Nick, Patsy realised now it had all been a lie: his trips to Scotland supposedly to see his nana, when in actual fact he had been meeting this young woman – his lover. The very woman who he was going to leave Patsy for. It seemed like they had their whole life ahead of them and everything had been going his way as always, until that Christmas night when someone had shot him dead outside the community centre that bore the Diamond name. The police were still investigating the shooting and Patsy had already been questioned many times as the wronged wife.

Taking a deep sigh and putting on a brave face, Patsy tried to put all that to the back of her mind for now. But who had killed

Nick Diamond? The question still hung in the air and on people's lips. There were no witnesses as far as they knew. It was all a complete mystery. Pulling herself together and remembering why she was here, Patsy continued.

'Have you heard anything about your son? Jimmy, is it?' Frowning, Patsy waited for an answer.

'His foster carer sends me photos and stuff. He's having some form of counselling, but personally I think they're making it worse reminding him about that awful day all of the time. He still doesn't know what he's done and feels he's being punished because he can't live with me. He doesn't understand.'

Tears brimmed in Natasha's eyes and she quickly brushed them away and looked around the room to see if any of the other prisoners had noticed. Natasha's bottom lip trembled and she moved closer to Patsy for privacy.

'He's a little boy. He thought it was just a game of Cowboys and Indians when he shot Steve, but how could he have known that the gun was real? They had played that game so many times. It was an accident – pure and simple and now' – Natasha looked down at the table and rubbed her swollen stomach – 'now, he's in foster care with strangers. I don't know when I'll see him again. He's being punished for an accident, Patsy. A bloody accident.'

Playing for time, Patsy got up and bought a chocolate bar for Natasha. Her gut instinct told her Natasha was having a hard time in prison, or worse, being bullied. She was pale and as thin as a sparrow, apart from her pregnant belly, and it looked as though she hadn't eaten in weeks. Of course, above everything else, was Natasha's tell-tale black eye.

Natasha looked around the room as she waited for Patsy to come back. People were casting glances towards her and whispering to each other. She knew they were talking about her. Time and time again she had been taunted and bullied over her little

Jimmy being a murderer. Some even went so far as to say she had stitched her own kid up for a murder she had committed. These past few months had been hell in prison and being pregnant didn't stop the bullies. It was pretty obvious to her when they cast their furtive glances towards her and Patsy Diamond that they had a whole new piece of gossip. Who was that well-dressed woman? Patsy had well and truly thrown the cat amongst the pigeons now and they would all want to know who she was. Thankfully, the short time she had spent in care homes had prepared Natasha for the prison regime; all institutions were the same. Holding her hand out for the chocolate, she started ripping open the sweet wrapper and putting the chocolate in her mouth.

Natasha put her elbows on the table and rested her chin on her hands. 'You still haven't said why you're here Patsy. What do you want from me? The small talk and the chocolates are all very nice but can we just get this over with?' Even though the sugar rush was making her feel better, she was still curious and nervous as to why Patsy was here.

Now faced with what she had said so many times in her head, Patsy felt nervous. She didn't want Natasha to start screaming and shouting, and considering the number of listening ears in the room, she had to be careful about what she said.

'The police are still investigating Nick's death. They are no wiser than they were four months ago, but they are now digging into Nick's past to see if he had any enemies that might cast a light on his murder. I don't know where his money is.' Patsy lowered her voice so it was barely above a whisper. 'If the police find it they will keep it and it will all go to the government for ill-gotten gains or something. There, I've said it.' Patsy threw her hands up in the air and shrugged.

'And you think Nicky has left me all of his money or some-thing? You've come here for money?' Pushing her chair back,

Natasha was going to stand up and leave when Patsy grabbed her arm, stopping her. She had expected this outburst.

'Who's going to look after your baby Natasha? Is that what you want, another kid taken into care?' Patsy hissed.

'No touching!' The warder shouted towards them and Patsy pulled away, waiting for Natasha to say something.

Natasha's eyebrows furrowed. 'I'm hoping the same foster carer who has Jimmy will take it in, so that they can be together. I don't know. I could face another year in here for possession of a firearm. They're even suggesting that I had the intent to kill Steve and set Jimmy up to do it. But I didn't set him up Patsy, I swear!' Her eyes swam with tears. 'I wouldn't use my own son to do something like that. I liked Steve. I was good friends with his wife Sheila; I had no gripe with them.' Natasha's lips trembled and she fought to hold back the tears as her emotions got the better of her.

'I know, love.' Soothingly, Patsy patted her hand while casting a glance at the prison warder, waiting for a reprimand, but none came.

'What do you care anyway?' Confused, Natasha pulled away again. 'You say you want Nick's money. Well, I'm sorry Patsy, I can't help you.'

'Yes, you can Natasha, but you just don't know it yet. Has anyone else visited you while you've been here?'

'Maggie's been a couple of times, even brought Beryl with her once, but it's quite a trek here from Glasgow and Beryl is no spring chicken. Anyway, the conversation is a bit one-sided. They can't exactly ask me what I've been doing can they? And I really don't want to hear how well everyone is getting on without me and who's moved into my flat. I'm homeless now. I presume you know that; you seem to have done your homework.'

'Something like that, but I wouldn't expect them to keep your flat. They don't know how long you're going to be here and I presume the council want their rent. You were in care weren't you?' Patsy had got snippets of Natasha's background from Beryl, but nothing of any importance. She was a waif and stray who had clung to Nick like a limpet. Maybe she had thought he was going to be her knight in shining armour, Patsy mused to herself while looking directly at Natasha. They had both shared the same man and as far as Patsy was concerned, they had both been used by Nick in some form or other. Nick had changed dramatically over the last few years. Patsy had hardly recognised him from the charming young man she had met and married. He had always been vain and selfish, but he had become cold and cruel in the latter years of their marriage.

'Bloody hell Patsy, you've covered everything. Why ask me all these questions when you seem to know all the answers?'

'Just an outline love, take the sulky look off your face. No wonder whoever is giving you that black eye feels like giving you another one. Lighten up lady, your fairy godmother is here. I want you to sign the baby over to me, tell them I'm long lost family or something. You can keep it in here with you for a while, but then what?' Holding the palms of her hands open wide, Patsy knew she was making it sound worse than it probably would be, but Natasha had become another statistic. 'Who is going to give you a job with a prison record?'

'Is that what you've come for? You want Nick's baby – you bitch!' Natasha screamed. 'You couldn't have his child and now you want mine. No! No! I'll never sign it over to you, you scheming bitch.' Natasha was becoming almost hysterical at the bombshell Patsy had dropped and reaching across the table, Natasha slapped Patsy's face. Instantly, the prison warders came over and pulled Natasha away. 'She wants my fucking baby!'

Natasha screamed and struggled, as the warders pushed her through the door and presumably back to her cell.

Smarting, and rubbing the side of her face where Natasha had slapped her, Patsy picked up her handbag under the watchful stares of the other prisoners and their families and calmly made for the door. 'Don't stare at me ladies, I'm free to walk out.' She gave her bravest smile and waited for the warder to open the door for her. Her heart sank as she headed for her car. Maybe she had gone in a bit strong, but visiting time wasn't long and she had to say what she needed to say. But it had all come out wrong, she accepted that. When she got home she would write to Natasha and explain that having the baby live with her until she got out of prison was her only intention.

In her mind's eye, she had thought it would give Natasha some kind of comfort, knowing her baby would be looked after and that she would have easy access to it when she came out of prison. She had thought it would be a peace offering, not a threat.

'Damn! Damn! Damn you, Patsy Diamond!' She hit the dashboard of the car with her hand. 'You stupid cow!' Starting the car, she headed for the motorway and back to London. She needed answers and fast. Where was Nick's money? It was nowhere to be found and she knew there were millions of pounds hidden somewhere. Someone had to know where it was, but who?

Her mind was working overtime as she sped along the motorway in her open-top sports car. Natasha was the link, she knew that. She just had to reach her. Catching sight of herself in the rear-view mirror, Patsy pushed her designer sunglasses on top of her dark hair and compared her made-up, ageing face to Natasha's young, smooth one. She was thirty-seven years old, over ten years older than Natasha. Nick had been flattered by the attentions of the younger woman and had visions of a new life with his mistress and baby. It saddened Patsy, but not as much as it should have done. Her marriage had been over long before herself and Nick had cared to admit it. They had plodded along for the sake of their social circle and status. She'd loved Nick and at some time he'd loved her, or rather she hoped he had. Otherwise, it would have been nothing but wasted years and a wasted life.

Over the last few years Nick had laundered hundreds of thousands of pounds through her salons, but no money had come to the salons over the last few months. Patsy had known the money must have something to do with drugs but had stupidly turned a blind eye. She hadn't been afraid of Nick, but she had shut up and put up. So where was that money going to now? Who was creaming it off the top? Everyone knew she was Nick Diamond's wife and yet no one had approached her. Her only solution was that she would have to find out who was involved and claim what was rightfully hers. Nick's grandmother, Beryl, had kept a very low profile since the funeral. So why had the old woman raised her ugly head and visited Natasha? Where this journey would take her, Patsy didn't have a clue, but she was determined to find out!

2

THE INHERITANCE

'Well? How did it go? You look shattered Patsy, let me get you a drink.' Victoria Diamond walked over to the drinks' cabinet and poured Patsy a brandy. She had waited all day for some contact from Patsy and none had come, and she could only presume things hadn't gone well.

Instead of going home to her London apartment, Patsy had decided to drive to Dorset to Nick's mother; she didn't feel like being on her own tonight. Kicking off her shoes, she accepted the drink and laid back on the sofa. She was indeed tired from the driving, but her mind was still alert.

'As we expected Victoria; she doesn't want to know. Maybe you should have gone; after all, you are that child's grandmother. You've certain rights to see it grow up, don't you? I'm sure a good solicitor would fight your corner given the circumstances.' Patsy was all out of ideas. Visiting Natasha had been her last hope.

'I spoke to Nick's accountant, and he thinks we should sell the community centre in Glasgow before the price drops. Only the weirdos and ghouls seem to visit there these days. After all, a man was shot outside of it; it doesn't represent the happy place it was supposed to be. Did you go?'

'No. I really can't face seeing it again. I'm not ready.' Patsy thought about Nick's beloved community centre in all of its splendour. The Diamond Centre. His nana had been so proud that he had renovated it into a place where the local residents could meet, play bingo and hopefully get the young hooligans off the streets. Instead, it had been Nick's drug den. A smoke screen. A place people frequented to sell their wares without knowing Nick was the feared local gangster the Undertaker, and the man they all worked for. On the face of it he was a respectable lawyer who had enjoyed playing games with the Glasgow residents and not one of them knew Nick Diamond and the Undertaker were the same man. Patsy almost wanted to laugh out loud, but thought better of it. After all, Nick had been laughing at them all for years.

'The accountant has done the sums. Although there was a grant for funding, there aren't as many people using it, especially as the police have been constantly crawling all over it – it puts people off. Beryl is still trying to hang on to it, but the accountant is insistent it will just be another millstone around our necks. He says he told Nick it was a bad investment, but we own the land and that should count for something... surely?'

'What? In that area,' Patsy scoffed and gulped back her drink, holding her glass out for a refill. 'Who the bloody hell would want to buy that dump Victoria? It's in a slum area and even the council had given up on it. After Nick's murder, they would only offer a pittance of what it's worth. If it can fund itself for the time being, I think we should let it carry on for now. Maybe when all of this blows over we might get a better price.' Patsy was adamant she wasn't going to sell the community centre. If anything, her gut instinct told her it was the key to the information she wanted. Nick hadn't bought that place as a charitable act, she was sure of that, but why had he ploughed so much money into it?

'Maybe this is a wild goose chase Patsy. After all, there are no answers and the police have no clues. Everyone around that area is keeping their mouths closed. We've all been interviewed time and time again and according to the police we all had motives for wanting to kill Nick. I'm sick of being dragged down to that police station while they interrogate me about my relationship with Nick. Don't they realise I've just lost my son?' Tears brimmed on Victoria's eyelashes. It had been a hard few months and she hadn't had time to properly grieve Nick's death.

'What about me! I'm the jealous wife with a gun in my pocket. They've already got me locked up and thrown away the bloody key Victoria. All they want is evidence. They want to know why I turned up that night out of the blue. Well, like I told them, why the bloody hell shouldn't I? No, there is more to this Victoria and I know we're going to open a big can of worms and find a Nick neither of us really knew. Where did he get all that money from? I would say it's pretty obvious he was dealing drugs; no one has that amount of money in cash lying around on a regular basis. You've already told me about that Billy guy. There's a connection, we just don't have the rest of the jigsaw puzzle yet. If the police dig up that information then they will claim all of the money they find, possibly even the community centre too. Anything in Nick's name can be claimed as drug money. Thankfully the apartment and my salons are in my name, but if there is any link whatsoever to Nick, I could lose everything. Absolutely anyone in that centre could have killed Nick that night. He was a selfish bastard!' Patsy spat out.

Billy Burke seemed to do nothing but ruin people's lives.

Victoria wished she had never told Nick about Billy, one of the worst criminals in Glasgow who ruled people by fear and drugs. She felt it was all her fault. Billy had date raped her while she was drugged and the result had been Nick. She had kept it a secret for so many years, but, when she found out that Nick was going to represent this man in court she felt bound to tell him the truth. He couldn't represent him; he was Billy Burke's son. Instead, Nick had joined forces with him and became the man on the outside in charge of the prostitution, racketeering and of course, the drug dealing. Nick had been drawn to him like a moth to a flame and it hadn't ended well for either of them. They were both dead now.

Victoria looked sharply at Patsy. 'You are in this as much as he was Patsy. You were laundering the money and you didn't do too badly from it. Is that all you care about, your bloody salons? You're a very rich woman thanks to Nick, and don't ever call my son a bastard!'

Holding her hands up in submission, Patsy nodded. 'Sorry Victoria, I'm just tired. Yes, I'm a rich woman for now, but we don't know how long this has been going on for. We have to stick together Victoria. We both need answers. Forgive me.' Patsy was genuine in her apology and standing up, she went and sat by Victoria on the sofa and put her arm around the other woman. Glancing at Victoria, she thought she had aged very quickly over the last few months. Her once perfect appearance had become dishevelled. Her face seemed constantly puffy from crying and it was as if she had simply given up. 'Think about it. When we find the money, we find the killer. The two are connected, I'm sure of it.' Patsy's soothing voice seemed to comfort Victoria and she watched her brush a tear from her eye.

'If you say so Patsy, but it's not just about the money. It's for Nick. Whatever he was up to, he didn't deserve that did he?'

Victoria wasn't sure. She had tossed and turned each night since his death. She liked to think of Nick as an innocent victim, but something inside her told her he wasn't. People who dealt with drugs usually ended up in some kind of fight or death. She watched the news; there were stories all the time about people like that. She just didn't want to think of her son being one of those people. 'Come on, you go to bed Patsy, you've had a long day.'

'What about you. You need to rest as well.' Patsy was concerned about Victoria. She didn't want her despair leading into something more. She was depressed, but it had even crossed her mind she could be suicidal. Patsy felt guilty about not feeling the same way. She was more angry than sad. If Nick had just confided in her a little more, then maybe she would have answers to the questions plaguing her, like who had killed Nick and, more importantly, who would be next?

Her apartment in London had been ransacked. She hadn't reported it because nothing was missing, well, nothing that she was aware of. But they had emptied drawers and cupboards and had even taken the skirting boards off, which was how she knew it wasn't a normal burglary. Someone was looking for something and she didn't know if they had found it. But someone knew something and they were afraid of it being uncovered. Would she be the next person with a bullet in her chest? Patsy was frightened. Any one of them could be a walking target.

'I don't sleep much these days, I just rest here on the sofa. Go on, I'll be fine.' Raising a smile, Victoria waved her hand towards Patsy, ushering her out of the room.

Yawning and feeling quite heady from the brandy, Patsy went to bed, leaving a forlorn Victoria behind her, idly staring at the flames on the log burner, as though hypnotised by them.

* * *

Patsy stayed with Victoria for a couple of days but seeing her in her numb state only depressed her even more. She had just one last thing to do before she returned to London. Driving to the local cemetery in Dorset, Patsy got out and went to Nick's grave. It didn't have a headstone yet. It hadn't been that long since his body had been released by the police and Victoria had been allowed to arrange a funeral. Laying a bunch of flowers on the grave, Patsy stared at it.

'Who did it Nick? You didn't trust me enough to tell me, did you? Did I mean nothing to you after all these years?' These were all the questions she yearned to ask him, but it was too late. 'Don't rest in peace Nick, I'm not done with you yet. You owe me answers and I'll get them. You can fucking rot in hell.'

Walking away, Patsy brushed angry tears from her eyes.

Mentally she had scanned everyone who had come to Dorset that day for the funeral. Any one of those who had attended could have been his killer. She had warned Victoria not to put when and where the service would be held on social media. She had found it strange when an unknown visitor had watched Victoria throw a bunch of roses on top of Nick's coffin and had then thrown a black Frisbee on top of it. No one had questioned it at the time. It had been an emotional day, but she knew now that she had to find that man and ask him what the message behind the Frisbee was.

No sooner had she unlocked the many safety locks on her new front door and switched off the alarm in her apartment than her telephone rang.

'Mrs Diamond?' the male voice on the end of the phone enquired. When she acknowledged them, they carried on. 'I'm the governor of the prison where Natasha Richards is staying. She has asked me to inform you that she has been taken to hospital with stomach cramps, spotting of blood and there is a chance the baby could be born prematurely or worse...'

Stunned, Patsy said, 'Can I come and visit her?'

'Yes, I could arrange that.' After giving Patsy more details about the hospital Natasha had been taken to, they ended the call.

Lighting a cigarette, Patsy was consumed with concern and guilt. Had her visit brought on this upset and caused Natasha to miscarry? Taking a deep sigh, she picked up her car keys. She would pick up a sandwich from one of the local service stations on the motorway. Bloody hell, she thought to herself as she set the alarm again. All she seemed to be doing these days was roaming the countryside like a bloody nomad!

It was evening when Patsy arrived in Edinburgh. It had been a better drive than expected and being spring, the nights were lighter and lasted longer, which made it easier. Once she had cleared security she was allowed to see Natasha, albeit only for a few minutes as it was so late.

Natasha was in a side room and she looked pale and tired. As soon as Patsy walked into the room she started to cry. 'I'm losing it Patsy! I'm losing my baby,' she sobbed.

Sitting in the chair at the side of her bed, Patsy held the younger woman's hand. 'Everything will be fine Natasha. What you need is rest. Don't upset yourself, I'm here now.' Her calming voice soothed her like a baby and she handed her a tissue from her handbag.

Sniffing and blowing her nose, Natasha wiped her face with her hands. 'Help me Patsy. I know I shouldn't ask but I need your help.' Her voice wobbled as she spoke and she gave a sideways glance at the warder sat at the other side of the bed.

'I'll do whatever I can Natasha. You just name it. But no more nonsense about losing your baby.'

Natasha bowed her head and played with her hands on the bedsheets. 'I've decided I'd like to sign my baby over to you. I spoke to a lawyer and he doesn't sound too optimistic about my court case. I don't know what will happen to my baby, possibly foster care.' Again she started to cry and tears rolled down her face.

'Stop it Natasha!' Patsy felt the softly softly approach wasn't working. It was time to take control of the situation. 'You've to remain calm and think of your baby. We can sort everything out, it's not a problem. That baby is a Diamond and Nick's mother will want to meet her new grandchild. Were you ever introduced to Victoria?' Patsy felt bringing Victoria into the equation might make things easier for Natasha to get her head around.

It obviously worked, because instantly, Natasha wiped away her tears with the screwed up tissue she was holding. 'I met her at the opening of the community centre. Just briefly though. Does she know about my baby?' Roused with curiosity, Natasha squeezed Patsy's hand and gave a faint smile. Her pale face was red from crying, but suddenly she had hope.

'Of course she does Natasha. That little person in there is her grandchild. I know for a fact she wouldn't want it going to anyone else but family. We're all family Natasha, in some form or another. We're Diamonds.'

'I'm not a Diamond though.' Natasha looked from under her eyelashes at Patsy.

'You're our rough diamond. You are having Nick's baby and that baby is blood to Victoria.'

'You speak very posh Patsy.' Natasha smiled, her own Scottish accent reminding her of the gulf between them.

Feeling quite sorry for her Patsy smiled back. Natasha

sounded almost childish. 'I've just had different opportunities Natasha.'

A nurse walked into the room and looked at her watch. 'You'll have to leave now and come back in the morning.' She wasn't rude or offensive, but she had a job to do and her main concern was Natasha and keeping her blood pressure down.

'I'll come back tomorrow. I'm going to book into a hotel nearby. When I know which one I'll ring and tell the nurses in case you need me. I'll leave them my mobile number on the way out. Get some sleep love.' Without thinking, Patsy kissed the top of Natasha's head and left.

Once outside, Patsy reached for her cigarettes in her handbag and lit one. Taking a huge drag and blowing out the smoke with a huge sigh, she welcomed the warm breeze in the dark night. This was all a mess. People would think she was crazy! She knew she should be wishing the worst on Natasha but this situation wasn't her or the baby's fault and she couldn't help feeling some empathy for Natasha.

Looking at her watch, Patsy saw that it was getting late; she needed to find somewhere to stay.

The hotel she found had plenty of rooms and Patsy ignored their stares when they saw she had no luggage. She was exhausted, emotionally and physically. After visiting the bathroom she opened the mini bar and took out a soft drink, almost gulping it down in one. She lay on top of the bed and must have dozed off, because her mobile ringing woke her.

Sleepily, she looked at the vibrating phone. She didn't recognise the number but answered it anyway. Hearing the ward sister from the hospital say her name suddenly brought Patsy to consciousness. Natasha had gone into labour and they were giving her an emergency caesarean. Dragging herself off the top of the bed, Patsy reached for her jacket and threw a comb through her hair to make it more presentable. Then, once more, she picked up her car keys and left for the hospital. By the time she had got there it was all over and the baby – a boy – was in the intensive care unit.

A boy, Patsy mused. Nick would have liked that. Swallowing hard to fight against her emotions, she went into the room where Natasha was resting. She was little drowsy, but relief seemed to wash over her when she saw Patsy.

'It's a boy Patsy. Have you seen him?' Natasha gave a weak smile. 'Do you think he'll live?' Tears rolled down her cheeks. 'Do you think we should get him baptised? We have to give him a name.' Suddenly she went into panic mode and Patsy stepped forward.

'Shush Natasha. You talk as if your son is dead already. They are working their socks off down there to keep him alive. Give the little bugger a chance will you!'

'Patsy, will you go to the baby unit and take some photos on your mobile phone please. I want to see him.'

'Yes, just stop panicking. The worst is over and he is alive. You've to be strong and get well.'

'Will you take him Patsy? Will you look after him for me?'

'Of course I will. As soon as he's strong enough I'll have him transferred to London, or possibly Dorset with his grandmother. I'll speak to the prison governor and see what paperwork there is to fill in. Stop worrying Natasha, we're here to help you.'

'Why are you being so kind to me? I don't deserve it. I'm sorry about Nicky.'

'Because, young lady, you owe me one. And you will pay me back. I have a favour to ask of you, but not now.' Casting a furtive glance towards the prison warder who was hanging around by the door having a cup of tea, Patsy put her finger to her lips. 'We'll talk soon. Don't worry now. Get some sleep.'

Patsy walked down the corridor to the nurse's reception point. 'Would it be possible to get a glimpse of the baby?' she asked.

The nurse nodded and Patsy followed her to the baby care unit. Her heart was pounding in her chest. This should have been the happiest day of Nick's life. He would have been here with Natasha, pacing the floor like all expectant fathers. Patsy tried to imagine his elation once he had learnt he had a son. She presumed he would have called his mother first and given her the good news. She felt saddened and robbed by the fact she had never shared that experience with Nick. Things could have been so different. On the other hand, given that he had changed so much over the last years, she was secretly pleased they hadn't shared a moment like this. Nick had become mean and ruthless and would only have used their baby as a weapon against her when she'd protested to his money laundering schemes. He would manipulate and charm the child to make it his own. Charming but deadly, that was Nick. Not exactly father of the year.

The tiny little baby, surrounded with tubes and wires, made her smile. He was so small, with his little woolly hat on. The machines above him were helping him breathe. Swallowing hard, she watched this little boy fighting for his life and turned towards the nurse. 'What are his chances?' she asked in a hushed whisper.

'Very good actually,' the nurse enthused. 'He made it to seven months, and he's a good size. But the next forty-eight hours will be crucial.'

Patsy took out her phone and, as promised, took photos of the baby in his incubator with the nurse's permission. 'Thank you for this. I'm sure you must think it's an odd situation,' Patsy said as she turned to leave. She suddenly felt sick to her stomach. This was her husband's baby with another woman and however brave she was, she couldn't help feeling that twinge of hurt. For all her bravado she was still a woman and a wife. Nick had paid the ultimate price for his moment of adultery. But she had other things to think about. She had just inherited his baby after all!

3

BEST LAID PLANS

Patsy had the photos of the baby printed out for Natasha. This way she could keep them whatever happened. Her next job was to telephone Victoria and tell her she was a grandmother. It was a painful experience, hearing Victoria gush and say she would go to Edinburgh straight away. She realised Victoria didn't know how hurtful it was to her; she was wrapped up in baby Diamond world. She had lost her son and now she had been given him back.

'I don't think you should come to Edinburgh Victoria. In fact, I have spoken to Natasha and she is prepared to sign the baby over to you and make you his guardian. Her court case is next week; I don't think they will put it off. I hope not, for her sake; she has waited long enough. What do you think?' The squeal of delight from the other side of the phone stabbed Patsy's heart.

'I would love that Patsy. Just think – Nick's baby is coming home.' Then Victoria faltered. Somewhere in her excitement, Patsy must have crossed her mind. 'I'm sorry Patsy. How do you feel about it? After all, this was your idea?'

'I still think it's a good idea. We will have to make arrangements for him to get to Dorset. But anything's possible. I'm going to go and see that lawyer of Natasha's today. She seems to think he is dragging his feet and can't be bothered, and then I'm going to the prison to see the governor. Speak soon.' Patsy couldn't wait to get off the telephone. She knew Victoria would already be organising some kind of homecoming for baby Diamond and building the biggest nursery she could.

As Patsy walked up the stone steps to the solicitor's office she raised her eyebrows in distaste. The windows weren't washed and the whole front looked unkempt. No wonder Natasha had no faith in this firm.

The receptionist, who sat filing her nails with her bright pink hair tied into a ponytail, didn't instil much confidence either. Her broad Glaswegian accent confused Patsy. She could hardly understand her.

'I'm looking for a solicitor called Larry, is he in?'

The receptionist tapped the computer and then picked up the telephone. Patsy presumed it was to let Larry know someone was here to see him.

A middle-aged man in a cheap, badly-fitting grey suit came into reception and looked at Patsy. 'Do we have an appointment, miss...?'

'Mrs Diamond.' She held out her hand. 'I wish to discuss Natasha Richards' case.'

Frowning, Larry looked around the empty reception with its dusty magazines and lazy receptionist and then back at Patsy. 'Come into my office Mrs Diamond.'

Patsy felt like dusting the wooden chair that he proffered for her to sit on. What the hell was this set up?

'I take it you're Mr Diamond's wife and not his mother,' he laughed, trying to break the ice.

Larry looked at the woman sat opposite him. This was a very

different clientele. She wore a red trouser suit that screamed money. Her white, silk blouse underneath it showed just a touch of cleavage to make him interested. He was intrigued; why would the wronged wife want to discuss the mistress's case?

Clearing his throat, and realising that Patsy wasn't in the mood for jokes, he got down to business. 'You know I cannot discuss my client with you Mrs Diamond. Although I am very sorry about your loss.'

'I know that, Larry the lawyer, so I am going to do the talking and you're going to do the thinking. That is, once you've taken your eyes off my cleavage! Don't fuck with me sonny, I've had a long few days and I'm tired. Now, what are Natasha's chances of getting off? No, stop. I'll start again.' She waved her perfectly manicured red fingernails in the air. She knew he couldn't tell her anything. 'She has just had her baby. She can stay at the hospital for a while, but her case is up next week and I don't want it postponed. Myself and Nick's mother, will be taking guardianship of the baby. I believe Natasha spoke to you about this on your last visit. There will be paperwork and I am going to give you the job of sorting it out. It looks like you could do with the work.' Sarcasm dripped from Patsy's mouth, as she looked around the room with its discarded newspapers and ran her finger along his dusty desk piled high with paperwork. It seemed all the pent up anger and upset she had felt over the last couple of days was spewing out like venom at this clown who called himself a solicitor.

Suddenly taking her seriously, Larry sat upright in his chair and straightened his tie, realising that no matter how feminine this woman looked on the outside, she was like granite on the inside.

'Well, off the record Mrs Diamond, they are still pushing for possession of a weapon, which can carry a sentence of a year, maybe more.' He shrugged. 'They are also saying that she endangered the life of her child by having the gun in the house. Although now Jimmy has had counselling and doesn't feel he is in trouble he has told them he stole the gun from Steve's house, not knowing it was real. Apparently he always played a shoot-out with Steve. So that could go in her favour.'

'Steve?' Patsy couldn't recollect him. 'Who is he?'

'The man who young Jimmy killed. Although it still begs the question why Natasha's fingerprints were on that gun. Why did she just discard it and not say anything to anyone? Was she hiding it for a purpose? I thought you knew all of this Mrs Diamond?' Puzzled, Larry paused. He felt he had said too much.

'Yes, of course. Sorry, it's been a busy few days.' Patsy swept her hair back from her face, feigning tiredness and stress. 'So Jimmy has admitted that he stole the gun? Surely that puts Natasha in the clear?' Patsy paused. 'Do you know where the boy is?' she asked.

'I believe social services have placed him with a good foster family. Why?'

Patsy's mind was working overtime. This indeed was a jumbled mess. It was as though the government wanted to pin this murder on Natasha to show justice was being done. 'I want you to get Jimmy back. Use our family ties if you must. He has a brother now and a grandmother. Surely they should all be together?'

Patsy's smug expression unnerved Larry and a frown crossed his brow. 'That's one angle I suppose, but I don't know if social services would agree to it. There would have to be a lot of supervised visits first.'

'That's okay. So, I have just commissioned you, Larry the lawyer, to get off your arse and stop reading the racing papers. Tell your receptionist to stop filing her nails, especially while a

customer is at the desk. You get on to social services about Jimmy
– he has a home and a family now. Sort out the paperwork
regarding the guardianship with this new baby. And as for the
court case Larry, I'll be there and I expect you to tell your
barrister friend to work his socks off and plead her case. I want
her out, even if it's on compassionate grounds. I don't give a shit.'

'Why do you care what happens to Natasha?'

'That's my business. Now, do we have a deal?'

'Yes, I can arrange your guardianship and find out more about
Jimmy, that's not a problem, but Natasha's freedom is in the
hands of the judge.' He shrugged and threw his own hands into
the air.

Patsy picked up her handbag and stood up. 'It had better not
be Larry. I expect great things from you. Here, take this.' Patsy put
down a wad of notes on his desk. 'There is five hundred pounds
sterling. Use it wisely and get me results. I'll see you in court
Larry.' Patsy turned and walked out of the room, leaving a waft of
expensive perfume behind her.

Larry looked at the money. Smiling, he breathed in her
perfume; this woman meant business and he knew if he did right
by her there would be more to come.

Patsy arranged to meet with the prison governor to tell him of
Natasha's intentions to sign the baby over to its biological grand-
mother. When she arrived, she found him unassuming and
gracious. He was happy to help, given the circumstances. He had
also organised Natasha's social worker to be there to discuss the
matter. Patsy informed them that she would like Jimmy also and
she had already organised a solicitor to start the proceedings.
Patsy had expected more opposition to her proposal, but none

came. They were all in agreement that the family should be kept together. The social worker, a nice lady called Angela, said she would put all of this in her report, but Jimmy would need further counselling and given Natasha's background he would always be under the watchful eye of social services.

'You see Mrs Diamond, there is a factor that I shouldn't disclose to you, but I feel I must. The case against Natasha is strong because as a young teenager she attacked a man by smashing a glass beer bottle and pushing it in his face. There is a history of violence and now she's been caught with a gun in her possession. It doesn't look good, does it? She has quite a temper I'm afraid. I am pleased that there is someone to look out for the new baby and little Jimmy and if you are prepared to do that, believe me it makes my life simpler.' She smiled.

Patsy was stunned by this revelation. 'Are you telling me she already has a record?'

'We like to call it a young offender's institution Mrs Diamond. But yes. Even though Natasha claimed she was acting in self-defence after an attempted rape, which was thrown out of court for lack of evidence, she stayed at the institution for six months.'

Doing her best to hold her composure while they both stared at her, Patsy smiled. She didn't know what else to do. This was a bolt from the blue. 'Thank you for being so honest with me Angela. I had no idea. Rest assured, my mother-in-law will look after those children as though they were her own. Also, I would like it noted that Natasha will have a home there too. That is until she gets on her feet. Make sure you put that in your report.'

Angela and the prison governor cast glances at each other across the table and smiled. This was indeed a strange situation, but this woman was clearly very kind and forgiving, with only the children's welfare at heart. It was nice to know there was still some good people left in the world.

'I understand your urgency Mrs Diamond, but there are checks to be made. The baby won't be going anywhere for a while and Jimmy is settled for now, but I'll do my best believe me.' Angela seemed genuine with her efforts to make everything run smoothly and as quickly as possible. As they all shook hands, Patsy felt that was another job well done. The only thing left to do was take the photos to Natasha and then she could go home.

Natasha seemed to have a little more colour in her face when Patsy arrived.

'I've brought you these Natasha, as promised.' Patsy held out the photos of the baby. 'I'm leaving today, but I'll come back next week for your court case if you like?'

'When do I sign the baby over to you? Have you changed your mind?' Natasha's lips trembled and there was panic in her eyes.

'Hush now and for god's sake, blow your nose. Here, don't you have a handkerchief? Every time I see you there is snot coming from your nose or tears from your eyes. You don't just sign babies away Natasha. There are procedures.' Patsy sighed and rubbed her eyes. 'Everything is in order. You just rest until you feel better. I'll see you next week.' As an afterthought, Patsy asked, 'By the way, do you have Beryl's telephone number?'

Natasha looked vaguely at Patsy. 'Yes, but surely you already have it?'

'You need to call her and tell her she is a great-grandmother.' Turning towards the prison officer standing by the door to Natasha's room, Patsy asked, 'Look, I don't know the protocol here, but the great-grandmother is old and I would like her to know about the baby... just in case...' Patsy trailed off, giving her a knowing look.

The officer nodded. 'I'll make the call and if need be I'll pass the telephone to you Natasha. Is that okay?'

Nodding, Natasha agreed.

'Just one more thing Natasha. Don't tell Beryl I'm here. Got it?'
Again, Natasha nodded.

Patsy smiled. Giving the officer Beryl's number, she waited with bated breath until Beryl answered. The officer checked who Beryl was and promptly told her the good news. She also informed her about the caesarean and that the baby was in intensive care. Kindly she gave Natasha her mobile. 'Say hello love and let her know you're okay,' the officer said, smiling.

'Hi Beryl, yes, I'm okay. I just wanted you to know. He's very premature.' She paused while Beryl said something on the other end. 'Maybe, but not for long. They don't want a lot of people in the baby unit.'

After a few more moments, Natasha said her goodbyes then ended the call.

Patsy didn't want Beryl knowing anything. Nick's grandmother couldn't keep her big mouth shut; she had learnt that in the past. The last thing she wanted was for the whole of that estate knowing she and Natasha were involved with each other. Patting Natasha's knee, like she would a small child, Patsy waved and left the room. She felt a little guilty about the smug satisfaction she felt as she walked out of the hospital. Nick would soon have tired of Natasha. She was weak and a limpet. He would have loved her adoration in the beginning, but he would soon have got bored with her. That she was sure of.

Driving through the night, Patsy felt better. The weather was still warm and there was hardly any traffic on the motorway. She needed to get back to her own life for a while. On the face of it, everything had to appear as normal as possible. She knew the police would be checking up on her and when it came to light she was taking charge of Natasha's children they would want to know why. But what could be more innocent than Victoria, the baby's grandmother, wanting to care for her grandchild? She had a week to gather her thoughts and prepare herself for the court case. In the meantime, she would have to prepare Victoria for any visits she may get from social services. She felt sure that as soon as they saw that mansion she lived in they would agree to her having the children live with her. She definitely wasn't after any kind of benefits. It was all for love and that was what they wanted to know.

Grinning to herself in the rear-view mirror, she knew she had drawn Natasha into her well-oiled plan. Maybe she would let her know how it felt to be stripped of everything you loved. Patience was indeed a virtue and Natasha would soon find out that Patsy had it by the bucket load.

4

GOOD NEWS

Beryl almost fell over her feet running out of the front door to Maggie's house.

'Natasha's had the baby! The prison officer just called me. He's premature and in an incubator,' she blurted out.

A little disgruntled at hearing the news second hand considering her friendship with Natasha, Maggie opened the door wider to let Beryl in.

'So she's had a boy then?' Maggie asked while making her way to the kitchen to put the kettle on.

'Yes!' Beryl clapped her hands together. 'I asked if we could go and visit and they said yes, but only a short one. He's not well.' Saddened by her own words, the happiness disappeared from Beryl's face. 'Do you think he'll survive?'

'If he's like his dad then, yes. He's a Diamond and they're fighters. He was just eager to come into the world and I doubt Natasha has been well looked after in that prison. When are you going?' Maggie probed. She wanted to ask the question that hung over them both but wanted it to come from Beryl.

As though reading her thoughts, Beryl chirped, 'Do you want to come with me?'

Relief washed over Maggie. She hadn't wanted to push the issue but was pleased that Beryl had asked her. Her smile was as broad as her face. 'I would love to Beryl. Thank you. Now let's have some tea and you can tell me what Natasha said.'

Once Beryl had talked her ears off, Maggie went to see Sheila. She felt it was only fair that the woman heard the news from her. Knocking on Sheila's door, Maggie felt pensive. It would hardly be good news to Sheila's ears; after all, Natasha's son had shot her husband Steve. Now a widow, Sheila had two daughters to feed and only a pittance of money through benefits.

Time and time again, Sheila had wished Natasha in hell. Why would a mother have a loaded gun in her home near her child? What kind of irresponsible mother was she?

'Hi Maggie, what can I do for you?' Opening the door wider, Sheila stood to one side to let Maggie in.

'I just want a word with you.' Sitting down on the sofa in the lounge, Maggie swallowed. 'Natasha has had her baby and I wanted you to hear it before the jungle drums started banging. I'm surprised Beryl hasn't shouted it from the balconies that she's a great-grandmother.' Maggie gave a weak smile.

'So she's had another killer kid has she? What makes you think I would be interested? I hope she rots in hell. She and that kid of hers have ruined my family!'

'Well, whatever fire and damnation you wish on her it has worked. The baby is in a critical condition by all accounts. It's premature and it must be bad because the prison officer is letting Beryl go and see it. It was a tragic accident Sheila. There was no malice.'

Sheila's face paled and she sat down on the chair opposite Maggie. 'I wouldn't wish any woman to lose her child Maggie, you know that. But I'm sure you understand how bitter I feel. There has been no justice for my Steve.'

Frowning, Maggie shook her head. She felt angry and it was in her maternal instinct to protect Natasha, especially now when she would be at her lowest ebb. 'I do understand, but you're wrong Sheila. You want justice you say... well, here is justice for you. Natasha has spent four months in a miserable prison because she took her eyes off Jimmy for a few minutes. He has been taken away and is living god knows where. I still wonder how Jimmy got that gun; it's not as though he found it on the floor or in a supermarket. He only went into my house and Beryl's, and of course yours...' Maggie dropped the bombshell that had been playing on her mind for months. Seeing Sheila's face turn ashen told her what she felt she already knew. 'We'll find out soon enough though, won't we? Natasha is in court next week; maybe the police have uncovered just where Jimmy found that gun.' Raising one eyebrow, Maggie looked directly into Sheila's eyes.

'You think it was Steve's gun? You think he was shot by his own illegal gun, don't you?' Sheila's voice was calm, although it wobbled slightly.

'Who knows love, but he was having a hard time on that moped doing pizza deliveries. Maybe it was just a little added protection for him?'

'If social services think I had a gun in my house, they will take the girls away, I'm sure of it.' Sheila burst into tears. She was afraid. 'At least when Steve was in prison I knew where he was and that one day he would come back, but he's never coming back now. And look at this, it came this morning.' Sheila stood up and took an envelope off the mantelpiece and waved it under Maggie's nose.

Confused, Maggie opened it. It was from the local council.

'They are offering you a terraced house in Edinburgh? Since when?'

'Steve applied for it months ago. He wanted us out of here, a fresh start so to speak. A lot of good that is going to do us now!' Maggie watched as the tears rolled down Sheila's face. She felt it was about time Sheila let out her grief. She had kept it inside for far too long for the sake of the girls.

'If that's what he wanted, why change things now? Maybe a fresh start after all of this would do you good. Think carefully, Sheila; this is an opportunity for you to start again,' Maggie stressed. 'They are asking you to make an appointment to go and view it. Beryl and I are going to Edinburgh tomorrow to see Natasha's baby. Why don't we all go together? A little moral support for you.'

'You think I should go don't you? But what's the point? It was supposed to be for us all as a family.'

'I think you should consider it. You've a chance here to start again, where no one knows about Steve and prison or his killing. You would just be a single mother with two kids. There's nothing strange about that these days. Concoct whatever story you like, it doesn't matter Sheila, but if it were me I would grab this chance with both hands.' Maggie could see Sheila's mind turning over as she listened to her wise words.

'Maybe I could come with you. But I'm not going to see her!' Sheila's voice was barely above a whisper. 'There's no harm in looking I suppose...'

'That's sorted then. And don't be too harsh on Natasha, you were good friends once. Think long and carefully about this opportunity Sheila and don't let pride come before a fall.' Standing up, Maggie took in Sheila's sadness. She hadn't had much luck in her life. Maybe things were about to turn around.

* * *

Beryl was up at the crack of dawn the next morning, knocking on Maggie's door.

Yawning and still in her nightdress, Maggie wrapped her dressing gown around her. She knew it would be Beryl; no one else around here got up that early.

'Are you nearly ready Maggie?' Excitedly, Beryl pushed her way past Maggie and made for the kitchen.

'Beryl, it's six thirty in the morning. Why would I be ready to catch an eleven o'clock train now?' Switching the kettle on, Maggie rolled her eyes at the ceiling. She knew she was going to hear the same stories she had yesterday about how the baby would look and how much she was looking forward to seeing it. It was all Beryl could think of.

'We don't want to be late now. It can take ages getting to the train station, and I'm a bit slow on my feet these days what with my rheumatism.'

'Beryl Diamond! You've been at death's door for the last ten years, and don't come with that rheumatism crap. You're quick on your feet when you want to be,' Maggie snapped. Beryl always played the 'I'm not a well old woman,' when it suited her. It was her trump card.

'Come on Maggie, aren't you the least bit excited?' Beryl fussed while Maggie made the tea. 'It might do you good if you cracked that miserable face of yours and smiled once in a while,' Beryl laughed.

Sitting down to drink their tea, Maggie saw the distaste in Beryl's face at being handed a mug. Beryl was old school and liked a cup and saucer.

Maggie felt this was a good time to mention Sheila was

coming with them. 'She has to go to Edinburgh Beryl, so why travel alone.'

'Because it's all her fault Maggie. Hers and that husband of hers. They were up to something; and let's be honest, neither of them were squeaky clean. Always in debt and running scams. I have a long memory about those two. Well, she had better not play the innocent victim with me or she will get the sharp end of my tongue!'

'Everybody gets the sharp end of your tongue Beryl whether they like it or not.' Maggie rubbed her eyes, then wrapped her hands around her mug of tea to keep them warm. 'She's coming on the train with us and then she has to be somewhere. Believe me,' Maggie scoffed, 'she isn't coming to the hospital to see Natasha. I would say that's the last place on earth she would want to be, given the circumstances.'

Maggie's icy stare seemed to stop Beryl short. It was early and she was in no mood for an argument.

'I'm going to make some toast. And then while I get washed and dressed you can make yourself useful and make some sandwiches for the journey. There's a flask in the cupboard, make some tea too. Those train prices are ridiculous and it's all hot water anyway.'

'Where is Sheila going? What business has she got in Edinburgh?' Beryl asked, suddenly curious. Sheila never ventured far.

'That's her business and if she wants to tell you she will.' Stubbornly, Maggie stuck her chin out and pursed her lips, making the wrinkles more visible. 'Now take off your coat and get cracking.'

A couple of hours later Maggie knocked and waited for Sheila to open the door. Pleasantly surprised, she could see that Sheila had made an effort. Her hair was combed, which was a bonus these days. Some days she spent all day in her pyjamas, but always made sure the girls were spick and span. They were the only thing that got her out of bed and Maggie sometimes felt that without them Sheila would have hidden under the duvet and taken the top off a wine bottle and never put it on again. She had given up and didn't care. But whatever Maggie had said, had sunk into Sheila's grieving mind. 'You look nice love. The taxi'll be here soon. I'll meet you in the forecourt when he beeps his horn, okay?'

A worried frown crossed Sheila's brow. 'What does Beryl think about me coming with you?'

'Who cares!' Maggie laughed. 'And don't worry about the cost of your train ticket, I have that under control. Well, that's all sorted then.' Maggie said, all matter of fact. 'We have some sandwiches packed up and I'm just making a flask, so we have something to drink. Come on Sheila... smile, this could be the first day of the rest of your life.' Pulling her black cardigan around her, Maggie left Sheila to her thoughts. She had thought to herself last night that something good had to come out of Steve's death. Sharon and Penny, Sheila's daughters, had been upset when there was no sign of their dad any more, but they were very young. They had asked questions, but as they were so used to life without him they just got on with it and Sheila couldn't bring herself to tell them he was dead. Maggie firmly believed she would tell them everything in her own good time. When she could face the truth herself.

The train journey to Edinburgh was lovely. They sat there with their picnic while looking out of the windows as the green meadows of Scotland whizzed by the windows. Maggie had breathed a sigh of relief when Beryl had joined in with the conversation and seemed at ease with Sheila.

Maggie had already checked out the bus Sheila needed to get to the house once she had given her the address and so on arrival at the train station, they all parted and went their separate ways. 'You've my mobile number if you need me,' Maggie shouted and waved at her as they saw her off. With a big sigh, Maggie took hold of Beryl's arm and linked it with her own. 'Come on Grandma, let's get our bus and see this wee laddie of yours.' She smiled.

Maggie couldn't help but stride towards Natasha in her hospital bed and hug her, almost squeezing the life out of her. She felt guilty for not visiting regularly while she was in prison, but it had depressed her and she didn't feel the visits did Natasha any good either. They had both sat avoiding the obvious subject and trying to think of something cheerful to say, when in fact there was nothing to make either of them feel better.

'You look well,' Maggie lied. She had had to hand the flowers and card she had bought to the prison officer, who in turn had checked them before handing them to Natasha.

'For goodness' sake, it's a bunch of flowers, what do you think is hidden in there?' Beryl snapped.

The prison officer raised her eyebrows and opened the card. 'You'd be surprised missus.'

Hearing the officer's comment struck a chord with Maggie. Not so long ago, Maggie had been sent to collect three mobile phones from the cemetery and had gone there with a bunch of flowers. She'd owed the gangland bosses that ruled Glasgow but had not known her best friend Beryl Diamond's grandson, with all his airs and graces, was the man they referred to as the Undertaker.

'I've been down already this morning to see him. Go and ask the nurse if she'll take you to see him, Maggie, he's gorgeous! He looks just like Nicky.' Natasha beamed.

These were the golden words Beryl had prayed for – she was itching to see her great-grandson. Maggie wanted to laugh out loud, because considering Beryl's rheumatism, which she constantly moaned about, she was out of that room like a bat out of hell when the nurse came to escort them.

But Beryl was greeted by disappointment, when she saw the many wires and machines helping the baby to breathe. She couldn't hold him as she had hoped, and he was laid in the incubator, wearing only a nappy and a little hat. Tears rolled down her cheeks. 'He's so tiny Maggie. He looks like a little doll.'

'He's going to be fine Beryl,' Maggie soothed. 'He's just a little early, that's all. He's in the best place, he was just too eager to come out and say hello to everyone. He'll be running circles around you in no time.'

Wiping her eyes and looking up at her hopefully, Beryl gave a weak smile. 'Do you think so?'

Patting her hand, Maggie gave her a reassuring nod, as the pair of them stood rooted to the spot, gazing at the little miracle before them, fighting for life.

Time had passed so quickly and once they returned to see Natasha they realised it was nearly time to leave. Reaching out, Natasha grabbed Maggie's arm. 'Will you be at the trial next week?'

'Of course I will love. I'm surprised it's still going ahead.' Maggie shook her head. 'Anyway, don't worry, I'll be there.' This wasn't the time to get into deep conversation. It was a happy time and a happy day for all, and personally, she didn't want to think about the outcome of the trial. What would happen to the poor little mite in the incubator? Only time would tell and she didn't want to ask all the questions that she desperately wanted to ask about the welfare of Natasha's children, should she end up in prison.

'Have you thought about a name yet?' Beryl interrupted.

'Yes Beryl, I am going to call him Nicky, and Jack after your son, Nick's dad, if that's okay with you?' Natasha grinned.

Over the moon and almost jumping for joy, Beryl clapped her hands with glee. 'That's beautiful Natasha. And don't forget his name is Diamond.' Beryl wagged a knowing finger at her. 'And that is what he is. A pure diamond.' Beryl went over and kissed Natasha; she couldn't remember feeling this happy.

As the officer handed them back their mobile phones, Maggie noticed a message. Reading it quickly, she saw it was from Sheila asking her to meet her at the new house. It had only been half an hour since she'd sent the message and so after a few more heart-felt hugs and tears Maggie yanked Beryl away and outside the hospital and quickly hailed a taxi. Arriving at the address given by Sheila, Maggie smiled as she saw the property. It was a two-up two-down terraced house with a tiny garden at the front.

Sheila greeted them at the gate; the wide grin on her face said it all. 'I wanted you to see it before I take the keys back. What do you think?' Sheila showed them both around the house.

It all looked clean and tidy and apart from a bit of cosmetic work, the house itself showed real promise. The council had put a new kitchen in and everything looked lovely. There were no broken tiles or fading lino. The house seemed to have a character of its own and was very welcoming.

Maggie put her arm around Sheila's shoulders and hugged her. 'It's lovely. You'd be a fool to say no and the house has a warm friendly feel to it. Go for it,' she urged, 'for Steve's sake. He would have loved this for his girls.'

They all opened the back door and looked out at the small back garden. The council workmen had left some of their mess from the kitchen refurbish outside and it also had old, discarded car tyres on the overgrown grass, but as Maggie pointed out, the council would move all of that and there was plenty of time to get the garden in order and make it somewhere nice for the girls to play.

Sheila couldn't help smiling as she looked around the house, mentally already making plans for it, although she felt a sadness because Steve wasn't there. This had been his dream and he would have loved it. 'The school is only around the corner and the main shops are in walking distance,' Sheila informed them. Her face was lit up with excitement. 'Do you think I should take it?'

Glancing at each other, Maggie and Beryl laughed. 'Why are you asking us, you've already made your mind up!'

The train journey home was full of good news and on the way home from the station they dropped in at the local council office and waited while Sheila signed the tenancy forms. It had been a much longer day than anticipated and they were all shattered.

'I've got some stew on the stove. It only needs warming up if you're interested,' Beryl chirped up.

'That sounds good to me Beryl; I'm famished,' Maggie agreed.

'Betty will have fed the girls, so I'll just grab a sandwich Beryl. But thank you.' Sheila acknowledged the gesture as a truce and was glad of it.

Beryl folded her arms in bossy mode. 'In that case Sheila, pop by mine first and I'll give you a bowl full of stew and then you can warm it up at home. You've had a long day and need some flesh on your bones. Come on lassie, let's get you fed and watered, you've a lot of planning to do.'

Sheila nodded gratefully. 'Thanks Beryl, I appreciate that.'

For the first time in months, Sheila could see the light at the end of the tunnel. There was hope, and maybe a future, but what it would hold was anyone's guess.

5

TRIAL AND ERROR

'You've got to come to Edinburgh for the court case Victoria,' Patsy stressed. 'It wouldn't seem right if you didn't. After all, you are a grandma now.' Trying to sound upbeat, Patsy still felt her heart sink at the beaming smile on Victoria's face when she saw the pictures of Natasha's baby. 'Anyway, while you're there you might be able to see the baby.' Patsy dangled the carrot she knew would make Victoria change her mind.

'Well, I suppose I could go with you. But I would need my hair doing.' Victoria ran her hand through her dishevelled hair. She knew she had let herself go of late. 'Do you think they would allow us at the hospital to see the baby?'

'Come back to London with me first. Let's get you all blonde and beautiful again. I'll make you the world's most glamorous granny Victoria.' Patsy laughed, feeling on firmer ground. The very idea of seeing her grandchild was intriguing Victoria and bringing other things other than sorrow to her mind. 'Will you write that letter to the judge I asked you to write?'

Patsy had already written a letter to the judge, explaining that Natasha would stay with Victoria, which meant she had a place of residence with family in Dorset. She had also suggested that she would give Natasha a job as an assistant hairdresser and she could go to college, thus helping her turn her life around. Patsy had felt all of this would go in Natasha's favour. She knew she was putting herself out for Natasha but she expected to be paid back in full.

All they needed now was lady luck on their side. Larry had surprisingly got back to her quite quickly regarding Jimmy and was organising a meeting with social services for Victoria to take guardianship.

Patsy knew she must look foolish in front of her friends and possibly family and she squirmed at the idea. She was the wronged woman. Her dead husband was the father of another woman's baby; why was she helping her? But she didn't care. Time was not on Patsy's side and she knew it. As soon as the police started digging into Nick's past, they would find out she had laundered money through her salons. Money laundering carried a long prison sentence, so a few sacrifices to make sure that didn't happen were worth it.

Breaking into her thoughts, Victoria smiled. 'Yes, I'll come to London with you, and I'll write that letter if you think it will help.' Standing up, Victoria looked into the mirror over her mantelpiece and stroked her face. 'I look old Patsy and I have dark shadows under my eyes.'

'Oh shut up; you're a beautiful woman and I am going to make you even more beautiful. Come on, pack a bag, come back to London with me,' Patsy urged. Seeing Victoria smile and leave the room, Patsy mentally ticked another box off in her head.

Patsy had only one goal in mind and that was to get to the dirty truth about Nick and the money, but mainly to keep herself out of prison. Whatever it took, she was prepared to do it and for now, Natasha was her only link to the Glasgow underworld.

* * *

Maggie sat in the courtroom and looked around. She hardly recognised anyone there apart from Sheila who had wanted to come to hear Natasha's fate. Maggie couldn't see the point, but if this was the closure Sheila needed, then so be it.

At last they brought Natasha into the courtroom. Natasha looked around and then spotted her and smiled. Maggie put her fingers to her lips and kissed them. Maggie could see that Natasha was trembling with fright as she held on to the railing surrounding the dock.

Natasha looked up and saw Patsy and Victoria, and was about to smile, but Patsy turned her head and ignored her, making Natasha frown and look down disappointedly.

Vaguely recognising the two other women there, Maggie glanced at them again. She was sure that was Nick Diamond's mum and wife. She couldn't understand why they would be here; this was nothing to do with them. Maggie was secretly wishing Beryl had come with her now to confirm it, but she had got a chest infection and had been forced to stay at home. Maggie felt sure the blonde one with the green eyes and the beautiful, soft pink skirt suit was definitely Nick's mother. You couldn't mistake those green eyes. The other woman with her had dark hair, but she had only seen Nick's wife briefly a couple of times and couldn't be sure. She was dressed smartly in a red trouser suit, and she was made up to the nines. Yes, that was definitely her, Maggie decided. That was Patsy Diamond. Maybe she had made a point of coming today to see Natasha sentenced to a life of hard labour! Being a woman scorned and all that.

Natasha was allowed to sit because of her recent caesarean and Maggie ached to hold her and reassure her. She looked so tiny sat there while everyone discussed her fate.

She was accused of possession of a loaded firearm, which inadvertently had killed a man. She had endangered the life of her child and others while concealing it in her home. She had been reckless and irresponsible. Maggie felt it wasn't going well, no matter how much Natasha pleaded her innocence. Her young son had killed a man with a young family of his own. It sounded so bad in black and white. To make things worse, the prosecution brought up the fact that this wasn't Natasha's first crime. Maggie sat shocked while he told the court she had spent time in a young offender's prison previously. Maggie felt slightly hurt at hearing this – Natasha had never told her that part of her life, not even in passing. She found that very strange considering they had become so close.

Natasha's face was red and blotchy from crying as the judge asked if she was able to stand while he passed sentence. Before he did this he told the courtroom about the letter he had received from Mrs Diamond vouching for Natasha and promising to take guardianship over her children.

The judge looked directly at Natasha and in a low unemotional voice spoke. 'Natasha Richards, the minimum sentence for possession carries a five-year sentence, but I feel you had no intention of using the weapon yourself whatever the circumstances.'

Maggie winced inside. Five years! She was stunned and trying to take in the rest of what he was saying.

'The court allows me to sentence you to three years, but I am going to suspend this for three years. Personally, given your recent situation, I think you may need to spend as much time with your baby as possible, but that doesn't excuse your actions or make the situation any better. A loving family have lost their husband and father.' The judge looked over at a stony-faced Sheila and acknowledged her. 'I have spoken to social services, who in turn have spoken to Mrs Diamond and they are all prepared to offer you support, which may mean you keep better company in the future.' They all hung on to every word he said. 'Each day for the next three years this sentence will hang over your head. You've served four months in custody, while awaiting trial, and that will be deducted from your sentence should you return to court for any another misdemeanour. But you've a long road ahead of you. What you do with your life now is in your hands. I hope this time in custody has given you time to rethink your lifestyle and build a better future for your children.'

Patsy grabbed Victoria's hand and squeezed it so hard her knuckles were nearly white. 'Your letter did the trick Victoria,' she whispered in her ear. 'He was ready to throw the book at Natasha and get some justice for that man's wife. Christ, he was a bloody jailbird himself by all accounts and that judge makes him sound like Mary Poppins.'

Dazed, Victoria leaned towards Patsy's ear. 'Does that mean she is free to go?'

Nodding, she whispered back, 'Yes. Suspended sentence. It's up to her now and more to the point it's up to us to find Nick's money and the people that wanted him dead. Come on, we have to go.' Almost pulling her out of her seat, Patsy headed for the door. She wanted to speak to the barrister and Larry, but she knew Victoria would want to go to the hospital with Natasha to see the baby. For now, all seemed to be going to plan and that pleased her. Natasha would stay at the hospital for the next day, while the hospital made arrangements for the baby to be transported to Dorset, which Patsy had arranged to pay for privately to speed up the process.

Natasha looked around the courtroom in floods of tears, clearly not understanding what the judge had said. Wiping her tear-stained face, she looked wide eyed at him helplessly.

'You are free to go,' he said sternly. 'And make sure you don't ever come back,' he added for good measure.

Almost crumbling to her knees, she leaned on the officer beside her for support as the tears rolled down her face. She was free! She couldn't believe it, she was free!

'How are you love?' Maggie reached out and held Sheila's hand.

Sheila shrugged. 'She didn't shoot Steve and Jimmy is too young to prosecute. She needs a chance to spend some time with that baby of hers. I think she's suffered enough, don't you? So Mrs Diamond is taking the baby off her then?'

'Just a guardianship, I believe, in case the worst happened, but at least now I know why she was here. She wants Nick's baby and so does Beryl. Poor Natasha doesn't stand a chance. But she has been given a home. It seems the Diamonds are responsible for her and she is under their charge. Her life will never be her own Sheila.' Maggie shook her head; she wasn't sure what was worse. Prison or Diamond prison. At least with prison you served your sentence and were free at the end of it to do as you pleased. In Diamond prison, your child would never be your own and you would have to be eternally grateful. There was no light at the end of that tunnel, Maggie felt sure of that.

The two women exchanged glances and smiled. 'Do you want to come back to the house and have a cuppa before you go back to Glasgow?'

'Love to Sheila, but if you don't mind, I'd like to say hello to Natasha.'

'No Maggie love. I'm tired of fighting and arguing. We will both say hello.' Standing up, Sheila and Maggie left the courtroom. Natasha had already been led away and was stood in the corridor with Victoria.

'Maggie!' Natasha waved and ran to her. 'Thank you for

coming.' Seeing Sheila, she stopped short and wiped her nose with the sleeve of her denim jacket.

'It's okay Natasha, I haven't come for a fight,' Sheila sighed and held out her hand to shake Natasha's.

'Thank you Sheila. That means a lot.' Embarrassed by Sheila's presence, Natasha looked down at her feet awkwardly and was grateful for Victoria's intervention.

'So Natasha, do you want to go to the hospital first and show me my lovely grandson, or shall we stop and have something to eat first? You must be famished.' Victoria smiled at the two women stood with Natasha. 'Victoria Diamond,' she said, holding out her hand to shake theirs.

'Maggie and Sheila, friends of mine from Glasgow,' Natasha said.

'It's lovely to meet you ladies. You must live near my mother-in-law Beryl Diamond. In fact' – Victoria looked at Maggie vaguely – 'we have met haven't we?'

'I thought it was you Mrs Diamond. Yes, Beryl and me are life-long friends. Known each other for years. How are you doing?' Maggie noticed a flash of pain cross Victoria's face. 'Sorry love, that was insensitive of me. Have you seen your grandson yet?' Quickly changing the subject, Maggie smiled and shook her hand. 'It sounds like Natasha is coming to stay with you, although, she could stay in Glasgow and have the wee laddie here with her when he's well enough to come out of hospital.' Maggie couldn't resist stating the obvious.

Irritated by her nosiness, Patsy jumped in quickly. 'Maggie's right, you're a free woman Natasha. That is as long as you stay out of trouble. I'm sure they would find you a hostel or something for the foreseeable future. You can't just stay with a friend, though, because you would need a proper place of residence for social services' approval, and after all, Victoria is family. It's up to you

Natasha, although Victoria has some lovely ideas she would like to go over with you about the nursery, and Peters the butler would love more than one person to arrange dinner for.' Sarcasm dripped from her mouth as she manipulated Natasha with dreams of a better life. Her sideways glance at Maggie spoke volumes.

Natasha's brow creased and tears welled up in her eyes again. 'Could I really stay with you Mrs Diamond? If they let my baby out of hospital, I won't have anywhere to take him and even then, I don't have any furniture or anything. They could put him in care until I'm back on my feet again and that could take forever.'

Victoria's soothing voice reassured her. 'You are my grandson's mother; where else would you stay? My home is their home and of course yours.' Impulsively, Victoria stepped forward, cupped Natasha's face in her hands and kissed her on both cheeks. 'Come and have a break from all of this, get some fresh Dorset air into your lungs.'

Natasha fell into her arms instantly and held her tightly. 'Thank you Victoria,' she whispered as her body shook with sobs.

Patsy felt sick and betrayed by the happy, emotional scene. It seemed everyone was on poor, little defenceless Natasha's side, but Patsy knew it was just a façade. She knew there was more to scheming Natasha than met the eye. Nick had a lifestyle and a bundle of money and oops! Natasha had got pregnant. It made her want to throw up the way they all fussed around her.

Patsy butted in again. 'I was thinking, Natasha. I have hair and beauty salons. Maybe you could go to college and train up as a hairdresser and in the meantime you could work at the salon I have in Dorset, gaining experience. You would have a job, an income and a home – something the authorities would look at kindly. Don't give me an answer yet, just think about it. Go to the hospital first with Victoria; I'll meet you back at the hotel later.'

Handing over her car keys to Victoria, Patsy looked around at the happy gathering. There wasn't a brain cell amongst them.

Victoria waited while Natasha said her goodbyes to Maggie and Sheila and then lovingly put her arm around her shoulders and walked her out of the court. Maggie leaned in towards Patsy. 'What's your game? Why do you want to look after your husband's mistress? You don't fool me love, there is something not right about this. I'll be keeping a firm eye on you lady.'

'Good!' Patsy snapped. 'Because I'll know where to find you then, wont I? My mother-in-law is ill; she has lost her son but found a grandson. All I'm doing is helping her get well again. I have to put my own feelings aside to do that. Her son was murdered on your estate; do you really think she wants her grandson living there?'

Maggie's jaw dropped; she hadn't thought of it like that. Of course Nick's mum was grieving. This new baby gave them hope. Something to cling on to like a life boat at sea. 'I'm sorry Mrs Diamond, I didn't see it like that.' Feeling foolish at her outburst, Maggie blushed slightly and made her excuses to leave with Sheila.

Breathing a sigh of relief now everyone had left, Patsy made her way over to Larry. 'I still want guardianship and shared parental responsibility over Natasha's baby with Victoria. Do what you can. Claim Natasha is unstable if you have to. And while you're at it, get her kid out of care!'

Larry had smartened himself up for today's hearing and had even bought a new tie, hoping that it would impress Patsy. 'I'll do my best, although I don't see it as too much of a problem. I take it you want all of this to keep her in line?' Raising his eyebrows, he smiled.

'Your best isn't good enough. Do better and don't smile at me. Believe me, I was charmed and smiled at by a professional all my married life; I won't be fooled again.' Having had enough for one day, Patsy stormed off, leaving a waft of her expensive perfume floating through the corridors and a reprimanded Larry watching her admiringly. A smile spread across his face as he watched her leave. Patsy Diamond was certainly a force to be reckoned with.

6

BASIC FOUNDATIONS

Not wanting to seem too eager, Patsy stayed in London and busied herself in the running of her salons, although each time she rang or heard from Victoria her heart sank. Victoria had whisked Natasha back to Dorset and she was settling in nicely, while the baby was being transported to the local hospital. Although Patsy had her goals in mind, she still felt a pang of sadness when she thought of the happy home scene at Victoria's house. She was the wronged woman and yet no one seemed to acknowledge that. She had been so busy helping others get their heads around Nick's death, it never occurred to them that she might need help or support too. Good old dependable Patsy, that was how they thought of her, and now it seemed they had replaced her without a second thought with little Nicky Junior in their midst. It actually broke her heart, the way that they could all be so flippant and live in their own bubbles. It was as though they were the only people that were hurting. Well, she thought to herself as she locked up the shop after a long day, she had a few surprises of her own to share, but that would wait until the time was right.

Although she was itching to go to Dorset and interrogate Natasha, she felt the softly softly approach would be better. She had already waited four months, what was a couple more weeks? Opening the door of her London apartment she told Alexa to put the lights on. Nick loved gadgets; she had felt that rather than going through all of this palaver it was just as easy to flick the switch. She kicked off her shoes, and was surprised that the room remined in darkness. She repeated the command to Alexa again, but still nothing happened.

'Come in Mrs Diamond. Don't bother shouting for anyone; it could be the last words you speak.' A voice from the opposite side of the room stopped Patsy in her tracks. 'Wi-Fi is such a good thing these days and so easy to disconnect. Forget the lights, sit down over there. I've put a chair out for you.'

Stunned, Patsy looked across at the shadowed figure in the corner of the room. Through the slit in the blinds behind him and the light from outside of her apartment, she could see the outline of a gun in his hand. Her heart was pounding in her chest, and she was in two minds whether to shout for help, although, the neighbours probably wouldn't hear her anyway.

'What do you want?' Her voice croaked as she swallowed hard. 'There is no money here.'

'What I want is for you to shut the door and sit down.'

His words drummed in her ears, but she did her best to remain calm. The voice was not one she recognised, and sounded foreign – possibly Russian or Polish, she couldn't be sure.

Fumbling in the dark for the back of the dining chair, Patsy found the seat and sat down while the man waited. She could see the gun in his hand pointing firmly at her and her palms began to sweat. Rubbing them together, she waited.

'What have you said to the police Mrs Diamond? What information have you given them?'

Frowning, Patsy looked at the shadowed figure in the corner. This man may have the upper hand with his gun, but it seemed he was more afraid of her and what she had told the police. Patsy took a moment before speaking as she gathered herself. 'I've just answered their questions about who might have wanted Nick dead and why. But like I told then, I know nothing. Was it you who broke into the apartment before?' she asked, trying to keep her voice steady and calm.

'I'm asking the questions Mrs Diamond. What names have you given them? Where is the rest of the stash? You will know, you took the deliveries. The Undertaker was very careful and secretive. Some people say he was a myth, but we know that not to be true, don't we?'

Undertaker? The word swam around in Patsy's head. Who the hell was the Undertaker? Her heart was pounding in her ears, but she knew that if she seemed of no use to this man, he wouldn't think twice about killing her. She wasn't sure which way to throw the dice. It was a gamble.

'What do you know about the Undertaker?' she whispered. She didn't even know if this was a ruse to find out what she knew. He could be playing her, but it was a chance she had to take.

'More to the point Mrs Diamond, what do *you* know about the Undertaker? Tell me.' His words echoed in the darkness.

Wringing her hands together to stop her palms from sweating, Patsy looked around. She had no idea what to say. She felt cornered, like a rabbit caught in the headlights.

'I know enough. Why do you want to know so badly? I haven't mentioned anyone's names,' she spat while shaking her head emphatically. She could feel the strength returning to her body. 'It's my house that has been turned over. It's me that has been marched down the police station day after day and accused of killing my husband.' Patsy looked towards the figure again. 'Did you shoot him?' she snapped. Although it was dark, her eyes were adapting and she could see more clearly. Blinking hard to focus more, she listened intently. This was a voice she would never forget.

'You had a lot to gain Mrs Diamond. How do we know that you didn't shoot him? We would have killed him eventually, it was only a matter of time, but it seems someone else got there first. Your husband was a very cruel, heartless man Mrs Diamond, but you already know that.' The man wavered slightly, letting out a huge sigh. 'Take this as a warning Mrs Diamond. Keep your mouth shut and keep out of our business. I'll give you a few days to remember where the rest of the stash is and I think that is very generous of me.'

Standing up, the shadowed man walked towards her. Patsy cringed inside as he stood beside her, while her stomach turned somersaults. He raised his arm and she shut her eyes tightly. The striking blow that followed as the cold, metal of the gun hit her head threw her off the chair on to the floor as she blacked out.

A loud knocking at the door brought Patsy back to semi-consciousness. Dazed, she raised her head and looked up at the light peering through the blinds at the windows. She felt numb and shivered from the cold. Her body ached and her head was throbbing. She could barely raise her chin from the carpet. The loud knocking at the door continued and, digging her hands into the carpet, she eased herself up on to her knees, spewing vomit as she struggled upwards. Her body felt like a dead weight, but with all of her might she stood up. Swaying slightly and holding on to any furniture nearby, she eventually managed to open the door.

The parcel delivery man stared at her. She looked drunk and it was only 10 a.m.

'Can you sign for these parcels please?'

Her eyes drifted back and forth as he spoke. Automatically, Patsy held out her hand and grasped his digital pen and scrawled something on the machine he was holding.

'What is it?' she slurred.

Looking down, the parcel man pointed to the three large cardboard boxes piled on top of each other on his metal trolley. Swinging the door open wide, Patsy nodded to the far wall inside of apartment. 'Leave them there.' Wheeling his trolley inside, the delivery man placed them where she requested, before looking her up and down with disgust and walking out.

Patsy shut the door and looked around the room. Her head was spinning, her legs felt weak and she didn't have the strength or inclination to open the boxes. She didn't care about anything at the moment. Whatever was in them could wait. Slowly, what had happened last night seeped through her brain. Shivering slightly, she walked over to the drinks cabinet and poured a large brandy. Her hand was trembling as she held the glass to her mouth to drink it. Without realising it, tears were falling down her cheeks and she began to shake. Staggering towards the armchair, she sat down. She knew she was in some kind of shock and didn't know what to do. Looking over at the carpet where she had spent the whole night, she saw blood. Reaching up, she felt her face and head. Her hair was stuck together with dried blood and underneath she could feel a swelling. Her head felt as though it would explode, it was banging so much. Sobbing, Patsy wrapped her arms around herself and rocked back and forth. She was frightened. She could have died last night and no one would have known. It was a terrifying thought.

After a few minutes, she stood up and walked into the bathroom. The reflection that stared back at her from the mirror horrified her. There was a dark patch on the top of her head where dried blood had matted in her hair and had poured down the side of her face, mixing with the smudged mascara around her eyes. Her suit jacket was covered in vomit and feeling a wetness behind her, she rubbed the back of her skirt and realised she had wet herself.

'Fuck you Nick Diamond,' she shouted at the mirror. 'This is only the beginning. Can you see what a fucking mess you've left behind you? This is all down to you!' Once she had let off steam, she turned on the bath taps and watched the water flow amongst the soapy bubbles. She got in and dunked her head beneath the water; it instantly turned pink from the blood. Cursing herself, she realised she should have showered first, but she had wanted to immerse herself in the hot bath to wash away all her fears. While soaking in the bath she contemplated going to the hospital to have her aching head checked over but thought better of it. Whoever was out there was watching her every move. She realised last night was just a warning and they would be back. The only thing keeping her alive was their presumption that she had the information they wanted. Where was this stash and what was it?

Lying there, up to her neck in pink bubbles, she replayed the conversation over in her mind. Who was the Undertaker? Was that man last night implying it was Nick?

A plan was forming in her head. There was no time to play softly softly with Natasha any more. She would get the information out of her if she had to wring her scrawny neck! After all, she had been the one with a gun pointed at her head and no one had protected her. She would get to the bottom of this Undertaker business once and for all. What a fucking name, she laughed out loud to herself. Couldn't Nick come up with something better than that! Pouring herself another drink, she held the glass in the air, as a kind of salute. 'Burn in hell Nick Diamond, the Undertaker. They may have been frightened of you, but they haven't met me yet. Bollocks! Bollocks to the lot of them!'

Wrapping her white towelling bathrobe around her, she took two paracetamol and a large gulp of brandy. She didn't care if it was the right thing to do or not; either way, her body needed to rest. Walking into the bedroom, she almost threw herself on the bed and wrapped the duvet tightly around her as sleep took her back into unconsciousness.

'What did she say?' Angrily, James listened to what Noel was telling him. The only place they could talk properly was at the ice-cream warehouse. They had both been in partnership with the Undertaker and they had a fair idea that Nick Diamond and the Undertaker were the same man. Albanian Noel wanted to take over the drugs empire and everything else since Nick's death and suddenly he didn't want a partnership with James any more. The only thing that stood in his way was Patsy Diamond. James, on the other hand, didn't like Noel's anger towards Patsy Diamond. For all of his criminal activities he had never vented his anger on a woman. He was no Billy Burke, even though he had known and worked with Billy for years. In that sense they were poles apart. Eyes and ears were all over the place since Nick's shooting and the police had even offered a reward for information. This was not a good situation and James felt Noel was only making things worse.

'What is the problem Noel? We have another supplier and a good one too.' James was sick of it all and he really didn't like violence and threats towards women.

Noel's deep Albanian voice sounded agitated and angry. 'What does she know James? A woman like her who just lost her husband is going to sing like a bird to the police. I'm not going back to prison and neither are my men.'

'Your men! We're partners Noel! And your men shouldn't be turning up with guns scaring the shit out of a woman. I don't like it.' James was getting sick and tired of Noel's continuous whining about Patsy Diamond. She had become the thorn in his side. Over the last four months he had talked of nothing else.

'She owns the community centre. Have you forgotten? That is our biggest output at the moment. Even the brothel above it is earning good money. With a click of her well-polished nails she could take all of that away from us. She has Nick's contacts and she has that never ending supply of drugs he had stashed away. He must have told her something.'

'For Christ's sake Noel, she also owns the pizza shops, unless you've forgotten that. Okay, they are not doing as much business but with still selling gear through them and the street dealers we're doing okay. If you kill her, who owns all of those places? Someone who wants to sell the lot and have done with it. You should never have stopped the money going to those salons. All you've done is cause suspicion and bad feeling. If you had paid up we wouldn't have to worry about Patsy fucking Diamond!'

Shouting and pacing the floor in the ice-cream warehouse, James was angry. 'Promise me now, that you will not go near her again. I mean you or your so-called men!' James laughed out loud. Since when did men go around scaring women with guns and leave them for dead! He had only just heard about Noel's stupid plan to scare Patsy Diamond into some kind of confession. James felt all Noel had done was push her straight into the coppers' arms for protection. She would be down the police station within the blink of an eye confessing everything that stupid Albanian friend of Noel's had done to her, James was sure of it.

'Don't push me Noel,' he warned, 'or Patsy Diamond won't be the only person you have to worry about.' Pulling up the shutter door of the ice-cream warehouse, James stormed out into the forecourt where the vans were parked. Lighting a cigarette, he took a huge drag of it and blew out the smoke into the air. He was sick of it all and mentally made his mind up to send half of his share to the salons. He wished he had never discovered where the money was being laundered. It had only been by accident he had found out from one of the delivery men when they had asked him which salon they were delivering to this month. He should have kept it to himself, rather than tell Noel. He had been bloody stupid!

Walking around the yard, a thought struck James. What if that mad man had actually killed Patsy? He didn't know for sure. All he had been told was that she had been hit on the head to give Noel's man time to get away. James wasn't going to be dragged into a murder charge, and after the many years he had spent in and out of prison he knew how easy it could be for the police to come up with some trumped up charge by association.

Impulsively, he took out his mobile phone and dialled Patsy Diamond's number. It hadn't been hard to get; they had got one of the prostitutes that worked for them to go into one of Patsy's salons in London and pose as someone looking for a job.

Nervously he waited while the telephone rang. Suddenly a woman answered, whom he presumed was Patsy Diamond. Ending the call and satisfied that she was still alive, he felt better.

7

THE JIGSAW

The two-hour journey to Dorset gave Patsy time to think. Plans were forming in her head and she was rehearsing what she was going to say to Natasha and Victoria. After playing many scenarios in her head she decided no more lies. She was going to tell them the truth. Why should she always be the strong one? Why should she go through all this terror alone?

The family scene that greeted her as she walked into the lounge almost stopped her in her tracks. Patsy's jaw dropped. Natasha was laid full length on the sofa with a pink blanket over her, watching television. The maid was putting down a tray of coffee and cakes on the table beside her. It made Patsy's blood boil. Who the hell did Natasha think she was? Lying there being waited on hand and foot. She was Nick's mistress and that was all she was.

Victoria was fussing around the lounge, filling her vases with freshly-cut roses from the garden. 'Patsy darling, how nice of you to come.' Victoria kissed her on the cheek.

Patsy couldn't help the sarcasm as it dripped from her mouth. Straightening herself up to her full height and taking a breath, she turned towards Natasha. 'Don't get too comfortable Natasha; everything you have here is on loan. I do hope you're healing well.'

Startled by her interruption, Natasha began to sit up when Victoria stopped her.

'Lie down, you have to let your scar heal. You've just had an operation.' Victoria rushed to Natasha's side. Sitting on the arm of the sofa, she stroked Natasha's blonde hair in a motherly fashion. 'Don't you think she's looking a little better Patsy? She has more colour to her face now.'

'Yes, much better than the bruises that surrounded her eyes the last time I saw her in prison.' Shooting Natasha a glare, Patsy helped herself to a drink and sat down. 'We have business to attend to. I've done my bit Natasha, now it's your turn.' Patsy wagged her finger in Natasha's face. This whole scene was making her feel sick. She wasn't sure what was making her angrier, the fact that Natasha was laid there like a member of the family or the fact that Patsy had organised it all. 'You're out of prison and you've your son in a nearby hospital. Now is the time for you to start paying back your favours or you find yourself somewhere else to squat!'

'Patsy!' Victoria shouted in disgust. 'How dare you waltz into my home spitting venom about who stays here. Natasha is my guest and if you don't like that, well maybe you had better leave.' Victoria's face flushed with anger, highlighting her blonde hair. 'What the hell is wrong with you?'

'I'll tell you what is wrong with me!' Patsy shouted back. 'I am Nick's widow! She is just some tart he screwed for a couple of months. If she had never got herself knocked up, would she be lounging on your sofa right now? No! She wouldn't. That is not why I brought her here and you know that Victoria. There is business to attend to and I only have a short time to come up with answers before whoever killed Nick shoots me too. Come to think of it, they could shoot either of you two as well! Look at you both, without a care in the world, while I am held at gunpoint and left for dead! I don't have time for happy fucking families!' Disgusted and hurt, Patsy sat down. She was already regretting coming so soon after her ordeal. She wasn't in the right frame of mind to have this conversation.

Victoria put her hand over her mouth in shock and gasped. 'My god Patsy, you've been held at gunpoint?' Victoria paled and sat down. 'Whatever for? Are you okay?'

Natasha's jaw dropped and she stared wide eyed at Patsy. 'Do you think someone is trying to kill us?' She began to tremble. 'Why would they want to kill me?'

Patsy threw Natasha an icy glare. 'You stupid bitch. Information! Nick was one sleazy bastard, by all accounts. The man who held me at gunpoint called him by another name – the Undertaker. I have no idea what that means, but he was up to his neck in whatever dodgy dealings were going on and my guess is, it was drugs. Good old Nick was drug dealing and money laundering and someone is very afraid about what we might know, and I mean all of us. Victoria, pour some brandies. We need to talk.'

Angry, but feeling a little calmer, Patsy filled them in on what had happened to her, as Victoria and Natasha sat there in amazement. Patsy felt better once she had told someone. It had scared her and she was afraid for her life.

'What makes you think he was drug dealing Patsy? He had money; he comes from money.' Natasha waved her arm around the grandeur of Victoria's house. For once, Natasha's input seemed sensible.

Feeling a little subdued, Patsy cast them both a furtive glance. 'Well, Nick was laundering money through my salons. Huge amounts of money. But since his death, those deliveries have stopped and I don't know who is collecting that money now, but whoever it is thinks we know more than we do. That's why we need to put our heads together and piece this jigsaw together. The police will find out about Nick's extra activities sooner or later and then we're doomed.' Patsy ran her hands through her hair, wincing when she accidentally touched the swelling on her head.

Pursing her lips together, Natasha butted in. 'You mean you're doomed Patsy. I never laundered Nick's money. I don't have a penny to my name. What has all of this got to do with me? From where I stand Patsy, this is all about saving your skin, not mine.'

'Be very careful Natasha,' Patsy shot back at her, 'otherwise that tongue of yours will choke you, and wipe that fucking smirk off your face. How do they know what Nick's Scottish tart knew? Maybe he talked in his sleep!' Patsy pointed her finger angrily at Natasha. She was ready to tear Natasha's eyes out. She was sick of this naïve, poor little girl act.

Standing up quickly, before this argument turned into a brawl, Victoria had to act as the peace maker. 'Ladies, ladies, let's remain calm.' Victoria stood in the middle of the room between them and held up her hands to stop the argument getting out of control. She knew there was more to Patsy's anger than Nick's past. It was the present that was hurting Patsy. The very fact that his mistress was in the family home. She had known this was a bad idea when Patsy had suggested it. In theory it had sounded okay, but in the cold light of day Patsy was smarting. Not only had she been replaced in Nick's affections, Victoria realised she felt she had been replaced here too. That most definitely wasn't the case.

'This is my home and I won't have two wild cats fighting in it. Let's all take a breath and start again. Let me close the door so the staff can't hear this conversation, and I'll pour us all another drink.'

Natasha and Patsy glared at each other from across the room but followed Victoria's stern orders.

Handing each of them a drink and taking a sip of her own, Victoria sat down. 'Right young lady, you've something to say and I want to hear it. And I mean all of it. Let's clear the air once and for all.'

Patsy looked across at Victoria. It was the first time she had ever seen her fired up; her eyes flashed as green as Nick's did when he was angry. She hadn't realised just how like his mother Nick was.

Rolling her eyes up to the ceiling, Patsy let out a huge sigh. All of this shouting had made her head ache again. She felt tired and stressed. It had all seemed clear in her mind but saying it out loud would sound like a jumbled mess. 'It's a melting pot Victoria, there are pieces that need filling in, which, as you know, is why I agreed to help Natasha. I'm sure she must know something about Nick that he kept from us. There must have been a time when his mobile rang and he answered it in front of her, possibly calling the person on the other end by name. What we need are names,' Patsy stressed. 'Who are these foreigners that are stalking me?'

'Are you telling me I'm just bait?' Natasha screamed across the room. 'I thought you wanted to know your grandson,' she shouted accusingly at Victoria.

'Bait?' Patsy scoffed. 'Don't make me laugh. You're living in the lap of luxury in Dorset's answer to Downton Abbey! You didn't have to come here Natasha. Your friend Maggie, or whatever her name is, was right. You could have stayed in Scotland and made your own way. Why did you come here? Are you hoping for a nice settlement because you've had Nick's kid? Well, he dropped his trousers quick enough for you; it makes my head spin wondering how many other little Nick's there are out there in the world. And you're no innocent, are you?' Patsy spat out. 'Do you think I haven't done my homework on you? Larry Kavanagh is a half-decent lawyer. I'm quite surprised actually.' Patsy laughed and took another sip of her drink. 'I thought he was a joke in his off the peg suits, but he is quite thorough. I'm impressed.'

Natasha's face dropped and her face flushed to the roots of her hair, highlighting her blondeness. Patsy had obviously hit a raw nerve. Avoiding Victoria and Patsy's stare as they looked across the room at her, she stammered, 'I don't know what you mean.'

'My first thought was that maybe Jimmy's father would want to take Jimmy, as Jimmy's only family member outside of prison, that would be the first port of call for the social services wouldn't it?' Patsy had a secret and bit by bit she watched Natasha squirm as the words left her mouth.

'You fucking bitch!' Natasha jumped off the sofa, flinging her blanket aside, while striding over to Patsy, bending over to meet her face. 'Have you been spying on me? You jealous cow. Just because you're a dried up old hag and your husband wanted me. Yes, me!' She pointed to her chest and laughed. 'Not you with your red lipstick and false nails. He didn't give a fuck about you! He told me he didn't know what sex was until he met me, not some fucking old statue in bed like you.'

Their faces were so close together, their noses were almost touching.

Brushing her aside, Patsy stood up and started clapping her hands together in applause, a wide grin on her face. 'Well, well, will the real Natasha please stand up? It's taken some digging to get beneath that façade you've created, but this is the real you, isn't it? Evil, vindictive and a fucking tart. I was surprised when my good friend Larry the lawyer showed me your social services file. Bloody hell, you couldn't make it up. And as for the sex Natasha. Once he'd left Scotland and we had a romantic dinner together he was back in my bed. Statue or not,' Patsy sneered, watching the shocked look on Natasha's face as her revelation of Nick sharing her bed again seeped through her brain.

Shocked and puzzled, Victoria looked from one to the other. She had no idea what secret they shared, but she had a feeling she wouldn't like it. Standing between them and raising her hand, she slapped both of them across the face hard in turn, stunning them both into submission. Victoria rubbed her hand, feeling the sting on her palm.

'Listen to me you pair of fools. Whoever is out there, are getting just what they want. We're arguing with each other. We need to stand together against the enemy! Don't you get it? Now the pair of you, sit fucking down and you Patsy, spit it out. I'm sick and tired of this cat and mouse game. If we're going to help each other, we have to be straight with each other.'

Victoria wanted the truth. After all, she had her own story to add to this can of worms. Her words were slow and articulate, as though talking to a child. 'And Natasha. Any confessions you've got, let's hear them. For god's sake, my nerves are frayed enough.' Tired of the constant bickering between Nick's wife and mistress, Victoria wanted to clear the air.

A strange silence hung in the air as each of them considered what Victoria had said. Of course she was right. The enemy was outside, not in here. Whatever grievances they had against each other were not more important than saving their lives. Whoever Nick had upset wanted vengeance and it was only a matter of time before each of them faced their own fate.

Sulkily, Natasha sat down on the sofa. 'You tell her Patsy,

seeing as you've got all the answers. If I tell her I might miss something out.'

Lighting a cigarette, Patsy blew the smoke into the air. 'Okay, if that's what you want. Jimmy's father is a married man.' Patsy waited for some reaction from Victoria. But there was none. 'The father wants nothing to do with Jimmy, although the lovely Natasha here has been making him pay maintenance, haven't you?'

Natasha's looked down at the carpet then shot a piercing glance at Patsy. 'What's so unusual about someone paying maintenance for their child?'

'Well, to start with,' Patsy drawled, 'you've never told the benefits people you are getting extra cash and secondly the father feels it's blackmail. You say you'll tell his wife about Jimmy if he doesn't keep up the payments.' Turning to Victoria, Patsy grinned. 'It seems she makes a habit of picking married men and getting herself pregnant. Larry went to see the father and had a talk with him. His wife knows nothing about Jimmy and he wants to keep it like that. Jimmy's father thinks you've insecurity problems and want to latch on to anyone's family because you don't have one of your own... is that right?'

At last, Victoria interrupted. 'And did he say how Natasha forced him into her bed and made her pregnant or was that a miracle of nature? The man knew what he was doing when he dropped his trousers Patsy, and he should pay for his child, although I agree, she shouldn't have lied to the authorities about it.'

'Yes, maybe so, Victoria, but the man in question is her ex-foster carer's husband. Just before she was due to leave. She didn't want to leave the happy home and so her plan was to get pregnant and stay with her baby.' Patsy shot a glance at Natasha. 'You were a grown up and didn't want to live on your own, but you were surprised when they moved you on anyway. For god's sake, is that all you do, latch on to other people's families? You're pathetic and manipulating.'

Natasha burst into tears. 'It wasn't like that, you evil cow! They had said I was family and the minute I turned of age they were already planning my replacement. All I was to them was money. They didn't care about me. I was hurt and confused.' Natasha let out a sob, which annoyed Patsy even more.

'You've one hell of a shady past and you cover your tracks well, I'll give you that. Do you know you could go back to prison and finish your sentence for blackmail and fraud? But the real question is Natasha, is he the father? The man told Larry that he was drunk and it was the first and only time he'd cheated on his wife, but he can't actually remember what happened between you. So Larry organised a DNA with social services, and he's not the father is he?'

Stony-faced, Victoria turned to Natasha. 'So you lied about Jimmy's father? Have you lied about my grandson being Nick's child? I want the truth now. Don't even think of making a fool out of me. You're on a suspended sentence and I have parental responsibility over that little baby fighting for his life. I have also given you a home to satisfy the authorities, but remember dear, anything that is given can be so easily taken away.' Fuming inside, Victoria did her best not to show her disappointment and anger. She felt she was being taken for a fool.

'Nick is the father of my baby Victoria, I swear.' Natasha stood up to make her point. 'There must be a hair brush of Nick's, or something lying around. Do your own DNA test! I loved Nick and I believe he loved me, whatever she says.' Humiliated and embarrassed, Natasha lowered her eyes to the floor. Her voice became no more than a whisper. 'So what's your verdict Victoria? Patsy, I'm sure you know the rest of my sordid past and have already

decided what an awful person I am. Jimmy's father was some
bloke I used to hang around with. We used to drink vodka in his
dad's garage. He said he loved me but we needed money to start
our life together. He soon fucked me off when I got fat and he was
frightened of his dad finding out about me being pregnant. That
is why I lied and blamed my foster carer because I needed the
maintenance. But I haven't taken a penny off that guy in ages. For
Christ's sake, I've been in prison for four months!'

Weighing up the situation, Victoria nodded. Everyone's
temper had seemed to get the better of them. They were all red
faced and upset. 'What do you want Patsy?' Victoria asked. 'I
appreciate Nick treated you badly and you want a whipping boy.
But no one forced him to sleep with Natasha.'

'I want us all to be honest with each other and I am sick of her
butter-wouldn't-melt-in-your-mouth, hard-done-by act. She is as
hard as nails and I want her to stop bursting into tears simply to
get our sympathy. We're all in this together and the last thing I
need is miss pure and innocent here pretending to be a victim,
turning on us and making friends with our enemies to suit
herself. So come on Natasha, what is it to be? You've bought your
way in to the Diamond family home with biology. We're prepared
to give you a life, but for that we want your loyalty.' Trying to
think straight again after her jealous outburst, Patsy wanted to
stress that they needed Natasha on their side.

'Fair enough Patsy, I understand that.' Natasha nodded. 'I am
grateful for this fresh start. No one has ever given a shit about me
and I agree, having little Nicky gave me a sense of belonging. So I
guess we're family, in some form or another, and family stick
together.' Walking towards Patsy, Natasha held her hand out.
'Deal? Whatever we do, we do together. I'll help you if I can.'

Satisfied, Patsy held out her hand and shook Natasha's. 'Deal.
Right, let's all get another drink, you sit down and I want you to

think of any business contacts Nick ever spoke of. Did he ever tell you where he was going...?' Patsy faltered and then threw out the ultimate question. 'Have you ever heard the name, the Undertaker?'

Natasha looked deep in thought. 'He once answered the phone to a man and called him James, but that could have been anyone. But the Undertaker? It rings a bell. I never paid any attention to it before, but now you mention it...' Natasha drummed her fingers on her chin. 'I have heard that saying, but I can't think where.' Natasha looked up at the ceiling. The puzzled frown on her face convinced Patsy she wasn't lying or hiding information.

'What's an undertaker got to do with it, Patsy?' Victoria was confused. The conversation had got way ahead of her now and she knew she needed to catch up.

'I think that was Nick's code name. I don't know though. That's what we need to find out.' Shaking her head in disbelief, Patsy sighed. 'What was he up to Victoria, who was he involved with?' She was totally exasperated by it all and she felt half sorry that she had subjected Natasha to her insults. Natasha's skeletons were her own. And Patsy had her own skeletons, none of which she was prepared to share.

'I might be able to help you there.' Thinking about it, Victoria had an idea. 'I don't know if any of this is connected, but as you know, Jack Diamond wasn't Nick's real father. Maybe I should fill you both in on the rest of the story. It might help, it might not. But my gut instinct tells me that either way, it's a starting point.'

Stunned, Patsy and Natasha listened in awe and silence as Victoria told them the story of Nick's real father, Billy Burke, and how Nick had become his lawyer. 'It all seems so sordid saying it out loud, but we are all sharing our secrets.'

They talked into the night, and the alcohol was getting the

better of them. The ambience steadily improved as they each swapped stories. For the first time in her life, Natasha felt she had found friends and it felt good to open up about the baggage she had carried around with her for so long. She felt free; there were no more lies.

As for Patsy, she too felt they had all bonded. She didn't particularly like or trust Natasha, but she hated the people who were threatening her even more. This was how it had to be if they were going to survive whatever ordeal lay ahead of them. And she was pleased for Victoria and the new lease of life her grandchild had breathed into her. She supposed with a weird quirk of fate, they were all in this mess because they had all loved the same man. Nick Diamond seemed to have controlled all of their lives in some way but Patsy was determined that was the past. It was her turn now; whatever he did, she could do better. She would play these men at their own game and take everything they had. After all, she was a Diamond too.

8

A NEW LEAD

'Patsy! Patsy, wake up.' Natasha was shaking her awake. In the darkness of the bedroom and still in her tipsy state after all the drinks they had drunk, Patsy sat up, startled by the urgency in Natasha's voice.

Fear and panic rose inside her. Had her assailants followed her to Victoria's house?

'I've got it Patsy. I've remembered!'

'What is it? What the hell is going on? Put the lamp on for god's sake. What time is it?' Stirring, Patsy turned and glanced at the digital clock beside her bed. It was 4 a.m. 'What the hell are you talking about?'

'The Undertaker!' Natasha almost shouted in her face. 'I've remembered where I've heard that name before!' Turning the lamp on as instructed, Natasha waited, while Patsy sat up in bed. Her eyes were bleary, more from brandy than sleep.

'Sheila. Sheila said that name to me once and I never paid any attention to it. I didn't know what she meant. But she said something about Steve, knowing who the Undertaker was. That's all I know.'

Being woken in the early hours of the morning, Patsy had expected more information than that. 'Who the hell is Sheila?'

'You know, the woman who was at court. Little Jimmy shot her husband, Steve!' Natasha urged. 'She mentioned the name to me and said she was afraid of what Steve would do.' Rubbing her arms and shivering slightly, Natasha felt she had been too hasty waking Patsy in the middle of the night. By the look on Patsy's face, she realised it maybe could have waited until a decent hour.

Alert now and curious, Patsy pulled back the duvet and almost jumped out of bed. 'We need to talk while this is fresh in your mind. Here, put this on.' Patsy threw a dressing gown at Natasha. She could see the goosebumps already rising on her arms.

Patsy pushed past her and made her way downstairs, leaving Natasha to trail behind her. Walking along the long corridor, Patsy stopped at a small room and switched on the light. 'This is the kitchenette. It has the basics, should anyone fancy something in the middle of the night without asking the staff.' The small square room was surrounded by worktops; it had a sink, a fridge, a kettle and a microwave. Once opened, Natasha could see the cupboards were stocked with cups and plates, but also a stash of biscuits and nibbles.

Switching the kettle on, Patsy took out two mugs and started making coffee. She pointed to the long metal stools under the worktop, which served as a breakfast bar-cum-table, for Natasha to pull out and sit on. 'There is a blow heater over there; plug it in and switch it on. Close the door, it will keep the heat in and no one can hear us. Also, there is a stash of cigarettes in that drawer. Victoria doesn't like smoking in the house, so this is also used as the smoking cupboard.' Patsy grinned while opening the drawer and taking a packet out.

'But you were smoking earlier in the lounge.' Natasha raised her eyebrows and plugged in the heater.

'Yes, well. Sometimes rules are meant to be broken. Here.' Putting the mugs of coffee on the worktop, Patsy lit a cigarette and offered Natasha the packet. 'So this Sheila woman. What exactly did she say?'

'We were good friends once. Our kids used to play with each other and we would have a cup of tea and a catch up. A couple of days before Steve was killed...' Natasha looked down and picked up her mug. She felt awkward saying Sheila's husband was dead because of her son. 'She was worried. She kept saying that she and Steve were just getting on their feet again. They had loads of money problems... but that's another story. Anyway,' Natasha continued, 'she said, that Steve thought he knew who the Under-taker was. I think Sheila thought I knew what she meant, but I didn't and I let her carry on. You know, nodding in all of the right places.'

'Yes, but does *Sheila* know who the Undertaker is? Did Steve ever tell her?'

Looking downcast, Natasha shook her head. 'I don't know, she never said. But she was afraid of what Steve would do. He'd just recently come out of prison and he blamed the Undertaker, said that it was all his fault. I'm afraid that is all I can tell you Patsy. Sorry, it doesn't seem like much now, does it?' Biting her bottom lip, Natasha waited for another sarcastic comment from Patsy.

'Oh, but it does! That is our starting block Natasha. That Sheila seems to know a lot. We need to pay her a visit.'

Spluttering and almost choking on her coffee, Natasha shook her head. 'We can't! She won't talk to me Patsy. She hates me.' Although Natasha wanted to shout, she knew she had to keep her voice low, in case they were overheard. Wrapping her hands around the hot mug, she stared wide eyed at Patsy.

'She spoke to you at the court. Didn't I hear that she's moved house or something?' Excitement rose in Patsy. She was fully awake now. This was the lead she needed.

'She's moved to Edinburgh. I don't know the address, but Maggie does. She knows everything.'

'You mean that old witch at the courthouse? Beryl Diamond's mate? You're going to have to get the address off her, she definitely won't tell me.'

'I can't just ask Maggie for the address out of the blue. She'd want to know why I wanted it. She might even want to come with me to visit Sheila. I don't know Patsy, I think you're treading on dangerous ground.'

Patsy's sneer was enough to chill Natasha. 'You've lied all of your life love. What is one more? Tell Maggie you want to write to Sheila or something. You know,' Patsy urged. 'To make peace about the circumstances. Let her know how sorry you are. We need that address. So sell your fucking soul if you have to. You're going to visit your old friend Maggie and get the information we need.'

'Do you have to keep being so nasty Patsy? I'm trying to help you. You're no innocent in all of this. Laundering money carries a hefty prison sentence. Even I know that. I'm still unwell, I need to rest, and what about the baby? I can't just leave him and go to Scotland. What will Victoria say?'

Patsy's face hardened and she reached for the cigarette packet and lit another one. 'I might be saving myself, but I'm also trying to save all of us. Someone has the upper hand and they don't care who they frighten to shut us up. Your baby is in an incubator at the hospital with Victoria close by. She will understand that you want to see old friends and take Beryl some photos of her great-grandchild. Why shouldn't you?' Patsy raised an eyebrow and smiled. To her it all made perfect sense. 'Grow a backbone,

Natasha. Don't you want to find out who killed Nick? I thought you loved him!' Seeing Natasha's face pale, she realised she had touched a nerve.

'Do you think, whoever these people are, they're the ones who killed Nick?'

'Of course. Like I said earlier. No money is being delivered to the salons to launder any more. So someone is cashing it in and they don't want us knowing who they are. Personally, I think whoever Nick upset wanted a bigger share of the money and that is where the bad feeling came in.'

Natasha contemplated Patsy's words. 'Okay, I'll go tomorrow, but I can't promise she'll give me the address. Stop bullying me Patsy, I thought we'd got over that. I'll do my best... okay?'

'Do better than your best Natasha. I know you can do it. I'll drop you off at the station in the morning.' Looking at the clock on the wall, Patsy yawned. 'In the meantime, I think we should get some sleep. Come on back to bed. You've got a long day ahead of you.'

'What are you flapping about Victoria? She's going to see Beryl and her old friends for a day or so. For god's sake, you would think she was being sent to Australia or something.'

'I just want to make sure she has a good breakfast and she's feeling well enough to travel. And I had a photo framed of baby Nicky for Beryl. Natasha can take it for me. Are you sure you can carry it?'

Seeing Patsy's bored expression, Natasha took the silver photo frame. 'I'll be fine Victoria. I promised Beryl that I would go and visit and she is Nick's family. I know it's sudden, but I just thought about it last night when we were discussing families and all. I

don't want her feeling pushed out.' Natasha's wide eyed inno-
cence assured Victoria and made Patsy feel physically sick.
Picking up her car keys, Patsy walked to the car.

While Natasha was waving at Victoria, Patsy couldn't help but
comment, 'My, what a cool liar you are Natasha. You almost
convinced me it was all for Beryl's welfare. Well done. I'll drop
you off at the station. If you get the address, call me as soon as
you can. I'll go to Edinburgh and meet you there, but make sure
Beryl and that Maggie woman know nothing of when you're
thinking of going. Top secret now.'

'Don't you have businesses to run? I thought you would be
sorting them out.'

'That's what good managers are for Natasha. Everything is in
order. Don't worry about me, I can take care of myself.'

Natasha sat the rest of the journey in silence. There was no
point in reaching out to Patsy's good side, there wasn't one. What-
ever you said, she always gave a snide retort. Musing to herself,
Natasha cast a sideways glance at Patsy. Her make-up was perfect
and her designer white skirt and black top suited her to perfec-
tion. Looking down at her own denim jeans and jacket with a T-
shirt underneath, Natasha felt shabby. She still had a baby
tummy and felt quite the frump beside Patsy. Whatever had Nick
seen in her? Patsy was a beautiful woman. What had gone so
wrong in their marriage that he had strayed? She loved and
missed Nick, but she found it hard to understand why Nick
would walk away from his wife.

As Patsy dropped Natasha off outside of the station and gave
her a handful of money to sort herself out, her mobile started
ringing. She instantly recognised the number. It was her manager
from the salon. 'Janine love, what's the problem?'

'Nothing, it's just that you've had a special delivery. Two large
cardboard boxes, but the delivery man said they were for you and

not the salon. I thought I'd better tell you. Do you want me to open them? It's probably just something from a sales rep or something.'

Alarm bells rang in Patsy's ears. It was strange her getting a special delivery at the shop. 'No Janine. I'm coming up later today, so just put it aside for now. Thanks for letting me know.' Perplexed, Patsy drove on. This was very strange indeed, and she felt an eerie sense of foreboding. Suddenly she remembered the delivery of the boxes at her flat. Her mind had been all over the place and she had never opened them. Making a mental note, she decided to open the boxes in her flat as soon as possible.

* * *

Maggie almost scooped Natasha up in her arms when she saw her. Since she'd rung her and told her she was coming to visit, Maggie had been like a cat on hot bricks. Her excitement had spread to Beryl who couldn't wait to hear the news about little Nicky. 'Oh it's good to see you Natasha. How are you feeling?' As she steered her into the lounge, Natasha could see that Maggie had already set the coffee table out with biscuits and cakes. 'I'll just go and put the kettle on love, you sit down. I want to hear all of your news. Beryl's here. She's just in the loo.'

'There you are lassie. Oh my, you look beautiful. Absolutely beaming.' Maggie and Beryl stood back, admiring Natasha. 'Motherhood suits you.'

'She was mother before Beryl; she's got little Jimmy too, remember?' Maggie scoffed. 'I'll go and make the tea.'

'Here Beryl, Victoria sent this for you.' Handing over the tissue-wrapped parcel, Natasha watched as Beryl eagerly ripped it open. Once she saw the photo of the baby in its silver frame, a large gasp escaped her.

'Oh my, it's lovely. Look here Maggie. Come and see what Vicky has sent me.'

'Sit down Natasha and drink this. You've had a long journey. How is life in Dorset? Are you enjoying it?'

'It's very nice Maggie, Victoria is being really kind and little Nicky is doing really well.' Natasha couldn't believe how awkward she felt. It had only been a short space of time, but suddenly she felt uneasy.

'You should come home love. Back where you belong. Don't you think so Beryl?'

'How can she do that Maggie? Victoria has vouched for her as a family member. You know she might even get little Jimmy back. Bloody hell, Maggie, apart from us, what's around here for her but bad memories?'

Natasha looked from one to the other. 'What about all of my stuff?' It had never occurred to Natasha that someone would already be living in her flat. Things had moved so quickly lately, she hadn't had time to take a breath. Panic rose in her, and tears brimmed on her lashes. 'Where's all my stuff?'

A frown crossed Beryl's brow. 'The council were going to clear it all out, but Victoria contacted me and said that Patsy thought we should put it in storage, because no one knew what was going to happen. I thought she would have told you?'

'That all seems very suspicious if you ask me. Not telling the wee lassie where her stuff is. You should definitely come home to your own people. Not those strangers.' Maggie looked across at Beryl. 'You're her family Beryl. What does she know about your daughter-in-law and Nick's wife? Why are they so interested anyway?'

'Because of the baby. Victoria has offered her a home. A good home. I hate to say it, because she is a stuck up cow at times, but she has a good heart and Nicky is her grandchild. She is only trying to do what is right by her son Maggie. I am surprised they didn't tell you though Natasha.' Beryl looked at Natasha, who seemed to have worked herself up into a state. 'Calm down love. All yours and little Jimmy's stuff is safe.' Beryl was doing her best to pacify Natasha.

'Well, I still don't see what that Patsy has to do with it all. Bloody weird if you ask me. The wife looking after the mistress,' Maggie snapped. 'It's not natural.' She pursed her lips in disapproval.

Natasha looked down at the floor and bit her bottom lip. 'Actually Maggie, I haven't seen Patsy. It's only been a few days and I've just been resting,' Natasha lied. 'I came back the first chance I got. I'm starting to feel much better and Victoria gave me the train fare.'

'See Maggie!' Beryl snapped. 'She hasn't even seen Nick's wife.' Turning to Natasha and ignoring Maggie, Beryl smiled and changed the subject. 'Is my grandson putting on weight Natasha? Is he getting better?'

'He's stable for now Beryl and that's all they're saying. Let's have our tea and a catch up.' Natasha grinned, happy to have Beryl there. She had a feeling if it had just been herself and Maggie, it would have been an interrogation. 'I've missed you both.'

Suddenly Patsy's words filled her ears. *What a cool liar you are Natasha...* And here she was proving her right. 'I'll go and make us all a refill Maggie; this one has gone a little cold.'

Picking up the mugs, Natasha walked into the kitchen and switched on the kettle. While waiting she looked around and like magic, saw a piece of paper on Maggie's cork board hanging on the wall. There, smack bang in the middle, was Sheila's name and new address in Edinburgh. Natasha couldn't believe her luck. This would stop a lot of questions. She wouldn't have to ask

Maggie or give her reasons why she wanted it. Quickly, she took out her phone, pointed the camera at the piece of paper and took a photo of it, without being seen.

Pleased with herself, she waltzed back into the lounge holding the cups of tea. 'Here you go ladies, just like old times.'

She felt much better now she had achieved her goal. She could relax and the afternoon seemed to flow much easier. Beryl was telling her about the community centre and what had been happening there lately when suddenly the sound of the mobile shop horn interrupted their conversation, making Natasha jump. It felt strange being back. It had only been a few months, but she had already forgotten things that had been so normal to her. The mobile shop, which served the community and brought groceries to the door, was like a glimpse into hell itself. It sold drugs of any kind, but gave you credit you could never pay off. The interest rates were sky high. Once it had you in its power there was no turning back. She shivered at the very thought of it. People pawned all kinds of things and others sold them stolen goods just for a bread loaf and a packet of cigarettes.

'It's only the mobile shop Natasha. Are you okay? Do you want to go and have a lie down? You seem quite jumpy.' Maggie went over and sat on the arm of her chair. 'It must feel strange coming back here, to the scene of the crime so to speak. Your last memories of this place aren't very good ones, are they? I understand now, why you didn't want to come back.' As a gentle smile spread across Maggie's face, Natasha felt better.

'I'm fine Maggie. It's just been a while since I've been out on my own. The estate feels so big and open. I suppose that comes from being banged up in prison. Everything seems strange.'

'Of course it does love. Sorry, I didn't mean to be a grump on your first visit here. Let's have some of those cream cakes, shall we, and fatten you up a little. You are staying the night, aren't you? Beryl has cooked some of her special scotch broth. How long is your train ticket for?'

Although it was an open ticket, Natasha felt another lie coming on. Weakly, Natasha smiled. 'Of course I am but my return ticket is for tomorrow afternoon,' she stammered when she saw Maggie's face drop.

'She has to get back to little Nicky, Maggie. She won't want to be parted from him for long,' Beryl piped up, not wanting to be pushed out of this friendly reunion. After all, Natasha had given birth to *her* great-grandchild, not Maggie's.

9

THE BEST OF ENEMIES

When Patsy got to the salon she was pleased to see her little bit of paradise was all in order. It was full, which was usually the case on pension day. 'Well, Janine, how's the blue rinse brigade?' She laughed. Each week was the same, her golden oldies would plough through magazines full of different hairstyles, but they also stayed with the same hairstyle they'd had for the last ten years.

Diamond Cuts was Patsy's safe haven and she had worked hard building this place up. Standing at the teak, horse-shoe-shaped reception desk she felt a sense of achievement. This had been her first shop, and she loved it.

The telephone was ringing and the bookings were rolling in. The five stylists she employed were run off their feet tending to the ladies lounging in the cream leather chairs under the hairdryers, flicking through magazines and drinking their tea. As all the women were regulars, they all knew each other and the gossip flowed. Sometimes the comments and banter they shared were enough to make your hair curl!

As soon as Maud spotted Patsy she pressed the button on her

electric wheelchair and moved towards her. 'How you doing Patsy love?' She was one of Patsy's oldest customers, and way into her eighties. She liked her hair done like the queen. Sometimes Patsy felt they had grown old together.

'I'm fine thanks Maud. You're looking very glamorous today. Has Amy painted your nails?' Always playing the hostess, Patsy took Maud's hand and held it.

'She did Patsy love. Dream pink. What do you think?'

'You're a heartbreaker Maud. There will be no stopping those old soldiers down the legion pub tonight.'

'Get away with you Patsy Diamond. I've had three husbands and they were all bloody useless. Why would I want another one? Pass me my hat would you.'

Turning around to the coat and hat rack, Patsy smiled and winked at the hairdresser behind her. It was always the same. Maud spent an hour and half having her hair done and then she would put her hat on. You rarely saw her without it, but if the queen could wear her hat with the wide open brim on her freshly styled hair, then so could Maud.

Once Maud had plonked her hat on her head and stabbed the hat pin through it to keep it on, she beckoned Patsy towards her and whispered in her ear. 'Widowhood isn't that bad love, I know. I've been there. Time is a great healer. This is for you.' Looking down, Patsy saw the pound coin Maud had preciously placed in her hand. 'You're a good 'un Patsy. Take care.'

'Thanks Maud love.' Patsy walked to the double doors of the salon and opened them for her so she could get her wheelchair out. She had made the whole shop accessible and had even invested in the kerb being lowered outside for mobile scooters. It had set her in good stead and the dividends had paid off enormously over the years.

Walking back up to the reception desk, Patsy popped the coin into the large jar the hairdressers used for tips. Each in turn the ladies shouted to her and said hello, even though they couldn't hear her answer under the dryers.

'Patsy, you're here. I wondered what all the commotion was. I thought we had a celebrity walk in.' Janine laughed as she greeted her. 'Come into the back; there are a couple of things I want to go through with you. I'll put the kettle on.'

The cheers from the ladies who raised their mugs was enough to bring the house down. Laughing, Patsy followed Janine's lead. 'I've put those boxes in the office if you want to have a look.'

Walking into the office, Patsy saw the two cardboard boxes. She picked up a pair of nearby scissors and ran them down the brown tape holding the lid together. A gasp almost left her, and she looked around to see if Janine was behind her. The box was full of money! There were bundles of it, just as there used to be when Nick had been alive. Opening the smaller second box, she almost screamed and covered her mouth to silence herself. In a see-through plastic bag was a dead rat. Feeling the bile rise in her throat as the smell engulfed her nostrils, Patsy noticed a note. Carefully, she put her hand in the box and took it out.

This is what happens to people who rat to the police.

Tears stung at her eyes and she could feel herself tremble. She was afraid. If they felt like that, why had they sent the money? Closing the lid tight on the box, she gingerly picked it up and strode outside to the bins in the yard and threw it in.

'Are you okay Patsy? You're as white as a sheet,' Janine said when Patsy returned. 'Phew! What is that smell?' Janine walked over to the windows and opened them. 'It smells like somebody died in here.'

Patsy stopped herself short, before her mouth ran away with her. She was anxious and panicking but didn't want to show it. 'Sorry Janine, I'm just a bit temperamental at the moment. That box was full of samples from some cheap sales company. One of their hair dye samples had spilt in the box. It was a bloody mess.' Knowing full well she had to remain calm she painted on a smile to reassure Janine.

'Do you want me to throw the other box out?'

'No! No, that one is fine; it's some sales rep leaflets I'll look through.' Turning on the charm, Patsy hugged Janine. 'You're a treasure. I'll get my act into gear soon and sort things out... promise. Now, don't you think those ladies out there have waited long enough for their teas?'

Once Janine had left, Patsy shut the door and opened the other box again. Seeing the huge amounts of money in there frightened her. Her salons were no longer the safe haven she'd thought they were. Someone knew how to get to her.

Suddenly her mobile buzzed. It was a picture from Natasha. Looking closely, she saw the details of Sheila's address, and for the first time that day a genuine smile crossed her face. Natasha had done her job!

Thinking what to do next, she messaged her back.

Don't go back to Dorset. I'll meet you in Edinburgh. I'll message you when I get close. I'm sure you can amuse yourself with your friends until then.

Patsy sat in her chair. She had never felt so alone in her life. She felt tired of braving it out and smiling at people. She was being threatened and she couldn't go to the police with it. They would only dig even deeper into her life and she couldn't chance it, especially with a box load of money in her possession. Her suitcase was still in the back of the car. She'd empty it out and refill it with the money. It was the only thing she could think of.

When she took the case back to the boot of the car, she was glad it had wheels, because it was bloody heavy! She would leave for Edinburgh straight away. It was clear she wasn't needed at the salons and she had more pressing matters to sort out.

* * *

'Natasha, get in! I've had to circle this train station three times. You look like a street walker stood at the end with your bag.'

'It's raining. I'm soaked! Put the heating on. What took you so long? I messaged you when I was getting to the station; you said you were already in Edinburgh.'

'Oh stop moaning. You look like a drowned rat!' No sooner had the words left Patsy's mouth than she recalled the horrible scene in the cardboard box earlier. It made her skin crawl and she shuddered. 'Where is this place? Do you know or do I have to Google it?'

'Google it; I'm not sure. What if she won't talk to us? She doesn't know you and she hates me!'

'That's a chance we'll have to take. She knows a lot more than we do and anyway, bribery always works.' Remembering the money in her boot, Patsy felt sure that might grease the way into Sheila's affections. Confused, Natasha carried on drying her hair the best she could.

They both sat in silence for the rest of the short journey. Eventually they turned into Sheila's road. 'Well, it's better than I expected.' Patsy nodded and turned to Natasha. 'You go and knock while I park the car; she knows you.'

'What!' Horror crossed Natasha's face and she stared wide eyed at Patsy. 'She'll spit in my face.'

'Well, we haven't come all this way to sit outside, have we? Go on.'

Natasha bit her bottom lip. Her heart was pounding and her mouth felt dry. She hadn't worked out what she was going to say to Sheila; she'd thought Patsy would take the lead.

Gently knocking on the door, she mentally hoped there would be no answer, but instantly the door opened.

'Natasha, what are you doing here? How did you find my address?'

'Erm, me and a friend wanted to see you. We need to talk to you,' Natasha stammered, ignoring Sheila's questions.

As Patsy walked down the path, both Sheila and Natasha turned to look at her. She was dressed in a black trouser suit and a red, silk, crew neck blouse. Her hair was up in a French pleat and what with that and her perfectly made up face she was a sight to behold.

'I take it you're Sheila?'

'Who wants to know?' Sheila stood there with her arms folded.

'Let's go inside; we need to talk.'

'Now hold on a minute, lady. Just because you're stood there in your posh clothes, doesn't mean you can come around here barking orders at me. This is my house and you can clear off.' Sheila was about to slam the door in their faces when Patsy held up a handful of fifty-pound notes.

A frown crossed Sheila's brow. 'What's that for?'

'It's for you if you let us in and answer a few questions. There is five hundred pounds here. Take it or leave it.'

'Well, what do you want to know?' Sheila asked, almost hypnotised by the money Patsy held like a fan in her hand.

Patsy raised her eyebrows. 'Do we get an invite in?'

Nodding, Sheila opened the door wider to let them in. 'The kids are still at school but they finish soon. So make it quick. What do you want?'

She led them into the lounge and Patsy looked around. It was sparse and needed decorating, but it was clean and homely.

'Do you want tea or coffee?'

'Coffee please. Black no sugar,' Patsy answered, sitting down on an armchair. She hadn't fully thought about what she was going to say, but she was here now and this woman might just be able to help her.

Patsy and Natasha sat in silence until Sheila returned with her mismatched mugs. Natasha nervously played with her hands but was grateful for the hot drink. Wrapping her hands around it, she looked over the top of her mug at Patsy.

'I'm Patsy Diamond. I know you know of my husband, and we will say no more about him. I'm here because there has been some kind of fall out since he was killed. It seems he was into some pretty dodgy drug dealing stuff and your husband knew who he really was. Am I right? Have you heard the name the Undertaker before?'

'Get out! The pair of you, get out!' Sheila screamed.

Stunned by her outburst, Patsy and Natasha watched her as she stormed towards the front door and opened it.

'Will you leave me alone!' Sheila screamed, her face red.

Patsy picked up her mug of coffee and took a sip. 'Sit down Sheila; we're not here to cause trouble. But why do I get the feeling you've had some?'

When Sheila didn't move, Patsy stood, walked to the front door and shut it. Gently, she reached out for Sheila's hand. 'What's happened love?'

Looking at the back of the front door, Patsy saw there were three bolts, a chain and a Yale lock.

'Why so many locks on such a small door, Sheila? Someone has been here before me haven't they?' Patsy's gut instinct told her that Sheila was frightened.

Sheila burst into tears and brushed them away with the sleeve of her jumper. 'Are you one of them?' Her voice trembled as she stared Patsy in the eyes. 'Leave my kids alone Mrs Diamond. I beg you. They have already lost their father, they are innocent. Please Mrs Diamond, I'll say nothing.'

'We need to sit down and swap stories Sheila. I'm not here to harm you or your kids.' Steering her back into the lounge, Patsy sat her down on the sofa. 'Do you smoke?' Once Sheila nodded her head, Patsy lit one for herself and then handed her packet and lighter over to Sheila. She noticed how Sheila's hands trembled slightly as she took the packet off her. Whoever these bastards were had threatened her and her kids and she was terrified.

'Not long after I moved in, when I'd sorted out the school for the girls, the head teacher suggested they pop along for an hour to get to know the place in the afternoon. When I went to pick them up after an hour or so, Sharon came out but Penny was missing. I went to see the teacher and she said that she had already been picked up on my instructions. You can imagine how frantic I was and when I came back here she was sitting on the doorstep. We hadn't called the police. It was the teacher who suggested I go home first to check if she was there. Penny told me a nice lady had picked her up and bought her an ice lolly and then dropped her off home. I did call the police, but as she was okay and couldn't describe them particularly well, there wasn't much they could do. That evening a bloke in a suit came to the door; I thought he was from the police, but he wasn't.' Sheila broke down in tears. 'He said next time he left her on the doorstep she wouldn't be alive. I know I owe them money and I thought I could just skip town without paying. It was a stupid idea. Those people always find you.'

Intrigued, Patsy stopped her. 'Why do you owe these people money? Who are they and how do you know them?'

'How much do you know Mrs Diamond?'

'I have had a few visits from foreign gentlemen myself. I went home one night to a stranger pointing a gun at me. My house has been ransacked and today they sent a dead rat to my salon. Whoever this is thinks I have names and they are warning me off talking to the police and telling them what I know. What I want to know Sheila is who my husband really was.'

'Steve was 99 per cent sure Nick Diamond was the Undertaker. No one knew his real identity, and yet everyone did his bidding. He sent Steve to prison for disobeying orders. I thought the guy who came here just wanted me to work off what I owed them in the brothel above the community centre.'

'Brothel? What brothel above the community centre?' Patsy's mind was spinning. Trying hard to take it all in, she listened to Sheila as she told Patsy how the Undertaker organised a prostitution ring on her old estate. The mobile shop would pass on the information to the women about when they were going to be picked up, and then they were taken by hearse to the cemetery to meet the men paying for them.

'The flat above the community centre, Steve said it was supposed to be used as storage, but he was sure it wasn't. They are dealing drugs from there too apparently.'

In an instant Patsy felt her whole world crumble away. She had lived with this man but didn't know anything about him.

'Why do they fear him so much Sheila? If no one knows who he was, how come they did as they were told? Who passed the orders on? He must have had a deputy or something to give the orders.' Stumbling on her words, Patsy wasn't sure what she was saying; it all sounded like a jumbled mess.

'He had top men apparently. I don't know who they are but they were all being blackmailed, for whatever reason. Scared shit-less by all accounts and some of his tortures were merciless, so I've heard.'

Tortures? Patsy paled at this new revelation and she looked at Sheila with shock. 'I thought it was just drug dealing?'

'Drug dealing is big money, Mrs Diamond; that and prostitu-tion make people very angry and very nervous. There are turf wars and people need to be kept in line. That's why Steve went to prison; he disobeyed an order and the Undertaker set him up. Maggie might know more; she seemed to be on the inside of things at times. She knew a lot about what was going on.' Sheila lit another cigarette.

Patsy frowned. 'Maggie? You mean Beryl Diamond's mate? What has she got to do with it?' Patsy couldn't believe her ears. Patsy had wanted the truth, but this was way beyond her expec-tations.

'I don't know much, but Maggie always seems to be in the "know". Steve felt there was something weird about the knitting nanas group that Beryl set up.'

'Knitting nanas?' For the first time since Sheila started unrav-elling her story, Patsy laughed out loud. 'What the hell are they?'

Furtively, Sheila glanced across at Natasha. 'You know about them don't you?'

Natasha nodded.

'The nanas knit toys and then sell them in the area. But Steve felt there was more than stuffing in those little knitted toys they went around distributing on their mobile scooters, claiming it was all in the name of charity.'

'Are you winding me up?' Patsy stood up, still laughing. 'I'm sorry Sheila, but when I think of crime bosses and drug dealers, I don't envision old ladies on mobile scooters. What the fuck was Nick playing at?'

Sheila took a long inhale on her cigarette, before exhaling, letting the cloud of smoke fill the air. 'Look, Mrs Diamond, I have to go and pick up the girls. I'm sorry, but you're going to have to leave, and I think I've said enough, don't you?' Standing up, Sheila looked out of the windows first and then walked towards the front door. It was obvious to Patsy that she was edgy and nervous.

Patsy's face softened. 'I understand. You've been more than helpful. Maybe we could talk again sometime?' As an afterthought, Patsy turned back to Sheila and opened her handbag and gave her one of her business cards. 'If you get worried, come to London. The address of my main salon is on there, but so is my mobile. Any time you want me, night or day, call me.'

Taking the card out of her hand, Sheila gave a weak smile and looked at it. 'Beauty salons. Now I know why you look so pristine. I must look a fright in comparison.' Sheila ran her hand through her own dowdy hair. 'Thank you Mrs Diamond, I might just have to take you up on your offer one day.'

'Make sure you do Sheila, and call me Patsy. Mrs Diamond reminds me of my mother-in-law.'

Starting the car, Patsy held out two cigarettes. 'Well, what do you think to your precious Nick now? Not exactly the knight in shining armour you thought he was, is he. That woman is terrified of any fall out from him and he's been dead for four months. He was a bastard with a capital B!'

'Stop it. He loved me, I know he did, and I loved him. We don't know if any of that is true. You handed her a fistful of money; she might just be telling you what she thinks you want to hear. Don't speak ill of the dead Patsy. You sound bitter and twisted.'

Patsy raised her hand and slapped Natasha across the face.

The fiery sting on Natasha's cheek made her head fly backwards and hit the side window, bringing tears to her eyes. 'You fucking old bitch! No wonder Nick didn't want you any more.'

Natasha reached across to Patsy like a wild cat, pulling at her hair and shaking her head. The pair of them scratched and fought until a knock on the car window interrupted them.

Dishevelled and bleeding from Natasha's scratches on her face, Patsy turned to see a policeman stood at the side of the car. They were both breathing heavily and red faced.

Doing her best to control her breathing and remain calm, she opened the window and looked at the policeman.

'Is everything all right ladies?' he asked, knowing full well it wasn't. They looked as though they had been in a war.

'Yes, just a disagreement officer.'

'Would you mind stepping out of the car?'

Natasha, who was still panting heavily, opened the car door to get out. Patsy did likewise and the policeman asked to see her driving licence. Still shaking from her outburst, she handed it over. Natasha brushed away her tears and sniffed, wiping her nose with her sleeve, leaving a long line of snot and blood behind.

'Do you want to tell me what all of this was about ladies? It looked pretty fierce from where I was standing.'

'Men! What else?' Patsy tried her hardest to smile, although her cut lip hurt like hell.

'Maybe you should come down the police station and make a statement.' He looked them both up and down. They were a sight to behold. Both of their faces were covered in scratch marks and from the state of their hair, they looked as if they had been pulled through a hedge backwards.

Natasha instantly shook her head. 'No, that won't be necessary. We're okay now... aren't we Patsy?' she stammered. Her pleading eyes brimmed with tears.

Following her lead, Patsy nodded, knowing full well that Natasha was frightened because she was on probation. The last thing she needed was the police on her back.

'Sorry officer, just letting off a bit of steam. It won't happen again.' Patsy was now in full control again. She answered the rest of the copper's questions and reluctantly he allowed them to leave. Breathing sighs of relief, they got back into the car.

For the rest of the journey they travelled in an icy silence. Natasha looked up into the mirror and saw the deep imbedded scratches from Patsy's talon-like nails. Casting a sideways glance at Patsy she could see where she had scratched her face. Patsy's lip was swelling, although the bleeding had stopped.

'Why are you stopping here?' Natasha looked out of the window and saw Edinburgh train station. 'Aren't you taking me home?'

'No. My gut instinct says I should go to Glasgow and see what this flat above the community centre looks like.' Patsy's voice was sharp and crisp. She was still smarting over their argument.

'Why don't you just sell it? Victoria thinks you should.' Natasha realised she had sad the wrong thing again. It was none of her business what she did with the centre.

'Victoria knows nothing,' Patsy barked. 'Nick got that council property at a discounted price. Okay, it was a bloody mess, but he also got grant funding to keep it open. We can't sell it for five years; if we do, we have to pay it all back. The full asking price. To make matters worse, we have to offer it to the council first. All the hard work and money ploughed into that place and we wouldn't get half the money we paid for it.'

Natasha bowed her head and looked at her scuffed trainers. 'I didn't realise,' she murmured. 'How come Victoria doesn't know that?'

Stopping in the parking bay outside the station, Patsy looked directly in Natasha's face. 'Because it's none of her bloody business! I'm Nick's widow, I'm the one taking all the shit and being threatened. What I do with that place is my business, but for now my gut instincts are telling me to go there and find out what is going on. I'll make out I am popping by to see how Beryl is getting on and then I'll visit the place. Here' – Patsy opened her handbag and took out a wad of notes – 'take this money and get your train to Dorset. Don't tell Victoria where I am going or where we have been.'

Sulkily, Natasha took the money. There was a silent pause between them and Patsy continued staring out of the window. Accepting her fate, Natasha opened the car door and got out. As soon as she closed the door behind her, Patsy drove off. Not a wave or a goodbye.

* * *

Glasgow was only an hour away and so she reached Beryl's estate in no time. Turning her nose up at the estate and the people on it, she cast a glance towards the community centre. People were still coming and going. Patsy looked upwards to this so-called storage flat upstairs. How much storage did a place like that need? Intriguing as it was, she felt she had better cover her tracks and make her way to Beryl's flat first.

When she arrived, she inwardly sighed before knocking on the door.

'Patsy? Why are you here lassie? You've never come under your own steam before.' Beryl peered at her suspiciously through the slit in the door.

'I have some new suppliers up this way and Victoria said I should drop in to see how you are. Is that okay, or are you going to leave me standing on the doorstep all night?'

'Yes, yes, come in. Suppliers you say. What for?' Beryl had never been a fan of Patsy and even now, after everything that had happened, she couldn't hide it.

'For my salons. Different hair products and things, you know how it is. Sometimes you've to go a bit further to get a better deal. Sorry, I should have called but I didn't know how long my meeting would be.'

'Don't worry lassie, sit yourself down and I'll put the kettle on, unless... you'd prefer something stronger?' Beryl grinned.

'Oh indeed I would, but I'm driving, and as much as a drop of your fine malt would do me the world of good, good old fashioned tea it is I'm afraid.'

'It's getting rather late; are you going to drive all the way to London tonight?' As an afterthought, Beryl nodded. 'I suppose you'll be staying in one of those posh hotels wouldn't you?' she snapped as she walked into the kitchen.

Smiling to herself, Patsy could already see the hackles rising on Beryl. 'As a matter of fact, I haven't made any plans. I thought my meeting would be long over by now.' Letting out a huge sigh for effect, Patsy continued. 'Never mind, I'll drive with the window open, I'm sure that will keep me awake.' Giving a yawn to seal the deal, Patsy waited.

'Stay here lassie; if you want to, that is. This is Nick's home and you're still his wife. And we will have a wee dram and raise our glasses to Nicky.'

'I would love to. That is really kind of you, thank you so much. So yes, you get the glasses out and I can kick my shoes off and rest my feet.' Patsy winced inside at her own sickly charm.

'What happened to your face? That lip of yours needs some antiseptic. I'll go and get some.'

Beryl peered at Patsy from the kitchen doorway. She felt something wasn't right but couldn't put her finger on it. Fifteen years Patsy had been married to Nick and not once had she turned up for a visit.

Touching her face, Patsy smiled. 'Oh, women and work. You often get the odd wild cat who doesn't like what you say. I suppose it's the hazard of working with so many women. Maybe I should employ men; at least they don't pull your hair out of the roots,' she said, laughing.

'Did you call the police lassie? You can't have employees doing that kind of thing. For goodness' sake, are you all right? Here, a good gulp of this whisky will be good for the shock.'

Patsy was surprised at Beryl's concern. She had never seemed to care what happened to her before.

Standing up, Patsy looked at her reddened face with two long scratch marks down either side of it and nodded. 'Some good make-up on that and no one will ever know.' Picking up the glass of whisky, Patsy took a large gulp. As it warmed her throat she felt better. No sooner had she finished it than Beryl had filled it up again.

'Have you eaten? I have a shepherd's pie in the oven if you want some...'

The pair of them were walking on egg shells, which Patsy felt was a shame. They had known each other for years, but now they were alone with each other, it felt awkward.

Licking her lips with enthusiasm, Patsy grinned. 'That sounds great. I haven't eaten all day. Thank you.'

Beryl smiled and busied herself in the kitchen. Patsy followed.

'Did I tell you that young Natasha came to visit? She looks well enough and I'm sure Vicky will put some meat on her bones with all the fancy cooking that staff of hers does.'

'I haven't seen her; is she okay?'

'As well as can be expected under the circumstances. The baby seems to be a fighter, and he's doing well by all accounts. Vicky sent me a lovely picture of him.' Proudly, Beryl held up the silver frame Natasha had brought with her. Patsy politely agreed how lovely the baby looked and went along with her sympathy about Natasha. Although, mentally, Patsy wanted to laugh. Beryl wouldn't think Natasha was so lovely if she knew she was the wild cat that had scratched her face like that.

Leaving the room, Patsy washed her face and applied antiseptic. Its sting made her wince and her lip throb. She stroked her naked face, free of make-up. She looked tired and had dark circles under her eyes. It felt as if she was fighting a losing battle. Sitting on the edge of the bath, she rubbed her face. Sheila had given her a lot to think about and deep down it angered and saddened her. It seemed whatever Nick had in his life hadn't been enough; he had wanted more.

The smell of Beryl's shepherd's pie wafted through the air as Patsy opened the door, reminding her of how hungry she was. Although she was ready for a barrage of Beryl's usual insults she was surprised when they ate dinner and none came. On the contrary, it was quite a pleasant evening. Of course Beryl went on about the baby, but she was a great-grandmother and that was her privilege.

After eating her fill, Patsy felt it was time for bed. While closing the curtains in the bedroom, Patsy looked out of the windows at the community centre in the distance. What mysteries did that place hold? she thought to herself. It seemed the community centre held the key to all her questions. She would go there tomorrow and find out for herself. Climbing into bed in just her underwear, she slept. And whether it was the whisky or the fact that she was mentally drained, she had the best night's sleep she'd had in months.

10

A WOMAN SCORNED

The birds singing outside woke Patsy. Getting up, she opened the curtains and saw that it was a beautiful spring morning. She felt refreshed and ready to fight the world. She could hear Beryl busying herself in the kitchen, singing along to some old song on the radio.

Looking around for something to cover herself with she opened the wardrobe. Inside was a dressing gown. As she reached for it off the hanger, she noticed a bulging holdall at the bottom of the wardrobe. She knew she shouldn't but curiosity got the better of her. Carefully unzipping it, she gasped. Bundles and bundles of cash filled the bag. Looking past it, she saw another bag. Eagerly, she unzipped it and again saw that it was fit to bursting and full of money.

A knock on the door startled her. 'Are you awake Patsy? I've made some tea.'

Trying her hardest to zip the bags back up again and push them to the back of the wardrobe, she shouted, 'Just coming!'

She closed the wardrobe doors, put on the dressing gown and

opened the bedroom door. Her mind was in a whirl. How could Beryl have all that money stashed away in the wardrobe?

Beryl put her hand to her chest. 'My you gave me a fright Patsy, standing there in Nick's dressing gown.'

'Nick's dressing gown?' Patsy looked down. 'Sorry, I didn't know and I certainly didn't mean to frighten you. I should have asked.'

'Don't be silly. Look, there are his initials on the pocket. Come and sit down, I've made some toast.'

Looking down at the breast pocket Patsy saw Nick's initials. She grimaced at the thought that he had worn it and now it was wrapped around herself.

'I've got some spare clothes in the boot of my car; I'll pop down after breakfast and get them. How are things at the community centre? Do people still use it or is it treated like a haunted palace or something?' Trying to make light of the situation and seeing that Beryl was in a talkative mood, Patsy broached the subject nonchalantly.

'Och, no lassie. Us Scots don't scare easy,' Beryl scoffed. 'It did go quiet for a while but it seems to be getting back to normal now and I have my bingo evenings back.' She laughed.

'I might pop down there myself later, just to see how things are. Whoever has been in charge lately has taken a lot on and done a good job I'm sure of it, but I would like to thank them for their kindness in keeping everything running for Nick's sake.' Patsy spied Beryl over the rim of her cup as she held it tightly in her hands. She knew she was on rocky ground and needed to weigh up the situation.

'That will be Greek Paul. He's the chef there and he's been keeping it running, along with his brothers, although one of them is totally stupid and has been relegated to caretaker.' Beryl laughed. 'Yes, that would be nice Patsy. Everyone likes to be appreciated.' Beryl smiled, thinking that maybe she had been wrong about Patsy all these years. They had hardly spent more than an hour in each other's company before, and even then it had been with Victoria or Nick. This was their first time alone and secretly Beryl was enjoying the company.

Wrapping her dressing gown tightly around her, Patsy went out to her car. Thankfully it still had wheels on it. In a place like this she had half expected to find it on bricks. Looking around the huge grey tower blocks covered in graffiti, she laughed to herself. This was Nick's empire? His crowning glory?

Realising that Beryl was her ticket into the community centre, she asked her to go with her. Beryl was the key here and as they were on such good terms it seemed the safest option.

It was strange walking up to the community centre and seeing her name above it. Patsy's mind drifted back to that fateful night when Nick had been gunned down outside. Today in the sunshine it didn't seem as scary as it had that dark December night.

Linking arms and marching Patsy up to the food counter, Beryl shouted and waved a man over. 'Paul, this is my daughter-in-law Patsy... Nick's wife. She wanted to come and thank you for all of your hard work.' Beryl beamed.

Patsy looked on as a tall, fat, swarthy man wearing his chef's whites and hat came forward and nodded over the counter at her. 'I've seen you before Mrs Diamond,' he mumbled in broken English. There was no smile or pleasant greeting, which unnerved Patsy. She had at least expected him extend his hand to shake hers, but there was nothing.

'Two teas when you're ready Paul. I'll take my usual seat over there with the girls.' Walking away and leaving Patsy, Beryl sat beside some other older ladies.

Raising one eyebrow, Patsy smiled. Girls indeed. It looked like the pensioners outing. There wasn't one under seventy!

'Could I have a word with you Paul? Maybe in the back somewhere where we can talk privately?' Patsy felt nervous and didn't know what to expect, but this was what she had come for. This was her goal.

Paul put two cups and saucers on top of the glass display counter, which was hot and lit up, displaying all kinds of sausage rolls and dishes of stews and chili con carnie for people to choose from.

Picking up the saucers, Patsy walked towards Beryl's table and put her tea down. 'I'm just going to have a word with Paul. I won't be long.' Walking back to the display counter, Patsy could feel everyone's eyes boring into her, whispering as she walked past with her head held high. She knew she looked out of place in her blue skirt suit.

Avoiding eye contact with everyone, she looked along the counter for Paul, but he was nowhere to be seen. Suddenly a side door near the counter opened and his huge bulk filled the frame of the doorway to let her in.

'What do you want Mrs Diamond?' Walking away from her he led the way through the kitchen to a small side room with a small desk.

Oozing with charm, Patsy parted her red painted lips and smiled. 'I want to thank you for holding the fort during our sad time. I'm afraid we haven't been much support for you and of course you will be reimbursed for your extra efforts.'

The mention of money almost broke a smile on Paul's face, but to Patsy it looked more like a grimace.

'Getting straight to the point, Paul, I would like the keys to the storage flat upstairs. I presume that you have them?'

Paul's eyes widened and Patsy knew she had hit a nerve.

'I don't,' he mumbled.

'Then how do you store things up there?' Reaching out, Patsy laid her hand on his.

'I think you should leave now.' Paul stood up to make the point that the meeting was over.

'If you don't give me the key, I'll call a locksmith. I'm sure he will open the door for me.'

Paul's dark eyes stared directly into her own. 'You can't do that; no one would come. You will have to ask Mr James. Now leave before I break your scrawny neck.'

Holding his gaze and not moving, Patsy moistened her lip. 'It's a shame we can't call the Undertaker isn't it? It's my name above that door Paul, and if you don't do as I ask I'll have this place closed down. You can tell your Mr James that!' Patsy spat out.

She wasn't sure if it was the heat of the kitchen or if Paul was just sweating, but he wiped his brow with the tea towel he had over his shoulder. He scanned the room, making Patsy feel nervous. There was something wild in this man's eyes that frightened her, but she held her composure. He became agitated and walked around the small office space. Taking a bunch of keys out of his pocket, he handed her two. 'You are a dead woman walking Mrs Diamond. Mr James won't like you interfering.'

'I've been a dead woman walking for a while. It seems all of your friends have threatened me in some form or another. I know you're going to make a phone call the moment I leave this room, so you might as well get it over with. You think Nick Diamond was a man to be reckoned with, well you haven't dealt with me.'

'What do you know Mrs Diamond?' A frown crossed Paul's brow and he waited.

'I know everything and from now on, you work for me,' Patsy bluffed.

A faint blush formed under his swarthy complexion. 'I'll break you Mrs Diamond.'

'No Paul, I'll break you. At the end of your shift. Close this place up. This is the last day of opening for now, and don't speak to me like that again,' Patsy spat, angered by this insolent giant.

His face froze. 'What about Mr James?' he mumbled.

'Fuck Mr James, whoever he is. If this Mr James of yours wants to speak to me then so be it, go and tell him. Who the hell is he anyway? You're talking to Mrs Diamond now.' Patsy pointed her finger in his face. 'Clean this place up and don't bother cooking any more.'

'But. But Mrs Diamond,' Paul stammered. 'The men. Their jobs. The people have nowhere else to go. Why do you do this?'

'Because I can!' Patsy stood up and walked towards the door. She was frightened that this huge bulk of a man might come after her. The knives and cleavers to cut the meat caught her eye and were duly noted. One move from that fat bastard, she thought, and I'll chop his fucking hands off. Her heart was pounding as she walked into the centre again, clutching the keys to the flat in her hand.

'Is everything all right?' Beryl shouted over.

Patsy's mouth felt dry and she swallowed hard. Her voice croaked as she spoke. 'Yes thanks. Paul's just asked me to look into something for him.'

She suddenly wished she had Natasha with her. If nothing else, she was back up, but at least Beryl knew where she was going if she never returned.

Looking around outside, she saw a door on the left and presumed this was the door to the flat. Nervously, she fumbled with the keys while looking around to see if anyone was watching. Her heart pounded in her chest as she opened the door and facing her were a few stairs that led up to the flat. Tentatively, she held onto the banister and walked up them, leaving the door open behind her. Not knowing what she was going to find upstairs sent a shiver down her spine. She had held the keys so tightly in her hand, her knuckles were white and the Yale key had imprinted itself into her palm. Reaching up, she put the key in the lock and turned it. She hadn't been sure whether to knock or not. Maybe someone was living there? Gently she pushed the door forwards. There was silence. Walking in, she could see that someone had been tipped off about her arrival – there was a cigarette still burning in the ashtray and the room was full of smoke – but she hadn't seen anyone leave.

Above her, the smoke alarm had been disconnected and was hanging from the ceiling. The sofa and chairs had clothing strewn over them. She walked through the modern lounge that seemed well kempt and into the kitchen. The breakfast bar had the semblance of a pub bar. It was fully stocked with all kinds of alcohol. Curiosity got the better of her now and she walked out of the kitchen towards the bathroom and bedrooms. To her surprise, it was a large flat and very well decorated and furnished, not at all like she had presumed... she had thought it would be some opium den or something.

Patsy stood outside a closed door, presuming it was one of the bedrooms. Summoning all of her courage, she took hold of the door handle and threw it wide open, making it hit the wall. Inside, was an unmade double bed and again, clothing was scattered everywhere. The blinds were closed and it stank of cheap perfume. The dressing table was littered with all kinds of make-up and an overflowing ashtray. The flat was deserted, but she knew for a fact Paul had seen to that.

Feeling braver now, she opened the next bedroom door and walked towards the window. It answered all of her questions. This bedroom had a small balcony outside, which led to a fire escape. That was how everyone had got out before she'd arrived.

She had missed her 'tenants', or whoever lived here, by seconds. A thought occurred to her and a sly grin crossed her face. She would play these bastards at their own game. Opening her mobile phone she searched for nearby locksmiths. Ringing the number she offered more than the amount he had quoted if he could come straight away. She had stressed its urgency and the man on the other end of the phone had told her he could be there within minutes.

Walking back into the lounge, Patsy picked up the discarded bras and G-strings scattered over the top of the sofa and gathered them all together. She made her way back to the bedroom with the balcony and threw them out of the window. There was a handbag with a purse inside it beside the bed. Patsy threw that out as well, thinking that whoever was outside would be needing it. Feeling angry now, she went around the rooms and gathered all of the clothing and did likewise, watching the scattered clothing land on the floor beneath her.

The knock at the door startled her, and she ran through to the lounge. 'Locksmith love.' Spying his work bag Patsy nodded and smiled at the workman with his ruddy complexion.

'I need the place securing. Change all of the locks, especially the one in the bedroom with the balcony windows. I'll pay whatever the price and more.' Taking out her purse, Patsy showed him the wad of notes she had.

'If you say so lassie. I was under the impression that this was some kind of bawdy house.'

'A what?' Patsy frowned; she hadn't heard that term before.

'Bawdy lassie. You know, a brothel.' Suddenly his face flushed. 'You're the customer miss, if you work here it's nothing to do with me. Sorry, no offence.'

A loud cackle erupted from Patsy and she shook her head. 'No mister, I'm no prostitute or madam, I just own the flat. As I say, the people have upped and left.' Still smiling to herself, she walked into the kitchen and left him to change the locks. That would certainly piss off whoever was in charge of this. They could probably pick the locks and get in again but it would anger them and hopefully they would come crawling out from under their stone. She was fed up with being frightened of shadowed figures and phantoms. She needed to face these people and end this reign of terror once and for all.

Lighting a cigarette, Patsy walked around the flat again. On closer inspection, she saw there was a drawer in the kitchen full of condoms. There were vibrators and whips in the bedrooms and the mirrored wardrobes left nothing to the imagination. In another drawer was a pile of unopened letters. Picking them up, she looked at the name; they were all for the same person: Karen Duret. The name didn't ring a bell, and if the woman lived here she wasn't in the habit of opening her mail. Ripping one of the envelopes open, she saw that it was a bank statement. The zeros at the end of the numbers amazed her; she didn't know there was that much money to be made in prostitution. The balance at the end of the letter showed five million pounds. Patsy checked it again to make sure she was reading it correctly. Scooping the rest of the letters up and putting them in her handbag, she decided to read them properly later. Now definitely wasn't the time.

Sauntering back into the lounge, she was stunned to see Maggie angrily glaring at her, standing there with her arms folded. 'Thought you might be behind this when I saw all those clothes flying through the air,' she snapped. The snarl on her face said it all.

Patsy's jaw almost dropped. 'Are you behind all of this

Maggie? You're Natasha's friend, you're Beryl's friend and now you're a brothel madam. Well, this place is full of secrets, isn't it?'

'I'm no madam lady muck, and don't use that tone with me.' Maggie wagged her finger in a threatening way. 'I'm here to warn you to back off. You're upsetting people and I've been asked to come and see what you're up to.'

'Just looking after my property Maggie. After all, it is my name above the door and on the deeds. As Nick's next of kin, this is all mine.' As an afterthought, and considering Maggie was clearly up to her neck in all of this, Patsy decided to ask the ultimate question. 'Did you shoot Nick?'

The look of horror on Maggie's face convinced Patsy she hadn't. 'Good god no. Did you? You had a reason to hate him; he was leaving you.'

'No I didn't, although clearing this trail of mess he has left behind him makes me wish I had. He lived quite the double life our Nick.'

'I had my suspicions something wasn't right. Call it gut instinct,' confessed Maggie. 'You need to leave Patsy, let sleeping dogs lie.'

'So what do you suggest Maggie, that I close the place down? Do you think I am just going to walk away and leave it? It's worth a lot of money and it's mine!'

'I'm sure they will pay you; they don't seem to be short of money, if that's all you're concerned about. Get out while you can Patsy.'

'Who are these people you mention and where would I find them? Do you know?'

Casting a furtive glance towards the locksmith, Maggie bit her bottom lip and shook her head. 'Lock this place up if you want, but the only people you're hurting are the girls that live and rely on this place. They're nice girls Patsy.'

'How many work here Maggie and how come you know them so well?'

'Six or seven. They have nowhere else to go. I have run a few errands for them and passed on messages, that's all.'

'This is my property and whoever is squatting here is taking the piss. It's not a free for all, let them find somewhere else, it's not my problem.'

'No, but it could be. I know what these people are capable of and it's not nice. I hardly know you Patsy, but I wouldn't wish any harm on you.'

Patsy burst out laughing. 'So that's their game is it? Send good old helpful Maggie to warn me off. Dear god, I would have thought they could do better than that. Did they call you and tell you to come here? For fuck's sake Maggie, wake up, you're being used just as much as these prostitutes. I take it you don't help out for nothing. All cash in hand is it?' Patsy's voice dripped sarcasm as she threw two fifty-pound notes at her. 'Take this for your services.' She couldn't believe it! Good old Beryl Diamond's friend was helping the very people who were threatening Patsy.

Ignoring Patsy's outburst and looking at the money flying in the air towards her in distaste, Maggie shook her head, her face burning with embarrassment. She had thought Patsy to be some overly made up Barbie doll, but now she could see that she was as hard as nails.

'All done lassie.' The locksmith touched the peak of his cap as a form of respect.

Ignoring Maggie, Patsy took a bundle of money out of her bag. 'I think that will cover it, don't you? Keys please.'

'Any time you need anything lassie, just give me a call.' Spying the two women glaring at each other, he put his business card on the table and left without another word.

As an afterthought, Patsy ran after him. 'Go and have a smoke in your van or something. I want you back again in ten minutes. Go on!' she barked. She was angry and Maggie had definitely got her ire up.

'Why did you say you had your suspicions about Nick? What was your gut instinct Maggie?'

Maggie looked down at the floor and shook her head. 'It was just something he said and did,' Maggie stammered. 'It was when he encouraged Beryl to put marijuana in her knitted toys. I thought it was odd, him being a solicitor and all. I know Beryl is a bit bonkers at times, but he shouldn't have encouraged it; on the contrary I thought he would have warned her against it.' Maggie shrugged her shoulders; she didn't know what else to say.

'That was his idea?' Looking at her in disbelief, Patsy gave a large sigh. This just got worse and worse. 'I have had enough of all this shit. Do you know who this Mr James is? That Greek chef kept mentioning him.'

'No, not really. All of this is run by the Albanians; they deal with the comings and goings of the girls.'

The mention of the Albanians reminded Patsy of the man in her flat. Pushing past Maggie, Patsy opened the door for them to walk through and then locked the mortice lock behind them. Downstairs she did the same thing.

'Right, let's show them who's boss shall we?' Patsy was fuming, and she wasn't thinking rationally.

Confused, Maggie watched her walk into the community centre, clap her hands loudly to get everyone's attention and shout at the top of her voice, 'Everyone, get out. This place is closed for the time being!' No one seemed to pay her an ounce of notice and so she shouted again. 'Everybody get out now or I'll call the police and have you removed. Get the fuck out!' she bellowed. Walking over to a trolley full of dirty cups and plates, she kicked it over. The smashing noise of the cups crashing onto the ground seemed to bring everyone to their senses.

'What's wrong, Patsy?' Beryl shouted towards her. 'Why you are so angry?' Beryl and her friends couldn't understand this outburst. Beryl had never seen her like this before.

'Fire!' Patsy shouted. 'There is a fire in the flat upstairs.' It was all she could think of to make them listen to her. Suddenly everyone stared at her wide eyed and made for the door. Even Paul and the other cooks came from behind the counter and made for the door.

'I'm the fire warden,' one of the cooks said.

'Good, well piss off outside then until it's all clear.'

The young cook looked at her confused, but then went running into the toilets, shouting. Eventually everyone had left, leaving Patsy standing alone. She looked around. She was sick of this millstone around her neck.

Walking out, she saw the locksmith's van. 'Oi you,' she barked. 'Change the locks on the main doors and the shutters and do it now.' To the crowd, she shouted, 'Go home everyone; the show is over for today.'

Paul strolled up to her and she could tell that he was angry. 'Mr James will hear about this Mrs Diamond. You will regret it.' His face was stern, probably from being duped by her cries of fire.

'I already do, you pompous prick. Now go and tell your mister fucking James I'm in charge and he can fuck off. Tell that coward from me I am selling everything and he can sell his drugs and prostitutes elsewhere.' By now Patsy was hysterical, shouting and screaming at the top of her voice. Turning towards Maggie who was stood beside Beryl, Patsy couldn't help herself. 'And you can fuck off too, you two-faced cow. Stay away from her Beryl, she's poison.'

'For god's sake Patsy, get a grip. What's going on?' Confused and embarrassed at Patsy's outburst, Beryl turned to Maggie and the crowd, shaking her head in sympathy. 'I know what this is. It's coming back here where Nicky was killed. It's all been too much for her. Come on lassie, let's go home.'

As Beryl held out her hand to lead her away, Patsy's mobile rang; she didn't know the number but answered it anyway. 'Yes, who is this?' she snapped. She was red faced and shaking with anger, but the voice on the other end shocked her more.

'Patsy, it's me, Sheila. I have to get out of here; they know you've been to see me. My house is trashed and they've sprayed graffiti all over my living room walls. They've been in my house Patsy!' Sheila screamed down the phone hysterically. 'I've just bought an old car with the money you gave me and I'll sleep in it if I have to. You said I could come to you!'

Walking away from the crowd so she couldn't be overheard, Patsy waited for a gap in between Sheila's hysterical cries. 'Sheila, do you think your car will get you to London? I'm still in Glasgow at the moment, but I'll text you my address; I'll meet you there. Are your girls okay?'

'Yes, but I need to get away now; they're not safe. I'll fucking walk if I have to.'

'Calm down, I'm sending my address now. Don't worry about your belongings, we will get what you need later. Right, I've sent the address, have you got it?'

'Aye, it's just come through. I'm leaving now. It's all your fault Patsy Diamond; you should never have come to my house. You've put my girls in danger.'

'We'll argue about that later.' Doing her best to compose herself, Patsy walked over to Beryl who was patiently waiting for her. 'I have to leave; something urgent has come up. Thank you for letting me stay.' She put her arms around her, all the while giving Maggie an icy glare over the back of Beryl's shoulders.

* * *

On the drive home, Patsy called Larry.

'Mrs Diamond, what can I do for you on this lovely spring day?'

'You can stop talking shit for a start. I want you to look for someone for me: a Karen Duret. I've just found a whole load of unopened letters for her and I don't know who she is. Find out what you can; if it's a dead end no worries. You will still get paid.'

'Is that all you have – a name?'

'No. Wait a minute.' Patsy pulled over and took her phone off the dashboard. Taking the opened letter out of her bag, she took a photo of it. 'I'm sending you a photo now; it's a bank statement.'

'I've got it, but the address is your community centre in Glasgow, isn't it? Can't you just ask around there to see if anyone knows her?'

'No, I can't. Can you do this or not? I'm not in the mood for playing games,' Patsy snapped.

'I'll do my best, but there are no guarantees.' No sooner had he finished his sentence than Patsy ended the call, put her phone back on the dashboard and drove off. Someone must know who this mystery woman was, she thought. This was a woman worth millions. She was eager to know what Larry Kavanagh could come up with. She hated admitting it to herself, but he was pretty good at his job. Thinking again, she pressed the quick dial button on her mobile and waited for Victoria to answer. 'Victoria, I need a favour. A friend of mine has two daughters and they need looking after for a couple of days. Can you come to London tomorrow to pick them up? Oh and get Natasha off her bony arse and bring her with you.'

'What kind of trouble Patsy? Are you okay love, you sound

distraught.' Victoria's soothing voice of concern made Patsy feel better.

'I'll explain more tomorrow if you can come.'

'Of course I'll come if you need me, you know that.'

'Thanks Victoria.' Patsy ended the call before Victoria could ask any more questions. It wasn't much of a plan, but if she could get Victoria to take Sheila's children to Dorset they would be well out of harm's way, plus they would have a holiday to boot. Maybe they all needed a break – God knows Patsy did!

11

_____

KEEP YOUR ENEMIES CLOSE

'Do you know what that Diamond woman has done? She's cost us thousands. She's closed the community centre and thrown those whores out on the street. I should have murdered her when I had the chance. You're too soft James; she needs to be put in her place... I'll sort her out.' Noel was fuming as he paced up and down. 'She sent a message to tell you to fuck off.'

'Calm down Noel, your shouting is getting us nowhere. I know she's closed the place down, Greek Paul told me. It's just her way of hitting out, she'll calm down.'

'I have prostitutes with nowhere to work. I've sent them to the pizza shops for now, but how long will it be before she closes them up too? The woman is a loose cannon; she knows too much.'

'She does, I agree, but the more you make the situation worse, the more you are pushing her right into the hands of the police. As far as I'm concerned, she's made her point, closed the centre and gone home. It's no big deal; we managed without that place before; we can do it again.'

'You mean I managed. Without you,' Noel spat out.

James frowned. 'Are you saying you want to dissolve this partnership?'

'I'm saying James, there is no partnership. The Undertaker is dead and buried and his turf is up for grabs. Well, I'm taking it. I'm taking all of it. We're done!' Noel had feared the Undertaker, but with him out of the way, there was nothing to fear and no repercussions.

'You're double crossing me Noel? We've been in this together and now you're letting a woman come between us?'

'I'm a businessman James and you are worthless to me now, so I suggest you leave while you can. I'm not paying money out to a dead weight like you. Take this as a warning.'

Noel turned his back to him and beckoned to someone James couldn't see. Two men carrying baseball bats appeared from the shadows. Heart hammering in his chest, James made to run for the exit, but the metal shutters came down before he could escape.

Noel said something in Albanian to the two men holding the baseball bats. James was terrified. He had walked straight into an ambush.

'Noel, there is no need for this. We've been friends a long time. I'll leave and it can all be yours,' he begged, knowing full well that he was pleading for his life. The stony-faced look that Noel gave him showed James there was no friendship between them and there were no second chances. Tears rolled down his face as he begged Noel for mercy, but it was futile. Falling onto his knees, in a prayer-like stance, James screamed to Noel to let him go.

Noel simply nodded at the two men and they came forward, raising their wooden bats, raining blow after blow upon James's body. Kicking out at them only made it worse and they laughed with each other as they beat him. James didn't stand a chance.

Pain shot through him like bolts of lightning as he heard his ribs crack. His howling screams echoed around the warehouse.

In a state of semi-consciousness, James heard the shutters roll up and just one last command from Noel. 'When he's dead, have the floor cemented over. It will cover the blood stains.'

A dark mist fell over his eyes and he passed out.

* * *

Fin, Beanie and Spider watched from a distance at the old ice-cream warehouse with its vans parked outside. James had called Fin before he'd gone to meet Noel.

'Why are we here Fin?' Beanie asked, yawning. 'I've been working all night distributing around the clubs; I'm knackered.'

'Because James said he wanted back-up. He said there was something strange about Noel's voice and his gut instinct told him it wasn't good.'

'So what are we supposed to do?' Spider looked across at the old warehouse. The unit next door was all boarded up and he didn't like the look of the place. 'Look, there's a bloke coming out.' Spider pointed.

'Get down, don't let him see you. Is James anywhere around?' Fin narrowed his eyes to get a better view.

'Wait until that bloke drives off and then we'll move a little closer. I think James was right: this stinks.'

As the man got in his car and drove away, the three of them made for the warehouse. One by one, they hid around the ice-cream vans for cover.

'Shit. What is that?' Spider's face paled. He could hear screams coming from inside the warehouse. 'Someone is in there Fin and it sounds like they're getting the shit kicked out of them,' he whispered.

They all cast a glance at each other and swallowed hard. 'Look down there. The shutter isn't closed properly. Come on.' Without thinking, Fin knelt down and squeezed his hands under the metal shutter, encouraging Spider and Beanie to do the same. With all of their might, they heaved it up.

Before them were two men holding baseball bats dripping with blood. They looked over at the three of them in surprise.

Fin wasn't sure of his next step, but as the two men began to run towards them he was glad he had taken along his old time protection from when he'd distributed around the clubs. You couldn't carry weapons, that was too obvious, and if you were searched, you were arrested. But bottles of water? Now that was a different matter.

Putting his leather gloved hands in each of his jacket pockets, he quickly took out two bottles, flicked the lids off and squirted the liquid towards the men, spraying the so-called water up and down them.

Instantly, their hands flew to their faces and they screamed in pain, rubbing their faces and falling to the floor.

'Here give me one.' Beanie reached out his hand for one of the bottles, but Fin held on to them, still squirting the acid in the direction of the men until at last they were empty. The men were writhing on the floor in pain, but Fin didn't care; he didn't know what these two men were capable of and out of fear he carried on regardless.

'Pick up the bats and hit the bastards. That's why I'm wearing gloves, so I don't burn my hands.' Spider and Beanie looked at the howling men on the floor, screaming in pain. Already they could see that the acid was burning into their faces and the more they rubbed, the more disfigured they became.

Spider and Beanie picked up the blood-soaked bats and beat the men who were already writhing in pain. The more they beat

them, the more helpless they became and eventually they
stopped moving. Covered in blood they lay there, but Fin wasn't
satisfied. Taking one of the bats, he hit each of them hard on the
head, just in case they were faking it. Sometimes, no matter how
much you hit someone, the pain from the acid kept them awake.
Once he had heard their skulls crack he felt better.

'Oh my god Fin, you've killed them.' Spider stared wide eyed
at the pool of blood surrounding the men and their red, burnt
faces. Their shirts, although covered in blood, had holes in them
where the acid had burnt through, burning their torsos.

'Fuck them. Go and see if there's anyone else here and check
on James while you're at it,' Fin shouted. He was feeling more
assertive now, and it wasn't the first time they had committed
murder. It was an occupational hazard sometimes. Kill or be
killed.

'He's still breathing,' Spider shouted while Beanie ran around,
checking to see if anyone else was about, but the warehouse
appeared empty.

'All clear here Fin, but there's a huge cement mixer at the
back. Why the hell would they want one of those in an ice-cream
warehouse?'

Frowning, Fin dropped the bat and strode towards Beanie. At
the very back of the warehouse there was indeed a cement mixer,
with bags of cement and sand beside it.

'They were going to bury him somewhere, that's why,' Fin
said, looking at them both. 'But where? Where would you bury
somebody around here?' Fin walked around the warehouse, but
there was nothing obvious. And just when he was about to give
up, he walked over a metal manhole. 'Give me a hand lifting this
up lads.'

Beanie stepped forward and looked at it. 'You've got to be
joking; those things are cast iron, and it will weigh a tonne.'

Fin's icy stare said it all. 'You've three choices: move this, do a life sentence for murder or wait for that bastard to come back in his car and discover you've just killed two of his men. God knows where he would bury you,' Fin snapped.

'Fair point; let's move it, although I doubt we can.' Flabbergasted, Beanie bent down on his hands and knees. It was a huge, round rusty manhole drain and it obviously hadn't been raised in ages. It took the three of them to break it free from the surrounding debris. The rust didn't help, but eventually it began to move. Breathless, Beanie stepped back for a moment while Spider and Fin pushed it aside.

Panting, they wiped the sweat from their brows and sat in silence for a moment, then Fin spoke up. 'We haven't got long. God knows when that bloke will come back. Spider, start that cement mixer; me and Beanie will carry those two over here and put them down there. It looks like quite a drop.'

'I don't know how to mix cement Fin, what do I do?'

Fin pointed to the bags of cement and sand. 'Put that lot in and add water. There's the sink. Fuck, it's like baking a cake. Come on, we have to get out of here and sort James out or all of this will be for nothing,' Fin stressed.

Working quickly and silently, Fin and Beanie took hold of the dead men and dragged them towards the manhole. 'Thank god they aren't fat bastards or we'd never get them down there,' said Fin, trying to lighten the situation, but no one smiled.

Dangling one of the men over the hole, Fin pushed, until eventually the dead body slid down it. Beanie dragged the other man over and did likewise. As the second man dropped down, Fin and Beanie glanced at each other and nodded. Spider switched off the cement mixer and wheeled it over, letting it hover over the hole. He had put far too much in the mixer and it spilled out onto the floor. 'Why don't we just put the lid on Fin, why do we have to pour cement in?' Spider was confused; he couldn't see the point.

'Simple Spider; dead bodies decay and smell and we don't know how far down that drain thing goes. The cement will stop the smell, or some of it at least.' Fin wasn't sure, but he felt if they were turned to stone, it would be better than rotting flesh. The cement was watery and pouring everywhere. 'Fuck, look at my trainers, you prick. Let's pull the lid back on.'

Once that was done, Fin looked around and saw a sweeping brush. 'You two get James out of here and I'll sweep the rest of that cement along the floor. If nothing else it will cover some of the blood stains. Go on move, before you turn into statues.' Fin felt fully in charge of the situation; the only problem he had now was getting James somewhere safe. 'Spider, go and see if there's a car around you can steal; we need transport.'

'Why search, when we have a car park full of ice-cream vans? I'll go and hot wire one.' If nothing else it lightened the mood and they all laughed. Once the ice-cream van had started, Spider backed it up towards the shutter, then ran back inside to help Beanie put James into the back. Fin waited until they had left and started spreading the wet cement around on the floor. It did the job and covered the blood. Pulling the shutter down, he jumped into the back of the van as Spider pulled away.

'Anybody want an ice lolly?' laughed Beanie while opening the freezers in the back of the van and looking through them, taking his pick.

'Hold one to James's mouth, let's get some water inside him.' Fin sat on the floor beside James and tried shaking him. 'James, can you hear me mate? It's Fin and the lads.' It was useless; he was still unconscious. 'We're going to drop him off at the hospital and scarper. We have no choice; he could have internal bleeding.'

The blood was drying and sticky on James's head, and his breathing was laboured. Fin wasn't sure he was going to make it.

Spider drove up to the front of the hospital and turning his head towards the back of the van, he shouted, 'We can't drop him here Fin; there's too many people milling around. We'll get spotted by someone and we're all covered in blood. Where the hell do you want me to go?'

Standing up, Fin looked out of the windows. 'Drive to the main visitor's car park around the corner, see if anyone is in there.' Although the car park was fit to bursting, there didn't seem to be anyone around. 'Open the back doors Spider. The best we can do is kick him out and hope some good Samaritan will find him.'

Horrified, Spider shook his head. 'We can't just leave him there, Fin; it could be hours before somebody finds him.'

'We have no choice. Look at us!' Fin shouted. 'There are hundreds of people coming and going, someone will find him. Look over there; let's drop him as close as possible to that parking meter. Loads of people will use that. Open the doors and let's get him out.' Fin looked down at James's battered body and pursed his lips together. 'Wait a minute, take his wallet and that wedding ring off his finger.'

'You're going to rob him? Nah Fin, I don't want none of this; the poor bastard's dying and you want to steal off him? Count me out.' Beanie looked at Fin with disgust.

'I'm not stealing off him you prick, but why would anyone go to so much trouble mugging him and beating him up and then leave him with his wallet and anything they could sell? It's too suspicious.'

Once they thought about it, they all agreed it made sense. James would just look like another victim of assault. Going through his pockets, they found his wallet and anything else of value, including his watch.

Spider remained in the driving seat while Beanie and Fin opened the back doors of the van. Looking around, they each took one of James's arms and pushed him out onto the tarmac.

'Drive Spider, and let's get the fuck out of here.' Fin looked out of the window at James's discarded body lying there. Fin's heart sank. He felt guilty about leaving him, but they had no choice. Hopefully, if and when James recovered, he would understand.

'We'll call the hospital later to see if he's been admitted,' said Beanie.

Rolling his eyes up towards the ceiling, Fin couldn't believe his ears. 'And just why would we ring the hospital and ask if he'd been admitted? Now we have to think about sorting ourselves out. We need to torch this van – our fingerprints and blood stains are all over it.'

'I've got a girlfriend; we could go to her place.' Beanie looked down at the floor, blushing.

Both Fin and Spider turned to him in amazement. 'You've got a girlfriend? Since when? Who would want to go out with you, you moron! Will we be okay once we get past her guide dog?' Fin laughed.

Beanie lowered his voice. 'I've been seeing her a while now; she works as a barmaid at one of the clubs, but I have a key.'

Stunned by this revelation, Fin sat open mouthed. 'Spider, keep your eyes on the road. Well, go on then lover boy, give us the address.'

They eventually arrived at a ground-floor flat on the other side of town. It was one of the better estates in the area. 'I'm impressed Beanie; she lives in a decent area. God knows what she sees in you. You go first and see if she's in.'

'I'm a sex god. She can't resist me.' Beanie beamed and polished his fingernails on his shirt.

'Well, you're right about that, because you're a prick!' Fin and Spider laughed.

Beanie knocked on the door first and when there was no answer he used his key and walked in. After a few minutes he came back to the door and gave Fin and Spider the thumbs up. 'Let's take the van around the corner and torch it.'

The grass verge opposite the flats looked like somewhere the kids would play, or where they would hold their bonfire night. Parking, Spider got out. Fin was already lighting paper and cardboard boxes from the back of the ice-cream van. Once they saw that it had taken hold, Fin threw a load of paper towards the driving seats and jumped out of the back, shutting the van doors behind them as they fled. Turning back they could already see the flames getting higher through the windows. 'We had better run; all that gas and stuff to keep the generators working to cool the ice-cream is going to make one hell of an explosion.'

Beanie had left the front door of the flat open while he had a shower. Running in, they darted to the windows and looked out. Black smoke filled the air and suddenly, they heard an almighty explosion. Wide eyed, Spider and Fin looked at each other and gasped. They could already hear fire engine sirens making their way to the fire.

Beanie got out of the shower and rushed into the lounge. 'What the hell was that noise?'

'The van!' Fin and Spider shouted at him in unison.

'Shit!' Rushing to the window, Beanie looked out at the sky covered in black smoke.

Fin and Spider burst out laughing. 'Is that the best you can say? Come on Spider, let's get showered.'

'Hey lads, put your clothes in the washing machine, my girlfriend's got one of those dryers as well,' he boasted. 'Then we can go home in the same clothes we came out in.'

Shrugging and grinning at each other, Fin and Spider walked towards the bathroom. Hopefully they would get away with it and James would be okay.

* * *

Noel went back to the warehouse and raised the metal shutters. Looking inside he felt satisfied. The floor was wet with cement, even though he could see brush strokes running through it. A wide grin spread across his face. James was dead, he was certain of it; his men wouldn't do half a job. They must have dumped his body somewhere; he didn't care where. Now this was his turf and his alone. Closing the shutters again, he walked back to his car and noticed one of the ice-cream vans was missing. Well that solved the mystery – his men had taken James's body away in the van. Realising what day of the week it was, Noel laughed to himself so much his shoulders shook: James McNally died on an ice-cream sundae!

12

A GUARDIAN ANGEL

Patsy's brain was spinning. There was so much to think about, and now she had an angry Sheila to contend with. And who the hell was Karen Duret? She had racked her brain but she couldn't recall ever hearing the name, even in passing. The long drive back to London was tiring, and she just wanted to relax in a hot bath, but she knew she couldn't.

She noticed the petrol gauge was showing the tank as nearly empty, so she turned into the nearest garage, filled up and got back in the car. Setting off again she looked at the clock on the dashboard – another half an hour and she would be home, although it didn't feel like home any more; it had become a place of horror and she dreaded being there.

Looking into the rear-view mirror she saw a man sitting in the back seat. Just as she was about to cry out, he threw a leather belt around her neck and tightened it, causing her to swerve.

'Drive carefully Mrs Diamond, we wouldn't want you to have an accident now, would we?' He laughed. The familiar foreign voice sent chills down her spine. Her heart was beating so fast she could hardly breathe and the leather noose around her neck seemed to get tighter and tighter.

She was tempted to put the hazard lights on, hoping that it would attract someone's attention, then she thought of sounding the horn.

As though reading her mind, the man behind her said, 'No tricks now Mrs Diamond, I am not in the mood.' The serious tone in his voice deterred her.

'Where are we going?' she croaked. The leather belt was so tight it bit into her neck. She held onto the steering wheel to control her trembling hands and noticed her knuckles had turned white.

'Home of course. Isn't that where you are going?' The only eye contact they had was through the mirror and as Patsy glanced up she could see that his were cold and full of hate.

'Why are you doing this? Is it money you want?' Spit dribbled down the side of her mouth and her eyes bulged.

'No Patsy Diamond, *I* ask the questions. Now shut up and drive and no tricks; I know where you live, remember.'

Her stomach was doing somersaults, and she wanted to be sick, but she knew she needed to concentrate. She cursed herself for getting out of the car to fill it up with petrol. For the rest of the journey they drove in silence until she turned into the underground garages of her apartment.

'There are security men down here. It's private parking; they will see you and so will the cameras,' she warned.

'Then maybe this will help you keep your mouth shut and silence the security.' Feeling his arm at her shoulder, she saw the gun he was holding and heard the click of the barrel as he was preparing to fire it. Pulling hard on the tail end of the belt, he pulled her head backwards, almost strangling her. She could hardly breathe and reached up to the noose around her neck to try and free it. 'Do as I say Mrs Diamond. Nice and easy now.' Looking out of the window, he gave a harsh laugh and pointed his gun towards the windscreen. 'So much for your security Mrs Diamond. They are nowhere to be seen.'

Forlornly, Patsy looked at the security guard hut where they usually stood to let the barrier up. There was no one and the barrier was already raised; her heart sank.

Leaving the noose around her neck, the man got out of the car. Patsy thought about making a run for it, but to where? Stepping to her side of the car, he opened the door and took hold of the tail end of the belt and roughly pulled her out. Lashing out, she slapped him, but he laughed and pulled tighter on the belt while pointing the gun in her face.

'I like my women feisty,' he laughed and walked quickly ahead of her, pulling her along, making her stumble and trip over her high heels. A feeling of dread ran through her and she wanted to cry. Was he going to rape her before he killed her? She looked like a dog on a lead as he marched her through the parking bay and towards the lift.

Her last hope was that there would be someone coming down from their apartment to the parking bays, but there wasn't. The disappointment on her face when she saw the lift was empty was apparent to him. 'Not your lucky day, is it?' Raising one eyebrow, he cocked his head and grinned.

Outside of the apartment he held his hand out for her keys. Opening the door, he pushed her forward. 'Ladies first.' The sarcastic grin on his face made her shudder. As she stepped forward into the hallway, he pulled on the end of the leather belt in his hand, making her jerk backwards and fall onto the hallway table. A large porcelain vase went crashing to the ground and smashed beside her.

'Get up you bitch!' he snapped.

Patsy could barely breathe as bile escaped from her mouth and dripped onto her clothing and the floor. She struggled to stand; her legs were like jelly, so she scrambled towards the lounge on her hands and feet. As she crawled, she cut herself on pieces of the vase, making this maniac laugh even more.

'Now, take a good look at me Mrs Diamond, or can I call you Patsy. I am the last thing you are ever going to see. I'm not going to kill you; you are going to kill yourself. You are so distressed by your dear husband's death, distraught even, that it has all become too much for you. So you are going to take an overdose along with a lot of alcohol.'

Coughing and choking, Patsy looked up at him. 'What about the bruises that will be around my neck? Don't you think they'll look suspicious?'

'Not really; maybe you tried hanging yourself first. After today's display in Glasgow, they all know that you are not in your right mind. Crazy woman shouting and screaming her head off.' He walked over to a side cabinet and picked up the vodka bottle. 'Come, Patsy,' he coaxed and held out his hand to help her to her feet. 'Sit on the sofa. Here's your vodka and these are your pills.' Reaching in his pocket, he took out a small plastic bag full of tablets and waved it in the air, then handed it to her.

Weak and helpless, Patsy looked at the bag. 'What are they?'

'Don't worry, I'm not a cruel man, you will just go to sleep and never wake up. Then we will all be rid of Patsy Diamond and her stupid ways.'

Sitting in the armchair opposite her with his back to the door, he waited while she opened the seal on the plastic bag.

Realising she had no choice, she took a sip of the vodka and put a pill in her mouth. Her neck was swollen and throbbing where the belt had cut deep into her and she found it hard to swallow.

'We're not going to do it one by one are we? I don't have all night.' His Albanian voice floated around the room in a sardonic way.

She looked at the tall man properly for the first time. He was around thirtyish, but the cruel grin on his face and the icy stare he glared at her with made him look much older. Was this the last voice she was ever going to hear? Was this it?

'I can't swallow properly yet,' she croaked. Trembling with fear, she put her hand into the plastic bag again, taking out two pills this time. But her hands were shaking so much she couldn't hold them.

Pointing his gun at her, he looked bored. 'Just take out a handful of pills and swallow the bastards, I haven't got all night to waste on you... now fucking swallow them!' Standing up, he grabbed at Patsy's hair, pulling her head backwards. Forcing her mouth open with his other hand, he poured the packet of pills into her mouth. He took the vodka bottle out of her hand and forced the bottle between her teeth, pouring the liquor into her open mouth, making her cough and splutter. She kicked and tried turning her head away but it was useless, he was too strong for her, and his vice-like grip on her hair and head made it impossible for her to move.

* * *

Sharon and Penny ran down the well-lit, carpeted corridor; they had never seen anything like it. Sheila walked along behind them, carefully looking at the numbers on the doors and checking her mobile to make sure she had the right address. Looking around she thought it looked like a hotel – how the other half live eh?

At last she got to Patsy's door and noticed the front door was already slightly ajar. Maybe she had left it open for herself and the girls, she thought to herself. She was about to push it when her gut instinct told her something was wrong. Frowning, she put her finger to her lips to the girls and knelt down.

'We have to be quiet; this is a surprise for Patsy,' she whispered. They nodded excitedly and stood back. With her finger, Sheila gently pushed the door; she could hear a mumbling of voices, but couldn't make out what was being said. Then she spotted the shattered remnants of what looked like a vase on the floor. The door to what she presumed was the lounge area was closed and, pausing for a moment, she took the girls by the hand and walked them further up the corridor. 'You two stay here and be quiet. Don't move.'

Making her way back to the front door, Sheila pushed the door again, gently tip-toeing inside to avoid the shattered vase. She listened at the lounge door. She could hear a man's threatening voice and a woman coughing and choking. She knew that would be Patsy; who else could it be?

Sheila didn't know what to do; if she called the police it could be too late. She heard Patsy cry out, and knew she had to do something. Looking around the fancy hallway, she saw a samurai sword mounted on the wall. Moistening her lips, she reached up to try and lift it from its mount, without being heard. It was long and heavy and she almost dropped it. Her heart was beating in her mouth. She didn't know what she was going to face and prayed to god it wasn't just the television on too loud with some crime movie on.

Summoning up all her strength, she grabbed the handle with both hands and took a huge breath. Then, with her elbow, she pushed down on the handle to open the door. Sheila's element of surprise had worked. She could see Patsy, with her head backwards while a man was shouting at her and pouring drink down her throat. As he turned and looked up, Sheila ran forward, raising the sword and with all her strength and one fleeting blow, she hit him around the head with it. He stumbled backwards and fell to the floor.

Sheila looked at Patsy and could see she was drowsy and covered in vodka. Stunned, Sheila looked down and saw two pills. 'Patsy! Patsy! Wake up.' She slapped her across the face, but the glazed expression in Patsy's eyes as they started to close made Sheila panic. Running into the kitchen, she flung open the cupboards. She'd seen this many times with addicts and thankfully knew what to do. At last she found what she was looking for – salt. Reaching for a mug, she half filled it with salt and water and ran back into the lounge. Patsy was unconscious now and hanging over the arm of the sofa.

Sheila did her best to pour the solution into Patsy's mouth; it oozed and dribbled out as Sheila shouted her name again and again. She wasn't even sure if any had gone down her throat. Rubbing her throat and windpipe, she felt Patsy swallow. At last Patsy started coughing and spluttering and Sheila ran to the kitchen and did the same again. Salt and water, anything to make Patsy vomit. The horrible mixture started working and vomit spewed from Patsy's mouth like a volcano erupting. Sheila rubbed Patsy's back as Patsy emptied the contents of her stomach onto the lounge floor.

Suddenly Sheila remembered the girls standing outside. Leaving Patsy with her head down, she ran to the front door. She didn't know what she was going to do; her own jumper and shoes were wet and covered in vomit.

Looking out of the door, she saw them. 'Sharon! Penny! Come here.' The pair of them ran towards her and, kneeling down, she hugged them both. 'Listen to me carefully. Patsy is not well and has been sick. It's horrible,' she laughed, trying not to frighten them. 'Were going to go inside, but this is hide and seek. I want you to close your eyes tightly so that you don't see it and then we'll run to the bedroom, until she's better and I can clean it up. Is that okay?' Thinking about the man lying on the floor, Sheila could think of nothing else to stop them from seeing him. She had no idea where the bedrooms were or what was in them.

'Yuck, is that like when I had a belly ache?' Both girls squirmed and made disgusted faces and stuck out their tongues, which made Sheila laugh.

'Worse, much worse. Come on.' Once Sheila had stepped inside the hallway, she looked down. 'Okay, here we go. One... Two... Three... Eyes closed!' She held their hands tightly. Looking around, she saw there was a hallway to the left and ran down there and kicked a door open with her foot. Thank god, she thought to herself. Not only was it the bedroom with a large four poster bed, it had what all kids loved... a television! 'Okay, open wide, yay!'

She could hear Patsy coughing and spluttering in the lounge and needed to get back to her without causing the girls alarm. 'Here Sharon, put the television on, I'll be back in a minute.'

Panicking, she ran into the lounge, and although drowsy, Patsy was stirring. 'Drink some more of that shit Patsy.' Patsy shook her head and pushed the cup away. 'I'm not asking. I am telling you. Now fucking drink it. I want your guts on that floor. It's that or die Patsy.'

Half nodding her head, Patsy reached for the cup and held the handle, taking another gulp. She instantly spewed it back out.

Sheila looked over at the unconscious man laid on the floor. He was still alive but out for the count. Running back into the kitchen, Sheila opened the cupboards and fridge. There was a large bottle of lemonade and a huge tin of chocolates on the side.

Picking them up, she grabbed two mugs along the way and went back into the bedroom.

'Surprise!' she shouted to the girls, throwing the tin of chocolates and bottle of lemonade on the bed. Looking at the television on the wall, she smiled. Thankfully, they had found the cartoon channel and were very happy with that.

Running back into the lounge, she could see that Patsy was breathing heavily and still heaving. Her eyes were still glazed and drifting. 'Come on Patsy. Where is the shower? I presume you've one in a place like this.'

Drowsily, Patsy pointed her finger towards the other side of the room where there was a door and on opening it, there was another hallway.

'Fuck me, this place is like the Tardis in *Dr Who*. Can you stand?' Sheila could see she was floppy, almost like a rag doll, and rushed to help her up. She put her arm around her shoulders and almost dragged her down the hallway. Pushing each door open, she finally found the bathroom. It was a walk-in shower and Sheila opened the doors and let Patsy drop to the base inside it. Not knowing how to turn it on, Sheila fumbled with the knobs until at last, water poured out, almost drowning Patsy in the process.

Leaving her there, Sheila ran back to the lounge; she wasn't sure how long the man would be unconscious for. She could see he was still breathing, so for good measure, she picked up the two tablets from the floor and, opening his mouth, she shoved them inside and poured what was left of the vodka in the bottle down his throat. Holding her hand over his mouth for a moment, she waited. If nothing else, she knew they would dissolve in his mouth and make him even drowsier. She knew exactly what they were: Librium.

Adrenalin coursed through her body as she ran back into the

shower room. Patsy had been sick again but was sitting with her back to the tiled wall as the water rained down on her. Taking a breath and looking around her, Sheila didn't know what else to do. The only thing she could think of was to clean up the lounge where Patsy had vomited. Looking around in the many kitchen cabinets, she found a dust pan and brush and some black bin liners. That would have to do for now. Running back into the lounge, she knelt down and grimaced at the sight of the vomit. She could hear the girls laughing in the bedroom, so she started scooping the vomit up into the dustpan and pouring it into the bin liner. She couldn't find a washing up bowl to wash the floor with so she used a mixing bowl and poured the hot soapy water onto the floor, diluting the thick, yellowy mess. She could see that some of the tablets hadn't quite dissolved yet and she breathed a sigh of relief.

She sat back on her haunches for a moment to catch her breath. She had done the best she could. She looked around the soaked carpet to check for any spots she'd missed and noticed the butt of a gun peeping out from under the sofa. Putting it in one of the cabinet drawers, she went back through to the shower room to check on Patsy. She seemed fully awake now and was sweeping her hair away from her face. 'Stay there, I'm going to find you something to wear.'

Running back into the bedroom, she smiled to herself. Although there were empty chocolate wrappers all over the bed, Sharon and Penny were fast asleep. She looked around and saw two thick white towelling dressing gowns on the back of the bedroom door. Grabbing both of them, she went back to Patsy and turned the shower off. The tiled floor was flooded and Sheila grabbed a couple of towels and threw them down to soak it up.

'Can you talk Patsy? Can you hear me?' she asked. She could see that Patsy was more coherent and her eyes looked clearer.

'Yes,' she answered.

'What's my name? Who am I?' Sheila asked, to see if she could really hear her.

'Sheila. My fucking guardian angel,' Patsy croaked. She tried coughing to clear her throat and raised her hand to it. The bruising around her neck was clear and Sheila gasped at the sight of it.

'Bloody hell lassie, that looks nasty. Do you want me to take you to the hospital?'

Shaking her head profusely, Patsy said huskily, 'No! I'll be fine soon. Help me get up.'

Sheila leaned into the cubicle and helped Patsy to her feet, out of her dirty clothing and into the fluffy towelling robe. Shock was starting to set in and Patsy started shaking and crying. Sheila reached out and hugged her closely. 'It's okay Patsy love, I'm here. Let it out.'

Patsy's sobs shook her body uncontrollably as she held onto Sheila.

'I'm going to take you to bed now. I'm not going to leave you; I'll sit with you all night. Come on Patsy, you can do this.'

Almost hobbling through to the bedroom, clinging on to Sheila, Patsy flopped onto the bed.

Sheila put pillows underneath her head. 'You've to sit up a bit Patsy, in case you're sick again. You could choke on your own vomit.'

Nodding her head, Patsy pushed the pillows behind her to help her sit up more. Her eyes closed instantly. Sheila felt satisfied that she had done her best and that a lot of the drowsiness would be from the alcohol. But she needed rest.

Walking back into the lounge, Sheila hovered over the man, then she spotted the belt he'd used on Patsy. Bastard! she thought to herself. Kneeling down, she wrapped it around his legs and buckled it, then she went into the bedroom and looked through the drawers. There, she found some of what she presumed were Nick's belts and ties in the wardrobe. Taking a couple out, she went back into the lounge and rolled the man over onto his back and tied a belt around his hands and buckled it, then for good measure she shoved a tie into his mouth. She had no idea what they were going to do with him, but that was something to think about later. For now, she had to get him out of the way so the girls wouldn't see him. With all her might, she pulled and dragged him into the shower room, wedging one of his shoes underneath the door as she walked out. If nothing else that would keep him in there. Puffing and panting, she wiped the sweat from her brow. She was shattered, her own adrenalin now wearing off. Putting on the other towelling robe, she checked on the girls and pulled the duvet over them.

Going back into Patsy's bedroom she could hear her breathing and mumbling. Putting her ear closer to her mouth, she heard her words. 'Nicky, Nicky,' she said again and again. Sheila shook her head and laid on the edge of the bed beside her. Sheila gave a deep sigh. What a fucking night.

Welcome to London Sheila, she mentally thought to herself before sleep finally took over.

13

THE COLD LIGHT OF DAY

'Oh my head, it's banging.' Patsy held her head in both hands. 'It feels like my brain is going to explode.'

Sheila stirred instantly; she had spent most of the night walking from room to room, checking on the girls and listening at the door of the shower room.

'How are you feeling?'

Patsy blinked hard to open her eyes properly. The room was spinning and her head felt like workmen were drilling inside of it.

'Like shit.' She smiled and reached out for Sheila's hand. 'You saved my life last night. I would be dead now if you hadn't turned up. Thank you Sheila.' Tears brimmed in Patsy's eyes.

'Och, now enough of that Patsy Diamond, especially as we have a worse problem ahead of us.'

'What problem? What could be worse than this?'

'Erm... the fact that we have a man tied up in the bathroom. Have you forgotten about him or do you often have men tied up in your home?' Sheila grinned.

'Oh my god, I'd forgotten about him!' Her eyes widened in

horror as it all came flooding back like some horrible nightmare. Patsy sat bolt upright. 'Is he alive?'

'I think so. I didn't want the girls to see him so I dragged him into the bathroom. I didn't know what else to do.' Sheila shrugged. 'But what do we do with him now?'

The pair of them looked at each other in silence.

Patsy threw back the duvet. 'We need to see if he's alive first, come on.' Still groggy from the night before, Patsy walked to the bathroom and listened at the door.

'He's bound and gagged,' whispered Sheila. 'We can't just let him walk out of here; he'll only come back and finish you off. We have to open the door.' Seeing the horror in Patsy's face, Sheila ran back into the lounge, opened the drawer of the cabinet and took the gun out. 'Right, you hold this and I'll open the door. If he looks like he's coming towards us, just shoot!'

'Where the hell did you get that from?' Patsy looked at the gun. Frowning, she shook her head. 'I can't hold a gun, I don't even know how to shoot one.'

'It's his, I think. Don't go all wimpish on me now Patsy, I've done more than my fair share. Just pull the bloody trigger.'

Listening to Sheila brought Patsy to her senses. 'You're right, of course. Give it to me.' Holding the cold metal in her hand, Patsy was shaking. Neither of them had any idea what faced them. Taking the shoe from the bottom of the door, Sheila held the door handle and looked up at Patsy and nodded. Sheila threw the door open wide. The man was awake, although drowsy, and his angry glare left nothing to the imagination. He was writhing and wriggling on the wet floor and trying to move his hands out from the belt that was holding him.

Patsy froze; memories of the day before gripped her with fear. This man had tried to kill her. She felt afraid of him even though he lay there tied up.

Sheila could see Patsy's hands trembling. 'Give me that,' she said, taking the gun off her. She shot at his leg. The sound of the bullet seemed to bring Patsy out of her hypnotic state. 'There, you bastard, you're not going to run now are you?' Sheila walked over to him and hit him over the head with the gun and watched him slump back into unconsciousness.

'Patsy, we can't keep walking in here and hitting him over the head for fuck's sake. We need to think fast. Do you think anyone heard that gunshot? Christ, let me check on the girls.' Running through the lounge and into the bedroom, Sheila could see they were both still sound asleep. Looking at the clock on the wall she saw that it was only 5 a.m.

When she returned to the bathroom, Patsy whispered, 'What time is it?'

'Five o'clock. Why?'

'We need to get him out of here.' Through her brain fog, Patsy tried to think straight. 'We could take him to my car now, but we need to stop the blood from his leg: it will make a trail.'

'Do you have any cling film?' Sheila asked.

Patsy nodded.

'Well, go and get it then!'

Automatically, Patsy did as she was told and returned with a roll of cling film. 'My feet are all wet, what happened to the carpet?'

'You spilled your guts out on to it. Here, cut this towel – we need to wrap his leg and then we will wrap it in the cling film tightly.'

'I've got some bandages, it will be easier, wait there.' Disappearing again, Patsy came back and held out a first aid kit. 'How do you know such things Sheila?' Patsy was surprised at Sheila's proficient ways.

'Because I come from Thistle Park; you need to know how to

look after yourself. My husband was a thief, an addict and a dealer and at some points so was I. It becomes part of daily life, and don't even think of judging me.'

'I'm not judging you. God knows what I would have done without you... That reminds me: Victoria, my mother-in-law, is coming today.'

Wrapping the bandages around the man's leg, Sheila looked up and snapped, 'Well, she'll have a nice bloody surprise when she comes for a shower then, won't she? Now get your arse into gear and start wrapping that cling film around his leg. Anyway, why is she coming?'

'To take your girls home with her.' Patsy bent down and started unravelling the cling film and wrapping it around the man's leg.

'She's what?' Sheila stopped what she was doing and stared at Patsy. 'What the hell do you mean, she's taking my wee lassies home with her? When did you organise this?'

Still in a dazed state, Patsy continued to wrap the film around his leg. 'Yesterday after you called. They will be safe with her; she lives in Dorset.'

Amazed, Sheila questioned her again. 'What and you never thought of asking me first? I don't even know her.'

'She's a good woman Sheila, and believe me, she lives in a mansion. Lots of spring sunshine and fields for the girls to run around in. And she has a lot of staff; they will look after them. I thought that was what you wanted, to keep them out of harm's way. It was all I could think of.'

Slightly put out, but understanding Patsy's reasoning, Sheila nodded. 'Well, I'll think about it when she gets here. I'm not just handing my daughters over to strangers.'

Looking down at the man's leg, Sheila felt satisfied that it was well and truly wrapped. 'He looks like a well-wrapped chicken. Now, how do we carry him to the car?'

'They have one of those metal trolley things that they bring heavy parcels and stuff up with in the basement. I'll be back.'

As Patsy left, Sheila went and checked up on Sharon and Penny again and then walked back into the lounge. She'd not noticed before, but there were three large cardboard boxes by the wall.

After what seemed an age, Patsy returned with a metal trolley.

Sheila looked down at the trolley, it looked like a metal baby's pram. 'Well, it's better than nothing. You take his legs and I'll take his arms.' Seeing Patsy's hesitancy at touching him, Sheila reached out and grabbed her. 'He can't hurt you now Patsy; come on love.'

Between them, they lifted and pulled the dead weight of the man on top of the trolley. Once done, they both stood back and took a breath.

'Phew, thank god he's not a fat bastard,' remarked Sheila. 'Okay, let's push him to the lift and keep quiet. I don't want the girls waking up.'

It wasn't easy pushing the trolley over Patsy's shag pile carpet, but they pushed and tried steering it in the direction of the door and at one point almost laughed.

'For fuck's sake Patsy, why can't you be like the rest of us and have thin carpets, or laminate? By the way, have you just moved in?' Sheila puffed as she tried pushing the trolley over the thick carpet.

'What makes you say that?' Patsy frowned.

'Those boxes in the corner; I thought you hadn't unpacked properly yet.'

Patsy followed her gaze and saw the boxes. 'Christ, I'd forgotten about them. They were delivered a few days ago.

They're from Nick's office at the solicitors. I was going to have a look through them and then I saw the stamp of the law firm on them. When I called his partner about them he told me they have cleared his office out and thought I might like his possessions.' Patsy looked towards them curiously. With everything going on, they had completely slipped her mind.

'Well, he must have had a lot of crap in his office, looking at the size of them.'

Deep in thought, Patsy nodded. 'Mmm, he must have.' She looked away and carried on pushing the trolley towards the front door.

'Put your coat on and give me one; we can't go down there in these dressing gowns.' Sheila then told her to look out the door to check there was no one around and press the lift button.

Once Patsy had given her the all clear and the lift doors were open, Sheila pushed the trolley inside. 'Bloody hell Patsy, I'm knackered.' Mopping her brow, Sheila leaned on the handle of the trolley and took a breath.

The car park was deserted and they ran to Patsy's car and opened the boot. Patsy saw all of her discarded clothes and the case that was full of money.

'What's all these clothes doing in here? Christ, we're never going to fit him in there.' The pair of them looked at each other for a moment.

'Where's your car?' Patsy looked around.

'It's three up from yours.' Sheila pointed with pride. 'Come on, let's go.'

Patsy's heart sank when she saw Sheila's old Vauxhall. The back doors weren't even the same colour, and it had been sprayed with normal spray paint cans from the shops. The rust around the wheel rims made her shudder but following Sheila's lead, she walked towards it. This was their getaway car? She was surprised it had made it this far.

'Which key is for the boot Sheila?' Patsy reached out her hand for the car keys and waited.

'There isn't one; the lock is broken. You've got to stick your finger through the hole where the lock used to be and fiddle about a bit until you feel the lever.'

Patsy was horrified; she had never heard anything like it. It was a heap of junk. 'What? Are you crazy? This car is a death trap; why the hell did you buy it? Oh no Sheila, there is no way I am getting into that thing.'

'What kind of car can you buy for two hundred pounds? Do you know how much the petrol cost to get here? For Christ's sake Patsy, get off your high horse. If you don't want to get into the car, that's fine with me. You stay here with an unconscious man wrapped in cling film with a bullet hole in his leg, and I'm going to take my girls and drive off in my rusty old car.'

'No, no Sheila. I'm sorry, it's just a shock that's all. I didn't mean to be rude. Do you think we'll get him in the back?'

Satisfied with Patsy's apology and casting her a dirty look, Sheila looked inside the boot of the car. 'Yes, loads of room in there. Put this bag with the kids' stuff into your car and then we'll try and get him in, but it's going to take a lot of lifting. I hope you're up to it. Be careful now, Patsy love, you might just break a nail,' Sheila shot back at her and grinned.

Between them, they pulled under his arms and tried balancing half of him on the rim of the boot, but they couldn't manage it. Each time they pulled one side of his body, and the other side nearly fell onto the floor. 'We can't do it Sheila; he's a dead weight.'

'Keep going Patsy, we have no choice. If we can just put half of him in, we can shove the rest in. Come on! Just one big heave and we're done,' Sheila screamed at her. 'Remember: this bastard was going to kill you. You fucking hate him!'

Patsy looked at Sheila and pursed her lips. She was right. This bastard deserved everything he was going to get and with every ounce of strength she had left in her body, Patsy took a large intake of breath, grabbed his legs and lifted and pulled until, eventually, they got him high enough to roll into the boot.

Sheila pushed his arms and legs a little more so that she was able to shut the lid of the boot. 'Come on, we need to dump him somewhere. We have to be quick though, the kids are in bed, and I'm not leaving them too long. You drive, you know the area. I have no idea where we're going.'

Frowning, Patsy just looked at Sheila. She couldn't believe how calm she was being about all of this. When Patsy got in the driver's side, her eyes widened. 'Oh my god, it's a toilet. There are wrappers, cans and god knows what else. There are holes in the upholstery.'

Sheila folded her arms and turned. 'I am getting sick of your moaning Patsy. Don't fucking push me, because I'll leave you in this shit. I have done a five-hour journey with two kids. The car is not fit for scrap and I didn't have time to clean it, but then I didn't know I would have the queen sat inside of it, did I?'

Without another word, Patsy started the engine. She was trying to think where they could dump a body without being seen! 'What if we drive by the river somewhere and push him and the car in?' She held her hand up to stop Sheila's outburst. 'I am not saying anything about your car, but you said yourself it's not fit for scrap.'

'And people in London are used to two women driving along the Thames and pushing a car into the river are they?' Sheila glared at her. 'Just keep driving. We'll see something; he's not going to tell anyone what happened even if he is found alive, is he?'

'What's that noise?' Patsy strained her ears. 'Can you hear that Sheila?'

'Oh it's probably the exhaust falling off, just keep driving. Let's drop him off under a bridge or something. That's what they do in the movies isn't it?'

Thud, thud.

'There it is again! Did you hear that?' Suddenly they both froze and glanced at each other. 'He's awake!' they shouted in unison. The thudding got louder and louder.

'Let's just park up somewhere and leave the bloody car at the roadside.' Patsy swerved to park and hit the kerb. Suddenly the entire windscreen shattered. It was like an explosion. Bowing their heads, they raised their arms to protect themselves from the shattered remnants that flew into the car and into their hair. Slamming her foot on the brake, Patsy stopped the car completely. They were both shaking and covered in glass. Suddenly, there was a knock on Sheila's side of the window. Frozen to the spot, she wound the window down. She could see by his attire that the man was from some car rescue service.

'Are you ladies all right? Do you need an ambulance?' he asked. 'Come on, get out of the car carefully.' Pulling at the door, he opened it and reached out his hand to Sheila. Wearing only an overcoat and a towelling dressing gown and trainers, she got out. She was shaking and pieces of glass were falling off her.

'I'm okay. Thanks.' Patsy rubbed her face. She was bleeding from a few splinters and shaking, but otherwise okay. Suddenly, she heard the thudding again. Her blood ran cold. What if this good Samaritan called the police or something?

Patsy saw a blue light flash behind her. Putting her hands in her hair, she could have wept. The bloody police were here now; could anything else go wrong today?

They police asked if an ambulance was needed and what had happened. 'I don't know officers, one minute we were driving and the next the windscreen just shattered. Scared us half to death,' she lied. She could see the policemen walking around the car and tutting. They wanted to see her licence, but she told them she didn't have it with her. Then they informed her she couldn't leave the car where it was.

'I can tow you back home. I can put the car on the back of my truck, that's not a problem.' The rescue man shrugged. The police seemed satisfied with that and after checking Patsy and Sheila were okay again, got back in their car. The mechanic had convinced them that there must have already been a crack in it, for it to shatter like that and both policemen had agreed. Sheila told them she would pop around the police station later with her details and kept apologising for the mess. Once they had left, Patsy took a sigh of relief, but she was more concerned about the noise coming from the boot of the car.

'I'll go and get my bag out of the boot, Mr... what is your name again?' Sheila smiled.

'It's Angus. I'm surprised to come all of this way and hear an accent like yours though,' he laughed.

Curiously, Sheila stared at him. 'You're Scottish. What is a Scotsman doing in these parts eh?'

'Part of the service miss; if people break down we have to drive them to a nearby garage or their destination. It's just that mine happened to be coming to London. I was on my way to get some breakfast when I saw you two ladies. I was behind you. Thank goodness I was too.'

'We're not members of your firm Angus,' Patsy piped up, 'but rest assured I'll pay you for your help.'

They both paled as the mechanic started strapping up the car and mounting it onto his truck. They glanced at each other but didn't speak a word.

Sheila undid the buttons on her coat, widening it somewhat so that it displayed an ample amount of cleavage. Patsy stood, confused, wondering what on earth she was doing.

'I'm going to sit up front beside him in his truck Patsy and you're going to agree with everything I say and shut your mouth... got it?' With both eyebrows raised, Sheila looked her square in the eyes.

Sheila bounced in the truck beside Angus and gave him Patsy's address. Patsy's heart sank. After everything they had done, they were going back home! She couldn't believe it. Mortified, she listened as Sheila chatted and charmed Angus. She had no idea what Sheila was up to but flirting with a mechanic at a time like this certainly wasn't on the agenda and as much as she wanted to say something, she remembered Sheila's words.

'It's a shame we don't know any scrap yards Angus. I can't afford to have this car fixed and I only got it yesterday. I doubt the insurance will pay me anything. Do you think I would get anything in scrap for it?' Sheila buried her head in her hands and started to cry. 'Oh my god, my husband has only been dead a few months and my wee girls have nothing and now I've lost everything,' she wailed.

Angus had one hand on the steering wheel and promptly put his other arm around Sheila. 'There lassie, it's not all bad.' His brows furrowed and he shook his head. 'To be honest, the car's a death trap. It looks to me like a cut and shut.'

'What's a cut and shut Angus?' Sheila's watery eyes looked up and gazed at him adoringly.

Angus let out a huge sigh and shook his head. 'It's two cars welded together. It's not fit to be on the road. It's a police matter.'

Patsy's jaw dropped at the very mention of the police and Sheila sat there stunned. 'I can't tell the police Angus; I'll get into trouble. Come on, you're a countryman. Help a wee Scots lassie. What can I do? I spent every penny I had left from the funeral on that car.'

Patsy wanted to be sick; whether it was from last night's sickness or Sheila's bad acting, she wasn't quite sure. There was a pause as Angus carried on driving.

Sheila waited for some indication that Angus might help her. Seeing Angus cast a furtive glance to her well-displayed cleavage gave her hope. If he wasn't interested, he wouldn't be looking.

'Why are you in London?' he asked cautiously.

'My friend Patsy, she's just lost her husband and was in a bit of a state last night. That's why I bought this piece of junk and drove straight down with my two lassies. A mission of mercy, you might say.' Again, Sheila buried her head in her hands and gave out soulful sobs.

Patsy rolled her eyes and looked out of the window, wondering what this man must be thinking. Two women, both with recently dead husbands and driving around in their dressing gowns? It was beyond anyone's imagination. You couldn't make this up if you tried.

'It sounds to me like you're in deep shit lassie. Maybe I can help. There's a scrap dealer not far from here; he might give you something for scrap weight.'

Instantly Sheila beamed with delight. 'Oh Angus love, that would be great. Can we go now?'

Chuckling to himself and enjoying the attention, Angus turned off the road and took another route. The nervous tension between Sheila and Patsy was electric. Although Sheila knew she was playing a dangerous game, she felt anything was better than nothing. She presumed Sharon and Penny would be awake by now and frightened waking up in a strange place without her. She felt nervous and worried, but she had to see this through.

Driving into the scrap yard, Angus blew his horn. He obviously knew the man who owned it. Pressing the button on his truck, he lowered their car onto the floor. Patsy listened carefully, but she couldn't hear any noises coming from it. 'I'll just go and have a word with Mick over there. You two ladies stay in the warm.'

'Wait!' shouted Sheila as he was about to walk away. 'Can they really scrap big cars into little matchbox ones?' she asked with a stupid grin on her face, and Patsy wondered what Sheila wanted now. Angus was nodding and laughing as he walked towards the scrap dealer's hut, with his arm around an excited Sheila.

A few minutes later, Sheila came running towards the side of the truck where Patsy was sat and whispered, 'I've just convinced that dealer and Angus how interesting it would be to see the car crushed and he is going to do it now to show us.' Patsy widened her eyes and stared at Sheila. 'He's going to crush it with everything... and I mean *everything* in it,' Sheila emphasised.

Patsy stared at her, open mouthed, and then looked towards Angus. 'Sheila, you're a fucking genius. Are you sure he's going to do it now?'

Sheila nodded and, clapping her hands excitedly, ran back towards Angus.

Within minutes, the car was being hoisted upwards and crushed. To a sounding applause from Sheila, who encouraged Patsy to put a smile on her face and do likewise. Patsy winced when she thought about the body inside it, but then remembered he would have done the same to her. Patsy felt like getting on her knees and praying, thanking god for intervening. Sheila kept up the presence and fawned all over Angus.

'How will you be getting home now Sheila?' he asked as they drove away.

'Well, I'm staying with the lassies at Patsy's for a few days and then I'll be going back to Edinburgh... why?' she asked innocently, knowing full well what was coming.

'I'm going back in the morning. But I'm staying in a hotel tonight...'

'Oh! You could meet me for a drink later if you want? I'd like to thank you for all of your help, and I know how grateful Patsy is, too.' Sheila gave him a knowing look and Angus burst into smiles; this was what he wanted to hear.

'I'd like that.' He nodded as they turned into Patsy's car park.

Patsy jumped out and went to her car. Opening the boot, she took out a handful of fifty-pound notes and ran back to Angus. 'Here, Angus, thank you ever so much for helping us. And thank you for helping Sheila. I don't know what we would have done without you.'

Angus refused to take Patsy's money, but she insisted and so with the blush rising from his neck he took it.

'I'll meet you down here at about 8 p.m.' Sheila smiled.

Angus nodded, got back into his van and left the car park. They waved him off. Suddenly, they both let out a huge sigh of relief. Their heads were pounding and they were tired.

'Shit! Sharon and Penny!' Turning, Sheila ran towards the lift and pressed it. Hot on her heels, Patsy followed. At the door, they could hear voices and the pair of them looked at each other, eyebrows raised. Patsy's heart sank at the thought of another assailant in her house, but then they heard laughter and what sounded like a hoover. Opening the door, they saw Victoria and Natasha talking to Sharon and Penny. Natasha had the carpet cleaner and was soaking up the water from the floor. There was a smell of cooking coming from the kitchen and much to Patsy's and Sheila's relief, everyone was safe. Sharon and Penny ran towards Sheila and gave her a big hug.

'Victoria, you're early…' said Patsy, avoiding her eyes.

'Come and have some coffee.' Victoria's calm, soothing voice assured Patsy all was well. 'And it's a good thing I was early, if you're going out in the morning with two little girls in bed.' Holding up her hand to stop any explanations in front of the children, Victoria added, 'We will discuss this later, and all of this mess. Okay? Come on you two.' Taking Penny's and Sharon's hands, she led them to the kitchen table.

Feeling something was needed to break the ice in a very awkward situation, Sheila wrapped her robe tightly around her and picked up her mug of coffee. 'I've got a date tonight,' she announced.

Victoria looked up while she poured more coffee. 'If that's the case, I must take an early morning walk with my dressing gown on too.'

Instantly, they all erupted into laughter.

14

A TURN OF EVENTS

'I've got a bunch of grapes; everyone takes grapes to hospital.'

Fin and Spider turned towards Beanie. 'Grapes? You can't go to the hospital. Are you crazy?' Fin couldn't believe his ears. The last thing he wanted to do was attract attention to himself. Leaving James to be found in the hospital car park was one thing but visiting him was another.

'Too late Fin. I needed to know if he'd been found alive. Well, he has and he's in a pretty bad way. I think we got him there in the nick of time. He's wired up to everything.'

'Are you stupid Beanie? How did you find him? Was anyone suspicious?'

'I picked up a white doctor's coat and put it on, then I walked around the intensive care unit... I presumed he'd be there because of his injuries, and true enough ladies, there he was.' Proud of his achievement, Beanie stood there smiling, while taking a grape out of the brown paper bag and eating one.

'They thought you were a doctor?' Fin flopped on the sofa, unable to believe his ears. 'Well if you're the best we can do then the NHS is fucked. You're an idiot, you look like an idiot and they believed you!' Fin burst out laughing. 'How come you still have the grapes then?'

Defensively, Beanie stuck out his chest, proud of his achievement. 'At least I went back to see if he was alive. I asked one of the nurses what his name was and she said anon, whatever that means. But she said she wouldn't know until he regained consciousness. He's on a lot of medication and his legs are in plaster.'

'Anon, means anonymous I think,' interrupted Spider. 'That means that Albanian bloke must think he's dead? There's been nothing on the news about a body being found in the car park or anything.'

Fin listened to the conversation carefully, deep in thought. 'If the Albanian lot think he's dead, they won't come back for him... but if they find out we were there and what we did, we're going to end up in the bed beside him. We need to get him out of hospital. Did that nurse say he was dying or anything?' Doing his best to think on his feet, Fin paced the floor of his flat. 'What he does once he's well again is his own business, but we need assurance this isn't going to backfire on us.'

Confused, Beanie couldn't see what Fin's point was. 'Why can't we just leave him where he is? The nurse said he would be going to a normal ward once he wakes up properly.'

'The police will want to find out who he is. When he wakes up they'll ask his name and then we're fucked. The Albanians will know someone helped him and will want to know what happened to their two goons. How do we know those Albanians haven't already been sniffing around the hospital? We need to cover our tracks. We haven't seen James and we don't know anything about what happened to him. And we need somewhere for him to stay where he can't be spotted.'

As though reading his thoughts, Beanie shook his head. 'No

way Fin, he's not staying at my girlfriend's house. Don't even ask. I'm not dragging her into this.'

'Don't worry Beanie, no one has asked your invisible girl-friend for a bed for the night. James needs to be out of the way. Let's be honest, all he's going to do is sleep and rest and we can get our hands on what he needs. Actually, I have an idea.' Fin tailed off. His mind was elsewhere. Who did he know who would keep quiet and nurse James? Suddenly Fin knew just the person.

As predicted, Kathy, James's wife, was informed about a man who had been attacked and was in the hospital. The police had invited her to go along and see if it was him. Kathy looked through the window of the hospital room and saw her husband half asleep, with his limbs in plaster casts. She'd had enough of his stupid lifestyle after all of these years, and she knew this was no chance mugging. Whatever had happened to him, he had brought it upon himself. 'Can I take a closer look officer?'

'Of course, Mrs McNally.' Opening the door, they all walked to the bedside where James laid helpless. Half opening his eyes he looked up at Kathy. He could see she wasn't pleased to see him, if anything she looked angry. For an instant, their eyes met.

'No, that's definitely not my husband.' Turning, she walked out of the room, without a backward glance. Finally, glad to see the back of him.

Hearing her words echo in his ears, James felt saddened. He wanted to try and speak to her but she had washed her hands of him. There was no turning back now. Closing his eyes again, he felt a deep despair. His wife had just disowned him. The pain he felt in his body was nothing like the pain he felt in his heart.

* * *

'Natasha, would you mind awfully taking the girls to get them some sweets or something? There's a lovely shop opposite the apartments and this place also has its own cinema I believe.'

Sharon and Penny got all excited when they heard there was a cinema. They started shouting out which movies they would like to see.

'Natasha? Would you mind?' Victoria winked at her. She badly wanted to talk to Patsy and Sheila and couldn't do it in front of the children.

Nodding and understanding the situation, Natasha joined in with the girls' enthusiasm and asked Sharon and Penny what they would like to see and if they would like popcorn. They jumped up and down with excitement and ran to get their coats.

'Here you go, just give me enough time to sort this mess out.' Victoria handed over some money to Natasha.

Patsy and Sheila waved them off with a smile and then turned to Victoria who sat in a chair like a head teacher ready to scold naughty children.

'Well, ladies, who wants to start this off?' she asked.

Sheila was amazed. She'd half expected Victoria to blow her top and ask what had been going on, but instead she sat there calmly waiting.

'I want the truth now,' Victoria warned. 'I've never thought of myself as stupid before, but maybe I am. From the beginning, okay?'

Patsy reached for a cigarette, contemplating where to start. 'Well, Sheila saved my life Victoria, but how she did that starts with me being car jacked and threatened by one of Nick's associates.'

Victoria's face never moved all the time Patsy recalled what had happened to her. Then Sheila took over because what had happened at the flat was still mostly a blank for Patsy. Taking a deep breath, they both nodded and decided to tell Victoria what they had done with the assailant's body.

Victoria's eyes narrowed. 'How did you come to upset maniacs so much? What have you done?'

'Nothing Victoria, well... apart from close the community centre. I admit with hindsight I completely lost it. Do you know what they were using the flat above the community centre for? A bloody brothel!' Patsy shouted. 'They have been playing us and we have been paying for it. I threw them out and changed the locks.' Angry and breathing heavily, Patsy cast Victoria an indignant look and stood up to leave the room.

'Sit down Patsy love, you've no enemies here. What about you Sheila, why did you come here?' Victoria was shocked that they had crushed a man to death, and to be honest, it horrified her just thinking about it.

'This gang knows I know things. I've had my daughters threatened and my house destroyed. My Steve knew them all, but he also worked out that your Nick was the Undertaker. Your son was a cold-hearted man Victoria. I don't know why these people followed his orders, or what he had over them. Some of those bastards could have snapped him like a twig, so what made them kowtow to your son?'

'I only wish I knew Sheila. But I have my own story to tell and it's just as pretty as yours.' Looking up at the frown on Sheila's face, she held up her hand to stop her interrupting. 'All will be revealed; as I say, it's not a pretty story. But I do know the kind of man Nick got involved with; maybe that's what led to all of this trouble? But Nick is dead now, so why are these people so determined to make your lives miserable? Never mind what Steve knew, Sheila, it's what they think you and Patsy know that frightens them. As you say, these people live in a different world, but unlike the actors in those films they use real guns with real bullets, you've seen that for yourself first hand. I don't want to lose you Patsy, not for the sake of money. Let them have the community centre and with my blessing. Personally I think you should call the police and tell them what you know. Of course, I would leave the part about crushing a man to death out of it.'

'Not a chance Vicky lass,' Sheila piped up, almost making Victoria laugh. Suddenly her mobile rang and Sheila answered it without thinking. A smile crept along her mouth and she handed it over to Patsy. 'Sorry, mine has a purple case too. Sounds like Sean Connery on the phone for you.'

Snatching the mobile off her, Patsy answered, 'Who is this?' She was in no mood for fun and games.

'Mrs Diamond, it's Larry.'

'What do you want?' she snapped. After all of this soul searching she was in no mood for more bad news.

'I was wondering about that woman you asked me to find. She is definitely a woman of substantial means and I wondered if your accountant would be able to shed any light on things? Why is her address the community centre? What did she have to do with it and was she paying rent? I doubt it, not with the amount she has in the bank. If you could ask the accountant to check, I'll carry on digging.'

Patsy had almost forgotten about the mysterious Karen Duret. It had been a long night and she wasn't thinking straight, but Larry had a point. Was Karen Duret the madam running the brothel? If so, she was making one hell of a profit. Five million pounds is a lot of commission, surely she could have found somewhere better than Thistle Park community centre. None of it made sense and Patsy thought she would go mad if she thought about it for much longer. 'Larry, thank you. I'll be in touch.' With that, Patsy ended the call.

'Who the hell was that? Oh my god Patsy, he sounds gorgeous. That gravelly voice of his is enough to get anyone's knickers twitching,' exclaimed Sheila.

'Sheila! Victoria's my mother-in-law, do you mind. And for your information, your knicker twitcher is my solicitor Larry. He wears off-the-peg suits and permanently has a sandwich carton on his desk.' Patsy tutted.

Folding her arms indignantly, Sheila scoffed at Patsy's snobbishness. 'Aye, there you go again, judging a book by the cover. He may be all that and more, but your husband wore expensive suits and went to expensive restaurants, and he's the reason we're all running for our lives.'

Humbled by Sheila's words, Patsy flashed a glance at Victoria for support, which didn't come.

'You have to admit Patsy: she has a point. I know Nick was representing a man called Billy Burke. A drug baron, a thief and a murderer. He wanted to get to know him better because... he was Nick's real father.' Casting a stern look at Sheila, Victoria carried on speaking. 'From the moment Nick met Billy he changed a lot, didn't he Patsy? We will never know what they discussed, and both of them are dead now, but whatever went on between them I would say all this trouble has something to do with Billy.'

Patsy felt herself about to cry but stopped herself. She couldn't believe her life had turned into this. 'How did Nick fool us all for so long, Victoria?'

'Nick was very persuasive Patsy, that's why. And we can all sit here and fire blame, but the fact is we have to be united. It's them against us,' Victoria stressed. 'Now, I'm going to take your children with me to Dorset if that's okay with you Sheila? And I think you should go back to Edinburgh; we need to make it look like nothing has happened, and nothing has changed.'

Sheila looked up, horrified. 'You're sending me back after everything I've done for Patsy? They'll kill me; don't you get it?'

Victoria cocked her head to one side and shrugged. 'The way I see it, someone must have known that man was coming to kill you Patsy. He's followed you up a motorway and left his car where? We don't know, we can only presume someone dropped him off and are waiting for him to report back. So if we all carry on as though your paths never crossed with him then neither of you can be linked to his disappearance, can you?'

Turning to each other, Patsy and Sheila felt Victoria made a lot of sense, even though going back to Edinburgh was the last thing Sheila wanted to do.

'You amaze me, Victoria. We've just told you we killed a man and you sit there as calm as a cucumber. I'm astonished. Most people would be having a panic attack by now.'

'Well, I am glad I am a revelation and not a disappointment Patsy. I'm sixty years old, give or take; do you really think I don't know what goes on in the world? What you and Sheila have done was by force, you had no choice, and you were damned lucky Sheila's man came to the rescue,' Victoria laughed. 'What were the other options?'

Again, they both knew she was right. The three of them agreed to play it low key for now.

Sheila was worried though. A frown crossed her brow and she wrung her hands together. 'Can I come and visit my kids Vicky? I don't even know where you're taking them to.'

Victoria burst into laughter. 'For goodness' sake Sheila, of course you can. I'm taking them home for a holiday not prison. Ask Natasha; she'll tell you the truth about my home. I promise, they will come to no harm.' Victoria made the sign of the cross as she spoke.

'Speaking of Natasha, are we going to tell her all of this Victoria?' Patsy asked.

'Yes. We're going to keep her in the loop; you never know when you might need her. Whatever gripe you've got with her Patsy, I suggest you get over it. Nick wasn't worth arguing over. Oh, I know I shouldn't say this, after all he was my son. But with everything we're uncovering about his other life, it doesn't make him very pretty does it? And I think Natasha has already paid her dues. It's time to move on.' Victoria's voice of authority made Patsy think. She was right of course, there was more to deal with than a cheating husband.

Clapping her hands to end the conversation, Victoria smiled. 'So, Sheila, what time is this date of yours?'

Feeling a little embarrassed, Sheila turned towards Patsy. 'I meant to ask you: I need to wash my jeans for tonight. I have nothing else with me and they are stiff with vomit. Can I use your washing machine?'

'I can do better than that Sheila. Come with me.' Patsy walked Sheila towards a door at the end of the bedroom. To Sheila it looked like an airing cupboard, but when Patsy opened it her jaw dropped. 'My god Patsy, it's a walk-in wardrobe... and look at those clothes!' Sheila walked down the aisle and ran her hand along the rails of clothes.

'Help yourself to whatever you want, Sheila.' Patsy smiled but seeing Sheila's face as she turned back to look at her, her smile dropped. 'What's up Sheila?'

'I can't wear these Patsy; it's not me. They're beautiful designer clothes, but I can't carry these off. Sorry.' Walking past Patsy, Sheila wandered into the kitchen. Picking up her jeans, she put them into the washing machine.

'Well what did you pick Sheila?' asked Victoria. Seeing Sheila shake her head and shrug, she smiled. 'Good. Because if there is one thing I like when I come to London it's shopping. Let's find you something that suits you.'

'We're back!' Natasha shouted on entering the apartment.

Sharon and Penny came racing through to find Sheila, their excitement and happiness filling the apartment with joy.

'Don't bother taking your coats off girls, we're going shopping,' shouted Victoria. 'We're going to buy lots of clothes. Come on, let's have some fun.'

Seeing their eyes widen with excitement, Sheila turned to Patsy. 'I guess I'm going to need a pair of jeans if you've any; we can't go out in our dressing gowns.'

Lightening the mood, everyone laughed.

Sheila patiently listened to the girls' stories about the movie they had seen and how much they had eaten. It sounded like a sugar overload but looking over at Natasha she mouthed a 'Thank you,' and smiled at her.

Then they all piled in the car and set off. When Victoria parked the car, Sheila looked around and gulped. It was in a main London high street full of clothing shops. She had never seen anything like it. 'Oh my god Patsy, I feel like pretty woman going on a shopping trip.'

'Make that six pretty women Sheila,' Victoria laughed. 'Come on girls, let's strip these stores. Get whatever you want.' Taking Sharon's and Penny's hands, Victoria walked ahead, then half turned her head to see Natasha, Patsy and Sheila all laughing with their arms linked, as they followed her into the store. Victoria smiled. Nick wasn't so bad. After all, without knowing, he had given her a family of daughters and baby Nicky. She had a lot to be grateful to Nick for.

15

THE GREAT ESCAPE

'He's been in hospital for ages and now it's time to get him out. Are you both with me on this?' Fin was adamant. He was worried because his usual stash of drugs hadn't been delivered and he wondered if there was some kind of suspicion surrounding himself and the others.

'Yes, we're both with you mate. There is going to be one hell of a drought, if we're not earning. Do you think he'll pay us for all of our hard work?' Sitting in the corner of the pub, all three of them looked towards Chalky the landlord. Even he didn't seem himself. Normally he would shout insults towards Fin and they would banter, but not today. Something was seriously wrong.

'I've asked Midge and Joe to lend us the mobile shop. I didn't tell them what for but said I needed a good cover and driving a mobile shop near a hospital isn't going to cause much suspicion. They think we're burgling some houses somewhere and as long as they get a piece of the action they don't care.'

Beanie took a sip of his pint of lager and looked around to see if anyone was listening. 'Where are we going to take him, Fin?'

'I've sorted that, but I'll leave that until later.' Fin couldn't tell them, because he was still waiting for an answer. He knew he was taking a big chance, but for his own sake it was worth it and maybe if James felt grateful enough for all of their hard work they might earn something out of it. James already owed him five hundred quid, which is what he'd promised him to follow him to the warehouse. Fin could have cursed himself for not getting the money up front.

After they had all gone their separate ways Fin went back to his flat and waited for half an hour in case he was being watched. Then he left, popping a bag of sugar under his coat. Knocking on Maggie's door, he waited.

'I wondered when you'd turn up.' Standing at the door, she wrapped her black cardigan around her tightly, then folded her arms.

'Can I come in Maggie?' Showing her the proper respect, he gave her a weak, helpless smile and after looking him up and down, she opened the door wider to let him in.

'Have you thought any more about what I said the other day? We all need your help. I need your help and after all, we are related.' Fin looked down at the floor. He knew this was a taboo subject never to be mentioned, but these were exceptional circumstances. She was his aunty Maggie. His mother, Maggie's sister, had dumped him on his grandmother and disappeared into thin air. There was a lot of bad blood between the family and Maggie hadn't known about Fin for a long time. Maggie never mentioned her sister, and never acknowledged him as family, even though if he was really in trouble, she did her best to help him. But to Maggie, Fin was trouble. Always stealing, always in prison and smoking and shoving whatever dust he could up his nose. She had washed her hands of him, but, sometimes, like now, when he mentioned their connection she was prepared to listen. He had kept his word and not one person on the estate knew they were related, which seemed odd to Maggie considering they were a load of nosey bastards. That one had slipped through the net.

Casting him a dark glare, she started her interrogation. 'You say you've a friend who needs to go into hiding for a while, but you never do anyone any favours Fin, so what's in it for you?'

'Possibly my life Maggie.' Fin shot her a glance. 'Things are not good around here at the moment; they're changing, you know that. And this bloke, well, he's not exactly a friend, just an acquaintance. He used to work for the Undertaker and now he's in shit. If we get him back on his feet again things might turn back to normal.'

'This is the first and last time I am going to mention this Fin. When my sister dumped you, I hadn't spoken to her in years, I didn't even know who you were until your nana was dying and she told me. I'll help you, but any trouble comes to my door and your friend is out, do you understand me?' Maggie pursed her lips to make her point.

'Thanks Maggie. Out of interest, where are the girls from the community centre? Are they okay?'

'Not really, thanks to that Patsy Diamond. Poor cows are working above the kebab shop, and it's a shithole. Not fit for animals. I know they aren't earning much.' Maggie's face softened somewhat and she pointed to the sofa for Fin to sit down. 'I agree, there is something in the air these days that's making us all watch our backs, including me. Beryl thinks Patsy Diamond is having some kind of mental breakdown.'

'Maybe if we get this bloke back on his feet things will return to normal... maybe eh?'

'When were you thinking of bringing him here?' Curiosity was now getting the better of Maggie. She had no idea who he was, but if he was a friend of the Undertaker, well, he had helped her once. Maybe this was the time to settle the score for good.

'Tomorrow, late evening. These spring nights don't help and he can't be seen coming in here. Is that okay?' Raising his eyebrows, he half expected a reprimand, but instead she nodded and stood up to show him the door.

'Why have you got a bag of sugar under you jacket, Fin?' Perplexed, she couldn't help noticing that he was taking it out of his jacket and holding it in his hand.

'Because, if anyone sees me leaving here, they will just think I'm on the scrounge again.' Giving her a smile, he opened the door to leave.

'You're always on the bloody scrounge,' she shouted after him as he walked away.

* * *

Sheila was back in Edinburgh and Patsy had given her a few hundred pounds to take with her. She had been reluctant to take it, but Patsy had insisted.

Victoria and Natasha had left with Sharon and Penny and now, alone in her apartment once more, Patsy felt very lonely. This place gave her the creeps but following Victoria's instructions she had decided to go back to work and carry on as normal. But first she had wanted to see Tom, the accountant, as suggested by Larry.

Entering Tom's office on her own felt strange; in the past Nick was usually with her. She had thought it was a 'couple' thing, to look after her, but now she realised it was only to make sure all the money laundering had gone through properly without raising suspicion. Tom probably presumed Patsy knew more about Nick's business than she actually did.

'Tom, it's so nice of you to see me at short notice. I have a couple of things to go through with you I'm afraid. Firstly, is the community centre making any money? It's past the first quarter now and I know you're keeping an eye on the receipts in my absence.' Patsy looked down, then peering up under her well-mascaraed eyes, flashed him a smile. 'Secondly, the pizza shops, I'm not sure I want to keep them. Scotland is such a long distance from London, and anyone could be ripping me off. Nick never mentioned staff or anything like that with me. He seemed to have it all in hand and I never got involved.'

Patsy was slowly working her way up to her main question but didn't want to blurt it out straight away. Playing the forlorn widow gave her the upper hand and she was pleased when Tom reached over the desk and patted her hand. 'You know Mrs Diamond, whatever I can do for you, you only have to ask.'

Patsy felt he had that puppy dog look on his face, which annoyed her. Now Nick was dead it seemed most of the men she knew suddenly thought she was fair game. Nick's partner John, at the law firm, had called her constantly. Now Nick was dead, he would have to buy her out of the law firm and it was going to cost him a fortune. He had suggested keeping the solicitors running as it was, but as he and his colleagues were doing all the work, he had suggested Patsy take 30 per cent out of the business instead of the 50 per cent she was entitled to.

Tom started typing on his computer and beamed a large, satisfied smile. 'Well, from what I can see, the community centre is a valuable asset. Up to now, you're in the profit margin.'

Choosing her words carefully, Patsy said, 'For the present time Tom, I've closed it. It seems there were some unsavoury people hanging around there without anyone in charge.'

Tom stared at her oddly. 'Well, in my opinion, you should open it again. Why lose that income? And from what I see, there is someone looking after it. Mrs Beryl Diamond and the chef Paul. He is the one who is keeping all of the invoices and receipts for the food and sending them on. I have applied for grants from the council and they have allowed them for crèche that's there and I believe once a week there is an education class. Teachers come from the local college and teach computers and English to help the local residents. The grant payments are for the use of the community centre, if you know what I mean. It's all cash and council funded, why turn it down?'

Patsy's jaw almost dropped and she did her best to hide it. 'Who is the tenant of the flat upstairs Tom? Maybe I should introduce myself to them?' Thankful that Tom had brought the subject up, she felt this was her chance to get the information that she wanted. All those letters had been for Karen Duret, maybe she was the named tenant.

'As far as I know, it's a Polish lady.' Tom laughed out loud. 'Don't even think of asking me to pronounce the name Mrs Diamond.' He joked and shrugged his shoulders, turning the computer around for her to see it.

Patsy's heart sank; a Polish woman with a name Tom couldn't pronounce was not what she was looking for.

'What about the pizza shops? Are they making money? Would you say they are a good investment?'

Tom carried on typing on his computer. 'Ah yes, Mrs Diamond, they are doing fine also, but I'm afraid you couldn't sell them off without buying Nick's partner out first.'

'Nick's partner? I didn't know he had a partner, who is it?'

'It's a... let me see... a Karen Duret.' Avoiding Patsy's gaze, he carried on typing on his computer. His face flushed, and he ran his finger along the inside of his shirt collar and straightened his tie.

Patsy sat there stunned for a moment. She had come for the

truth, but this bombshell rocked her world. 'How do we find her Tom? How long were they partners?'

Coughing to clear his throat, Tom swallowed hard. 'For quite a while I believe. As for her address, I believe she lives abroad. In Paris to be precise.'

Patsy felt dazed; her brain was spinning and she didn't know what to say. She felt sick and she could see that Tom felt uncomfortable too. More to the point she felt humiliated. How could she have lived with someone for so long and know nothing about them? Nick had become a stranger to her. Rubbing her palms together, to try and dry some of the sweat off them, she asked Tom what he thought about John's proposition of 30 per cent.

'Don't take it Mrs Diamond. Nick was the senior partner, and I would get a solicitor to look into that side of things for you. But you are entitled to Nick's full share. What with this and your own successful salons, you're a very wealthy woman.'

Yet again, the cheesy smile Tom gave her made her cringe inside. She didn't know what else to say. She may be rich, but her whole marriage had been based on lies. Reaching out her hand to shake Tom's, she needed to think things through properly. But suddenly another thought occurred to her. 'I'm thinking of selling my apartment. I'm sure you can understand, I don't want to live there any more.'

'That's between you and the estate agent Mrs Diamond. But if you need any financial assistance, of course I would be more than happy to help.'

Suddenly Patsy felt overwhelmingly uncomfortable in his presence; she wanted to get out of there and she couldn't breathe. 'Thank you for your very valuable advice Tom, I'll be in touch. And thank you for keeping an eye on things for me.'

Standing up, Patsy's first impulse was to run as fast as possible out of there, but for her own dignity she walked slowly, trying to maintain her composure.

Once back in her car, she lit a cigarette. She didn't know what to think, although she had a starting block. Picking up her mobile she made a call. 'Larry, it's Patsy Diamond. I just thought you should know that the name of the woman I gave you was apparently Nick's partner. She lives in Paris and it's even more important that I track her down now; she owns half of the shops in Scotland!' Patsy was half talking and half shouting down the telephone.

'Okay, Mrs Diamond. I'll carry on looking into it when I get back to Scotland. These things take time you know.' His calm voice made her feel better.

'Where are you? What do you mean when you get back to Scotland? I'm not paying you to take a bloody holiday!' All of her hurt and pent up anguish poured out and tears brimmed on her lashes. She needed to get it out of her system.

Ignoring her outburst, Larry carried on. 'I'm in London Mrs Diamond. It may have escaped your notice but I am a criminal lawyer, and I do have other clients. Rest assured, everything is in hand, and I won't let you down. I never have, have I?'

Patsy took a deep breath. He was right. Larry had always gone that extra mile for her. 'Can I see you when you've finished with whatever it is you're doing? I need to explain things to you.' Her voice shook as she spoke.

'Yes Mrs Diamond, but you sound like you're going to have a panic attack. Slow down; whatever it is we can fix it. It's all come as a shock that's all.'

'I don't know what to do, Larry. Help me sort this... please.' Tears rolled down her face and she could barely speak.

'And I will. Let's say about 3 p.m. I should be done around here, where do you want to meet?'

'Come to my apartment, I'll text you the address. I don't want anyone else overhearing what I have to tell you. This is strictly between you and me... understand?' Patsy waited for his answer and once he had agreed she took a sigh of relief. Looking at her watch, she could see that it was just after 1 p.m. Not too long to wait.

'Mrs Diamond, I'll be there as soon as I can. Promise.' With that, Larry ended the call.

As usual, the traffic in London was back to back and it seemed as though she had to stop at every traffic light along the way. Everything that Tom had told her went through her mind again and again. It seemed no sooner was she home and had calmed down a little that Larry turned up.

'Thanks for coming. Do you want a drink or something to eat?'

Larry surveyed the enormous, swanky apartment and although he was impressed, his heart sank. He liked Patsy very much. She was a beautiful woman with spirit. He looked forward to her calls, even if they were usually abrupt and rude, but just looking around the apartment he knew he didn't have a chance in hell with her. He wasn't a poor man, but he didn't live like a millionaire either and that was what she was used to.

He looked at Patsy as she walked away. She was wearing a powder blue skirt suit and matching shoes. The colour high-lighted her long dark hair and make-up. He felt a flush of embar-rassment rise from his neck to his face and needed to concentrate on the matter in hand, but what was going through his mind right now was far from professional. 'Just a coffee please, milk no sugar. I don't have too long Mrs Diamond, my train is in a couple of hours, but it's long enough for you to give me an outline of what's happened.'

Patsy offered him a seat and went through to get the coffee

which was already prepared in her expresso machine. 'I don't know where to start Larry,' she confessed, taking a huge sigh and lighting another cigarette. 'Do you come to London often? Why do you catch the train rather than drive?'

'Because I can read my files, have a coffee and it's less stressful. Anyway, you were telling me about the information you've discovered about Karen Duret.' Picking up his cup, he waited. He could see she was agitated and distressed, but bit by bit her meeting with Tom unfolded.

'If her share of the profits are going into an account and we have seen the bank statement, what makes him think she lives in Paris? All we have is a sort code and an account number. Personally, with what you've told me I would say Tom knows a lot more than he's told you. Maybe he's trying to spare your feelings.'

Pondering his words, Patsy frowned. Larry was right – what did make Tom think she lived in Paris?

'As for the other stuff, Mrs Diamond, I agree, why let the community centre sit there empty, when it looks like you're making profit? Open it again and blame your outburst on the menopause or something. I find women usually do that,' he laughed.

Patsy smiled; it all seemed to make sense when Larry said it. 'Yes, you're right, but what about the flat above the community centre? This Karen person didn't live there and yet her mail goes there.'

'But someone was at least paying the rent. I'll have your mystery woman traced but remember Mrs Diamond, I am a lawyer not Agatha Christie. Your husband buried his secrets deep. Deep enough never to be found and he knew the law. This will take time, so I suggest you get on with life and leave the thinking to me – that is why you're paying me. You know how these things work Mrs Diamond; you were married to a lawyer long enough,' he pointed out. 'And I might have some good news for Natasha. Social services are preparing to set up a meeting prior to her seeing young Jimmy. It will be maybe monthly or weekly supervised meetings in the beginning, but we have to start somewhere. How is the baby doing?'

'I thought you didn't get involved in family law, Larry.' She grinned. 'It seems you've worked very hard and I appreciate it. The baby is doing okay by all accounts, thanks for asking.' His genuine concern touched her. Why should he care after all? 'I'll pass your message on to Natasha and Victoria; at least that is one problem I can tick off my list.' Patsy felt much better now she had got it all off her chest and Larry had made sense of everything. 'You've bought a new suit Larry, am I paying you too much?' They both burst out laughing.

'Well, I can't represent the famous Mrs Diamond and look like I've got dressed in the dark can I?'

Although the words 'the famous Mrs Diamond' stung a little, she knew he meant no harm. She felt easy in his company, and as they drank more coffee and chatted, Patsy realised it was the first time she'd actually had a proper conversation with Larry.

Looking at his watch, Larry stood up. 'I didn't realise I had been here so long. I have to go; my train leaves in one hour.'

'I'll drive you to the station. Sorry, I've kept you far too long.'

But the traffic was horrendous and it came to the point where they were both watching the clock as Larry's departure time loomed. 'I should have got the tube.'

'We'll make it Larry, were nearly there. Stop panicking.' Tongue in cheek, even Patsy wasn't sure if they could make it, although they could see Kings Cross Station in their sights. At last they were in the drop off parking bay around the back.

'Right, I'm off.' Larry had already undone his seatbelt and was jumping out of the car.

'Wait! I'm coming with you in case you miss it,' she shouted.

As they both ran towards the gates, Larry shouted at one of the station men, 'Which one for Scotland?' Seeing him point his finger to the one in front of them, he breathed a sigh of relief. 'Two minutes to spare Mrs Diamond.' He was about to walk away when he turned back towards Patsy at the gates. Impulsively, he looked into her large brown eyes and, putting down his briefcase, he placed his hands on the sides of her face, leaned in and kissed her on the lips.

'I know I'll get sacked for that,' he shouted as he ran, 'but it was worth it.' Leaving Patsy shocked and confused at the gates, Larry boarded the train just in time.

Speechless, Patsy watched the train disappear into the distance, and then looked around at the other people stood there. Embarrassed at their stares, she walked away, not really sure what had happened. Had Larry really kissed her? She didn't know what to think, although looking closer at her windscreen as she got to her car, she raised an eyebrow and let out a deep sigh. Larry's hurried departure and kiss had just cost her a parking ticket.

16

NEW PARTNERSHIPS

'Why do we have to go at visiting time – the busiest time of the day? How are we going to sneak into the hospital and kidnap James?' Pushing his hat back, Beanie gave out a huge sigh. What Fin was asking was impossible. They would all get caught for stealing a patient.

'That's the whole point Beanie, it will be full of strangers coming and going, so us three walking in won't look suspicious.' Fin knew it was a big thing he was asking of their friendship, but if he supplied them with enough drugs for courage, they wouldn't remember anyway.

'But three of us plus a patient in a plaster cast might look suspicious, especially still drugged up and half-conscious.' Spider shook his head. Fin was one of his best friends, but sometimes he could be stupidly impulsive.

'We're going to use a wheelchair!' Fin spat out. 'For god's sake, you idiots, take another sniff of that cocaine and grow some balls. Come on laddies, whatever is happening around here lately is shit. We can't get our hands on any decent stuff to sell, those Albanians have seen to that. I nearly got beaten up the other night for trying to sell that crap. We need to get James back on his feet. He will sort all of this out, you'll see, and we will get something for our trouble, I'm sure of it.' Fin knew he was winging it, but he needed to sound confident for Spider and Beanie to help him.

Bending over towards Fin's battered wooden coffee table, they each took a straw and sniffed a long line of cocaine and then wiped their noses. Their eyes watered and stung. 'Where did you get that from Fin? It's not bad?' Spider looked towards Fin. 'How come your stuff is okay?'

Agitated by their constant complaining, Fin paced the floor and moved the old Celtic flag from the windows to see if the mobile shop had turned up yet. He heard its horn blow as it drove onto the estate and saw Midge open the shutter to serve any customers. Fin nodded to Spider. 'Come on, were leaving.'

Midge opened the back doors of the van to let them in once the last customer had left.

'How come you've got a black eye Midge? Who you been fighting with?' Beanie was surprised to see Midge's face. He was like one of those Jack Russel dogs: a fighter who rarely got beaten.

'It's nothing... just a bit of trouble.' Avoiding their stares, Midge locked the back doors and Joe drove off.

'Is someone giving you grief? We're mates, you know that. If you need some muscle, I'm with you.' Concerned, Spider looked around the back of the van for a show of camaraderie from the others and they all agreed.

Helping himself to a chocolate bar and then passing a couple more to his friends, Fin spied Midge. He usually had so much to say, but today he seemed very tight lipped. 'I do hope you haven't spilled your guts and told anyone what we're up to Midge. You seem a bit edgy to me. What's the problem?'

'I'm no grass Fin. It's just that lot that have taken over the sales for the shop. Every time the takings are down, one of us gets a beating to keep us in line. We threatened to leave, but we got a beating about that too. You can see for yourself how short the queues are at the van now. The drugs are rubbish, I'm not even sure they are drugs, but those Albanian ice-cream men are making our lives hell!'

Listening to Midge's outburst Fin realised why he had agreed to help him. They were stuck between a rock and a hard place and presumed Fin had all the answers, or rather, as leader of the gang, they hoped he did. Mentally, he knew he didn't, because as much as they were hoping he could help them, he was hoping for the same from James.

Joe parked the mobile shop in the forecourt of the hospital and Fin, Spider and Beanie jumped out of the back.

'If you get moved on we will meet you in the visitors' car park,' Fin shouted as they all ran through the doors. There wasn't a moment to lose; they needed to get James out and get to Maggie's.

Getting into the lift, they all put their heads down and their hoodies up to avoid the CCTV cameras. Visitors were pouring through the doors with their bunches of flowers, which pleased Fin. No one was paying any attention to them. Seeing a wheel-chair in the corridor, Fin started pushing it towards James's bed. He was still half-conscious and there was a drip in his arm and his leg was in traction. Grimacing, he felt he had bitten off more than he could chew. He felt tempted to leave, but then he saw Beanie who had nicked a white doctor's coat and was quickly closing the curtains around the bed for privacy. Giving Fin a wink, he smiled and started taking the needle from the drip. Spider started taking James's plastered leg out of the traction that was holding it upright. That cocaine had worked wonders, Fin thought to himself and smiled.

* * *

The passers-by surrounded the mobile shop, especially as the word had spread that they had half price, cheap cigarettes from abroad. Clearly their chocolate and drinks were much cheaper than the hospital shop's and they were doing a roaring trade. 'Joe, you carry on serving, it looks like there's something trapped on top of the van. I'll be back in a minute.' Midge got out the van and promptly started climbing up the side of the brick wall near the van and threw himself on top of the van. Joe heard a thud as he landed but thought nothing of it and carried on serving.

* * *

James was a dead weight as the three of them heaved him up and tried to get him into the wheelchair. A low moan escaped James, as he dropped into the chair and his head fell back.

Fin peered through the curtains to see if there was a doctor or nurse hanging around. 'All clear.'

Beanie parted the curtains and, standing there in his doctor's coat, he pointed towards the exit. 'Over there please porters,' he ordered, with all the authority he could muster without laughing, while striding ahead. Grabbing the handles tightly, Fin started to push while Spider held on to James so he didn't fall out of the chair. It was awkward with his plastered leg sticking out in front of him and even harder to turn him without hitting someone or knocking something over.

Although some of the visitors looked them up and down, seeing Beanie in his white coat assured them and made them dismiss the charade and carry on talking. Half walking and half running they headed for the lift, bumping into everything in their path as they tried to steer James steadily. Thankfully, the lift doors opened and people were just getting out of it and so they didn't have to wait.

Puffing and panting and doing their best to hold James up, Fin warned, 'When we get down to the ground floor, I want no eye contact with anyone. Walk through there with your head held high and confident. Whatever happens, keep walking towards that bloody van wherever it is.'

The lift doors opened and someone was about to get in.

'No room, contagious,' Beanie snapped as he pressed the button to close the lift doors again. 'I've always wanted to do that; I've seen it on the television.' Beanie grinned. Fin and Spider caught each other's eyes and shook their heads. There was nothing to say.

Striding through the hospital towards the exit, they avoided the curious stares from members of staff, and increased their pace when they saw one of the nurses walking towards them. Their adrenalin was at an all-time high as they pushed past everyone in the crowded hospital. They rushed out of the doors, nearly dropping James in the process.

'Phew, there's the van. Run for it,' Spider shouted. The van was exactly where they had left it. The back doors were half open, waiting for them. They glanced at each other; they couldn't get the wheelchair in with all of the stock in the back, so they tipped James out and dragged him inside.

'Drive, you silly bastard!' Fin shouted to Joe as he was pulling the back doors closed.

Joe instantly ignored who he was serving and got into the driver's seat, started the engine, and sped off, leaving confused customers standing there. They were all exhausted, breathing heavily and lying on the floor beside James, trying to catch their breath.

Spider looked around. 'Where's Midge?'

Hearing some banging and shouting, they all looked up to the skylight in the roof of the van where they could see Midge's body. He was lying face down on the top of the van as they raced off.

'I'm not stopping, not with that bloke in the back. He will have to hang on till we stop at some traffic lights,' Joe shouted.

As soon as they stopped at the traffic lights, Spider jumped out. 'Midge, jump! Come on mate, I'll catch you.'

Scrambling to the edge of the van, Midge jumped, landing on Spider and making him fall to the ground. Picking themselves up they got into the back of the van and slammed the doors behind them. Midge was grinning from ear to ear.

'Wow, laddies, that was the best buzz ever. I was surfing through Glasgow!'

They all burst out laughing. 'You made this van look like a bloody helicopter with your arms and legs stretched out like that,' Fin said.

Wiping the tears of laughter from his eyes, Joe shouted out from the driver's seat, 'Are we taking him back to yours Fin? We have to get the van back. Those bastards wait for us at the ice-cream warehouse. It's where we have to park it now.'

A worried look crossed Fin's face. It was still light; he couldn't take him to Maggie's yet. 'Can we pick up a shopping trolley along the route or something? The lift is working, but we need to get him to it first.'

Spider butted in, still laughing at Midge. 'We'll make a stretcher. Do you have an old blanket Fin? It will be easier to carry him on that. We can also cover his face so no one can see him.'

Thinking about it, Fin nodded.

Once near the estate, Fin ran to his flat and grabbed the duvet off his bed. Laying it on the floor outside of the van, they opened the doors and rolled James on to it. Folding the duvet over him, the three of them started carrying James towards the lift.

'Thanks Joe, thanks Midge. I owe you both a large drink,' Fin shouted.

James's straight plastered leg did not help matters as they tried pushing him in the lift. The lift doors opened before Fin's floor and stood in front of the doors was Maggie with her arms folded. Shocked to see her, their jaws dropped.

'What a load of prats you look.' She tutted and wrapped her black cardigan around her. 'Come with me. And don't drop him.'

Doing their best to grab the edge of the duvet and wrap it around their hands, they followed Maggie to her flat.

'Do you think people don't have windows you bloody fools? Go on, get in, let's hope they think you've just been stealing again.' Maggie took great pleasure in watching the three of them struggle to carry James in. The sweat was pouring down the sides of their faces and they wanted to stop and take a break, but Maggie had marched ahead like a military sergeant.

'Put him in there,' she barked and pointed to a bedroom. Even though Maggie had been expecting them and had watched the farce from her window, she was angry that they had done it in broad daylight. She had needed to step in and sort it out, before anyone else saw them. She had already made up the spare room for James. 'Do you have any medication for him?' she asked as they almost threw him on the bed. James let out a groan as they rolled him onto his back. 'Christ, he looks in a worse state than you said Fin, or have you three done this to him?' Maggie looked at the three of them stood there gasping and trying to catch their breath. 'Are you done, you bloody wimps! Fin, I want medication, and you two' – Maggie pointed her finger in Spider's and Beanie's faces – 'were never here. You never saw me and you didn't bring that body here. Do you understand? One wrong word and I'll have your balls cut off!' she warned. Her thin pale face was almost touching theirs.

Wide eyed, they nodded and headed for the front door. Fin reached into his inside pocket and took out two bottles. 'That's tramadol for the pain and clonazepam to help him sleep. I'll see what else I can get.' Fin knew he had messed up again, but Maggie was keeping her word and that was what mattered. For all of Maggie's brash ways, she had a heart of gold and was a good woman. Life just hadn't been kind to her and she had built a brick wall around her to save her from more hurt and pain.

Snatching the pills from Fin, she looked at James's battered body. 'What are you going to do when that cast needs to come off?'

Clearing his throat, Fin met her eyes. 'If you let him stay that long, I'll do like they do in the hospitals and cut it off with a saw.'

Maggie nodded. 'He can stay; you obviously think he's worth it. Well he had better be and you're paying his food bills my laddie. I'm not a charity.' Maggie walked towards the front door and opened it for them to leave without another word.

17

CHANGING TIMES

'Are you sure you want me to do this Patsy?' Standing above her with her scissors, Janine felt nervous.

'I am Janine and if I was going to trust my hair with anyone it would be you. I've been back at work for two weeks now and every time I look up into those mirrors above the salon chairs I see Mrs Nick Diamond. Well, I am not her any more, am I? I am Patsy Diamond and she deserves a new hairstyle. I want it long on the top, with a wispy fringe and short into the neck.' Patsy instructed.

Although a professional, Janine winced as she raised her scissors and cut the first lock of dark wavy hair, watching it fall to the ground.

Bowing her head while Janine worked her magic, Patsy thought over the last couple of weeks. Strangely enough, life seemed to have returned to normal. There had been no more incidents of strange Albanian men turning up at her apartment. She had spoken to an estate agent and the apartment was on the market for sale. As agreed, she had sent the keys to Beryl Diamond to open up the community centre again, much to her sheer delight. Patsy had telephoned her and agreed that it was the stress of recent times and everything had got too much for her.

No doubt Beryl would have spread the word quickly and the centre would have been opened up as soon as the keys were delivered. If that is what it took to get these animals off her back for now, Patsy felt it was worth it.

Sheila checked in every other day to make sure she was safe and to see how things were going. They were both lonely in their own ways, although it seemed Angus, the car rescue man, had become a frequent visitor and was helping Sheila redecorate her house. The thought of Sheila made Patsy smile. She had become a good friend and didn't mince her words, and even Victoria found her amusing; she was far from what she was used to but she'd brought a smile to her face when she had visited her daughters at Victoria's house.

Natasha was healing well and the baby was doing fine. He was a fighter and Natasha texted photos of him regularly. It seemed so much had happened. Her arch rival had suddenly become the nuisance younger sister, revelling in Victoria's attention, and Sheila had become the middle sibling. It was all very odd but seemed strangely natural. Victoria was the mother hen and kept the peace between them all. Her house was full of gaiety and laughter and if nothing else it gave the staff something to do. Victoria seemed much happier these days, and it was true what they said: *not all medicine comes in bottles.*

'There you go Patsy, what do you think?' Janine stood back and marvelled at her own handiwork. 'You look amazing. If anything, you look younger. Good choice of style.'

Patsy hardly recognised herself as she looked up into the mirror. Her short haircut looked feminine and wispy. Patsy turned in the chair and stood up, shaking the apron around her shoulders, letting all of the cut hair fall to the floor. 'Thank you

Janine, you've done a marvellous job as always. It looks great and I feel so light headed.'

'I bet you do. We could make a wig out of that lot on the floor,' Janine laughed. 'I'm going to put the kettle on. I haven't had one since the staff left; I must admit, I wondered what I'd done wrong when you asked me to stay behind after closing.'

'You've done nothing wrong Janine, quite the contrary, but I wanted us to be alone for this.' Patsy cleared her throat. 'In fact, I know you've been covering for me all of these months but I wondered if you would take over as general manager of the London shops permanently. I'll still pop in from time to time of course, but I am going to be fairly busy sorting out Nick's affairs and even though I am captain of the ship I need a good right hand like yourself. Of course, there is extra money in it for you and a percentage across the shops.' Once she had finished her speech Patsy felt better. She had thought about this for the last couple of weeks and there were only so many balls she could throw into the air and catch without dropping them. Her mind was on other things these days and she didn't want the shops to suffer. She had worked so hard building up the clientele over the years, and it would break her heart to see it all go to waste.

'For goodness' sake Patsy, you sound like you're never coming back. You know I'll take care of things for you, if you're happy with that. All the books are in order, you can see that for yourself, but I don't need a percentage Patsy. That is more than generous.'

Taking her coffee mug from Janine, Patsy took a sip and smiled. 'No, I want you to take a percentage, because that is the incentive to keep things running. The more profit you make, the bigger the bonus.' Patsy laughed and carefully chinked her coffee mug against Janine's.

'Cheers,' they both shouted in unison.

Feeling a huge weight lifted from her shoulders, Patsy drove home. The place gave her the creeps these days and she never felt safe there. She had even kept the gun left behind by her assailant by her bedside. This time she was determined, whatever happened, she would shoot any bastard that threatened her life. Driving along, she kept looking in the rear-view mirror at her new hairstyle. It felt strange having short hair, but she felt better for it. This was a fresh start in her life.

And perhaps the people who were threatening her life would find it harder to recognise her like this too? Woken from her thoughts by her mobile, she saw that it was Larry. They hadn't spoken since that day at the train station, but he must know by now she hadn't taken offence because she hadn't sacked him. Accepting the call from her mobile on the dashboard, she waited.

'Mrs Diamond... is that you? It's Larry from the solicitors.'

'Yes, I know Larry, because I have your number and name in my mobile. What can I do for you?' A smile crept along her face when she thought of that kiss at the train station. She could hear by the tone of his voice he was nervous about calling her.

'If you've the time Mrs Diamond, I would like you to come to Scotland. I think I may have found your Karen Duret... No guarantees now,' he faltered, 'but Duret isn't a common name and I really need you to be here when I visit her. As I said, I can't be 100 per cent certain, but I think this could be the one.'

Patsy pulled the car over to the roadside. 'You sound very secretive Larry. Where does she live?' Patsy couldn't believe her ears. Larry had found Nick's mysterious partner!

'Calm down Mrs Diamond, I only said I think I have, remember? No guarantees. She is in Glasgow and I think you should come as soon as you can, to see her for yourself. I'm not divulging any more information until you come.'

'Don't play games with me Larry, I'm really not in the mood,' she snapped.

Larry gave her no more information, no matter how hard she tried to squeeze more out of him.

'I'll be at your office some time tomorrow, depending on the traffic.'

Now he'd given her the news, his voice became softer and concerned. 'That's fine. Why don't you take the train and then you can relax,' he stressed, but he knew she wouldn't listen.

'Because I need my car Larry. I'll pop by to see what Beryl is up to as well and then I'll go to Edinburgh to see Sheila. Then, once I've met this woman, I can tie up the loose ends and move on.'

'Indeed.' Clearing his throat, he muttered something Patsy couldn't hear.

'What did you say Larry? My phone cut out and I couldn't hear you.'

'I said it will be nice to see you again Mrs Diamond; it's been a while,' Larry trailed off, as though waiting for some rebuke.

A warm feeling rose in her stomach, and she smiled. 'I'll see you tomorrow Larry,' she said and ended the call.

* * *

The drive to Scotland was long and arduous, although she knew the roads well enough by now as she had travelled them so many times. Pulling up outside Larry's office, she went in, and not waiting for the receptionist to announce her arrival, she walked straight to his office. She didn't care; she had put enough revenue into this firm to be able to waltz in when she felt like it.

Looking up, Larry smiled and gave a low whistle. 'I love the new hairstyle; you look amazing Mrs Diamond.'

'Are you saying I didn't look amazing before? I'll take that as a compliment but I'm not sure it was one.'

Hearing the tone of her voice, he stood up. 'Don't bother sitting down, we're going out. I'll drive.'

'Just give me the address Larry, I have Google maps and I'm sure I can find it.' Her stubborn expression as she stood there with her hands on her hips annoyed him and he bit his tongue, for fear of saying something he shouldn't. Picking up his keys, he walked ahead of her, leaving her with no choice but to follow him.

Once in his car, Larry took a breath before starting the engine. 'Right Mrs Diamond, before we do anything else I want you to promise me two things. Firstly, don't ask questions. Secondly, do as I say. Once all is revealed, you can ask as many questions as you like, but for the time being just do as I ask.' Glaring at her, he waited for another retort from that sharp tongue of hers, but none came.

Puzzled by his manner, Patsy nodded and made the sign of a zip closing her mouth. Satisfied, Larry drove on in silence. Once they arrived at their destination, Patsy raised her eyebrows and turned towards him and was about to speak, when Larry held up his hand to stop her.

'Remember your promise Mrs Diamond,' he warned.

Nodding, she stopped what she was about to say and looked up at the address he had driven her to. She was confused; this mystery tour of Larry's filled her with foreboding and although reluctant, she waited until Larry got out of his car and opened the door for her.

Hesitantly, Patsy followed him. Her mind was all over the place and looking around at the scenery made her feel worse. They both walked in silence for what seemed an eternity, although it was only minutes. It suddenly dawned on her that Larry had already been here, because he knew exactly where to go. Stopping, Larry pointed. 'There Mrs

Diamond. There is your Karen Duret. There are no guaran-
tees and the private investigator I have hired on your behalf
is still looking to see what he can find, but the trail stops
here.'

Stunned, Patsy looked down at the headstone in the grave-
yard. She shivered slightly as she read the name... Karen Duret
R.I.P. When Larry had marched her through the cemetery gates,
she had been confused but this chilled her to the bone. Not able
to take her eyes off the headstone, she found her voice. Her tone
was low and shaky. 'How can this be Larry? There must be some
mistake. Those bank statements are only a few months old. For
god's sake, tell me you're wrong, because I just don't know what to
think.'

The blood had drained from her face, and even under her
make-up Larry could see how distressed she was. 'Look at the
date of birth on the headstone Mrs Diamond; it matches with
what we already know. Duret isn't a common name.' He
shrugged. 'It's either one hell of a coincidence or the truth is, the
trail stops here. I trust the investigator I've used. I have used him
before; he's usually right. I couldn't tell you this over the tele-
phone; you needed to see it for yourself.'

Patsy felt dizzy and thought she was going to faint, but Larry
put his arms around her shoulders to steady her.

'Let's go back to the car Mrs Diamond, although there is
something you haven't noticed.' He pointed again to the
headstone.

Puzzled, Patsy looked. 'You mean the date of death? That was
only four years ago.'

'No Mrs Diamond. Someone has laid fresh flowers here.
Look.'

Following his gaze Patsy looked again. She couldn't work it
out; someone must know who this woman is, but who? 'Who is

she Larry? Does she have a family? What else do you know about her?'

'I have a file on her Patsy, but first let's get you to the car; you've had enough shocks for one day.' Steadying her as he linked her arm through his, they walked back to the car.

Still in shock, Patsy looked out of the window while Larry drove away. The streets of Glasgow seemed to pass by in a blur. 'Where are we going?'

'I'm taking you to my house; you need to gather your thoughts. I'm not letting you drive like this.'

Patsy nodded. She felt numb and didn't know what to say. Eventually, she saw trees and houses. They were in the suburbs. 'You live around here?'

'Yes, I do. I may be a lowly solicitor to you, but I'm still a solicitor on a decent wage. Did you think I lived in a bedsit somewhere or in one of the tenements? You really do have a low opinion of me, don't you?' He cast a quick glance at her.

Patsy looked out of the window and felt embarrassed by her own assumptions. She had never thought about Larry's life away from the office. She'd had so much on her mind lately, she was ashamed to think it hadn't even crossed her mind.

She was surprised at Larry's large semi-detached house, with its carefully mowed lawn. The paintwork on the garage and outside of the house was pristine. Giving Larry a weak smile, Patsy got out of the car and followed him into the house. Inside was just as pristine, she noticed. Passing the large wooden staircase in the hallway, Larry led her into the lounge. It was bright and airy, with its huge comfortable beige leather sofas.

'It's a lovely house Larry,' she acknowledged, and indeed it was. Looking around, she was impressed. It was homely.

'Well, as you're giving it the once over, come into my crowning glory while I get you a drink,' he laughed.

Curiously, Patsy followed him through the long hallway and into the kitchen. Her eyes widened with surprise. 'My god this is lovely: a real chef's kitchen.' Patsy looked around at the stainless steel worktops and smoked glass double ovens. Kitchen utensils and pans hung from a ceiling shelf, held up by a pulley. Patsy marvelled at it.

'I like to cook Mrs Diamond. It's a hobby of mine and I've been working on this kitchen for months to get it just the way I want it.' Proud of his achievement, although slightly embarrassed by his confession, a pink flush rose in his cheeks.

'You built this?' Patsy stammered, amazed at his handiwork. She walked around the breakfast bar and admired it. 'So this is your man den?'

'Yes, I suppose it is,' he stammered. 'Let me get you that drink Mrs Diamond. Tea or coffee?'

'Brandy if you have any.' She smiled.

'Well, maybe a weak one; you are driving later after all. Or you can stay if you like. It has four bedrooms.' Suddenly he stopped short. 'Oh, I didn't mean to sound impertinent, Mrs Diamond, it was just an idea... sorry.'

'Thanks Larry, but I have things to do. You don't have to nurse maid me, I'm a big girl.' Touched by his politeness and concern, she walked back towards the lounge. And Larry followed with two brandies.

'So Larry, what do we know about this woman? How can she be dead and yet have a bank account and own half of the pizza shops? Surely when she died they would have been sold off or something.'

Taking a gulp of his own brandy, Larry sighed. 'It's not the first time I have come across this Mrs Diamond. Fraud and stolen identities. Your husband seems to have had a lot of money to distribute and using different identities could have been a solution.'

Patsy frowned. 'Are you saying Nick picked names out of a cemetery and gave them bank accounts?'

'Yes, and surprisingly enough it can be quite easily done if you know how, and it seems your husband knew a lot of things. He literally buried his secrets deep.'

'Do you think I'm a criminal Larry?' Throwing her hands in the air, she let out a huge sigh. 'Oh I don't blame you if you do; my life is a mess at the moment.' Casting her eyes downwards, she paused. 'I am guilty Larry; I laundered some of Nick's money through my salons. I'm a stupid gullible woman and believe me I have been more than humiliated. Nick was married to me and yet, there was Natasha and now this Karen woman. Was she his mistress too? Was my marriage a complete sham?'

'I think you've been naïve and manipulated to a point, but love and loyalty make us do stupid things. I also know that you're ignorant of whatever dealings Nick had, or else you wouldn't be spending money on detectives trying to trace business partners, be they dead or alive. Whatever you think, I'm not stupid. Don't be too harsh on him hiding money in different accounts, people do it all of the time; why do you think the rich and famous have offshore accounts? And if I may say so Mrs Diamond, you've your own skeletons too, don't you?'

Shooting a glance at him, her eyes flashed. 'Have you been checking up on me Larry? What the bloody hell gives you the right? You work for me! Whatever you think you know about me I suggest you keep it to yourself.'

Calmly, Larry waited until she had stopped her hurl of abuse. 'I like to know who I am working for Mrs Diamond and it's amazing what you uncover about people. But don't forget, I am your solicitor and that puts me in a place of trust. Confidentiality is the key; I'm like a priest. So with that in mind, can I ask you something?'

Not knowing what to expect, Patsy shrugged her shoulders. 'What do you want to know? Surely you have all of the answers already.'

'Did you kill Nick? Did you shoot him? You had more than good reason to, but between us here and now, did you?'

Patsy's jaw dropped. 'What?' She shook her head emphatically. 'No. No, Larry, I didn't kill my husband. If anything, we'd made our peace that night. I did turn up at Christmas to give Natasha a piece of my mind. Fifteen years Larry! And I was cast aside for a younger, pregnant woman who satisfied his ego. When I got there we exchanged words, but then I heard Natasha had been taken to the police station and I saw the worried look on Nick's face and knew I'd lost the war. I went outside to him, hoping to save something of our relationship. I asked him if we divorced if he was going to take my salons and leave me penniless. I know that sounds silly, but they are my babies.' Giving a weak smile and trying hard to not sound too pathetic she carried on. 'He said no, but now I'm not so sure. But I wished him well, we shook hands and I accepted defeat. He kissed me on the cheek and we hugged. Do you know what he whispered in my ear while he held me?' Tears began to fall down Patsy's face and her heart sank as she wiped them away. 'He said, "I'll always love you Patsy, just not enough for a lifetime."' Sobs wracked her body as she cried. She had kept that to herself for so long that in some way she felt better to be able to get it off her chest and say it out loud.

'I hate to admit this Larry, but at last I can say it: I think he really did love Natasha. Although after what I've discovered about him I'm not sure he really loved anyone. Laughing at us all like fools for believing everything he said and did behind that charming smile he hid behind. In answer to your question Larry,

I didn't kill Nick, although there have been times when I wish I had!'

Getting up, Larry sat beside her and handed her a tissue. He was satisfied now but had felt the need to ask. He was sure by her reaction she was telling the truth; he'd mixed with enough criminals in his career to be able to know the difference. Her outburst convinced him of that. Putting his arms around her, he held her tightly. 'Shush, Patsy. I'm sorry I had to ask.'

Feeling the warmth of his strong, muscly arms around her, comforting her, impulsively, she kissed his neck and nuzzled closer to him until they were cheek to cheek.

Reluctantly, Larry pulled away; her closeness and the scent of her perfume intoxicated him. 'I'm human Patsy; don't do anything you'll regret,' he whispered. 'I've dreamt about holding you in my arms, fantasised even, but I won't take advantage of your present situation.'

Their eyes locked and Patsy moved closer to him, putting her arms around his neck. Suddenly their lips met and tentatively, they kissed. The yearning feeling to be needed aroused her and they kissed again. Each kiss became more ardent and passionate as she held him tightly while his hands roamed over her body.

Lying back on the sofa, she felt his warm lips kiss her neck as he unbuttoned the front of her blouse, letting his tongue trail down to her breasts. Greedily, he teased them, feeling her nipples harden under his kisses. They were both excited and breathing heavily, as Patsy closed her eyes and let out a gasp of sheer pleasure. Their lips met again as he pushed his tongue inside her mouth while his hands reached under her skirt to stroke her thighs. His fingers slid beneath her black lace panties and she arched her back, thrusting her hips higher towards him as he stroked her. Burning sensations shot through her trembling body and she reached down to rub his crotch, feeling the arousal and excitement growing within him.

'I want you,' she moaned. Her hands searched for the belt on his trousers.

'I want you too,' he whispered.

Suddenly, they heard a noise and stopped. Looking at each other, they waited before they heard it again.

'Lawrence are you home?' a woman's voice bellowed down the hallway.

'Dad! Where are you?' a boy shouted.

Springing up off the sofa, Larry started fastening his belt again and tucking his shirt into his trousers.

Confused, Patsy sat up and did likewise with the buttons on her blouse. Their faces were flushed and their breathing unsteady. As Larry stood before her, Patsy could see the presence of excitement through his trousers.

Clearing his throat, he shouted back, 'Yes, I'll just be a minute!' Running his hands through his hair, he did his best to compose himself and walked to the doorway of the lounge. 'I'm in here, I didn't expect you back so early,' he croaked, trying to clear his throat and inject some form of casualness into it.

'The shops weren't very busy, and this misery guts wanted to come home and play his boring games. Are you all right Lawrence? You look flustered.'

Patsy heard the woman's voice again and straightened her clothing. Sitting up on the sofa, she curiously listened to the conversation.

'I'm fine, I have a visitor. A client. We were just going through some things; you put your shopping away I'll be through in a minute.'

Patsy turned towards the doorway. A young woman popped her head around the doorway and greeted her. 'Hello, I'm Jenny

Kavanagh, nice to meet you. Do you want some coffee?' She smiled, totally oblivious to Patsy's unease.

Patsy's face burned with embarrassment; Larry was married! She had never thought about that, and he had never mentioned it. He had a wife and son and had just been about to have sex with her in his own home while they were out. The cheating bastard! Her heart was thumping in her chest and she shook her head.

'I'm just leaving,' she stammered, trying to keep her voice steady while casting a piercing glance at Larry. Nodding, the young woman picked up her shopping bags and walked towards the kitchen.

'Dad, I'm going upstairs to play on my game; give us a shout when dinner's ready,' his son shouted. Catching a glimpse of him in his school uniform, Patsy reckoned he was about ten or eleven. Angrily, she picked up her bag and walked towards the front door, pushing past Larry and making a point of digging him in the stomach with her elbow. She felt embarrassed and humiliated but felt better when she saw him wince.

'Wait, Mrs Diamond. I'll drive you back to your car,' he shouted as she stormed up the driveway. Running after her, Larry stopped her. 'Don't leave like this Patsy, let me drive you, you don't know where you are.'

'Fuck off Larry, or is it Lawrence? And it's Mrs Diamond to you. You've just told Jenny that I'm a client. Do you fuck all of your female clients? I'll find my own way back; there must be a taxi company around here. Just fuck off and leave me alone.' She stormed off, not knowing where she was going. Once out of sight, she took out her mobile. She was shaking and tears of anger rolled down her face. She found a taxi number and asked them to come straight away. She couldn't believe she had made such a fool of herself and Larry had put her in an impossible situation.

Once in the back of the taxi, she thought about how she had brought this on herself. She had kissed him and let things go too far. He was weak and pathetic and couldn't refuse sex when it was laid out on a plate before him. How bloody stupid she was. Cursing herself as the taxi drove, she listened to the driver's idle chatter and looked out of the car window, desperate to get back to her car. Texts from Larry came one after the other, but she ignored them and declined his calls. She shook her head. She would find another solicitor straight away, she decided, and she would never have to see Larry again.

18

REPERCUSSIONS

'How's he doing Maggie?' Fin stood in Maggie's hallway. He had done as requested and stayed away for the last couple of weeks and Maggie had made a point of ignoring him, which was nothing unusual. Curiosity had got the better of him and he couldn't stand it any more. Standing there with his hands in his pockets and bouncing from one foot to the other, waiting for another lash from Maggie's sharp tongue, he felt like a kid in front of the head teacher. He was surprised when she actually half smiled and opened the door wider.

'You had better come through.' Maggie showed him into the bedroom where James was sitting up. 'As you can see he's much better. I've stopped the sleeping tablets and just give him something to ease the pain. He's eating soups to keep his strength up, aren't you James?'

Sitting on the wooden chair at James's bedside, he grinned. 'How you doing James? You look better than you did. Maggie's nursing seems to have worked wonders.'

'Thanks to you and your friends Fin. I'll pay you back, I promise.' James held out his hand and shook Fin's. 'I'm still having trouble breathing; my ribs are still healing. But Maggie has bandaged them as tightly as possible. She's a saint.' James smiled at Maggie and there was a pregnant pause, indicating to Maggie that he wanted to talk to Fin alone.

Maggie walked away, understanding they must have a lot to talk about.

'I don't remember too much Fin. What happened when you got there? Fill me in.'

Fin told him what had happened in hushed whispers.

'So, they were definitely going to kill me... I thought so,' James whispered back. 'Even my wife has disowned me. I guess she's had enough after all these years and this is as good an excuse as any.'

Fin frowned but said nothing and was glad when Maggie made her presence known by rattling cups and talking loudly. 'Tea time James. You must be ready for a drink by now.' Turning to Fin, she added, 'I've made you one too.'

Fin tried to think of something to say to Maggie. 'I see that Mrs Diamond has been staying at Beryl's.' Excitedly he turned towards James. 'Oh god you don't know, do you? That Diamond woman went berserk and closed the community centre, changing the locks and throwing clothes out of the windows. She completely lost it!' Fin laughed.

Only Maggie noticed the serious look on James's face, as he listened to Fin's story.

'Is the community centre still closed?' James asked. 'Why is she staying with Beryl Diamond?'

'No James, they re-opened it and I don't know why she's here, probably just visiting old Beryl.' Fin shrugged.

Raising her arm, Maggie cuffed Fin's ear, making him wince. 'Old Beryl? Have some bloody respect,' Maggie snapped. 'I think Patsy wants to apologise for her outburst. Beryl put it down to some form of mental breakdown after everything she's been through. Why do you ask, James?'

'Could you get her to come and see me? I need to speak to her; it's important.' Looking up at each of them in turn, James stressed again, 'Please Maggie, Fin, I need to speak to her.'

The urgency in James's voice perturbed Maggie. 'Not in your state laddie. Anyway, she wouldn't come, we don't get on too well.'

James reached out his good arm and held Maggie's hand. 'Please Maggie, I have no right to ask any more of you. You've been so kind to me, but at this moment in time, Mrs Diamond is my only hope. I have to speak to her, make her see sense.'

Maggie looked down at him and cast a furtive glance towards Fin. 'What can she do that we can't James? She's not one of us, she doesn't see things the way we do.' The last thing she wanted was for James to make himself unwell again, worrying about Patsy Diamond.

'She might, if I explain.' James's forlorn look as he lay back on his pillow and let out a deep sigh made Maggie think.

'Patsy Diamond is not interested in the woes and cares of others, only herself.' Maggie patted him on the shoulder. 'But I'll try and think of something James, I just don't know what yet. In the meantime, get some rest and stop worrying.'

A weak smile crossed James's face. 'I'm very grateful you took me in Maggie. I was a dead man, but unfortunately I still am, and that is why I want to speak to Mrs Diamond.' James's eyelids began to droop and Maggie beckoned to Fin to leave the room.

'What does he need her for Maggie? What can she do?' Fin was curious; it all seemed very cloak and dagger to him.

'I don't know.' Maggie shrugged. 'I'll see if Beryl can influence her to come here, though god knows what they're going to say about me harbouring a fugitive.' Maggie felt agitated; she didn't know what to do. But she knew if she asked and Patsy Diamond refused she could at least tell James she had tried. It wasn't much consolation, but it was all she had. 'You'd better go Fin; I need time to think.'

* * *

Knocking on the door, Patsy waited for Sheila to open it. 'Sheila, I'm sorry it's late. I just wanted to go somewhere, anywhere, before going back to Beryl's flat,' she blurted out.

'Patsy, what's wrong? You look awful and like you've been crying. Come in lassie, come in.' Sheila steered Patsy towards the lounge and went into the kitchen to put the kettle on.

Seeing Sheila's state of undress, Patsy apologised. 'I'm sorry, I didn't realise you would be in bed. I didn't notice the time.' Sitting on the armchair, Patsy looked around the lounge. 'You've painted,' she called out. 'It looks lovely Sheila.'

Coming through with two large mugs of tea, Sheila put them down on the little side tables near the chairs. Wrapping her dressing gown around her and taking the elastic band off her wrist, she pulled her hair back and tied it into a pony tail. 'Magnolia. It's cheap and cheerful and if the kids ever dirty it you can always get another tin. Angus stripped and sanded the walls; he's handy like that.' Walking into the hallway she shouted up the stairs, 'Angus! Come on love, it's time to go.'

'Oh my god Sheila, is Angus here? I'm so sorry, it never crossed my mind. I just started driving and I ended up here. I'll go.' Patsy stood up.

'You sit your arse down Patsy and drink that tea. Angus has got to be at work soon anyway. Angus, get down here!' Sheila shouted at the top of her voice. Patsy heard the footsteps on the stairs and looked up at the doorway where Angus was stood in his T-shirt and boxer shorts. He was a huge, well-built man, almost the size of the doorway, but not fat. Scrutinising him a little more, Patsy noticed that he'd shortened his beard. It was still bushy and long but now it just laid on his chest past his neck. 'Hello Angus, I'm sorry to inconvenience you, I really must be going.' Patsy picked up her bag; it was blatantly obvious she had turned up at an inappropriate time.

'No my wee lassie, you drink your tea. I have to be at work soon anyway, I'm working the night shift. I'll just go and get properly dressed if you'll excuse me.' Blushing slightly at his state of undress, he turned towards Sheila.

'That's right Angus, this is women's time. We need to talk about you and discuss women's problems love.' Reaching up, Sheila gave him a quick peck on the lips and slapped his bottom. 'Go on sexy, get dressed before you get Patsy all excited,' she laughed.

'Will you let me know what you think about the car Sheila? The man needs to know as soon as possible. We can work out the money, you know that.'

'It's nice Angus, and so are you. We'll speak later. Go on, scoot!' She clapped her hands together and gave him a playful shove.

'I didn't mean to interrupt Sheila. I'm so sorry.' Biting her bottom lip, Patsy shook her head. She could feel the tears brimming on her eye lashes. She'd had an awful day and now she had ruined Sheila's.

'Och, don't flatter yourself Patsy. Angus has had his fill for one night. And what are the tears for, have you had some trouble?' A flash of concern crossed Sheila's face. She could only imagine the worst.

'Nothing like that Sheila.' Patsy lowered her voice so Angus couldn't hear her. Avoiding the subject until Angus had left, Patsy instead asked Sheila what Angus had meant about the car.

Sitting down beside her and wrapping her hands around her mug of tea, she explained, 'Oh that. His friend's got a car for sale; it's very nice and of course Angus has checked it out. Angus said he would loan me the money, but I don't want him to. He's good company, and I feel safe with him around but there are no promises or commitments. We fill gaps. I have gaps, he has gaps and we fill them together. Although, I must confess Patsy that beard of his does keep your tits warm in bed!' It was the first time Patsy had laughed all day.

'I noticed he's trimmed it a little,' Patsy laughed. Suddenly she felt so much better. If anyone could lift her spirits Sheila could.

'Oh yes, I soon got my scissors out; I was nearly tripping over it. It was like kissing Father Christmas.' Sheila laughed and then her voice softened and took on a serious tone. 'It's strange, but I've never been with a man like him before. When he's not here I don't worry that the police are going to kick the door in looking for him and I don't get a call from the police station in the middle of the night. I loved Steve, truly I did, but I could never rely on him. Some weeks we had a thousand pounds and he would buy all the latest gadgets and the next week he was selling the new television on the cheap. Only when he came out of prison the last time, did he get a proper job, and he tried hard, he really did. Although it is strange Pats.' She giggled. 'Steve was eleven stone dripping wet, and Angus fills the whole of the bed. No wonder I have to spend so much time on top.' They were both laughing like school girls when Angus came through into the lounge again.

Coughing to make his presence known, Angus stood there in his illuminous rescue service uniform. 'I'll be going now Sheila. Nice to see you again Patsy.' He nodded.

'I'll just see him out, give him one last grope and then I'll make us a fresh cuppa and you can tell me all about what's bothering you.'

Sheila left the room and Patsy could hear giggling and kisses coming from the front door and then she heard it close.

Bustling back into the lounge, Sheila rubbed her hands together. 'Right, that's Angus sorted. We'll have tea and you can tell me why you look like shit. Although, that hairstyle is amazing; it really suits you.'

Patsy had almost forgotten her new hair and ran her fingers through it to smooth it down. 'I saw Larry the lawyer today. I asked him to see if he could trace a mystery business partner of Nick's. Well, he has found Nick's mystery business partner, Karen Duret. The only problem is, even though she has bank statements from only a couple of months ago, her latest address is at the cemetery. According to the headstone, she's been dead for ages. How can that be Sheila?'

Sheila's jaw dropped and she stared wide eyed as Patsy filled her in on the rest of the story. 'Are you sure this detective bloke has got it right? Where is this file Larry says he has?'

It suddenly dawned on Patsy she hadn't picked it up from Larry. 'Oh, I've forgotten it, would you go and get it from the solicitors tomorrow for me Sheila?'

Sheila narrowed her eyes and looked at Patsy. 'Why can't you go? You're on your way back to Glasgow. I live in Edinburgh. What is it that you're not telling me?'

'Oh Sheila, I've made such a fool of myself. I can't see Larry again, but I do need that file. Please go.'

With a little more urging, Sheila got the whole story of Patsy and Larry and their torrid afternoon, including his wife and son. 'That's weird Patsy, I have never known a married man take someone back to his house before. This calls for a proper drink; he's a bloody dark horse and he's got more front than Selfridges.' Sheila opened the battered cabinet and produced a small bottle of whisky and put it into their mugs.

'Just a small one for me Sheila, I'm driving to Beryl's next.'

'No you're not lassie, I don't have much but you're staying here tonight. You can have my bed and I'll sleep in the kids' room.'

Sheila's kindness touched Patsy. It was true, she didn't have much but whatever Sheila had you were welcome to and that meant a lot to Patsy.

Kneeling beside her on the floor, Sheila took a sip from her mug. 'I'll get your file for you, but you have to face him Patsy. Don't be a chicken.' As an afterthought, she looked across at Patsy, a cheeky grin on her face. 'Was he good?'

'I told you we didn't get that far, thank god. I think I humiliated myself enough, don't you?'

'Is he a good kisser? Come on, tell me. That voice of his makes me want to cream my knickers, and if he can back it up with everything else, that's a bonus. I've told you about Angus; I deserve the same confidence.'

Patsy looked down. 'He was okay.' Feeling Sheila's eyes burning into her, she looked up again. 'Satisfactory.'

'Oh for fuck's sake Patsy, you sound like you're buying a sofa. Satisfactory? What the hell does that mean? Did he shove his tongue down your throat? Did you get a feel of his dick?' She laughed. 'You know what, your upper class politeness makes me laugh. Say it as it was Pats. There's only me here.'

Patsy could feel the flush rising in her face and she nodded. 'Yes and yes. And that is all you're getting. Anyway, it's all irrelevant now; he's married and made a fool of me.'

'No he hasn't, he's made a fool of himself. He's been well caught out and feels like a total prick. I bet the minute you left that wife of his had a few questions to ask. She might not have argued in front of you out of politeness, but I bet he got a right thump. I would have done; you can always tell when someone has been up to naughtiness and this was in her lounge. His dinner will be in the dog, believe me.'

Feeling a whole lot better, Patsy laughed. 'Maybe you're right. I hadn't thought of it like that. Call it women's intuition, I suppose.'

Chinking their glasses together, Sheila said, 'Here's to Larry, the last of the great lovers with his nuts kicked in.'

They continued talking into the early hours of the morning and Patsy realised that even though their lives had been so different, they were in fact parallel. Sheila didn't have the money, but she had been left alone constantly, the same as herself when Nick had disappeared on business matters. It all amounted to the same thing. Steve had lied to her about his dealings in the past and she had had to fight for survival to feed her kids. Patsy realised that although they were two very different women from different backgrounds, they were also, in many ways, exactly the same.

19

THE BITTER TRUTH

Washed and dressed again, Patsy felt better. 'Thanks for last night Sheila, and I'm sorry about interrupting you and Angus.' Patsy put her arms around Sheila and hugged her.

'Och, it was nothing you silly woman. Mates before dates. As long as you're feeling better, that's all that counts.'

'I am feeling better. And I was just wondering, do you have a bank account Sheila?'

'Not much of one, but yes. Do you need some cash or something?' Startled at her question, Sheila opened the biscuit tin on top of the work top. 'This is where I keep my housekeeping cash; there's about thirty pounds. Here, take it.'

Patsy laughed and waved her hands at Sheila. 'No you silly woman, that's not what I meant but thank you. Do you have online banking?'

Frowning at the line of questioning and not knowing where it was leading, Sheila nodded. 'The banks are miles away from here and it's only my benefits that go in it. Why?'

Taking out her phone, Patsy started typing while Sheila waited patiently. 'Give me your account details.'

Still confused, Sheila did as she was told.

'There love, buy Angus's car. I'm sure he'll make sure it's safe for you, and if you ever break down you know just the man.'

'No! No way Patsy. You can't spend your life buying people and I have been for sale too many times. I thought we were friends.' Sheila felt hurt and insulted that Patsy felt she had to pay her for her friendship.

Taking her hand in her own, Patsy smiled comfortingly. 'I'm not buying you Sheila; but the car sounds like a good idea and I don't want you owing Angus anything if you decide to end your torrid affair. Anyway, it will be easier when you decide to see the girls. Have you been to Victoria's yet?'

'Have I? Oh bloody hell, it's a castle! They have clothes coming out of their ears and toys I could never have bought them in a million years. I felt like the bloody chamber maid!'

'I told you they would be safe there, and it will do Victoria the world of good having the house full of laughter. Get the car Sheila; you never know, I might need you one day at short notice. Take it, please. Anyway, I must go, I'm sure Beryl has got something to say about my disappearance.'

Nodding, Sheila felt humbled. She had never known such kindness.

Once Patsy had left, Sheila looked at her bank account and saw that Patsy had put 3,000 pounds into her account. She gasped at the sight of all those zeros and had to count them again to make sure she hadn't made a mistake. Suddenly, her phone buzzed with a message.

For petrol and insurance! Even the chamber maid gets wages xx

A broad smile appeared on Sheila's face and a warm feeling of friendship overwhelmed her. She could feel a tear forming and brushed it away.

* * *

'Hi Beryl, I'm back,' Patsy shouted and walked into the lounge.

'Where have you been? You could have bloody called. Hotel Beryl isn't a free for all, you know.' Beryl sat in her armchair with her arms folded with a stern look on her face.

Realising her mistake, Patsy grimaced. 'I'm sorry Beryl. I had to go see Sheila on an errand for Natasha. She wants them to be friends again, and it got late so I stayed over,' Patsy lied.

'Is Sheila okay? They used to be good friends until that awful business.' Beryl tutted and shook her head.

'She's getting by, one step at a time, but I think I've made her see reason and she'll talk to Natasha.'

Instantly Beryl's attitude changed once she realised Patsy had been on a mission of mercy. 'Well, you could still have telephoned me,' she muttered under her breath.

'I'm sorry, but once Sheila put a drop of her whisky in my tea, time just passed. Sorry... it was thoughtless of me.'

Patsy hated lying like this, but for the moment she had no other option. She didn't know who was on her side. 'Let me make you a fresh cup of tea.'

While in the kitchen, Patsy could hear Beryl talking at the front door.

'Make that another cup of tea Patsy! Maggie's here,' Beryl shouted through to her.

As much as it set Patsy's teeth on edge knowing that woman was in the living room with Beryl, she decided to be polite as she was already in Beryl's bad books.

Taking the tray in, she smiled. 'Here you go ladies, I'm just going to take a shower. Enjoy.'

'Aren't you having a cup of tea with us? Especially when we have a visitor.' Put out by Patsy's snub, Beryl cast her another stern look.

Hiding behind a false smile, Patsy nodded. 'Of course, I just thought you ladies would like some time on your own.'

Beryl pointed her thumb to the sofa to indicate for Patsy to sit down, which she did immediately – the last thing Patsy wanted was to rock the boat.

Maggie cast a furtive glance her way. As usual, Beryl discussed the neighbours' gossip; she also dropped the bombshell that people were being charged to go into the community centre. Apparently it was towards the upkeep of the place.

Shocked, Patsy asked her to repeat herself. She knew nothing of this and didn't know why they would need to charge people as it had enough funding for the time being and was making money.

Nodding in agreement, Maggie echoed Beryl's words. 'They have people on the door now charging an entrance fee.'

Patsy's mind spun. 'Why didn't you tell me about this Beryl? You have the keys. How is someone else taking the place over?' Standing with her hands on hips, Patsy glared at Beryl. 'Who have you handed the place over to? You don't own it Beryl, it's mine. Just what are you playing at?' Patsy had had enough of this blood Diamond clan. They were all twisted and thieves.

'I didn't want to bother you love, you've enough to worry about. But if it keeps the community centre running it will be worth it.'

Patsy felt for all of Beryl's wily ways she was being very naïve or stupid when it came to that place. 'Can't you see it's corrupt? Or are you in on it like your bloody grandson?'

'No, Patsy. I have nothing to hide and believe me I know about

Nick, but the wee kiddies still need the creches and the parents have to work and have nowhere to leave them. If it's council funded, the parents get a payment to help them with childcare costs. I just want to help people and make the best of a bad job.' Beryl looked down at the floor.

Patsy nodded, satisfied that this had nothing to do with Beryl. If anything, it sounded as though she was being bullied and didn't want to admit it. The strong, feisty Beryl Diamond was afraid.

Patsy had seen the last time she had stayed there that Beryl had bags of money stashed in the wardrobe; surely that would pay for the upkeep of the community centre? She decided to check if it was still there when she next went into the bedroom.

Beryl carried on trashing the neighbours with her vicious tongue, while Maggie and Patsy nodded and agreed in all the right places, although Patsy felt there was an underlying unease or tension in Maggie. Once she'd drunk her tea, Maggie stood up. 'Well, I'd better be off now Beryl. I'll see you soon.'

'I'll see you out Maggie.' Beryl stood up.

'No Beryl, you stay there and drink your tea, Patsy can see me out.' Maggie glanced at Patsy.

Realising there was something wrong, Patsy stood up. 'I'll go. You finish your tea and don't eat all of the good biscuits.' She laughed light-heartedly. Following Maggie to the door, she opened it. Maggie beckoned her to follow her outside.

'I know you don't like me Patsy, but I have a message for you. I want you to come to my house as soon as possible. There is someone who wants to meet you.'

Stunned, Patsy shot a piercing look at her.

Holding her hands up, Maggie assured her. 'You're not in any danger, I promise, and you will see that for yourself. Please come Patsy. I promised I would ask you and I have. I'll say no more for now, I don't want Beryl getting suspicious.' Wrapping her usual black cardigan around her, Maggie walked away without a backward glance, giving Patsy a lot to think about.

'Maggie looks well, doesn't she Beryl?' Patsy commented once back inside the flat.

'Well enough I suppose. I haven't seen her for a while. She only came because she saw you're visiting. Nosey cow!'

Patsy smiled as she took the tea tray away. It was good to know some things hadn't changed and Beryl's sharp tongue was as cutting as ever. But Patsy had got the answer she wanted. What was Maggie hiding? Why hadn't she seen Beryl lately, when they were usually as thick as thieves?

Patsy knew she couldn't leave straight away, which was what she wanted, but had to bide her time and give Beryl some company and find out exactly what it was Maggie wanted from her. Making her more tea, this time Patsy poured some whisky in it. Beryl always had the bottle on hand so it wasn't hard to find.

'Here you go, this will warm your bones.'

Leaving her to it, Patsy walked into the bedroom and opened the wardrobe door. She was surprised to see all the bags of money were still stashed at the back, just as she had left them. Opening the zipper of one, she noticed nothing had been taken. She actually wondered if Beryl even knew the cash was there. Patsy couldn't make her mind up, so closed the zipper and walked back into the lounge.

Seeing that her plan had worked, she felt satisfied. Beryl was dozing off in her chair; she could hardly keep her eyes open. Looking at the cup on the table beside Beryl she saw that she had drank the lot. Waiting a little longer until she could hear Beryl snoring, she carefully slipped out of the door and towards Maggie's.

* * *

'Well? I'm here, so what's the big secret?' Patsy snapped, showing her distaste.

Maggie looked from side to side, up and down the balcony, and ignoring her slight, more or less pulled her in. 'Follow me lassie.'

Curious, Patsy followed Maggie into a bedroom. She looked at the battered and bruised man in bed with the duvet rolled back. Maggie pulled out the wooden chair at the side of the bed for her to sit on. 'Sit down lassie. James, this is Mrs Diamond.'

He held out his good arm to shake her hand. 'Thank you for coming Mrs Diamond.'

Patsy's lips and throat felt dry; she wasn't sure if she had walked into an ambush, and half wished she had taken Beryl with her.

'No need to worry Mrs Diamond. As you can see, I am in no state to attack you or anything.' The man's Scottish accent filled her ears and inside she wanted to make a run for it.

'Who are you? What do you want from me?' Her voice was barely above a whisper and she swallowed hard.

'I was in partnership with the Undertaker,' he began. 'I believe that was your husband Mrs Diamond.'

Stunned, Patsy felt the blood run from her face. Suddenly a form of recognition came to her mind. 'You were the man at the funeral. You threw a Frisbee or something in the grave, am I right?'

'You should have looked closer; it wasn't a Frisbee, it was a top hat. Top hats do that. They flatten down and pop back up when you need them. He was the Undertaker and all good undertakers should have a top hat.'

Patsy's heart was pounding in her chest. 'Is it you who has been trying to kill me?'

'No, I don't hurt women. I fight turf wars with people who are just as guilty as myself. But I did send you the money that got delivered to your salon.'

Finding her voice a little more, Patsy nodded. 'Yes, and I remember the rat full of maggots stinking the place out too... and that message.'

'I was trying to keep you safe. Noel and his Albanian gang want you dead. You are trouble to them and to be fair, you've kicked off and made their life hard. The problem is, without the Undertaker they felt they didn't need me as a partner any more.' James faltered and held his ribs while he took a breath. He tried to sit up in bed.

Impulsively, Patsy held her hands out to help him and put the pillows behind his head. 'So why do they want to kill me?'

'He was your husband Mrs Diamond. You've been in and out of the police station many times. What are you telling them? Are you giving them the recordings? Everyone is frightened and fear breeds hate.'

'What recordings are you talking about?' Trying hard to hide her ignorance of what he was talking about, Patsy sat back in the chair and listened.

'Don't play coy with me Mrs Diamond. We both know what we're talking about.' He smiled weakly. 'Your husband was black-mailing a lot of violent criminals to do his bidding. When he said jump, they asked how high. That is a lot of power to hold over someone, don't you agree?'

Nodding, Patsy remained silent. She had wanted the truth and now she was getting it with both barrels.

'No one knew who he really was, but I knew it was him. There were times when we spoke that he let his mask slip. When some

of the men were facing a jail sentence, Mr Diamond always repre-
sented them in court. He represented myself and that's how we
met. We all had a lot to be grateful for and paid him back
numerous times, knowing he could always find the evidence to
put us away for a very long time. But his demands were getting
out of hand and his punishments getting worse. The Undertaker
had Noel's young brother nailed to the front door to show him
who was boss. Like I say Mrs Diamond: turf wars. But if you're
going to ask me who killed him, it wasn't me, although Noel and I
probably would have done in the end.'

Patsy's stomach somersaulted and she wanted to be sick. Nick
had ordered someone to be nailed to a door? That was
unthinkable.

James began to cough and eased himself up a little more.
Patsy handed him a glass of water from the bedside table. Her
hands felt clammy; she rubbed them together and let James
carry on.

'When he gave the order for Billy Burke to be murdered in
prison, we all went along with it, because he was becoming a
liability, but it did make us wonder if he would do the same with
us in time. He had no conscience Mrs Diamond. I know he was
your husband and I don't want to speak ill of the dead, but I can
only tell you how it was.'

Stunned at this revelation, Patsy listened. She couldn't believe
this man was talking about her husband. Charming, suave Nick
was really a monster. 'You still haven't said what you want from
me James. I can't be held responsible for my husband's actions,
surely?'

'I'm a dead man, that is why I look like this. Noel didn't like
my objections about killing you. As far as he is concerned, his
men beat me to death and buried me under concrete, but I have
friends too and thankfully they helped me. That is how I ended

up here, still alive. He thinks he can take over everything now, but the only thing standing in his way is you. I may be dead Mrs Diamond but you're a dead woman walking.'

The colour drained from Patsy's face and impulsively, she picked up the glass of water and took a sip herself.

'So I am going to tell you what I want from you. My wife has disowned me and I am officially a missing person. I need money to get myself back on my feet again. I can't stay here forever.'

'Money! All this is about money? Surely with all of the dealings you've done over the years you've got money for fuck's sake. Is that what this sob story is all about?' Patsy stood up and was about to leave when James stopped her.

'Please Mrs Diamond, hear me out. I cannot touch my own money without people knowing I am neither dead nor missing. For now, that is what I want them to think. Believe me, I have had a lot of time to think while lying here. I just want the money back that I sent you that day. You're the only person I can ask. I'll get my revenge on Noel, but the element of surprise is better than him looking over his shoulder for me. The Undertaker recorded every one of the men's confessions over the years on his mobile phone and used it against them. They have lived in his shadow for eight years; I think they have served their sentence now he is dead. As insurance, he told them all, if he was mysteriously killed, the details of the recordings are in his will to be used accordingly. Where are the recordings Mrs Diamond? I presume the will has been read by now?'

Patsy's brain was trying to soak up all of the information James was giving her, but she couldn't quite take it in. So Nick was still blackmailing them, even in death. She didn't want to admit to James, but she knew nothing of the recordings. 'The will has not been read properly yet James. There is a lot of property to sort out and these things take time, so for now your friends are safe.

Although, I presume, whoever Nick instructed to read the will would know what to do. I don't know. As I say, it hasn't been read officially yet.'

James seemed satisfied with her answer. 'What about the money?'

'Why should I give it back to you? Whatever you've done, you've brought it on yourself,' Patsy snapped. 'How do I know this isn't a trap?'

'Because, quite frankly, whoever I take my revenge on, will stop coming for you. Noel won't stop until he's stopped. I hear he has taken over the community centre and is charging people to walk through the doors. As far as he is concerned, he's in charge of it all and you're just an obstacle in his path now.'

Taking in his words, Patsy nodded. At last she had a name – Noel – and she presumed that this was the Mr James the Greek chef had been shouting about. Part of her thought about going to the police with this information. James was incapable of going anywhere. Maggie was hiding him, and this Albanian Noel, they all knew how to find him. Case closed. Or would it be? There was still her own involvement. What did they know about her? James knew where to have the money delivered to, didn't he? Standing up, she held out her hand to shake his.

'Well, you've been very frank James, but I'll need time to think about it and by the look of things you won't be going anywhere for a while.'

'That's just the point Mrs Diamond. I cannot put Maggie in danger for much longer; she's a good woman but they would kill her for helping me. I need that money,' he pleaded,

'And what do I get in return apart from an empty space in my bank account?'

'What do you want Mrs Diamond? Why do I have a feeling

that the Undertaker's assistant wishes to fill the gap in his empire?'

His words hit hard and Patsy blushed. 'I'm no drug dealer James. Let me think about it.'

A plan was forming in James's head but for now he wanted to keep it to himself. He didn't want to push her further. 'Then all I can say, is thank you for coming Mrs Diamond.'

'One thing does bother me James: you say you disliked my husband and his ways but you speak of him with respect. He is either the Undertaker or Mr Diamond. You never insult him. Why?'

'As I said Mrs Diamond, your husband helped me more than once and he gave me an opportunity to earn money, as long as I did as I was told and didn't cause waves. Plus, I won't speak ill of the dead. We made a lot of money together, although we were never friends.'

As an afterthought, Patsy asked him if he had heard of Karen Duret.

'I only know mail turned up at the flat above the community centre. I was told to box it up and Mr Diamond would pick it up when he visited.'

Patsy had heard enough for one day. Walking into the lounge, she saw Maggie sat there knitting. Patsy knew she had been eavesdropping. That was her nature. 'What is your part in all of this Maggie? Who are you to that man in there?'

'No one. I am doing a favour for a friend, that's all.' Turning away from Patsy, she looked out of the window.

'Why do I feel you're up to your neck in all of this Maggie? You worked for the Undertaker too, didn't you? You took his orders and manipulated people, the way he manipulated you,' Patsy spat out.

Solemnly Maggie nodded. 'Suppose I did, but I didn't know

this drug boss was your husband, although I did have my suspicions. But Beryl saw nothing wrong in Nick; the sun shone from the pretty boy's arse didn't it!'

Ignoring her comments, Patsy left. She had more than enough to think about. James obviously presumed Nick and herself were partners in all of this and didn't feel he was speaking out of turn. Her mind was troubled, but she knew he was right on one subject: she was and would be forever in danger. She would spend the rest of her life looking over her shoulder and afraid to live in her apartment, never knowing when the next evil bastard would turn up to kill her.

Sitting with Beryl gave her time to contemplate her actions and she had already made her mind up about what to do when she went to bed. Opening the wardrobe, Patsy looked at the bags of money stuffed inside. Waiting until Beryl went to bed, Patsy heaved the bag out as best as she could, mentally wondering how money could be so heavy. Dragging it along by the handle and sneaking out into the night, she reached Maggie's and gently tapped on the door.

She saw Maggie part the curtains to glimpse out first and then she came to the door. They looked at each other and then Patsy looked down at the bag.

'Give this to him. I'm sure you heard why this afternoon.' Walking away, Patsy felt she had done her bit by James and whatever happened now might just save her own skin. What bothered her were these mystery recordings James had spoken of. There was nothing in her apartment, as far as she knew. Wracking her brains, she thought of every cupboard and drawer in her house where Nick might have hidden something. Then a thought struck her.

She knew she would need help in her venture and picked up her mobile and rang Victoria. 'Hi Victoria could you be at my apartment tomorrow sometime; there is something I need to discuss with you. Can you leave the children with the staff?'

'Yes, of course. What's wrong Patsy? You haven't been hurt again have you?'

'No, nothing like that, but I do need your help. Bring Natasha too. We all have some talking to do. I can't tell you any more now. I'll see you tomorrow sometime. Bye.'

She needed to get home.

* * *

Sheila had gone to Glasgow to Larry's solicitor firm. They weren't going to let her in without an appointment, but she caused such an argument Larry and one of the other solicitors came out into reception. Recognising him instantly, Sheila looked at him. 'Do you remember me Larry? We met in court when you were representing Natasha.'

Nodding, he ushered her into his office. 'What can I do for you, erm...' He was doing his best to recollect her name, and so she prompted him.

'Sheila. Patsy asked me to come and pick up a folder on that woman your private investigator was finding out about. Can I have it please?' Holding out her hand, Sheila waited.

'No, you can't. Firstly, the investigator needs paying and no money has changed hands yet. And secondly, this file is to be handed to Mrs Diamond only; whatever she decides to do with it after that is her business. Kindly pass the message on will you Sheila.'

'All right snotty, I'll tell her. Considering you've been such a low down rat, it surprises me you've the affront to be so pompous. Men like you make me sick. If it was down to me I would cut your balls off and use them as earrings!' Flouncing out, Sheila immediately called Patsy. 'He won't hand it over without the money Pats. You'll have to come and do it. He's a nice looking bloke; better than I remembered. Oh and that voice, even when he's being all stern...'

'I get the point Sheila, there is no need for detail. Okay I'd better contact him. If the man wants his money then so be it. Thanks for trying. Oh, by the way, something has come up and I've asked Victoria and Natasha to be at my apartment tomorrow. I don't suppose you could make it, could you? Could Angus release you from his grip for a couple of days?'

'Sounds interesting. I'll be there. Let me sort out the car business today with Angus and I'll tell him I am going to visit the kids. See you tomorrow.'

* * *

After speaking to Sheila, Patsy dialled Larry's number.

'Hello Larry, it's Mrs Diamond. I got your message from Sheila and of course I'll pay your bill. You could have given her the file; I always pay my debts. I'm on my way to your office now.'

'No you're not Mrs Diamond; I'm in court in half an hour and will be for the rest of the day. I'm not leaving the file in reception, it's for your eyes only. I'll come back to the office later. Can you be there at about 7 p.m.?'

Considering the snub, Patsy agreed to the time, but felt restless. That meant she had to stay for the rest of the day in Glasgow.

Determined to look smart when she saw Larry, she went to great pains getting ready. She always took a Chanel dress with her wherever she went, because it could be used for any occasion and it fitted so well. She blow-waved the top of her hair, giving it more height. She always wore her silver necklace with its large diamond in the middle and her diamond bracelet and rings set the whole presentation off perfectly. One pair of high velvet court shoes and she was done. It felt like she was wearing an armour to face Larry. She was hiding her shame behind designer labels and diamonds.

The solicitor's building was dimly lit, and she had to press the buzzer outside to be let in. She was surprised to see the reception area empty and she looked at her watch. It was 7 p.m. – the time she and Larry had agreed upon.

'Hello?' she shouted. 'Anyone there?'

'Mrs Diamond, sorry, I didn't realise the time.' Looking at his watch, Larry appeared. 'The files are in my office; I'll just be a moment.'

Patsy couldn't help but comment without thinking, 'Well, I must say, you scrub up very nicely. Where have you been hiding yourself?' she teased.

She couldn't believe her eyes. Larry was wearing a red tartan kilt and looked taller than usual in a tuxedo and bow tie. His hair had been swept backwards, showing more of his face. Patsy couldn't help but admire him.

Blushing slightly, he looked down at his attire. 'I have to go out later, so I thought I would get ready here. It saves me the time of having to fight my way through traffic. You know how it is.'

'Larry, if you're going out, why on earth did you agree for me to come here tonight? I could have come tomorrow if you had explained. Or you could have just given it to Sheila,' she said as she handed him a cheque. 'I have filled in the rest you just need to put the name of the recipient.'

'Thank you Mrs Diamond, I'll see that he gets it. I couldn't run it though our accounts for obvious reasons, unless you wanted the whole office knowing your business.'

'Yes indeed, I didn't think. Thank you. Oh Larry, I do hope I haven't spoilt your night.'

'No, not at all Mrs Diamond. After all, the client comes first. Now, if you will excuse me, I'll get your files.'

As Larry walked away, Patsy followed him to his office. She couldn't help admiring his tall stance and how handsome he looked. She thought back to that fateful day when his wife had come home early. He was a rat, but he was a good kisser, she couldn't deny that. A faint smile crossed her face when she remembered what Sheila had said about him; she wanted to laugh to herself but held it back.

'Here you are Mrs Diamond.' Larry handed over the cardboard folder as promised and for a moment there was that pregnant pause between them.

'Thank you Larry, I appreciate it. So where are you off to then?' Changing the subject, Patsy waited. It was fair to say Larry wasn't very happy to see her, in fact, he didn't look very happy at all.

'It's the law society dinner. Needs must and all of that.' He shrugged.

'Oh I remember those very well, when I used to go with Nick. Boring... but as you say, needs must and you've got to show your face... I do hope I haven't inconvenienced you holding you back. I'm sure Jenny won't thank me for it.'

'Why would Jenny care? I'm going alone, so you haven't inconvenienced anyone.' Patsy felt that he sounded almost embarrassed about it and wanted her to drop the subject. She also felt like he wanted her to leave. There was another awkward silence and having nothing else to say, she turned to leave.

'Enjoy your evening Larry. You never know who you might meet.' Patsy couldn't resist one last dig, although she couldn't see the sense in it. She had been as much to blame, and to be fair she had never asked him if he was married. There was no point in sulking like a teenager. She was a grown woman. The only thing that had hurt her more was that feeling of betrayal in her life again! But that wasn't Larry's problem. It was hers.

Hearing him cough to clear his throat she turned back to face him.

'Do you want to come with me Mrs Diamond?' Waving his hand in the air to dismiss his words, he added, 'I shouldn't have said that. You're my client and it's improper.'

'I can't come with you Larry; those dinners are usually black tie and ball gowns. Anyway, I am no one's mistress Larry. If your wife doesn't want to go, that's her choice, but I am no one's substitute.'

'Married?' Larry's eyes widened and he sat up straight. 'I'm divorced. I have a son and I see him every other weekend and in school holidays. It's not the best of arrangements, but it works. My ex-wife and I are on good terms, especially for my wee laddie Paul and her new husband is a very decent man.'

Patsy felt herself blush to the roots. She felt stupid and embarrassed. She'd been surrounded by lies and betrayal for so long she had forgotten that some people were genuine. She tried to compose her shocked state and pick her jaw up from the ground.

'She's married again? If you're on such good terms Larry, why did you get divorced, considering you speak well of her. Most of the divorced people I know usually insult each other and snipe at each other behind their backs.'

'What's the point Patsy? I was a workaholic and she was fed up of staying home alone and so she found someone to pass the time with. Shit happens. We have a son together, and it was an amicable parting. Well, eventually.' He grinned. 'Two years on, it works fine for all of us and the main thing is my son's happiness.'

Feeling foolish and not quite sure he was telling her the truth, she blurted out the burning question on her tongue, 'So who is Jenny then? Your girlfriend? Can't she come out to play tonight?'

Suddenly, the penny dropped and Larry looked at her, shocked. 'Oh my god, Patsy. Is that why you haven't answered my calls? Jenny is my younger sister who is constantly arguing with her partner. She then leaves him for two weeks to make him beg and then goes home. In the mean time she ends up on my doorstep in tears. I'm sure you get the picture.' Letting out a huge sigh and throwing his head back for a moment while running his hands through his hair, he straightened up and looked Patsy in the eye. 'You thought I would cheat on my wife in my own home? You really don't have a high opinion of me, do you? Now I understand. I think you had better go, you've said enough.' Now, Larry felt angry and hurt that she had instantly jumped to this conclusion without even asking him. He had been tried, judged and sentenced on a whim.

Patsy's face burned; she felt even more stupid than she could have possibly imagined. 'If I have judged you badly I am sorry. You must admit though Larry, it's a fair mistake to make.'

'Maybe so Mrs Diamond, but that is why adults talk to each other. If you had answered just one of my calls I could have told you. I'm sorry you feel that way because I really enjoyed our afternoon together. I have thought of nothing else since, but now I know what you've been thinking. It also ties in with why Sheila was going to use my balls as earrings. Thanks for that, Mrs Diamond.'

She tried to laugh, but felt it was strained. She had wronged him badly and not even given him a chance to explain. She owed Larry an apology and another chance.

'Okay Larry, if you don't mind that I'm not in evening dress, and if the invitation still stands, I will come with you tonight. I'll just need to make a call so everyone knows that I haven't been kidnapped.'

Startled by her answer, Larry couldn't believe his ears. She was agreeing to go out with him?

'Are you teasing me Mrs Diamond?' He half laughed. Surprised, Larry looked up at her, waiting for her to burst into laughter or give some sarcastic retort.

'No, not if you still want me to go with you, I have nothing special planned for tonight apart from reading through this file.' At Larry's nod and smile, Patsy called Beryl and explained she was at Sheila's house. Then she rang Sheila just in case Beryl rang her.

'Go on Patsy,' Sheila screamed down the phone. 'Rip his clothes off and get your leg over with Sean Connery and then, give him one for me.'

Cringing inside at Sheila's dirty laugh down the phone, and feeling her face burn while hoping that Larry couldn't hear Sheila's comments, Patsy replied, 'Yes, well thank you Sheila. I'll see you later.' Holding her poker face and ignoring Sheila's innuendos down the phone she ended the call. 'Shall we go Larry?'

The beaming smile on his face warmed her heart, as he held out his arm out for her to link hers through.

* * *

Walking into the hotel ballroom, Patsy nearly burst out laughing when she saw all of the men in kilts. 'Oh my god Larry, it's Brigadoon!'

'Well, we are in Scotland, and it's tradition that we wear kilts at the law society ball.' He laughed.

Surprisingly, she enjoyed the evening and found she had a lot more in common with him than she would have presumed. They laughed together and he introduced her to all of his friends and colleagues. 'This, Patsy, is my annoying little sister Jenny.' Raising his eyebrows, he looked at Patsy and cocked his head to one side, as though trying to prove a point.

'How lovely to meet you again. I am so sorry I burst in on you the other day. I really am. Lawrence should have called me to say he had company, I could have taken Paul for a burger or something.'

'Really, it's not a problem.' Patsy blushed and looked around her.

She noticed Larry had a wry grin on his face. 'See, I told you Patsy, she really is my annoying little sister and her annoying husband is also a solicitor,' he laughed.

'This is Georgie, my partner.' Jenny beamed.

'Nice to meet you.' Georgie stepped forward and held out his hand to shake hers. 'And don't worry, Jenny has told the world that she burst into a half-dressed Lawrence and a red-faced woman. There is no need to explain; it's probably been on the news.' He laughed. Patsy laughed too, although she also felt relieved. Sheila had been right. Married men didn't usually have their affairs in their own home.

Patsy liked the fact that there were no hidden sides to Larry; what you saw was what you got, unlike Nick. She didn't have to do the duty rounds and be polite to people she didn't care about, while being bored to death. These evenings had always been networking events to Nick, where he oozed charm and said the right things to hook the right clients. Tonight she was laughing and having fun; she couldn't remember the last time she'd laughed whole-heartedly like this.

During the last dance of the evening, Larry took her into his arms. There was a chemistry between them, she knew that, and holding her even closer, he began kissing her ear and the side of her neck.

'You're a beautiful woman Patsy Diamond and you deserve to be kissed and often,' he whispered, and kissed her on the lips.

'I think you've drunk too much of that cheap wine Larry.' Her heart was pounding in her chest and she gave a weak smile.

'I want you Patsy Diamond, I want you in my bed. I want your legs wrapped around my neck, not your arms.'

Stunned, Patsy looked at him and started to withdraw from him, but he pulled her closer.

'What are you afraid of? I know I'm punching above my weight, but this will be the only chance I get to hold you in my arms and tell you what I want and tomorrow, you will bark your orders down the telephone and we will greet each other like strangers again.'

'Am I so rude to you down the telephone Larry? And you're not punching above your weight. You're the well-schooled lawyer; strip me of everything and I'm just Patsy the hairdresser.' Her mouth felt dry and she ran her tongue across her lips to moisten them.

Larry's deep Gaelic voice in her ear was awakening emotions she hadn't felt for a very long time. In the months before Nick's death, she had done her best to seduce him and had faced constant rejection. She had felt unattractive and frumpy against the young Natasha, but tonight, she felt like a woman again. She wasn't doing the chasing for once; she was being chased and she liked it.

Slowly roaming his hands up and down her back and down to her bottom, he squeezed it, making her tremble slightly as he pulled her even closer to his body. Patsy's eyes widened as she felt his hardness from under his kilt pressing against her. His warm breath in her ear and the waft of his aftershave was making her feel heady and nervous like a young school girl on a first date.

He flicked the lobe of her ear with the tip of his tongue. 'That's for you if you want it Patsy, because god knows, I want you. I ache for you every time I think of you, which believe me is often.' Suddenly the lights were going up and the song was finishing and Patsy stepped back.

'I need to go to the bathroom, I'll be back in a minute.' Leaving him standing there, Patsy rushed off to the ladies. Her heart was pounding and she ran her hands under the cold tap, to cool herself down. She needed to compose herself before joining him again.

As she exited the toilets she noticed he was waiting in the reception area for her. Everyone was making their way out and saying their farewells. Jenny and Georgie were stood with him.

'Sorry, have I kept you all waiting? There was a queue,' she lied.

'I just wanted to say goodnight Patsy; it's been lovely meeting you again,' Jenny gushed. It was clear she'd had her fair share of wine and Georgie was steering her towards the doors.

'Do you want to share a taxi?' Georgie asked, while balancing Jenny with his arm around her waist.

'No, we'll get our own. Thank you.' Larry smiled and looked at Patsy as they slowly made their way outside. 'Are you coming home with me?' he whispered.

'No, I don't think so. I think we've both had too much to drink. It's been a lovely evening and thank you for asking me. I'll pop by your office first thing to pick up my car and that file.' Thinking about it, Patsy desperately wanted to go home with him. She wanted his arms around her, but inside she was afraid. Her fingers had been well and truly burnt by Nick. She still wanted

Larry on side as her lawyer and some silly one night stand could ruin that.

'You'll be lucky. Tomorrow is Sunday. But I'll meet you at the office for the file, just give me a call when you're on your way there.' Disappointed, Larry put his arm out for a taxi. 'You take this one, I'll take the next.'

'Oh yes, I forgot it's Saturday. Sorry, I'm going to spoil your Sunday. Look, leave the file for now. I'll just collect my car. I'm going back to London tomorrow.'

Larry's face fell. 'You're going home? When are you coming back?'

'I don't know, but I have people coming tomorrow and need to be there...' she trailed off as they looked into each other's eyes.

Leaning towards her, Larry wrapped his arms around her and kissed her passionately. Patsy surprised herself when she responded so ardently to his kiss. She held on to him and ran her hands through his hair as they kissed again.

'I have to go Larry. Goodnight,' she whispered once he had released her. Getting into the cab she looked out of the window and blew him a kiss. Her heart was pounding, and she was about to change her mind when she saw him get into the taxi behind her. She was tempted to call him on his mobile but felt foolish. Instead, she sat in the taxi while it drove her to Beryl's flat, mentally imagining what could be happening between them by now.

Patsy was in a turmoil; her heart said one thing and her head another. Trying her hardest to push Larry to the back of her mind she called Sheila. 'Are you awake and alone Sheila? Sorry it's so late.'

'Weren't you supposed to be having an evening of dancing and fornication?' She laughed groggily down the phone. 'Yes, I'm alone, Angus is working the night shift. Oh my god, are you telling me that Larry didn't suggest spending the night at his place?'

Sitting upright in bed, Sheila waited for the gossip as Patsy poured her heart out.

'You bottled it, didn't you?' Sheila laughed out loud. 'For god's sake Patsy. For a clever woman you're really stupid. He's gagging for it and so are you, what is the problem? He's a good looking bloke, you said yourself he has the equipment and those teeth of his, well you need sunglasses when he smiles.'

Feeling her heart sink, Patsy changed the subject. Sheila wasn't making her feel any better. 'Apparently his father is a dentist,' she said weakly. 'Anyway, why I am calling is I am leaving tomorrow and I wondered if you needed a lift to London.'

'Yes, okay, pick me up when you're ready.' As an afterthought, Sheila asked, 'By the way, just in case I need to contact Larry on your behalf at some point, send me his number. It will save me making a fuss if I ever need to go to his office again.'

'I doubt you will but I'll text it to you, just in case.' Patsy yawned. 'Night Sheila, go back to sleep.'

After ending the call Sheila sat up in bed and turned on the lamp. She waited for Patsy to send Larry's number and dialling it, she was surprised when he answered so quickly.

'Is something or someone keeping you awake Larry?' she asked seductively.

'It's Sheila, isn't it? What do you want?' he snapped, waiting for another tirade of insults. He wasn't in the mood for banter or anything else.

'I'm your fairy godmother Larry, and I have a long drive with a frustrated, miserable cow tomorrow who has bottled a night of passion and called me at 1 a.m. to tell me so. Forget you're her lawyer Larry and stop being polite. You've one last chance tomorrow when she collects her car; man up and do what is on your mind. This is for my sake as well as yours. The last thing I need is a bad tempered hell cat. Do us both a favour Larry, be a little forceful.'

'I wouldn't force myself on any woman Sheila. You do realise that kind of thing is against the law. You're suggesting the impossible.' He sighed.

'Are you a hot-blooded Scotsman or an impersonation of one? Stop thinking rationally and do what comes naturally. Night Larry.' With that, Sheila ended the call. She knew she had given Larry a lot to think about and the very fact that she had called after speaking to Patsy gave him hope.

* * *

Larry was already at his office when Patsy arrived the next day. She could feel the nervous tension between them and wanted to leave.

'Come in Patsy, I'll just get your file.'

Following him in, she could feel her heart pounding, and she couldn't help but admire how handsome he looked. His hair seemed to have lightened with the spring sunshine and the blue shirt he wore seemed to heighten his colouring. Not wanting to betray herself, she found herself looking at the shape of his lips, the very lips that had kissed and nuzzled her neck the night before and ran her tongue across her own lips to moisten them.

His cold professional manner disturbed her as she watched him opening his desk drawer. He handed the folder over to her. 'There you go, have a safe journey home.'

She felt a sinking feeling in the pit of her stomach; she wanted to stay in his company a little longer but had nothing else to say. All her confidence had left her; she felt young and embarrassed.

Larry walked around to Patsy's side of the desk. 'There is something else I have for you.' Raising one eyebrow, he smiled coyly. Pulling her roughly towards him and sweeping her into his arms, he kissed her passionately. Everything he had felt the night before came pouring out. Kissing him back just as ardently, their hunger for each other was aroused again.

Patsy felt like she had just swallowed a box of fireworks; her body was on fire as he held her and let his hands roam over her body. She could feel her excitement building as she clung to him for more. He unzipped the back of her dress and caressed her naked back. She trembled and slid her hands underneath his shirt to entwine her fingers in the hairs on his chest, then let her hands slowly reach down to stroke him. She could feel the hardness of his excitement as her own naked breasts were exposed and teased by his tongue. Her legs began to tremble, and she could feel her own moistness as he kissed her nipples.

Stroking his crotch, she pulled at his belt and undid it. His manhood sprung out and into her hand as she stroked it. She felt herself being raised as Larry roughly laid her on his desk and pulled the rest of her dress and panties away, throwing them on the floor. Their desire and excitement matched each other's as they tore away the barriers of clothing between them.

Opening her legs, she could see the burning desire in his eyes and reached out for him. Cheek to cheek, she searched for his mouth and kissed him. Suddenly she let out a gasp, as he mounted her, thrusting himself inside her again and again. Frenzied passion overwhelmed them both as Patsy egged him on for more. Folders and paperwork flew off his desk as he grabbed her legs and put them around his neck. Thrusting her hips towards him, Patsy moaned and panted. She couldn't get enough of him, as they both rocked in unison. Feeling a trembling sensation inside her, Patsy raised her arms above her head and held on to the edge of the desk tightly. She could feel her body about to explode as she reached her peak. She closed her eyes in ecstasy and cried out in pleasure. Stopping for a moment to let her catch her breath, Larry pulled her off the desk and turned her around, bending her over it. A moan of sheer delight escaped her lips as he thrust himself once more inside her. She pushing herself backwards to greet him. Wild with passion, he held her hips firmly, until again, he felt her body tense, and a moan of pleasure escaped her lips. Feeling his own release, he threw his head back, trying to suck air into his lungs. His body shivered with the intensity of it and panting, he rested his head on Patsy's back to catch his breath.

Patsy's legs felt weak as she tried to stand up and face him. Gently, she reached up and put her arms around his neck, kissing him, pulling him down on to the carpeted floor.

'Again Larry, I want you again,' she whispered with desire. Overwhelmed by passion, they both lied down on the floor, as Patsy opened her thighs to welcome him once more.

20

DISCOVERY

Seeing Victoria's car already in the car parking bay, Sheila turned towards Patsy. 'Lassie, do you want some advice?' Puzzled Patsy waited. 'If you don't want Vicky to know that you've had sex, take that dreamy look off your face. You've sung like a bird to every song on the way here with a big grin on your face. It's as plain as the nose on your face what you've been up to.'

Patsy burst out laughing. 'Back to business then Sheila, and thanks for the tip.'

'Victoria, Natasha, I'm sorry we're late, the traffic was terrible,' Patsy lied, casting a glance towards Sheila.

'No worries darling. You're both safe and sound and that is what matters. Natasha make some coffee for everyone,' Victoria instructed.

Looking towards Natasha, Patsy smiled. 'How is the baby doing Natasha?'

'Really well. He's putting on weight and breathing by himself,' Natasha gushed. 'Oh and I'm getting a supervised visit with Jimmy soon – I'm so excited.' She beamed and then went into the kitchen to make the coffee.

Once they had settled down, Patsy filled them in on her talk with James McNally. Stunned, they all stared at her wide eyed.

Victoria was the first to speak. 'Where do you think these recordings are Patsy?'

Looking towards the two unopened boxes near the door, Patsy nodded. 'Possibly in there. That is all of Nick's things from his office. I would put money on them being in there. Come on, let's open them.' Each in turn they pulled at the boxes and opened them.

'Have you seen this on that woman's file Patsy?' Natasha frowned and picked up the file Larry had given her on Karen Duret from the coffee table.

'What is it? There is only her name on the front Natasha – what are you talking about?'

'When I was in prison I did lots of puzzles – crosswords and sudoku. Look at the name of the woman.'

Patsy couldn't help her sarcasm. 'Wow Natasha, that is the best thing you learnt while in prison, how to do a bloody cross-word puzzle.'

'Shut up Patsy and use your eyes instead of your mouth for once,' Natasha snapped. They all looked up, surprised at her outburst, and walked over to the table. 'Karen Duret. It's an anagram. Move the letters around and it spells undertaker. Isn't that the name Nick used?'

They all stared at it in disbelief, and Patsy got a pen and paper and wrote the letters out to make sure.

'Oh my god, you're right Natasha. Do you think that was just a coincidence?' Frowning, they all cast glances at each other, while totally lost for words. 'Let's get these bloody boxes open. What other surprises are there in store for us?'

Fuelled by anger, Patsy put her hands in the boxes and brought out books and dictionaries and office stationery. She was surprised to find a framed photo of herself and Nick from when they were recently married and still very much in love. Staring at it, Patsy felt a fleeting stab to her heart.

There was a map of Scotland, and laying it on the floor, they could see Nick had put red dots on certain locations. 'That is where he did all of his dealings, isn't it? My god, it's so widespread. Did he rule the whole of Glasgow?'

Bewildered by it all, Patsy continued to tell them about James's conversation. It was only when she mentioned Billy Burke's name, did Victoria stop what she was doing.

'Did you say Nick was involved in Billy's murder? I knew that man would bring misery to this family. You remember him Patsy. I told you, he was Nick's real father,' Victoria blurted out.

Patsy knew she had heard the name before, but she hadn't been able to bring it to the forefront of her mind. 'He gave the order for the death of his own father?'

'I think I know why. He probably saw it as revenge for me. Somehow I feel very responsible for all of this mess. It goes back to my meeting with Billy Burke. If Nick had never wanted to meet his biological father, none of this would have happened, and if Nick hadn't found out I had been date raped, he would never have wanted the man dead.' Sorrowful, Victoria sat on the sofa and put her head in her hands. She knew Billy Burke had drawn Nick into his unsavoury world, but the apple never fell far from the tree and Nick was more like his father than she could possibly have imagined.

Sheila sat beside her. 'It's not your fault Vicky. He didn't have to carry on with it all, did he? He made the choices; he took the money. He loved the power he held over everyone. Billy Burke just lit the blue touch paper, but Nick knew exactly what he was doing.'

'Here's his laptop,' Patsy butted in. 'Let's charge it up and see what's on it.' Plugging it in, Patsy turned it on, but there were hardly any files on it. 'Do you think it's been wiped? It's just music, which I presumed he listened to when working.'

Natasha looked over her shoulders at the screen. 'What's all those numbers for Patsy? Look at that folder, it's just numbers, no names.'

Shrugging, they all looked at each other. None of it made sense. They didn't know what they were looking for and this seemed like a pointless task. Natasha continued typing on the keyboard, intrigued by all of the numbers and suddenly a file jumped out at her.

'Maybe that James knows what the numbers are Patsy,' Sheila butted in.

Victoria glanced at the boxes and the contents lying on the floor. 'My guess is whatever we're looking for is still in his office somewhere.'

Patsy shook her head. 'No Victoria. They cleared his office and this is all there was in there.'

Sheila started poring over the stationery, shaking books and laying everything out in order. 'Well, you would think for all of his money he would buy a better dictionary. Fucking cheapskate.' She held up a small book with an elastic band around it. 'And I was right, he does have a dead plant in here. Honestly Patsy, you should have opened these boxes ages ago.' She tutted.

'It's not dead Sheila, look.' Natasha pointed to the tiny leaves. 'That's one of those plants people don't water and they put in glass jars. You know, like cactus and stuff. What is the name for them.' Thumbing her chin, Natasha looked in the air for inspiration. 'Terrarium. That's it. The plant contains its own moisture in the glass jars.

Patsy held out her hand for it and looked inside the glass

bowl. 'Nick was no gardener, believe me. Look around this place, can you see a plant?'

As though seeing the place for the first time, they all looked around the apartment.

'Empty it,' Victoria said. She couldn't take her eyes off it. 'I have a strange feeling about this, but you're right Patsy, Nick didn't do plants, it wasn't his thing.'

Sheila tipped the bowl upside down onto some paper and waited while the stones and soil fell out. As if by magic two keys fell out of the bottom. Stunned, they all stood and looked at the keys on the floor. 'What do you think they're for?'

'I don't know,' Victoria said, 'but if that plant was in his office I'd say there is something in there that key opens. Do you still have access to Nick's office, Patsy?'

'No. They've cleared it and possibly moved someone else into it now. But even if we got inside, what are we looking for? These keys they look almost Victorian with the fancy ornate shapes on the top.'

Natasha couldn't help butting in. 'Why don't we ask a locksmith? There's a shop up the road here and surely the man behind the counter could give us some idea for what we're looking for. Surely, if keys are his business, he'll know everything. And what does funus mean?' she asked.

'I don't know. Give me that dictionary, I'll look it up.' Patsy snatched the dictionary from Natasha and ran her hands through the pages.

'For crying out loud lassies, you've Google on your mobiles, look it up.' Sheila tutted and took out her mobile and typed in the word. Immediately the blood drained from her face. 'Funus means funeral or death and considering Nick Diamond was the Undertaker, I would say this was his kind of sick joke wouldn't you? Where did you see that word Natasha?'

'On the laptop. It's a folder with all of those numbers. A lot of it is in Latin or something. I'm having to look it up.' Natasha jumped up and clapped her hands. 'Whatever we're looking for has a death theme. Those numbers have something to do with death, I'll put money on it. R3SG?'

They all looked at each other, bewildered. They had no idea what any of it meant; it was way beyond them.

'It doesn't come up on Google.' Sheila shrugged.

Victoria hovered over the map on the floor again. 'These red dots are all cemeteries, look.' She pointed. 'And if you've noticed, there is a similar number on that file of yours Patsy. What does that stand for?'

Looking at the folder, Patsy shrugged. 'I don't know. I'll ask Larry, let's see if he knows what it stands for.' Taking a breath she dialled his number. The others wanted her to put it on loud speaker and casting a furtive glance at Sheila, she waited till he answered it before quickly blurting out, 'Larry, you're on loud speaker. I have Victoria and the girls here...'

Instantly Larry took the hint. Addressing her properly, he answered, 'Mrs Diamond. How can I help?'

Sighing with relief, Patsy continued. 'We were just wondering what the numbers were on the side of the folder regarding Karen Duret?'

'That's the plot number Mrs Diamond. All headstones have numbers to make it easier to find where people are buried.'

'What would R3SG mean?' Patsy asked tentatively, looking at the others.

'That's simple, Mrs Diamond. That would be row 3 and SG would be St George's church, but that isn't where Karen Duret is buried...'

'Thanks Larry, I'll be in touch.' Patsy quickly ended the call and felt herself blushing.

Sheila rubbed her hands together. 'Firstly ladies, it's time for a stiff drink. Natasha, you're the crossword queen, go through all those numbers and letters on those files and see if you can match any up with cemetery names on that map. We still need to find those recordings and work out what that key fits.'

They all nodded in agreement.

'I'll go to the locksmith and see if he can help us,' suggested Patsy. 'I wish we knew a burglar, I'd happily pay someone to get into that office and search it for us.'

Smugly, Sheila folded her arms. 'I know a burglar if you're serious about paying?'

They all burst out laughing. 'For crying out loud Sheila, is there anyone you don't know?'

'My husband was a burglar and he always took a bloke called Fin with him. He'll come, if I ask him to.'

'Okay, if he'll come, then I'm willing to pay, but we can't tell him what to steal, because we're not sure ourselves.' Patsy sighed. It all seemed pretty desperate.

'I guarantee if there is anything in that office that Fin feels shouldn't be there, he'll find it. Call it gut instinct, but he and Steve were like sniffer dogs; they knew where to look.'

A frown crossed Victoria's face. 'But can we trust him? I'm sorry Sheila, I know he's a friend of yours, but...' Trailing off for fear of offending Sheila, she gave a weak smile.

'You can trust Fin. If he's doing a job for you, then he'll do it and you'll get your spoils. All he's concerned about is getting paid. You know Fin, don't you Natasha?' Sheila nodded in Natasha's direction.

'Yes, he's always treated me fair, he even got me a job at one of the pizza shops.'

Satisfied, Patsy nodded. 'If you both trust him, that's good enough for me. After all, who else do we have to ask? Make the call Sheila.'

Casting a glance at Maggie as she opened the door, Fin walked towards James's bedroom.

'You wanted to see me James. What's the problem?'

'There's no problem Fin. I have something for you. Here.' Putting his hand under the duvet cover, James took out 6,000 pounds. 'This is for you. I know it should be more but I just need to get on my feet first and then I'll see you right. You all deserve it and more. What price can I put on my life?'

Fin's eyes widened at the money as though hypnotised. 'Six grand?' He was astonished and sat on the side of the bed.

'Yes Fin, but there is one more favour I need you to do for me.'

'Anything. You name it, James.' Fin's smile almost lit up the room.

'I want you to get a saw or something to take these plaster casts off. I can't go anywhere to get it done, will you do it?'

Fin rubbed his chin and spied the casts. Nothing particularly bothered him, but mentally, he was frightened in case he cut deeper than the casts. 'They have professional saws for that, don't they? What should I do it with?'

James could see the apprehension in Fin's eyes, and half smiled. 'An angle grinder should do it. Go and find what you can; I just want them off.' Reaching under his pillow for his wallet, James took out 100 pounds and handed it over.

Scooping up his own money and tucking it inside his leather jacket, Fin took 100 pounds and ran outside where he squeezed his fists together and punched the air. Just then his mobile rang, interrupting his thoughts about what he was going to spend his money on. 'Hi Sheila, long time, no hear. How's things in Edinburgh?'

'Can you get to London tomorrow Fin? There is a job with your name on it and expenses.'

Fin thought about the things he had to do. He wasn't sure if James would need him again over the next couple of days. 'How long for Sheila?'

'That's up to you Fin. Can you come or not? I need someone with your skills.'

'I can, but where are you?'

'Ring me when you get close to Kings Cross Station, I'll give you further instructions then. Can't say a lot now Fin, speak tomorrow.'

'Okay Sheila, who is it for, can you tell me that at least?'

'Tomorrow Fin. All will be revealed.' With that, his phone line went dead.

Forgetting his good fortune for a moment, Fin was perplexed by Sheila's call. Why did she want him to go to London? And more to the point, what kind of a job did she want him to do? He trusted Sheila, they had been friends most of their lives, but her secrecy made him nervous. Shrugging it off, he shoved his hands into his pockets and walked to his flat. Pulling the air vent off the wall, he took out the old cushion he had in there, unzipped it and put his money inside. Replacing the vent, he checked it all looked in order again and left for the hardware shop.

21

A THIEF IN THE NIGHT

Standing outside Kings Cross Station, Sheila spotted Fin as he got off the train and waved towards him, but as usual he wasn't paying attention.

Striding over to the gate as he walked through, she punched him in the arm. 'Hey daydreamer, are your ears full of wax?'

'Sorry Sheila, I was miles away. It's my first time to London, I might even do some sightseeing while I'm here.'

'Do what you like afterwards Fin, but come on, we'll get a taxi, I have some friends I want you to meet.'

Fin bit his bottom lip, and a frown crossed his brow. 'What's all this about Sheila?'

'Come on and take that worried look off your face, all will be revealed. Trust me.'

Once they had arrived at Patsy's apartment, his throat felt dry and looking down at his clothing, he wished he'd worn something better. He did have his designer jeans on and hoped that would make the difference; the only problem was that he hadn't washed them in a week.

He stepped into the hallway and was quite surprised that Sheila just waltzed in. In fact, she seemed quite at home here. As she opened the lounge door Fin was surprised to see Patsy Diamond, Natasha and another lady who he thought might have been Nick Diamond's mother.

The three of them were sat on the sofa behind a coffee table. The way they looked at him reminded him of his many times in court. These women looked like the magistrates he had faced in the past and didn't have a hair out of place.

'Ladies, this is Fin.' She ushered him in and offered him an armchair. He sat down and looked around the huge apartment.

'I know you,' he said, looking at Patsy. 'You're Mrs Diamond.' Then Fin coughed, realising his mistake. Looking at Victoria, he smiled. 'You're Mrs Diamond as well...'

Victoria's soothing voice put him at his ease. 'Just call me Victoria and as you say, you know Patsy. Shall we just leave it on a first name basis before we all get mixed up?' She laughed, making him feel more at his ease.

'What we need Fin is a burglar. Someone with your reputation. I've told them you're the best and you wouldn't let us down.' Sheila deliberately boosted his ego and he fell into her honey trap straight away.

'Thanks Sheila, I appreciate that. That's why they call me Fingers Fin. But why do you ladies want a burglar?' He found this a very odd situation.

All matter of fact and business-like, Patsy finally spoke. 'Fin, you know some of the problems I've had in Glasgow and with the community centre. You also know who my husband was and the other name he was known by. Let's not play games. The point is, if you're as good as Sheila says, I want you to break into somewhere for me. It won't be easy, because to be honest, we don't know what we're looking for. We have a key, which, according to a locksmith, is supposed to fit a jewellery box or something. The locksmith said they were usually for jewellery boxes years ago. We really don't know, and I am not sure he does either.' Frustrated, Patsy threw her hands in the air. 'We think the box can only be in one place, but we know it's being well hidden. So tell me Fin, where do people usually hide things?'

Confused, Fin looked around the room. It felt like an ambush. He'd often fantasised about being the only male in a room full of women, but this wasn't what he'd envisaged.

'Well...' he started slowly and shot a glance at Sheila. 'Depending on what it is, they might hide things in air vents, skirting boards and even under the floor boards. So, you're looking for a jewellery box? An old one, yeah?'

There was a silence in the room as they looked around at each other. Lost for words Patsy shrugged. 'We don't know Fin. I was told there might be recordings, possibly mobile phones.' Letting out a deep sigh, Patsy stood up and walked around the room, as though looking for ideas. 'All I can say Fin, is that if you decide to do this thing. Anything you feel shouldn't be in a solicitor's office is probably what we're looking for. I know that sounds vague. Sorry Fin.'

Rubbing his face with his hands, Fin pondered on what she had said. He didn't know how he could help, but it was worth a try. They all seemed desperate and were clearly prepared to pay. 'I give no guarantees I'll find anything, but I'll take a look for you.'

'And we can't ask for any more than that.' Victoria gave him a smile.

Fin cleared his throat. 'If you don't mind lassies, I think I'll go and have a look around London for a couple of hours. I'll be back later. After all, I can't do my job in daylight. So if you don't mind...' Fin got up. He was glad to be out of there.

'Wait a moment.' Patsy took her purse out of her bag and

handed over 100 pounds. 'That's for your train fare and to get something to eat. Oh, and don't spend all day in the pubs; I want you sober for this job, do you understand?' Patsy's stern look was enough to make him think twice about his London trip.

'Business is business Patsy. I'll be back and I'll be sober. Actually, give me the address of the place you want me to rob and I can have a walk around and check it out in daylight.'

Satisfied by his business manner, Patsy gave him the address and told him where to find Nick's office.

After he left, Victoria clapped her hands together. 'Right ladies, let's eat. There is nothing we can do for the moment, apart from sit it out and wait for Fin to do his job.'

'Why the worried look Patsy?' asked Sheila. 'Do you think he's going to do a runner with your money?'

'No, not really, and if he decides to not come back well, he deserves his train fare. It's just that I've seen him around Glasgow... are you sure he's the right man for the job? Do you think he can keep his mouth shut about all of this once he goes back to Thistle Park?'

'He's exactly the man for this job Patsy. Like I said, he and my Steve did a lot of jobs together. If there is anything to be found, I guarantee he'll find it. As for gossiping about it, the answer to that is a definite no. He's a closed book our Fin, he'll keep our secret,' Sheila reassured her. She knew Patsy was anxious, but she had faith in Fin; for all of his weird ways, he was a man to be trusted.

* * *

Once inside, Fin was surprised by the size of the building; it certainly didn't look like any solicitor's office he had ever been in, with its long winding staircase. He'd sat outside for hours watching everyone leave. As an extra precaution, just in case anyone had stayed behind to work late, he called the office several times to see if anyone answered the phones, but it was only the answerphone every time.

Walking around the ground floor, he closed all of the vertical blinds, then, wearing a headband with a light on the front he wandered around the offices and then walked to Nick's office. He was slightly surprised that the sign on the door still read Nick Diamond. It gave him hope, because obviously no one else was using it yet.

Inside, the office was almost bare, with a large wooden desk with a telephone on it and a huge leather chair on either side. Opening the desk drawers, he rummaged around, but only found paperclips and a stapler. There was an air vent on the wall and as he pulled it away and put his hand inside, he found nothing. There was a painting on the wall of Edinburgh castle and tracing his hand around it in admiration, he realised it wasn't a picture at all. The frame was like an ornamental square plaster cast fixed to the wall. Taking out his Swiss-style multi-function knife set, he ran it around the picture. Instantly the picture came away and it was just a white wall behind it. Fin knocked on the wall to see if it was solid and a grin crept on his face when he heard a distinctive echo telling him it was a false wall.

Taking the jagged edge of his knife, he pierced the plaster board until it chipped away. Looking around for something harder, he saw a solid lamp stand. Picking it up, he bashed it against the wall until a bigger hole appeared. Taking out his mobile phone, he turned on the light and held it up against the hole. Taking a closer look, he saw a shelf and on it was a security box. He reached inside and tried grabbing at the box, but it was quite large and a lot heavier than he'd realised. For fear of dropping it, he looked around for something heavier to make the hole bigger. In the far corner was a small wooden nest of tables and picking up the smallest one, he smashed it against the hole in the wall and plaster dust and bits of plaster flew in the air and on the floor. Now he could almost walk into the wall and pick up the silver and grey box.

Satisfied with his achievements, he put the box on the desk and continued looking around the room. Kneeling down to the wooden skirting boards, he unscrewed the screws at each end with his faithful army knife. Pulling them away he could see there were no holes behind them, but he noticed a piece of the carpet was loose. He ran his hands along it.

Gently pulling at the frayed edge, which seemed unusual in such an establishment, it folded back easily, as though it had been pulled back many times before. Intrigued, Fin knelt down and with his headlamp and phone looked down at the floorboards and ran his hands over them. Again he grinned to himself. One of the screws was raised, which to his expert eye meant it had been unscrewed and the floorboard removed. Hastily he unscrewed the surrounding floorboards and pulled them up and looked down at the hole.

Fin leaned in and found large canvass holdalls stuffed inside. Using all of his strength, he pulled them upwards and rested each one on the floor beside him. Quickly unzipping one, he saw that it was full of more money than he had ever seen in his life. There were two more bags down there and with all of his might he heaved them up. He didn't have time to check them out, he felt he had stayed long enough. He dragged the bags outside the office then, sweating and out of breath, he looked at the desk again. Curiosity was now getting the better of him. Swiftly he opened all the drawers and pulled them out onto the floor. As he presumed, the bottom drawer had a false bottom and sliding the wood apart, inside he saw a folder full of envelopes. Scooping them up, he put them on top of the desk.

Looking around, he felt his work was done here; he was convinced there was nothing else to be found. This place was like a rabbit warren with all of these hiding places, but Patsy Diamond had been right when she had said look for anything that shouldn't be in a solicitor's office.

Out of habit, Fin took the screwdriver of his Swiss Army knife and took the door handles off. There was only one way to make sure there wasn't any finger prints left behind and that was to take the door handles with him. Picking up the security box and folder, let out a huge sigh. There was so much stuff to carry; it would be an impossible task. Then he remembered the supermarket across the road. Quickly running over, he put a pound in a supermarket trolley to release it and ran back to the office. Hastily he filled the trolley with the bags, folder and safety box. Contemplating what to do next he took out his mobile and rang Sheila. He was surprised when she answered instantly.

'Come and get me Sheila. I'm at the supermarket,' was all he said before he ended the call. Pushing the trolley across to the supermarket, he parked it near a group of shaded bushes and left it there while he ran into the shop.

Picking up a sandwich, he went back to the bushes and waited. Seeing headlights, he ducked inside of the bushes and peered out. From a distance he could see two women in a car and tentatively walked towards it. Breathing a sigh of relief when Sheila opened the window, he grinned. 'There's a lot of stuff Sheila, I need help.'

Patsy jumped out of the driver side of the car and walked towards him. 'What have you found?'

'Not here. Empty that trolley load into the back of the car. Come on, it's heavy.'

Stunned, Sheila and Patsy looked at the trolley then back at Fin. 'Well, move your arses, we haven't got all night,' he snapped. 'You do that, I've got something else to do, back in a minute.'

Patsy and Sheila watched as Fin disappeared and between them they struggled to load the boot of the car. Fin came running back to the car puffing and panting.

'Let's go!' he shouted, then as an afterthought he wheeled the shopping trolley into one of its parking areas where all the trolleys were housed and then ran back to the car. Patsy already had the engine revved up and was waiting.

Sheila couldn't help but ask, 'Why did you go to all the trouble of taking the trolley back? What does it matter for goodness' sake?'

'I wanted my pound back Sheila,' he said as he climbed into the back of the car.

Sheila and Patsy turned to face each other and, raising their eyebrows in disbelief, they shrugged and drove off.

After a couple of trips to load everything into the lift in the car park, puffing and panting the three of them stood back and took a breath.

Working in silence, they pulled the bags into Patsy's apartment. Patsy was surprised to see that Victoria and Natasha were still up and waiting for them.

'You three look like you could do with a stiff drink.' Victoria brought a bottle of whisky and some glasses over and put them on the coffee table and then looked at the bags on the floor. 'It looks like there was a lot that shouldn't be in a solicitor's office.' Raising her eyebrows, she looked at Fin and sat down on the sofa opposite him.

'You've got to see what's inside them; I couldn't believe my eyes!' Fin almost shouted and downed his whisky in one. The three of them watched pensively as Fin opened the bags. They all gasped with surprise.

Kneeling down, Natasha put her hand in the bag and took out a roll of money. 'Is this all real?' she asked, looking around the room in disbelief.

'Of course it is,' Patsy snapped. 'Nick went to a bloody lot of trouble if it wasn't, didn't he?'

Victoria held her hands up to stop another argument. 'Tell us what happened Fin. How did you find all of this?' She was curious, especially when Fin pulled out the envelopes and the security box and told them the whole story. This was beyond anything they had dreamed of.

Patsy looked at the box. It wasn't your average security safe box. 'What's in that?'

'Don't know Mrs Diamond and I didn't have time to check, but now I look at it, it's more like a strong box with all of those combinations and such.' He shrugged. Greedily, he held up a roll of money and rolled it in his hands. 'This is like winning the lottery,' he half whispered to himself.

Mesmerised by the strange box, they all stared at it. It wasn't a usual metal box, it was different. It was more of an orange or rust colour. 'It looks like cast iron to me, Mrs Diamond. That is an old box and fuck it's heavy. Look at all those weird hinges on the sides.' Fin gently roamed his fingers over it, marvelling at the old craftwork that had gone into it. Some of the hinges on the sides were held by leather corner pieces, but it was old. Very old indeed. 'It looks like something they raised from the *Titanic*.' Fin laughed and tried breaking the ice, but no one smiled. 'It's vintage all right, bigger than normal safety deposit boxes, but those combination locks are a mystery. I've never seen one like it.'

Patsy looked up at him. She too was intrigued by this square box that could hold a million secrets and the end of her journey.

She handed the key over to Fin. 'Open it,' Patsy instructed. Curiosity was now getting the better of her. She wasn't interested in the money; she knew whatever was in that box was worth more.

Half laughing and shrugging, Fin poured himself another drink. 'I'm no safe cracker; you need Spider for that. That may well be the key, but what about the combinations, do you have those? Look at it, it has more than one lock.'

'You're a thief who can't open a safe? What's the point of that?'

'I'm a bloody good thief Mrs Diamond and an honest one. I could have stuffed a load of that money in my pockets, but I didn't. Me, Spider and Beanie work together.' Turning towards Sheila, he looked at her for an explanation. 'You know I'm no safe cracker Sheila, why didn't you tell me to bring Spider?'

'Well, maybe, you brainless oaf, it's because I didn't know there was going to be a safe and I didn't want the whole world knowing what we were up to. We had no idea what you would find,' Sheila replied.

The whisky was now getting the better of Fin and he laughed out loud. 'I took these as well.' Holding up the door handles, he dangled them in the air and smiled. 'No fingerprints. Light fingered Fin, that's what they call me,' he boasted.

Confused, and knowing she was going to get a tongue lashing, Natasha asked the obvious question, 'Don't you wear gloves?'

A frown crossed all of their brows and even Patsy had to admit, she had never thought of that.

'I sometimes wear my leather ones, but I forgot them. I can't wear those acrylic ones, because of my eczema. I get the cream on prescription.' Holding up his hands to show them, they all stared at each other in disbelief. This was getting weirder by the minute.

'But,' Victoria asked, 'won't your fingerprints be all over the place? What was the point in bringing the handles? Your fingerprints will be everywhere.'

Gulping back another whisky, Fin nodded. 'Yeah, that's why when Mrs Diamond and Sheila were putting the stuff in the back of the car I ran back and torched the place!'

Their jaws dropped and they stared wide eyed at him for a moment. Sheepishly, Fin looked over his glass at them and paused for a moment. 'What was I supposed to do?'

'That's my fucking building!' Patsy spat out. 'It's worth a fortune, you bloody idiot!'

Fin shrugged. 'And it still is, Mrs Diamond. I presume you're insured. You'll get your money back.' Cocking his head, he winked at her, which annoyed her even more.

'Well, I hope they don't think it was me. Shit, I'm in my neck up to it, and now I'm going to be charged with arson!' Lying back on the sofa in disbelief, Patsy felt like crying.

Putting her arm around her shoulders, Victoria comforted her. 'I think we should all get some sleep. It's the early hours. Let's sleep on it and think again after we've rested.' Victoria stood up and tightened the belt around her dressing gown.

Fin coughed. 'Before we all part lassies, shouldn't we sort something out?' He coughed again and looked at the bags.

Patsy knew he was hinting for his payment for a job well done.

Standing up, she took a handful of the rolls of money out of the bag and then did the same again. 'Will that buy your silence Fin?'

Wide eyed, he stared at the money in his lap and looked up at her. 'Wow! Thank you Mrs Diamond. I only usually get paid a few hundred quid. That's amazing. Thank you,' he gushed, gripping the rolls of bills tightly.

Lost for words, Patsy shook her head in disbelief and rolled her eyes up to the ceiling. 'You've earned it,' she said calmly. 'Sleep on the sofa Fin, I'll get you a duvet.' Wearily, she walked out of the lounge and pulled Sheila by the arm alongside her. 'Get that fucking idiot on the first train back to Glasgow!'

22

A DOUBLE-EDGED SWORD

None of them slept well, and a couple of hours later they all emerged from their bedrooms yawning and reaching for the paracetamol. The loud snoring from a drunken Fin didn't help matters. Seeing the empty whisky bottle in his arms, Patsy started making some coffee.

Talking things over, they agreed they needed to see what was in that box and go through the envelopes. Victoria noticed there were numerous messages on her mobile. Listening to them, she gasped. 'Oh my god, Beryl's in hospital. It seems she's been hurt, a fall or something, but the police are involved and it doesn't look good. They've asked if I can go straight away.'

'We're all coming with you,' Patsy insisted.

Once Natasha and Victoria had left the room, Patsy looked at Sheila. 'Why do I have a bad feeling about this? Beryl was fine when I saw her and she's not unsteady on her feet, and why are the police involved? Something isn't right.'

Sheila tried making light of it. 'She's probably tripped over that tongue of hers. Still, there is no point in fretting. The sooner we get there, the sooner we'll have all the answers we need.'

'Why don't we take the box with us? Fin said his friend Spider can open it and it would save us a lot of trouble.'

'I agree lassie, let's take the box. I'm sure Beryl will be okay, she's a fighter.' Picking up her cup, Sheila looked towards the lounge. 'We may as well give him a lift back and to be fair, whatever you think Patsy lass, he did a bloody good job.'

'I agree, I'm sorry I snapped at him last night, it's just each time we think we're going forward we take two steps back. And you've got to agree Sheila, he is a sandwich short of a picnic.'

'He's got a lot more about him than you give him credit for and believe me, after what you gave him last night you've bought his loyalty for life.' She walked away laughing, giving Patsy a lot to think about.

Looking at her own mobile, Patsy saw there were numerous calls from Larry. Although she was pleased he had called her, she felt sad about it, too. Now was not the time to get involved with someone new, especially someone as nice as Larry.

Going into the lounge, she shook Fin. 'We're leaving for Glasgow. Get dressed,' she barked.

Looking at her through the slits of his eyes, he yawned and nodded.

After a long drive, they dropped Fin off near Thistle Park and went to the hospital. Victoria spoke to the doctors, but they were all surprised to see the police there in their droves. Patsy looked around and noticed the two detectives who were dealing with Nick's murder case.

Tearful, Victoria walked up to them in the corridor. 'Apparently, she was at the community centre and was knocked about by some Polish guys who manage the doors. She wouldn't pay to go in and an argument broke out and they pushed her. They haven't been arrested because they made a run for it,' Victoria sighed.

Shocked, Patsy held her hand to her mouth. She remembered her conversation with Maggie and Beryl. She had more or less accused Beryl of giving her keys to some thugs who were charging to enter the community centre. These must be the same people who had roughed her up. Poor Beryl, she hadn't deserved any of this.

'So why are those detectives here Victoria?'

Taking a huge sigh, Victoria shook her head. 'Apparently she wants to make a clean breast of it and confess to Nick's murder. That's why they wanted us here so quickly, she wouldn't do it without us here.' Victoria burst into tears and fell into Patsy's arms.

They were all stunned. 'I don't believe it Victoria. Beryl adored Nick. Can we see her?' Although comforting Victoria, Patsy's disbelief was apparent. Why on earth would Beryl murder her own grandson? Her mind whirling, she marched up to the detectives who were stood looking through the windows of Beryl's hospital room, deep in conversation.

'Are you that desperate to close Nick's case you're blaming an old woman you sad bastards!' Patsy shouted at them.

Staying calm, the detective in charge pulled her to one side and lowered his voice. 'We're as surprised as you are Mrs Diamond. But she asked us to come here.' Almost apologetically, the detective looked down at the floor.

Lost for words, Patsy silently walked back over to Victoria.

'I've just spoken to the nurse and it's not good. Apparently after her fall they think she had a stroke and she's only got hours left maybe. They can't do anything, especially with her injuries.

They are just making her comfortable.' Victoria sniffed. 'Let me dry my face, I don't want to go in her room like this.'

They were all shocked and horrified when they saw Beryl in bed with her oxygen mask on, surrounded by machines. The once feisty Beryl now looked like a frail old lady with a black eye and swollen face.

'Dear god,' Victoria wailed, 'what the hell has happened to her? Who did this?'

They all turned towards the policeman who just repeated what they had already been told.

'Well, they've done a demolition job on her that's for sure,' Sheila commented.

Victoria held Beryl's hand, and none of them could hold back the tears. Her eyes half flickered in acknowledgement of them all between the swollen slits. Suddenly the detectives walked in with another two police officers carrying a table with equipment on.

'What's that for?' enquired Patsy although she felt she knew the answer. 'You can't let her confess while she's like this. Surely it can't be legal?'

'Can you hear us Beryl? Do you still want to talk to us?' the detective almost shouted at her. Loosening her hand from Victoria's grasp, Beryl weakly reached up and pulled the oxygen mask down.

'Yes,' she replied.

Instantly, the officers set it up and told her to start whenever she was ready.

'I'll just turn off my mobile phone. Does everyone else want to do the same so there are no interruptions?' said Patsy.

Everyone agreed and the detectives thanked her for her consideration. She had her own reasons for this. While she was supposedly switching off her phone, she turned the volume off and put it on record and put it on the side table beside Beryl.

'I killed my beloved Nicky.' The detective was about to ask her questions, but she raised her hand. She wanted to do this in her own way. 'I loved him,' she gasped. 'But he had become mean and had changed. The night of the party, he insulted everyone and didn't think I'd heard, but I had.' Panting and breathing heavily, she raised the oxygen mask back on to her face and took a breath. The room was silent, apart from the machines beeping, as they all sat around the bed waiting for the next instalment.

'I'd gone back to my flat to get some whisky, and while I was there I put the bedroom lamps on as I always do. When I went into Nick's room I banged my leg on the wardrobe door. It was slightly open and when I went to close it, I could see there was a bag inside.'

Patsy blushed. She knew exactly what Beryl was talking about but kept her calm.

'There was some clothing, but there was also a gun,' she panted.

Inwardly, Patsy knew that to be a lie. The bags were full of money. Puzzled, Patsy held Victoria's hand and listened.

'He'd brought it to use on someone. Nobody carries a gun for nothing.' She pointed at Sheila. 'I heard Nick and Steve arguing and Nick threatened Steve. Maybe, he was going to kill your Steve, but little Jimmy got there first.' Sheila gasped and looked down at the floor and waited while Beryl took some more air from the oxygen mask. 'My Jack. My beloved son's name is above the centre. But the Diamond reputation was in tatters because of Nicky. He was into drugs and in with all kinds of bad people. I took the gun and was going to confront him about it, but he laughed in my face and without thinking I just fired it at him. I didn't want him to be in pain, so I shot him again.' She gasped and laid back on her pillow.

'Where is the gun now Mrs Diamond?' the detective asked.

'I threw it in the skip and then went into the back of the community centre to join everyone again.'

Stunned by this revelation, they each in turn looked at each other. No one seemed to know what to say.

'How do you know he was into drugs Mrs Diamond? Did he take drugs?'

Pulling her mask down, she shook her head. 'I don't think so, but he got me to sell them for him. Me and my knitting circle. And he was friends with the men who did this to me.' At this Beryl, started to cry.

'Enough,' the doctor intervened. 'You've had your confession and that is enough. Mrs Diamond is struggling to breathe; I can't let this interview continue.'

Both detectives nodded and stopping the recording, they stood up. 'Thank you Mrs Diamond. I'll leave you all in peace now.'

Patsy followed them out. 'What happens next officer?'

She certainly didn't believe Beryl's confession and wondered if they did. As far as she was concerned, there were more holes in her story than a tea strainer.

'Well, we can't argue with a confession Mrs Diamond, but there is a lot to look into. Did you know your husband was into drugs?'

Patsy looked him squarely in the face. 'I'm sure you know officer, there was a lot I didn't know about my husband and I rarely went to Scotland.'

Raising his eyebrows, the detective looked around at Natasha, Victoria and Sheila. 'I think it seems very strange that the wife is friends with the mistress and the mistress is friends with the woman whose husband was killed by her son.'

'That's because you're a man, officer. There are children involved and the mistress's son is my mother-in-law's grandchild.

Sheila and Natasha are making the best of a bad situation. What's the point in being enemies? I've always said women could sit down and end wars,' Patsy drawled in her snobbish way.

Disgruntled, the detective nodded and walked away. 'I'll let you know of any developments.'

Patsy walked back into Beryl's room and looked at the doctor.

'I'll leave you to say your goodbyes.' He nodded and left the room. Beryl's breathing became more laboured and she seemed to drift in and out of consciousness.

Victoria held her hand and kissed her forehead and Patsy did the same. It was a sad time and an awful end for such a matriarch as Beryl.

Suddenly Beryl opened her eyes and half dazed, looked around the sea of faces. Weakly, she raised her arm and pointed at Natasha. 'I want to talk to you... alone,' she mumbled.

Victoria ushered Patsy and Sheila out. 'Leave her to say her goodbyes ladies. We'll get our turn.' Patsy was annoyed at being overlooked for Natasha but bit her tongue.

Once the door had closed behind them, Natasha sat beside Beryl. 'I just want to say, Beryl: thank you for everything you did for me when I moved into Thistle Park. For me and little Jimmy,' she stammered, feeling her own tears running down her cheeks.

Beryl took hold of her hand and squeezed it. 'Show me my grandchild.'

As quick as a flash, Natasha fumbled for her phone and held it up displaying all the photos of baby Nicky.

'Look after him for me. I saw you Tash – that night I saw you.' Her hand released its grip and the machines started to beep loudly.

Before Natasha could reply, Victoria rushed in with the others hot on her heels as the doctors rushed forward. They all looked on while the doctors checked her over, but Beryl had died. Victoria burst into tears.

Glaring at her, Patsy moved towards Natasha. 'What did she want?' Patsy asked. 'What did she say?'

Natasha's face was red and she was blushing to her roots. 'She wanted to see pictures of the baby and didn't want to offend you.' Natasha showed Patsy her phone with the pictures. 'She just wanted to see her great-grandchild one last time before she died.'

'Mmm, so I see.' Patsy walked away and went to console Victoria. She had mixed feelings about what she had witnessed, but most of all she resented the fact that they had all been brushed aside so Beryl could spend her last moments with Natasha.

'Leave it lass,' Sheila whispered in her ear, 'the old woman just wanted to see photos of the baby without putting your nose out of joint. Let it go Patsy, just let it go.'

They were about to leave when the doctor popped his head around the door. 'Is this someone's mobile phone?' Waving it in the air, he waited.

Patsy looked towards him and nodded. 'Thank you doctor. I took it out of my bag when I switched it off.' A smile crossed her face as she took her phone back. Now she would find out for herself what Beryl's last words were.

Looking at her phone she could see that it was still on record, and she stopped it instantly without being seen.

* * *

When they arrived back at the estate, it was late and they were all tired. Patsy noticed Larry's car parked in the forecourt. Ignoring him, she got out of the car and was making a hasty retreat to Beryl's flat when he called after her.

'Mrs Diamond,' he shouted.

Thankfully, Sheila intervened and gave Patsy a cheeky smile. 'That's that lawyer of yours, isn't it Patsy? You had better see what he wants. We'll go in and put the kettle on.'

Getting in the car beside him, Patsy held her hands up. 'Look Larry, I don't need this now. Beryl has just died after confessing to Nick's death.'

Larry's face dropped. 'I know, Patsy. The police were looking for you earlier, which is why I called you. They wanted to know if I had another telephone number for you and told me the whole sorry story.'

'I just can't believe Beryl has confessed to killing Nick. A dying confession – does that mean the case is closed?'

'Most likely they will check on the things she has said, to see if it coincides with the events as they know them, but you and Victoria have been questioned numerous times. Sheila had no motive and was still in shock. The only person with a rock solid alibi is Natasha. I vouched for her myself when I took her to the hospital.'

Confused, Patsy stared at the windscreen. 'The hospital? I thought she was being questioned at the police station.'

'No.' Larry shook his head. 'She started bleeding and they thought she was having a miscarriage. They agreed that I should take her to the hospital and stay with her. When we got there they gave her an ultrasound and thankfully she hadn't lost the baby, but they put her to bed. She'd been so distraught, they gave her some sleeping tablets and told me to go back in the morning. I thought you knew all of this?'

Taken aback, Patsy stopped short. 'Oh sorry Larry; that night seems like a lifetime ago.' But Patsy's mind was working overtime. Natasha had never mentioned she had nearly lost the baby and gone to hospital.

It was dark outside, and Larry felt more at ease avoiding eye contact with Patsy. 'I've missed you Patsy,' he whispered and reached out for her hand and held it. 'I'm sorry, I know it's a bad time, but I had to call on you because you never call me.'

'I've just been busy Larry, and today hasn't helped.' She could see her excuses didn't convince Larry and she had to admit, she was very pleased to see him. Much more than she realised.

On impulse, she leaned forward and kissed him and was pleased when he kissed her back with more ardency than expected. Their passion for each other engulfed them as they kissed and stroked each other. Patsy undid his trousers belt and felt her seat fold back as she welcomed him on top of her. Her feet pressed against the dashboard and she pushed her thighs up to meet his thrust as he entered her. A gasp escaped her and she held on to him with all of her might as their lips met once more. It was over quickly but they were both gasping for breath and satiated. Looking over his shoulder, Patsy felt a movement.

'Larry, the car's moving,' she whispered.

'Oh, it's not moving Patsy. It bloody rocked. That was fantastic.' He grinned, looking her in the eyes, trying to catch his breath.

'No Larry, the car is moving!' she emphasised.

Larry looked over his shoulder and saw the car moving slowly backwards. Looking down, he pulled the handbrake up sharply as he tried getting back into his seat. Flinging the car door open, he attempted to get out and tripped over his trousers that were still around his knees. Patsy burst out laughing, as she saw Larry half sprawled across the pavement.

Standing up, he pulled up his trousers and straightened his clothing. Sweeping his thick head of hair back, he looked at Patsy forlornly. 'I'm sorry Patsy, not exactly the most romantic of endings was it.'

'It was memorable Larry, in both ways,' she laughed. 'I have to go; they'll be waiting for me. Give me a kiss before I go and I promise to call you.' Getting out of the car, she put a hand on each side of his face and kissed him tenderly, before walking to Beryl's flat. It had certainly been one of those days.

23

REVELATIONS

Although Patsy could see Victoria was upset by Beryl's death, she had other things on her mind. She did feel saddened by Beryl's horrible demise. After fifteen years of sniping at each other, they had talked and got to know each other more in the last few weeks than they ever had.

The next morning, Patsy announced she would go and tell Maggie about Beryl's death. 'After all, they were good friends,' she commented, but Patsy had her own agenda. She wanted to know if James McNally was still there. Maybe he could shed some light on Beryl's demise. After all, he was in with those Albanian gangs, whatever he said. She wanted to know more. She wanted to tell Maggie in front of him to see his reaction. Had James and his friends caused Beryl's death? Did they think she knew something to incriminate them? She was determined to find out.

'You're right Patsy love, I'm sure she's worried. Everyone knew Beryl and some even liked her.' Victoria forced a smile.

Walking up to Sheila, Patsy whispered in her ear, 'Bring that box with you and show me where that Fin lives. Natasha, will you look after Victoria while I go and have a word with Maggie?'

Seeing the still yawning Natasha pick up her coffee mug and nod satisfied Patsy.

Quickly, Patsy and Sheila dressed and knocked on Maggie's door. 'Morning Maggie.' Patsy smiled. 'Can I come in? I'm afraid I have some bad news.'

'Come in, Patsy. I've already heard that Beryl's dead, but I have to say it was awful to see. Those bloody doormen just pushed and shoved her around for sport. There was no one around and I was no competition for those bastards!' Maggie barked.

Walking into the lounge, Patsy saw exactly what she wanted to see. James was standing in the lounge, exercising his legs by moving them backwards and forwards and trying to do squats.

Watching him, Patsy folded her arms. 'You look well all of a sudden. It must be all of that haggis.' Sarcasm was on the tip of her tongue, but she held it back.

'Mrs Diamond?' James sat down, puffing and panting at his efforts. 'Can I just say how sorry I am about Beryl? Are you okay?'

'I don't think it's really sunk in James, especially as just before she died, Beryl confessed to Nick's murder.'

Seeing Maggie's, jaw drop Patsy was convinced that she was as shocked as the rest of them.

'Yes,' Patsy continued, 'her dying confession was that she killed Nick.'

'I don't believe it,' Maggie butted in. 'Never! Who threatened her to say that? Who is she covering for? Your Nick could have set the house on fire around her and she wouldn't have killed him and I'll swear to that in a court of law!' Maggie pulled her famous cardigan around her and sat down, shaking her head.

'Well, that's what she said Maggie. Out of her own mouth and who can argue with that?'

Maggie continued muttering under breath, as Patsy turned to James.

'I suggest you get that leg of yours up to speed James. You owe me, and I want vengeance for what happened to Beryl. She might have been an old witch at times, but she didn't deserve being beaten to death. You say you know people, well, get to know them again and find these men and then beat them to death,' she demanded.

James nodded. 'My disappearance could be your salvation. I know who those people were and I know their boss. It's the same man who had this done to me. I need to get myself back on form and make plans. Don't worry, you will get your vengeance, I swear.'

'Well do it soon James, or else I'll let it be known you're alive and well.'

Shocked at Patsy's threats, James glared at her. 'Well, I must say Mrs Diamond, there is more to you than lipstick and perfume. If I didn't know better I would think I was talking to your husband.'

'Good! I'm glad you realise that. He might be dead but I am alive and well. Now earn your money, because I'm not a charity.' Angrily, Patsy walked towards the front door. 'Come on Sheila, we need to find Fin. Let's leave Laurel and Hardy to their own thoughts.'

Embarrassed at Patsy's outburst, Sheila walked behind her. She felt she should apologise but given the mood Patsy was in, dismissed the idea.

'Wait!' James walked towards Patsy. 'What do you need Fin for?'

Looking towards Sheila, Patsy pointed at the leather bag she was holding. 'Show him Sheila.'

Unzipping the large bag, Sheila showed him the box inside. 'It was found in Nick's office; we need to open it. I know Fin has a friend who can open a strong box like this.'

Taking it out of the bag, James looked at the front of it. 'Christ, I haven't seen one of these in years.' He marvelled at it. 'Craftsmanship at its finest. Do you know there are five keys to boxes like these?'

James saw Sheila's and Patsy's faces drop. 'Five keys? We only have one and we don't have the combination.'

'I can work out this combination. Do you know what's inside?'

Patsy and Sheila both shook their heads.

James put the box on the dining table and put his ear close to it, fiddling with the wheel on the front. Patsy held her breath as she heard it click. Concentrating, James turned the wheel again and there was another click. Suddenly the box sprung open. They all shot a glance at each other.

'Open it,' Patsy whispered, handing him her own key.

'I don't need that.' James took out what looked like an oddly shaped pen knife and fiddled around with the locks inside. Little drawers opened from the side of the box.

Moistening his lips, James tentatively opened the door fully. Frowning, he looked closer at the contents inside.

Patsy and Sheila stared at the box and then at each other in shock. Inside was a mixture of mobile phones and numerous SIM cards scattered around.

Holding one of the phones in his hand, James looked towards Patsy. 'I think I know what these are, but we need to get chargers for these phones. You were right first time, go and see Fin and tell him what chargers we need and tell him we want them now.'

Sheila ran out of the door and returned minutes later with a cardboard box full of phone chargers. Emptying the contents on Maggie's table, Sheila laughed. 'I'm telling you: he's got loads more if we need them.'

'Of course he has,' James scoffed. 'I didn't mean go to Fin's to get him to go out and steal them, I expected him to have some. No one buys a stolen mobile without the charger.'

James instructed Maggie to put the kettle on while he fitted the chargers into the phones and waited for them to spring into life.

Patsy sat down, not knowing what to expect. 'What do you think is on them James?' she asked. Suddenly she felt nervous and the palms of her hands were sweating.

'I'd put money on these being the confessions from the people your husband was blackmailing. No wonder he kept them under lock and key, these were his insurance if people didn't do as they were told. Do you realise how much all of that information is worth? If it's what I think it is, those men will give anything to have those recordings back.'

Patsy stared at him, lost for words. 'Won't they all have passwords on though? How do we unlock them?' Patsy asked.

Suddenly Fin walked through the door. 'It's only me,' he chimed, totally oblivious to what was going on.

James nodded towards him. 'There is your answer. Fin, unlock these phones, we need to use them.'

Astonished, Patsy, Sheila and Maggie looked on as Fin fiddled about with the mobiles nonchalantly. 'There you are. What's going on?'

'Can you find any recordings on them?'

With ease, Fin picked one up and pressed play. They all listened as one man gave his full name and date of birth. They could hear Nick's voice asking him about a court case and encouraging him to tell him the truth. James was right, the man on the recording finally unfolded the truth about his crime and who he had brutally murdered.

They all sat in silence and listened to more recordings. Patsy felt sick to her stomach as she heard Nick calmly cajole and assure them he was their friend and that he would try and help them. It was sickening and she wanted to throw up.

'Enough!' she shouted and held up her hand to stop the recordings. 'I've heard enough. Do you know these men James? Fin?' Looking at each of them in turn, she paused.

'Yes, a couple,' James admitted.

Fin also nodded. 'Me too, or rather, I know of them.'

'Me too,' Maggie added, much to Patsy's surprise. 'I didn't know they were beholden to your husband though.' They all looked towards her, but Maggie just shrugged helplessly.

Trying to think straight, Patsy looked at the mobiles again. 'I'm taking these with me until I decide what to do with them,' she exclaimed and started gathering them together. 'You lot never heard those conversations. Do you hear me?' Casting a stern glare, she waited.

'What are you going to do with them Mrs Diamond? What are your intentions?' James couldn't help but ask. He was curious and knew somewhere on one of those mobiles would be his voice. Secretly he was scared. Those recordings could cause one hell of a war. Each criminal, giving names and blaming other criminals. Some making deals with the police, by informing on their friends. The very thought of it made him feel sick.

Running her hands through her hair, Patsy shook her head. 'I don't know. But I do know I can't let them out of my sight.'

Again, James interrupted. 'They are worth a lot, Mrs Diamond, but if people know that you have them they will come looking for them. Be careful,' he warned.

'The only people who know I have them, James, are the people in this room. Are any of you going to tell anyone?' Patsy snapped. 'God knows, I could tell my own story about you three.'

Solemnly, they all shook their heads.

As she left, Patsy thought about her own accidental recording of Beryl's last words to Natasha. She had done exactly the same thing as Nick had done. Tears brimmed on her eyelashes as Nick's voice played over in her mind again. It had felt as though he was with them in the room.

'How could I not know Sheila? Am I so blind and stupid, I couldn't see what was under my nose.'

Folding her arms, Sheila shook her head. 'No Patsy, you had an inkling. Where the hell were all those deliveries of money coming from? It didn't drop from the sky you know. Money like that, unless you've won the lottery, spells only one thing: drug dealing. And you knew it Patsy. You weren't that ignorant, so don't give me that.'

'I didn't know about the killings and beatings. I didn't know about everything Nick did. He was a manipulative bastard and I have been a fool, and after everything I did for him, he was going to leave me. I fucking hate him!'

* * *

Victoria and Natasha bumped into Patsy and Sheila as they were walking back into Beryl's flat. 'Where are you going? And what are you doing with my laptop?' Patsy looked down at the laptop case in Natasha's hand.

'We're going to the cemeteries. I want to check if I am right.' Stubbornly, Natasha stuck out her chin in defiance.

'Right about what? What are you talking about? Victoria, you should rest.' Patsy was about to steer Victoria back into the lounge when Victoria shrugged her off.

'You're not the only detective around here Patsy. Natasha has sat for hours with that map and those codes and we're going to check if she has the right gravestones in the right cemeteries. We might as well use the time in Glasgow for something productive.'

Patsy looked at Natasha. She was surprised that she had carried on with it but was secretly glad she had. 'Do you think you are on to something?'

Smiling broadly at for once being acknowledged as one of the team, Natasha replied, 'Yes, Patsy. I just need to check if I'm right and the only way to find out is to go to the cemeteries. Are you coming?'

'Too bloody right we are,' exclaimed Patsy, 'and then we'll eat. We haven't had a square meal since yesterday at the petrol station on the way here.'

'On second thoughts, why don't we go for some breakfast now? It could be a long day, searching all of those cemeteries,' Victoria announced in motherly fashion. 'We'll find somewhere to eat and then we will go on our mission.'

While they sat and ate, two burly men came up to their table. They were each in their forties; one had light brown hair and the other was almost bald. Their soiled T-shirts, bearing an ice-cream logo on the front, were stretched at the seams by their pot bellies.

Stopping mid-conversation, Patsy looked up. 'Can we help you?' she enquired.

'Are you the Diamond sluts?' one asked, pulling down the zipper on his jeans.

Startled, they looked at the men. 'Who the hell are you?' Patsy shouted at them, but the man promptly took out his penis and started urinating all over the breakfast plates and over their food, while his friend followed suit. It was disgusting, and Victoria stood up to avoid the onslaught of urine as it bounced off the table and on to her knee. Patsy tried getting around the table towards them, but she was trapped at the back against the wall, and could only get out if Sheila moved.

Shocked and outraged, Natasha stood up and threw her hot mug of tea in the face of one of the men, making him cry out.

Picking up her fork, she stabbed at the man's penis, making him stagger backwards.

'You fucking bitch!' Grabbing her roughly by the hair, the other man was about to punch Natasha when Sheila drew her arm back and punched him hard in the face. Natasha jabbed and stabbed them with her fork, making hole punctures in their arms which spurted blood and made him scream in pain. Victoria took off her high heeled court shoe and whacked one man around the head, drawing blood with her heel. Both men bolted for the door, clearly not expecting the onslaught from the women.

Not one person in the restaurant had offered to help them. Patsy, who was sat at the far side of the table and whose trousers were soaked in urine, stood up and in her anger, shouted to the crowd, 'What the hell is wrong with you all? We were being attacked and you did bloody nothing! You should be ashamed of yourselves, you bastards.'

Everyone averted their eyes and ignored Patsy's outburst. The table and their plates were swimming in urine. In her anger, Patsy tipped up the table, sending all of the plates and cutlery crashing to the floor and on to the next table. 'I take it you spineless bastards never saw that either!'

Shaken, and soaked, the women made their way to the door, pushing past the other customers and causing mayhem in their wake.

Reaching the car, they all got in and took a breath. 'What the hell was all that about? Who were they Patsy?' shouted Victoria who was badly shaken and was visibly trembling.

'We're going home, back to Beryl's,' Patsy rambled.

Sheila was still rubbing her hand, which was starting to swell, but managed to take out her cigarettes and pass them around. 'Come on ladies, this will help calm us. We need to change. There must be something of Beryl's we can borrow until our clothes are clean,' Sheila reasoned.

Tears of shock rolled down Victoria's face and she kept asking why those strangers would do such a thing until Patsy could stand it no longer.

'They are enemies of Nick's, Victoria, don't you get it? That is the sort of bastard he dangled on a string. The people he dealt his drugs to. They hate us, because we know too much. Hasn't that sunk into your brain yet?' Almost hysterical, Patsy shouted as she drove.

'Calm down Patsy. It's okay Vicky lass. We'll find some of that whisky Beryl had stashed away to calm your nerves.' Yet again, Sheila was the voice of reason as fear and emotions rose. They had all been frightened and shocked by the awful scene.

Once home, they calmed down, and one by one they showered. It seemed to work wonders, and once they emerged they felt better. The mood lightened even more when Sheila cracked dirty jokes about how small the man's penis had been.

Patsy walked up to Natasha. 'Thank you. You were the first to fight back while the rest of us were still in shock. Although, I presume he looks like a pin cushion now.' She grinned. 'And you, Sheila, would give a boxer a run for his money.'

'I'm used to it,' Natasha said. 'They throw urine over your dinner all the time in prison. They think it's funny, but after a while, you get used to it and learn how to fight back. They are just bullies trying to frighten you.' She shrugged.

'Nevertheless, you acted fast, while we were in a state of shock and for that I thank you,' Patsy said, humbly.

'Can we still go to the cemeteries to see if I am right about those numbers? I don't mind going on my own if you prefer.' Natasha stood there in her wide-eyed innocence and Patsy looked at her closely. This girly façade Natasha put on for the public didn't fool her. Natasha had already proven how strong she was, the way she had stood up to the men at their table. Memo to self, Patsy thought, listen to the recording between Beryl and Natasha.

Once they had all rested, they set off for the first cemetery on the map. Sitting on a bench, Natasha took out the laptop and looked at the numbers, then she pointed to a row of headstones. 'Try that row,' she said and then promptly shouted out the number for Victoria and the others to check on the side of the headstone. Against each number, Natasha typed the name from the headstone.

Victoria walked on the grass in between the headstones and suddenly Patsy heard her scream. Running over, she could see that Victoria's shoe had got stuck in the mud and she had fallen face down on one of the graves with an almighty thud.

'Oh my god Victoria, let me help you up.' Sheila jumped onto the grave to help Victoria and felt it move beneath her feet. Looking down at the ground, she could see by the grass edging surrounded by stone squares it had sunk a little. Looking at the others, she jumped on it again, and again it moved. 'That's not fucking right lassies. According to that headstone, whoever is below here has been dead for forty years; how come their grave is moving?'

Natasha knelt down and felt the grass. 'Look, this isn't real grass, it's that false stuff they use at kids' playgrounds.'

Patsy knelt down beside her and stroked the grass. 'You're right, it is. Why would they have that on such an old grave?'

Natasha ran her hands around the edges of the Astro Turf and pulled at it. To all of their surprise, it came away easily.

Natasha rolled it along. 'There are just boards with some compost thrown on it. It should be deeper than that, shouldn't it?'

'Of course it's supposed to be deeper, and if that person has been dead forty years, I would expect it to be more solid.'

They all looked towards each other, then back at the grave.

Patsy was the first to speak. 'There is something under there, there has to be. Quick Natasha. Roll that grass back; there is an old man coming this way with his dog. Put everything back as you found it, we'll come back later on when no one is around.'

'Why can't he walk his dog in the park like normal people? I bet he lets it shit all over the place,' commented Sheila while still brushing down Victoria and pulling her shoe out of the ground. 'If you're coming back tonight Vicky lass, I suggest you wear flatter shoes.'

Packing up their things, they hurriedly left without noticing that on a bench at the far side of the cemetery someone was watching them. James had been right. They were being followed.

* * *

'Noel!' Breathless, a man ran through the ice-cream warehouse towards Noel. He was panting from running. '*Grua Diamanti*,' he blurted out.

Noel walked sharply up to him and slapped him across the face. 'Speak English you fool. Why can't you just say that Diamond woman like anyone else? No wonder the police are looking for Albanian immigrants with you shooting your mouth off. Now calm down and tell me.'

Slowly, in broken English, the Albanian man tried explaining that he had seen Patsy and her friends in the cemetery and that they were acting suspicious. 'My friend – he walk dog and hear them. They go back tonight.'

Puzzled, Noel looked at the sea of faces before him. 'Why would they be spending their time in the cemetery and plan to visit it at night?' Walking up and down his line of vendors like a sergeant major, he stopped at random ones. 'Why do you think they are going back?'

'Because her husband was known as the Undertaker and him and that James visited each other in cemeteries. The English are sick people,' the man spat out with disgust.

'You're right.' Noel nodded. 'But James is long gone.' Noel tapped the cement floor with his foot and grinned. 'My guess is there is money or drugs to be found and they belong to me!'

He stopped in front of two men and slapped them hard across the face. The men didn't move.

'The police are swarming all over that Diamond centre because you killed that old woman. The best thing you can do is pack up your things and fly home. I no longer need your services. Now get out,' he ordered. 'I have already lost three men because of that Diamond woman. I hate that bitch! I sent Szymon to kill her, I gave him money to move away for a while, keep his head down until the heat was off, but she is still alive so I can only presume he took my money and fucked off back to Poland! Two other good friends of mine killed James and have had to make themselves scarce. I am losing men all over the place for one fucking woman. This stops here and now. I will kill her myself.'

Noel cast a furtive glance at a man at the end of the line and winked. 'Everyone, get to work. Why are you standing there when there are ice-cream vans standing outside? Go and sell my drugs.' He laughed out loud, in an almost manic way.

As everyone departed, Noel walked up to his friend and put his finger to his neck and ran it along his throat. His friend knew exactly what he meant and hastily walked outside and shouted to the two men who had killed Beryl Diamond to come back in. 'Mr Noel wants to give you some money for your flight.'

Eagerly, they stopped their engines and ran back into the warehouse. Noel walked past them as they entered and waved off the other ice-cream vendors leaving the car park. Hearing a loud bang, he turned and saw that his friend had already shot one of the men in the forehead. The other man looked at the lifeless body and stood there with his hands in the air, begging for mercy. Tears fell down his face and he dropped to his knees. A wet patch appeared on his trousers, where he was urinating himself in fear.

Noel took the gun out of his friend's hand. 'You've cost me money.' Firing the gun, he shot the other man through the forehead. 'Now get rid of them, and make it a warning to the others.'

* * *

Later that evening, the four women sat watching a film in Beryl's flat.

'God I'm bored, and it's only 10 p.m.,' Sheila exclaimed. 'Do you realise I could be at home now being groped by Angus?' She laughed, much to everyone's horror.

Just then, they heard screaming. Victoria turned down the television and listened again. It was definitely screams. Running to the front door, they could see that other people had done likewise. A woman was standing in the middle of the forecourt, pointing towards the community centre.

'Come on!' Sheila dragged Patsy by the arm and ran across the landing and down the stairs. Hordes of people were gathering and running towards the centre, then Patsy saw it for herself. Two men with bullet holes in their foreheads. Blood stained their heads, faces and clothing, as they swayed in the darkness with only the street lights to illuminate them. Nooses were tied tightly around their necks as they dangled in the air. The gory sight made Sheila and Patsy shiver. Crowds gathered, gasping and staring at the two lifeless corpses.

'I feel sick Sheila; why is everyone pushing and shoving to get a better view? Why doesn't someone cut them down?' Although Patsy was talking, she couldn't take her eyes off the sight before her.

As police sirens roared in the background and blue lights flashed, Sheila turned towards Patsy. 'You do realise, that could be us,' she whispered in Patsy's ear, making Patsy's blood run cold. She realised now, she was well and truly out of her depth.

24

THE LAST STRAW

Everyone was talking on their balconies about the men hanging from the community centre.

Agitated, Patsy walked around the flat. 'When are they going to go indoors? It's nearly midnight, for god's sake. Have they nothing better to do than watch the police? It's gruesome.'

There was a knock at the door and Natasha went to open it. She gasped when she saw a man with a hoodie pulled way over his head, nearly to his nose.

Fin popped his head around the door. 'Let us in Natasha, for fuck's sake.' Seeing him, Natasha breathed a sigh of relief. After the day they'd had, they were all on pins and needles.

Pulling his hoodie down, James stood there, much to everyone's surprise. 'Are you okay? I had to come and see you for myself.'

'Sit down.' Patsy offered him a chair, knowing it had taken him a lot to climb the stairs with his leg.

After making the introductions, James asked Patsy what her plans were.

'What do you mean, my plans? What has all of this got to do with me?'

Shaking his head slowly, James looked at her carefully. 'I know you were at the cemetery today. I asked Fin to keep an eye on you. And Spider and Beanie saw what happened at the restaurant. This is a warning, Patsy. His friends burnt Billy Burke to death while in prison, that is how dangerous they are,' he stressed. 'You've become obsessed with this mystery of your husband. I know you intend to go back to the cemetery tonight. What are you hoping to achieve?'

'Answers. Closure. I really don't know James. The mystery just gets deeper and I am trying to understand it all.' Tears slipped down her cheeks and she wiped them away. 'My husband is not the man I thought he was. Oh yes, I knew he was no innocent, but I had no idea to what extent. This was a carefully planned operation that goes back years, not some man who did a bit of dealing. He wasn't a crooked lawyer. He was a drug baron and I could go to prison for helping him launder his money. If I'm going to get found out and locked away, I don't want to spend my nights in a cell wondering what happened.' Another choke escaped her and Victoria put an arm around her.

'I'm sure you understand,' Victoria interrupted, 'this has been a distressing time for all of us.'

'I do, but if you're going there tonight, we're coming with you. Watch my lips, Mrs Diamond. You're walking into an ambush! In another couple of hours you could be dead. Do you understand?' Although he spoke calmly, James was trying to stress the severity of it all.

'I know, but I have to know. Do you understand? What is he hiding in that grave? Because I know there is something.' Turning towards the others, she smiled. 'You've heard what he said. You don't have to come; I'll go alone. It's dangerous, but I'll face this bastard. I cannot walk around in fear for the rest of my life.' Sitting down, Patsy broke down. She'd had enough and was distraught. Day in and day out she had carried this burden and now she was sick of it. Sick of being frightened of her own shadow.

'I'm coming with you.' Sheila stood up and folded her arms stubbornly.

'So am I,' Victoria said.

'Me too,' Natasha agreed. 'We're in this together and we either sink or swim together.'

'Okay,' James said. 'We'll need a spade if we have to dig, and put some dark clothing on.'

Patsy looked up. 'Where would we get a spade from at this time of night?'

'I think there's one at Fin's flat,' said Beanie.

'Just out of interest, Fin, is there anything you don't have in that flat of yours?' As an afterthought, James rubbed his growing beard and asked, 'Do you have a gun or, better still, guns?'

Sheepishly, Fin looked down at the floor. 'Maybe. I help a guy out who sells them sometimes.'

'Good man. Bring what you've got because I guarantee they will have some. Go on laddie, we haven't got time to piss about,' James commanded.

'You want to shoot people?' Victoria stood wide eyed listening to James.

Calmly, he turned towards her. 'Tell me, Mrs Diamond, and I mean honestly, if someone was threatening your family and waving a gun in your face and you had a gun. Would you shoot him?'

Victoria sat back down, realising James was right. 'Possibly,' she muttered under her breath.

Following James's instructions, they all went and changed

into something darker. As they returned to the lounge, Beanie came running back into the flat. 'Here's the spade, in fact, there's two and this trowel. The police are cutting down those men; it's crazy out there. You're right James, no one is going to pay any attention to us.'

James nodded. The mood was sombre and they were all nervous. None of them knew what lay ahead, only time would tell. The summersaults in their stomachs made them feel sick.

James's instructions were simple: he would go in the car with the women. Spider and Beanie could hot wire one and wait for Fin. That way they had back up in case Noel and his men were waiting for them.

Walking through the back gates of the cemetery, Sheila looked around. 'Why do people always go to cemeteries late at night? It's creepy, like some horror movie.'

'Because you're not supposed to be seen digging up the graves in the daylight,' James snapped. He ushered Patsy forward and continued looking around. He walked ahead of them, even though his leg ached. Waving them in the direction of the grave, he continued looking behind trees and bushes. His eyes darted everywhere he thought would be a good hiding place.

Unafraid, Natasha was the first to kneel down at the side of the grave and reach for the Astro Turf. As she started to roll it back, she looked up at the rest of them who instantly followed suit and knelt down. They worked in silence, their hearts pounding as they revealed the wooden boards. Natasha pulled and slid her fingers between the boards to get a hold on one and pulled at it. It was quite heavy and Sheila helped her pull it away. It was muddy and damp but came away easily. Victoria and Patsy took the board off them and laid it away from them on another grave.

'It's plasterboard,' whispered Victoria.

Patsy nodded her head and was grateful they had found Beryl's selection of woolly gloves she had stuffed in a bedroom drawer. Whether it be the cold night air, or fear, they were all shaking. Natasha pulled at the other boards which came away easily, but losing her balance, she fell into the grave, which seemed to be hollow and about three feet deep.

'Are you okay?' Patsy and Sheila quickly pulled away the last board. They were puffing and panting, trying to see Natasha properly in the darkness. The blackness of the grave made them shudder; they could hardly see her in her dark clothing.

Scrambling to her feet, Natasha looked up. 'Pass me the spade,' she whispered. Patsy lowered it down to her gently and threw the trowel in. 'This might help, I'm coming down there with you.'

'No don't Patsy.' Natasha waved her hand. 'We don't know how safe it is, it might not take the weight of both of us. I'm the lightest of us all. I'm okay, I just can't see much.'

Getting back on her hands and knees, Natasha started scraping away at the sides of the shallow grave with the trowel. 'It's compost, it's not mud.' Natasha discarded the trowel and started brushing the compost away with her hands. 'There's some more boards,' she whispered as they all stood at the graveside, watching her work.

Sheila nudged Patsy. 'It could be a coffin?' She grimaced.

'Not that high up it's not. It's only a few feet deep. I thought people were buried six feet deep?' Victoria commented without taking her eyes off Natasha as she worked away, pulling away at another board. These boards were smaller and almost plank-like.

'I need a light, I can't see.' Looking up, Natasha waited for someone to help her. Patsy went against everything James had warned her about and took out her mobile. Kneeling down and bending over the grave, she shone the light from her mobile into the black hole. Natasha pulled the planks away and handed them up to her to make room. They could see plastic boxes underneath.

Fear now left Patsy and curiosity took over. 'If you can Natasha, pull the lid off one. Can you get your hand in?'

Nodding, Natasha scraped the rest of the compost away with her fingernails and pulled with all of her might at the lid of the container. It was stuck. Panting now, she pulled with her broken, bloodied nails as hard as she could then sat back on her haunches, taking a breath. 'I need a minute, hang on.'

'I think that's far enough ladies. Thank you for doing the hard work. We'll take over now.'

Patsy's blood ran cold.

They turned to see a group of men behind them. Still on her hands and knees, Patsy was about to get up when she saw Natasha put her finger to her lips and crawl to a corner of the grave. As Patsy turned off the light from her mobile, she stood up.

'Who are you and what do you want?' Sounding braver than she felt, Patsy stared at the man, while scouring the area for James. Where the hell was he?

Two of the men were holding Sheila and Victoria from behind, with their hands over their mouths. Sheila kicked and struggled and bit one of the men's hands.

'You bitch,' he shouted, slapping her across the face. Shaking his hand and then grabbing her hair, he threw her to the ground and kicked her in the stomach. Sheila cried out and brought her knees up, groaning in pain. Victoria struggled free and the same man punched her in the face, sending her flying.

Patsy stood there trembling as she waited for James to intervene. Then a horrible thought crept into her mind. What if James was in on it and he had convinced her to go tonight? She wondered if he had tipped this man off.

Taking one last drag on his cigarette, Noel threw the butt onto the ground. Then, grabbing Patsy's jaw, he squeezed it hard, screwing her face up. Patsy fought to hold back the tears but couldn't help them escaping. 'I knew a nosey bitch like you wouldn't stop. So what now Mrs Diamond? You've found out that your husband was a drug dealing, murdering bastard and you've led us to his hiding place. We knew his supply was around here somewhere, it was just a case of which grave. Now they belong to me and tonight you die Mrs Diamond. It's just my luck that your grave has already been dug,' he spat.

Noel's sneering face annoyed and frightened her at the same time. Her mouth was dry and she licked her lips to moisten them.

Loosening his grip, Noel looked around at his men and laughed. 'Does anyone want a go at this high-class slut?'

Patsy looked him directly in the eye. She knew there was no point in fighting or kicking him in the balls. She was outnumbered. 'Let the others go. These women are no threat to you.'

'They are here and they have seen me and that is enough of a reason to die.' He laughed and turned to his friends to join in the joke. 'We will empty the grave of its contents first to make space for you all. Get inside and hand me what is in there. Kristian, look down there and see if you can see anything,' Noel commanded. Turning to his men, he instructed them to tie up Sheila and Victoria.

Patsy winced as she watched the men throwing blow after blow upon Sheila and Victoria, while their hands were tied behind their backs. The men laughed and threw insults at them, like some game. The darkness of the graveyard made everything seem so final and she realised tonight would be the last she would spend alive.

Kristian knelt down at the graveside and peered in, not being able to see anything he spoke in Albanian and turned to one of the other men to hand him a torch. It was pretty clear to Patsy that they had come prepared. They had rope, torches and in the waistband of Noel's trousers she saw a gun. She was frightened, her heart was pounding, and she could feel the sweat on her brow. Helplessly, she looked at Victoria and Sheila. Tears mixed with mud on their faces. Digging her fingernails into the palms of her hands, she was determined not to crumble before these bullies. If she was going to die, she was going to die with dignity. Not begging these low life junkies for her life.

Suddenly there was an almighty crash, and Kristian raised his hand to his head in a dazed state and fell into the grave pit. Noel ran forward and saw Natasha with the spade in her hand.

'Fuck you, you Albanian bastard,' she shouted angrily.

Angrily, Noel waved his men over. 'Get that fucking bitch out of there now!'

Natasha ducked and weaved away from the men who were on their hands and knees reaching out to her, while trying to avoid the spade she was waving around.

'Get in there and pull that bitch out,' Noel commanded again.

Natasha bit their hands and screamed as they yanked her by her hair and arm, ripping her clothing and hoisting her upwards. Once she was out of the grave, they slapped her and threw her to the ground.

'Maybe one of my men should teach you a lesson, you Scottish slut.' Noel strode forwards and although Natasha kicked and screamed as best as she could, Noel ripped at her top, exposing her naked breasts to his men. He burst out laughing. 'There isn't much there to satisfy anyone.' Looking up at his men, he threw his hands in the air. 'Do what you want with her.'

Natasha screamed and shouted as one of the men strode towards her and started undoing his belt.

'That's about your limit Noel, beating up women and threatening them,' James said as he stepped from behind one of the trees near the gravestones.

Noel paled when he saw James. 'So there are ghosts in grave-yards. Are you hiding behind these bitches' skirts now?'

James stood still while Noel peered closely at him. During his time at Maggie's, James hadn't shaved, and his bushy beard hid most of his face. Noel pulled at the end of it. 'Just checking. Where have you been hiding?'

Calmly, James smiled. Quick as a flash, he took out a gun and pointed it at Noel. 'Natasha! Stay still,' he shouted and shot the man who was astride Natasha, pinning her down on her back. He gave out a low moan and fell sideways. Spider and Beanie came out of the shadows with a gun in each hand and pointed them at Noel's men.

'Put your guns down, arseholes. You too.' Spider looked at Noel and fired a bullet into Noel's arm, making him cry out and clutch at the bloody mess. The blood ran through his fingers and he stumbled backwards. 'The next one will be in your head!'

Calmly, James spoke again. 'Do you remember when you organised your Albanian friends to burn Billy Burke to death, Noel? And do you remember how Billy used to boast about having a son?'

Swaying and gripping his arm, Noel shrugged. 'Of course I do. Billy Burke only ever talked bullshit. There was no son. He was a loser.' Panting to catch his breath, Noel glared at James. 'Are you a loser James? Is that why you've gone soft? Are you screwing this bitch, because that is all she is good for? She has caused us nothing but problems. I say we get rid of her and then the world is our oyster.' As he stepped forward towards James, Spider shot at the ground before him, making Noel quickly step back.

There was a noise from behind them all and then Fin appeared. He was deep in the shadows between two graves; only the moonlight and some street lighting from afar illuminated him.

'All of you women, get into the grave now, and bury your heads!' he shouted. 'Go on, get in.'

Spider and Beanie they walked towards Patsy and the others and almost dragged them to the end of the graveside. Natasha was breathing heavily and doing her best to stand up while attempting to cover her nakedness.

'You too, get in there. All of you, jump. Do as I fucking say!'

'Yes! A boy with common sense,' Noel shouted, almost relieved. Turning towards the women, Noel smiled then turned to his men. 'Put your guns back in your belts boys, our work is done.'

Patsy glared in Fin's direction. Her face burned at his betrayal. The four women walked towards the grave and took one last look behind them as Noel's men walked towards them and roughly pushed them into the grave. The women clung to each other and trembled as they stumbled and fell, not knowing how they were going to meet their end, or if they were just going to bury them alive.

Above them they saw a flash of light, almost like an explosion. There were flames and deafening screams from the men above. They all covered their heads to hide themselves, although it was hard to not glance up to see what was happening. The heat almost burnt Patsy's face and she could feel her jumper had caught fire. Doing her best to slap it with her hand to put it out, she could feel a burning sensation on her arm and winced. The heat and the light from whatever it was made it hard for her to see anything. They kept as low as possible to the ground, the heavy sounds above them making them all shake with fear, while the whole place was lit up like some wild bonfire.

Almost like magic, they were plunged into darkness again

The smell of burning bodies filled their nostrils, and the heat and smoke were unbearable, making them cough and choke. Only a few minutes passed, but it seemed like hours and they hardly dared to breathe. Afraid to raise their heads, they looked towards each other.

'Come on Mrs Diamond, give me your hand.'

Raising her head slowly, Patsy looked up. Wearing a full face mask, Spider was knelt down with his hands toward them.

'It's okay lassies, give me your hands.'

Visibly shaking, Patsy dribbled down the side of her mud-stained face, and she realised she had wet herself with fear. She could hardly stand; her legs were weak and trembling. They all held on to each other as they stumbled and tried standing upright. Victoria was moaning and in pain, rubbing her ankle. They all blinked and rubbed their eyes, to see beyond the haze of smoke in the air.

'You can come out now. You're safe.' James nodded and held out his hand to reassure them; he was wearing some kind of gas mask that was now propped on the top of his head.

Patsy held out her hand. Spider grabbed it and heaved her up. The others did the same.

'Be careful where you stand. The ground is hot,' James warned them.

Once above ground, Patsy looked around her. The smoke made it hard to see properly, but she saw bodies lying on the ground. Bile rose in her throat and she vomited. She could hear Fin shouting and swearing. Patsy tried her best to see what he was doing. Her eyes were still streaming from the smoke and she rubbed them. Her blood turned cold when she could see more clearly. Fin was chopping Noel's head off with an axe. Seeing her distress, James held her hand, while she bent over and vomited some more. Wiping her mouth with the back of her hand, tears streamed down her cheeks.

'It's okay Mrs Diamond. Let it out.' James rubbed her back gently before leading Patsy away from the gory sight.

Coughing, Sheila looked around. 'What happened here?' Her eyes were red and sore and she could barely see as tears streamed down her face.

The men's burnt bodies were smouldering in the darkness. Patsy closed her eyes tightly; she couldn't bear to look any more.

James guided them all to the other side of the cemetery where they sat on the grass to compose themselves.

'You took your fucking time,' Patsy spluttered. 'Were you going to let them rape us and torture us first?'

'No. I had to wait until Fin attached his flamethrower together. You were doing okay and don't forget, Mrs Diamond, you wanted to come alone,' James explained. He looked around at everyone. 'Is everyone here? Are you all okay?'

Everyone nodded and muttered to make their presence known. The mood was sombre as they all tried to make sense of what had just happened. Out of the blue Victoria spoke. 'What was all of that about Billy Burke?'

Sprawling out on his back on the grass, Fin let out a deep sigh. 'Billy Burke was my father and they cremated him in prison. Now I've cooked that bastard and chopped his fucking head off so I've had my revenge.'

Stunned, Victoria looked at him. If he was Billy Burke's son that also meant he was Nick's half-brother!

Looking at the night sky and avoiding their eyes, Fin carried on speaking. 'I never knew about him until I went into prison on remand and he was there. We shared a cell for a while, then he showed me a photo of his wife. It was a photo of my mother, He looked after me in prison, and when I came out he always saw to it that I had something decent to sell on the streets, but that was as far as fatherhood went for him. It was too late to become a reunited family, but he was my father and that bastard had him burnt in his cell, without giving him a chance to defend himself. Eye for an eye. Rest in peace Dad.' Brushing a tear away from his eye, he sat up.

Stunned by his confession, Victoria tentatively questioned him. 'What about your mother; where is she?' She had never heard about Billy Burke being married and it made her wonder if he had been married that night he had drugged and raped her – the night she had conceived Nick.

Taking a deep sigh and rubbing away the smears of the black soot and dust on his face, Fin replied, 'Don't know Mrs Diamond; she never left a forwarding address when she dumped me at my gran's.'

Everyone was quiet. James thought back to when he had arranged and agreed to kill Billy Burke with Nick and Noel, but that was something he would take to his own grave.

Breaking the stunned silence, Sheila spoke again. 'Where the fuck do you happen to have a flamethrower stashed away? And what is that backpack for? I've got singe marks on my clothes. Christ, it's a wonder we all weren't burnt to death. The flames from that thing are fierce.' Whether it be hysteria or not, they all smiled and laughed.

'The backpack, as you call it Sheila, is the tank for the flamethrower. It can be either petrol or diesel, but I used propane because it's easier to extinguish and more civilised.' Fin enjoyed giving them all the benefit of his knowledge.

Natasha pointed to a nearby tree. 'Look at that tree; it's nearly burnt to a crisp. That's a lot of paper gone up in smoke.'

'Oh god,' sighed Patsy. 'That is all we need: the eco queen!' Remembering how Natasha had done her best to defend them,

Patsy humbly changed her tone and smiled. 'You're right though, his flamethrower has done a lot of damage. All these headstones will be smoke damaged.'

'On a serious note, we need to hide those bodies,' said James. 'They should be cooling down now in the night air. Let's see what's in the grave and then bury them in it.'

Wearily, they all stood up and looked across at the still-smoking ground. The very thought of seeing all of those dead bodies made Patsy and the others cringe, but even she agreed they had to cover their tracks. It would be getting light soon and the whole point of them being here was to see inside that grave.

Victoria winced when she tried to stand and hopped a little, complaining about her ankle. Fin and James agreed she should stay put; she had probably broken it when she had been pushed into the grave.

Swiftly, the rest of them went back to the graveside. Suddenly their adrenalin returned and their eagerness to finish what they had started spurred them on. Avoiding the badly-charred bodies, the three women concentrated on the grave. James's leg wasn't strong enough to jump inside, so Fin, Spider and Beanie got in and started pulling away at some chipboard and compost, while Sheila, Patsy and Natasha held their mobile phones up to give them light.

The excited look on Fin's and Spider's faces told everyone that they had found something good. They were knocking on the wood beneath it, then their jaws dropped. Spider shivered. 'Holy shit, it's a coffin. I'm getting out.'

James urged them on. 'Come on, you can't look like wimps in front of these lassies.'

Fin looked up. 'It's a fucking coffin with padlocks on it. Tell me if I am wrong, but who the hell puts padlocks on a coffin?'

They pushed the debris aside and pulled at the coffin, which came away easily. Heaving it up as best as they could, they balanced it on the edge of the graveside while the others got onto their hands and knees and pulled at it.

James took a leather pouch out of his pocket. 'No self-respecting thief leaves home without one of these.'

Curious, the women watched him as he bent down and fiddled with the locks, which suddenly sprang open. 'Right, pull the lid off.'

Fin and Spider lifted the lid. Inside, it was full of small plastic bags. Picking one out, Fin shook it. 'For fuck's sake you lot, those tiny bags are full of pills and meth.' He held them out like the crown jewels.

Hobbling towards them, Victoria looked down at him with distaste. 'Burn it. Burn the bloody lot, it's disgusting.' The sneer on her face said it all. 'That stuff ruins lives. Burn it with your flamethrower.'

Fin, Beanie and Spider looked at her agog. 'Are you crazy? Do you know how much this stuff is worth on the streets? The only lives it ruins Mrs Diamond are the people who choose to use it. It certainly hasn't ruined yours!' Fin snapped. Wrapping his arms around a number of the bags, he glared at her. 'You burn what you fucking want, but we're having these for all of our trouble. We saved your lives tonight and I think some compensation is needed.' He was angry and he couldn't hold his outburst back.

'Calm down everyone,' James intervened. His voice was barely above a whisper. 'Let's all take a breath. Mrs Diamond, if we didn't sell it someone else would. Spider, Beanie,' he commanded, 'get all of that stuff loaded in the back of the car, we'll think about what to do with it later. In the meantime, let's clear this lot up and get the hell out of here!'

Numbly, they all followed James orders.

Once they had packed away everything into the car, it was

time to put the charred bodies into the now empty grave. James took some cling film that Fin had brought him and waved it in the air. 'They might not have much skin left on their bones, but it will rot and smell. Let's cover them in this stuff and keep them fresh for as long as possible. Here's another roll of cling film lassies, you do him over there. I and the laddies here will do these. Come on, move your arses!' he barked.

Wincing and almost vomiting at the burnt bodies, Patsy unfolded the cling film with trembling hands and attempted to wrap it around one of the men's faces. The ground was cold now and rain began to spit down. Natasha reached forward to help and pulled his head up so Patsy could wrap the cling film around it. Waking from their shocked states, Sheila and Victoria concentrated on the job in hand, almost baulking while they did it. The men had worked more swiftly. They had a job to do and got on with it. Once done, James walked around the area.

'What are you looking for?' asked Patsy. She was confused and trembling, be it from her ordeal or the cool night air. Looking down at her sleeve, she saw that there was a hole in it where it had been scorched by the flames.

'Debris Patsy. Maybe a shoe or a belt, who knows? But we need to check that there is no evidence that we, or they, were here.'

Realising he made sense, she too started looking around, and just as James had predicted, she found a watch on the floor. Thankful for his common sense and practical thinking, she urged the others to scour the area for anything else.

Rolling the bodies into the now deep grave, Fin picked up Noel's charred head and threw it in. They replaced the boards and then Natasha and James carefully rolled the Astro Turf back over the grave. It was a strange atmosphere. Apart from the stains on the headstones from the fallout of ash and smoke and patches of burnt grass in between the graves, it looked like nothing had happened.

'James.' Patsy lowered her voice and met his eyes. 'What's happened to the body that was in there? This grave is years old.'

Subdued, James shook his head. 'Don't think about it Patsy. Stop torturing yourself about something you cannot change.' With that, he took her hand and led her through the back entrance of the cemetery. Each in turn they walked in silence. There was nothing more to be said.

25

NORMALITY

A morbid silence hung in the air as everyone returned to the estate. Not a word was spoken between them. One by one the women went to shower; their reflections in the mirror showed more horror than they'd realised. The clothing was hanging off them and Natasha's was still torn from her attack. Their faces were sooty and tear-stained. They all realised what they had done tonight was murder, and even if they hadn't committed the crime they had helped clear away the bodies. This was a whole new ball game.

They all sat in the lounge, each having donned one of Beryl's winceyette nightgowns, and poured themselves some whisky.

Sheila broke the silence. 'I think I might pop home tomorrow. I'm sure Angus will wonder where I've been.' Her voice was quiet and still husky from the smoke.

Solemnly, Victoria took a sip of her whisky. 'Natasha and I have an appointment with the social worker. It's her first supervised visit with Jimmy. They are even talking about him coming home soon...' She caught Patsy's eye and bit her tongue.

Gulping back her own whisky, Patsy was angry. 'I think we

should all clear the bloody air! Do you realise what we did tonight? Or am I dreaming? The thing spinning in my brain is that all those headstone numbers that Natasha has on the laptop are also filled with drugs. Fin, as crazy as he is, isn't that stupid. We're sitting on a gold mine.'

Victoria was about to interrupt but Patsy held up her hand to stop her.

'I know, drugs are bad, but as James says, if we don't sell them, there's always someone out there who will. Let's leave it for now, but we need to think through our options.' Patsy's business brain was working overtime.

Sheila couldn't help herself as she listened to Patsy's crazy idea. 'You've shops and salons, so it's very easy to launder your money, but what about us? I presume you're including the rest of us in your mad scheme or are your new partners James and Fin?' she spat out.

'For god's sake no!' Patsy was horrified at the suggestion that she would drop her friends as quickly as that. 'We're all in this together, that is if you want to be. James and Fin would be colleagues and I'm sure Fin would sort Beanie and Spider out. I know what you mean though. You and Natasha are both on benefits, so my suggestion would be that your money for the time being would be clean money.'

Frowning, Sheila and Natasha both looked at Patsy curiously. 'How would our share be clean money Patsy? It's not possible,' Sheila scoffed.

'You, Sheila, take the money from the sale of my apartment, and you Natasha' – Patsy wagged her finger at her warningly – 'work hard and do your hairdressing college course. Then, you can have the Dorset salon.' Sheila was about to butt in but Patsy stopped her. 'I know what you're thinking. You're wondering what the police would say if I gave you both such a pay-out, am I right?'

Sheila nodded.

'Let's just call it guilt money. I'll tell them that I feel I owe you something for all you've both suffered at the hands of my husband. That it's my business what I do with my money, to clear my conscience.'

Sheila and Natasha were overwhelmed by her idea. They would be rich women in their own right. 'But to earn your money Natasha you've got to work hard, and you Sheila can buy a safe haven for your girls. It's up to you two; think about it.'

'Just one more thing,' Sheila interrupted her. This time her face was stern and she glared at Patsy. 'Don't ever bad mouth your husband again. We all know what he was and there is no escaping that. But what you're suggesting is the same thing. You're no better than him, now. None of us are. So we let him rest in peace...' Looking towards Victoria, Sheila trailed off, knowing she had made her point, and seeing Victoria's smile, she knew she had said what was on her mind too. Nick Diamond: rest in peace.

Blushing at her reprimand, Patsy nodded. It was true, she was no better than Nick. She had entered the underworld without realising it. Sheila was right, it was time to move forward and get on with whatever life threw at them.

Victoria was lying on the sofa with her leg up. 'What about me, Patsy? What do I get out of it?' She laughed.

Patsy smiled. 'Well, firstly, I think we should get your leg x-rayed in case you've broken it, but I think you've had your payment. You've a family and grandchildren. You don't need the money but your share is there in case you do. What else do you want?'

'I want to know why Beryl killed Nick. She loved him and always stood by him, through good and bad. Do you think she knew all about this? It's just a nagging feeling inside of me.'

Realising Victoria's need for answers Patsy agreed, 'I understand that Victoria, and I feel the same, but who knows what went through Beryl's mind that night. It's a strange one I grant you. But we're never going to find out. They are both dead now.'

Each in turn they all looked at Patsy. 'And what are you going to do?'

'Go home, like you. I have some things to do – same as you. You know, I do have a life. I'm leaving those drugs with James and Fin. I wouldn't even know how to start selling them even if I wanted to. They have earned it after tonight. Remember that before any recriminations, those men were going to kill us in cold blood and bury us alive or dead. If it wasn't for James, we wouldn't be here. Let's all have another drink, it might help us sleep. And Victoria, it may take some pain away.'

The next morning, they all hugged and before they went their separate ways, Sheila sidled up to Patsy. 'Are you going to tell Larry you're leaving? It seems like the decent thing to do.'

Pondering on her words, Patsy shook her head. 'I'll text him when I'm home; I hate long goodbyes. Anyway, I don't want him dragged into all of this.' Patsy frowned. 'Why do you care so much, Sheila?'

Sheila smiled. 'Because he's a nice man and I know you like him, and you deserve a bit of happiness lassie.'

Before leaving, Patsy put a note through Maggie's letter box. All she had written was thank you, and her mobile number in case James didn't have it. She didn't want to write anything else incriminating.

* * *

Life seemed surreal once Patsy walked into her London apartment, and suddenly very empty without the others there. On her answerphone were messages from estate agents and she couldn't be bothered to listen to them wanting to make appointments. Looking at her phone, she saw there were messages from Larry, too. She felt sad about him; for now she would have to leave him on ice. If he liked her, he would wait, she decided. Texting him quickly, she told him she was home and having to sort things out for Beryl's funeral. At least that wasn't a lie.

Being alone gave her time to think, but firstly she wanted to lie down. She ached all over and needed to sleep. Fully clothed, she lay on her bed and looked up at the ceiling. The last couple of days roared through her mind, reminding her how close she had come to death. She thought about the friendships she had made and the bonds that had formed between herself, Victoria, Natasha and Sheila.

They all needed some space, although Victoria would fill her time organising Beryl's funeral. She would give her a grand Scottish send off for all of her friends to say their final farewells.

As for Natasha, she had her first meeting with Jimmy and she had waited a long time for that. And then there was Sheila. Her children were safe in Dorset for the time being. She had Angus and it seemed like for the first time in her life she had a stable relationship even though it was still early days. A smile crept over Patsy's mouth. That made her feel better and as she closed her eyes, she drifted off to sleep.

26

THE LAST LINK

After a few days, and feeling refreshed, Patsy had finally organised the viewings with the estate agents. Victoria had made so many calls regarding Beryl's funeral that Patsy had told her it would be quicker if she drove to Scotland and they could discuss everything face to face.

Janine was running everything smoothly in the salons, and Patsy had visited to get a cut and her roots done. Looking into the mirror, she liked what she saw. She felt herself again; her nails were manicured and painted properly after her night in the cemetery.

Straightening the jacket of her blue trouser suit, Patsy smiled. It had been a good week; even the bags under her eyes seemed to have disappeared. The only strange thing that had happened was she had been sent a mobile phone in the post. She had been puzzled at first; she knew it must be from James, but she wasn't sure how he knew her address. Then it came to her: Fin. He must have given her address to James.

Patsy had had a lot of thinking time away from everyone and James had just confirmed what she needed to know. She was still in the gang, so to speak. James still saw her as a partner. Grinning like a Cheshire cat, she pondered the idea of running Nick's drug business. But under Patsy's rule it would be bigger and better. This would be her empire and for whatever reason, James needed her onside, which she felt gave her the upper hand. Her devilish plan had wormed its way into her brain over the last week, and she liked it. Patsy Diamond's empire and all of her rough diamonds doing her work for her.

Picking up her mobile, Patsy decided to charge it fully, and while doing so she wanted to delete any unwanted messages that could be incriminating. That's when she remembered the confession from Beryl still on her phone. Beryl's breathless, weak voice confessing to Nick's murder made her blood run cold, and then suddenly she was rooted to the spot and stunned by what she heard next. Rewinding the recording, she listened again.

Her mind was working overtime, almost giving her palpitations. James answered the phone instantly when she called him; she was pleased about that. This proved to her he had been waiting for her call. Although he was shocked at what she said, he agreed to it. Picking up her bag, she decided to go to Scotland earlier than planned. She wanted to get there before the others.

Entering Beryl's flat, her first job was to check the money Nick had stashed away in Beryl's wardrobe was still okay. Patsy was quite surprised that it hadn't been broken into, but she felt Fin, Maggie and James had made it a 'hands off' place, and like it or not, people respected Maggie, or were frightened of her, she wasn't entirely sure.

Telephoning Larry, she told him that she'd had a threat on her life. He was distressed and said he would inform the police about this and was surprised she hadn't already. She brushed it off, saying it was possibly a practical joke or something. But just as she had predicted, Larry took it very seriously and said he would report it. After a long farewell and promises to meet up, Patsy ended the call. Suddenly there was a knock at the door, interrupting her thoughts.

'Hi Patsy.' Victoria and the others smiled at her. Sheila had brought the girls with her and was bringing them home to stay. Victoria was going to be in Scotland for a week or so anyway for the funeral. It was a real, heartfelt greeting as they all bounced in full of gossip. Painting on a smile, Patsy greeted them, although her mind was spinning, as she spied them all.

'Aunty Patsy,' Sharon and Penny shouted as they reached up and flung their arms around her. 'Look what Nana bought us!' Showing Patsy their new dresses and doing a twirl, they laughed.

Hugging them, Patsy looked up at Sheila puzzled.

'It's easier if they call Vicky Nana. And you seem to like it don't you Vicky lass?' Sheila grinned.

'As long as I don't look as old as Beryl. Every time I think of the word nana, Beryl pops into my head.' Victoria laughed and kissed Patsy on the cheek. 'Get the coffee out Patsy and pour some lemonade for the girls. You're not much of a hostess are you? Just as well I stopped and picked up some shopping on the way.' Victoria picked up her carrier bags and walked past her.

They all busied themselves in the kitchen and Patsy put the television on in Beryl's bedroom so the girls could watch cartoons. As they sat around the lounge with their coffees, Sheila gave them a blow by blow account of her sex life during the week, which made them all laugh and squirm at the very idea of it.

'How did your visit with the social worker and Jimmy go?' Patsy asked, directing her question at Natasha.

Elated and excited, Natasha filled her in on all of the details and how well Jimmy was looking. He'd put on weight and the main thing was, he hadn't forgotten her. She was so relieved about that, it almost brought tears to her eyes. 'They said I could have another supervised visit in two weeks Patsy. Isn't that great! And little Nicky comes home next week. It will be amazing to actually hold him in my arms properly, without all those nurses watching.' Natasha couldn't help gushing, even though Victoria gave her a knowing look and a shake of her head to stop. After all, this was Patsy's husband's baby Natasha was talking about. Even now, Victoria felt it must cut deep.

Realising her mistake, Natasha stopped. 'Sorry Patsy, I didn't mean to go on…'

Patsy sucked in a huge breath. 'That's fine Natasha. It seems little Nicky has nine lives. He survives everything, doesn't he? It's a shame his father wasn't the same.'

'What do you mean?' asked Victoria. 'That's a strange thing to say.'

Patsy blew her cigarette smoke into the air and crossed her legs, while giving Natasha a stern look. 'Why didn't you tell anyone that you had nearly miscarried little Nicky the night of Nick's murder?'

Natasha's head shot up and she glared at Patsy. 'What makes you say that?' Blushing to the roots of her blonde hair, Natasha avoided Sheila's and Victoria's eyes.

Feigning innocence, sarcastic laughter erupted from Patsy. 'Am I wrong Natasha? I'm sorry, maybe Larry the lawyer who was defending you while at the police station the day Nick was shot has made a mistake.'

Natasha's jaw dropped. 'What did he tell you Patsy? Everyone knows you've been screwing him; is that how you pay your legal bills?' Natasha's nasty retort shocked both Victoria and Sheila.

'He told me enough. By the way, when the police gave me

Nick's things back they gave me this.' Patsy took out a small ring box and threw it towards Natasha. 'It seems he bought that on the day he died, so it definitely wasn't for me. He'd bought it for you Natasha.' Taking a long drag on her cigarette and blowing out the smoke, Patsy watched Natasha nervously open the box. It was an emerald ring.

Victoria and Sheila glanced at each other then looked on, puzzled. They both knew that Patsy had something on her chest she needed to get off, but they couldn't understand this attack on Natasha.

'Tell us about your miscarriage that night Natasha. It must have been an awful time for you,' Patsy drawled, never moving her eyes away from Natasha.

Natasha looked at the ring and tried it on. Tears ran down her face. 'What are you getting at Patsy? What do you want to know?'

'Ladies, what is all of this about?' interrupted Victoria. 'Patsy, what is your problem? Nick bought a ring for Natasha, so what of it?'

'I want to know the truth. Come on Natasha, tell us what happened. We're all friends here.'

'I don't know what you mean.' Natasha shook her head emphatically. 'I just had a little spotting, but everything was fine.'

'Was that before or after you left the police station and went to the hospital with Larry?' Sarcasm dripped from Patsy's mouth. The others sat there in stunned silence.

'You nearly lost the baby lassie, why on earth didn't you tell us?' Sheila's concern touched Patsy, but she wasn't giving up.

Taking out her mobile, Patsy pressed play on the recording. They all sat in silence listening to it.

'No! You fucking bitch, you were recording it! How could you?' Tears rolled down Natasha's cheeks and her face was flushed with anger. 'That Larry will say anything to get into your knickers. He's lying.'

'What about Beryl? Is she lying too?' Patsy kept her voice low and steady, while watching Natasha squirm.

'Natasha love, tell us what Beryl meant. She saw you. When did she see you?' Shocked at the recording, Victoria pressed Natasha further, but almost in a motherly tone. Comforting even. Then Victoria turned towards Patsy. 'Why did you record it? What are you trying to prove?'

'It's that fucking bitch, she hates me and always has. She was going to take Nick away from me. I saw them, hugging each other outside the community centre that night!' Natasha shouted.

'Stop it!' Victoria stood up and intervened. 'I don't know what all of this is about, but I suggest we stop messing about. Patsy, whatever it is you have to say, say it.'

'I don't need to Victoria, Natasha has already said it. She's right, she did see me and Nick hug. But I'd accepted my fate. He was leaving me for a younger woman who was having his baby. It was best to part as friends and so we hugged. But you saw it Natasha, didn't you? How did you see it? Tell us all; it's time you got it off your conscience.'

'You mean he wasn't coming back to you and dumping me?' Wide eyed, Natasha looked up. Her red, blotchy, tear-stained face looked around the room at the three of them.

Sheila glared at Natasha. 'I think it's time you spilled your guts lassie, because if what I am thinking is right, you're facing a long sentence. Now wipe your snotty nose and tell us how you saw them. And I mean it, the fucking lot or I'll wring your fucking neck.'

Wiping her face, Natasha reached for Patsy's cigarettes and lit one. 'I was stressed and upset... you've got to believe me!' she begged, but none of them said a word. Silence hung in the air and

Natasha knew she had no option but to tell the truth. Her hands trembled as she brought the cigarette to her lips. 'I was at the police station, and Nick had come and gone. Larry said they could keep me for twenty-four hours. I was distraught; they had taken Jimmy away.' A small hiccup left her mouth as she started to sob, but none of them moved to comfort her.

'I was allowed a toilet break during questioning. My only thought was to get to Nicky. I had to see him, I knew he would help me. I wasn't thinking straight.' Knowing she was beaten she carried on. 'Once in the toilet I took out my earring and scratched it against my leg. Once the blood appeared, I let the few drops fall on to my knickers, then I cried out.'

Stunned, they all turned to each other. They couldn't believe what they were hearing.

'You are a cunning bitch, aren't you Natasha?' Patsy grinned. 'Go on, you've started and now finish your story. Victoria has given you a home, the least you can do is be honest with her.'

Victoria's sat stony-faced. Gone was the pleasant smiling woman. Emotionless, she sat there listening.

Taking a drag on her cigarette between wobbly fingers, Natasha spied them all and carried on. 'I was desperate to see Nick. They were blaming me for Steve's murder.' Looking towards Sheila, she cast her eyes down. 'Seeing the blood, they stopped the investigation and said I had to go to hospital. I wasn't under arrest, so Larry said he would vouch for me and take me there. He had to sign papers and I pretended to have stomach cramps. I thought, if I could just get to Nick, we could run away somewhere. When I got to the hospital, they took me for a scan, but seeing my distraught state the nurses said they would keep me in overnight. They told Larry to leave and come back in the morning, because the tablets they were giving me meant I would be asleep all night. But I didn't swallow the pills. I took them out of my mouth and as

soon as the nurse left I got dressed again. There was no one
around when I looked out of the room door and so I walked down
the corridor. There were a lot of drunks in the reception area and
a Father Christmas outfit on the back of a chair and so I picked it
up and put it on and got in a taxi.

'When I got to Thistle Park, I saw you' – she pointed accus-
ingly at Patsy – 'hugging Nick. His arms were around you and he
was kissing your cheek! The bastard.' Letting out a huge sigh and
stubbing the end of her cigarette out, Natasha felt braver and
carried on. 'I went to Beryl's flat; I was going to call Nick from
there and ask him to come and meet me. She always had her
spare key on a bit of string through the letter box and so I let
myself in. I heard a noise and realised Beryl was coming in and so
I ran into the bedroom – Nick's room. I banged my leg on the
wardrobe door and when I opened it I saw a bag full of money.
There was also a gun. I decided to shoot you Patsy; I was going to
get rid of you once and for all,' she spat.

Victoria sucked in a breath and held it for a while. Patsy
rubbed her knee and gave her a knowing look, while prompting
Natasha to carry on.

'I took the gun and some money, then I ran as fast as I could
to the community centre, but Nick was outside on his own. Fire-
works were going off. I was angry and not thinking straight, my
head was all over the place. When I stood in front of him, I could
see that he was drunk and he didn't seem pleased to see me. He'd
been going to leave me rotting in that police station while he
played happy families with you!' She sobbed and pointed her
finger at Patsy. 'He'd said he loved me, but he'd been caught out
holding you in his arms. I raised the gun and I'd hardly pressed
the trigger and it went off. I was just going to threaten him,
frighten him maybe... I don't know. Seeing he was still alive, I got
scared. He would know it was me, and he would send me to

prison. He would hate me forever. The only thing I could think of was to finish the job and no one would ever know. So I shot him again. I went back to the hospital and got back into bed without being seen and took the sleeping pills.'

A low scream erupted from Victoria, building its way up to a high pitch as she flung herself at Natasha. Like a wild cat, she pulled at her hair and slapped and punched her. 'My baby, you killed my fucking baby you bitch,' Victoria screamed. Natasha was no match for her outburst and suffered blow after blow.

Sheila stood up and pulled Victoria away. 'Enough Vicky lassie, enough. Let's just call the police and put that scheming bitch away. What is it with her family and guns?'

Rubbing the blood from her nose and on her hands on to her jeans, whilst kneeling on the floor, Natasha looked up at them all. 'You can't put me in prison, I know too much about you all. I know who Nick really was. I know where you buried those guys with James. I can put you all in prison! You're no better than me, you're killers too!'

Agitated at her outburst, Sheila went to the bedroom to see if the girls were okay. She didn't want them seeing this.

Breathless, Victoria sat there and nursed the scratches on her face from Natasha. 'So what do we do now?'

Ignoring her threats, Patsy nodded. 'You're right, Natasha, you could put us all behind bars. I say, nothing is said. We know the truth now. You leave and we never want to hear from you again. We all have something to fear, so we won't say anything as long as you don't.'

Victoria looked at Patsy, shocked. 'No way is she getting away with murdering my baby. Everyone around here thinks Beryl killed Nick. She saw you leaving the flat, she possibly even looked out over the balcony to see you scurrying off like a thief in the night, but she kept quiet for her great-grandchild's sake. No way would she put the mother of her great-grandchild in prison. You heartless, scheming bitch. You were jealous and you killed my son. I have had you in my home, and you must have been laughing your fucking socks off at me.' Victoria broke down in tears.

Sheila shut the bedroom door, once she saw the girls were engrossed in their cartoons and walked back into the lounge. 'Eye for an eye lassie. You took Victoria's baby and she has guardianship over little Nicky. She has a son back now. Personally I think you and Nick deserved each other. You're both rotten to the core.'

Patsy's mobile buzzed. Looking at it, she put her mobile down, satisfied. All it had said was, 'Done.'

'I think emotions are running high. Natasha is right, it's a double-edged sword. She has us over a barrel and would sail us down the river to save her own skin.' Picking up her car keys, Patsy walked over to Natasha. 'Take my car and take your scrawny murdering arse out of here and leave. I never want to see you again!'

'What about my baby? What about Jimmy?' Natasha asked in disbelief.

'Just go Natasha and if I ever hear a word about this I'll sing like a fucking bird to the police and put a bullet in your head.'

Wide eyed and knowing it wasn't an idle threat, Natasha snatched the keys out of Patsy's hand and headed for the door, slamming it behind her. Victoria sat there trembling in Sheila's arms. 'I can't believe you're just going to let her go.'

'Letting her go? Whatever makes you think that?' She laughed. Reaching in her hand bag she took out a bottle of brandy. 'Here you go ladies, I think we could all do with one of these.'

Stunned, Sheila and Victoria watched her going about her

business without a care in the world. They couldn't believe she could be so heartless after what they had heard.

Natasha ran down the balcony as fast as she could before they changed their minds. She scanned the forecourt to see if they had telephoned the police already. She was panicking and afraid as she opened Patsy s car and got in. Putting the key into the ignition, and turning the key, the car burst into flames and glass shattered everywhere. Everyone ran out to see the burning car in the forecourt, but the flames were too high and fierce to be able to see clearly.

'Everyone get back in. The fire engines are on their way,' Fin shouted from over the balcony. 'Go on, get in, it's going to explode again,' he warned. People ran for their lives and hid indoors. The heat from the burning car was intense and no one could get near it.

Victoria and Sheila jumped up at hearing the explosion and ran outside onto the balcony, watching the inferno below them. Then Patsy joined them, holding their brandy glasses. 'Do you really think I was going to let her leave with all of that information on us and murder on her hands? Have a drink ladies.' She smiled.

Astounded, Victoria and Sheila paled and stared wide eyed at her. 'You did this?' they said in unison.

Standing at the iron rail at the end of the balcony, Patsy raised a glass towards the other tower block of flats at James, who was standing there opposite her, smoking a cigarette and leaning on the iron balcony railing, watching the firemen extinguish the flames, leaving the charred, steaming remains of Patsy's car.

Victoria looked down at the smoky devastation. 'I hope she

burns in hell. But why your car?'

'Oh that's simple. It gives us all an alibi. Larry knows I've been having threats made against me and has already informed the police. No doubt they will be here soon. That is my car and the bomb was obviously meant for me. The fact that Natasha was using it to go to the shops is a horrible accident.

'I knew she'd killed Nick the night Larry presumed I knew she had been let out of the police station. And then I heard Beryl defending her but letting her know with her last dying breath that she'd seen her. She held her tongue, and no way would she let her Nick's boy grow up without a mother. She had nothing to lose with her dying confession; all that stress and soul searching must have killed her. But it protected everyone. Beryl was a good woman who only wanted the best for her family. Hopefully now she will know that Nick has been avenged and his son will be looked after by you Victoria.' Patsy grinned. The sombre silence that followed was interrupted by a well-dressed woman walking towards them.

The woman was tall, blonde and wearing a long red camel coat and was dusting it down with her handkerchief. The French accent startled them all. '*Mon Dieu*, I have been here five minutes and I'm covered in smoke and glass.' She looked very out of place in Thistle Park. Looking at the three of them through the black smoke that was rising from the devastation, she waved her hand to clear it. 'I'm looking for Patsy Diamond. Someone said she would be here?'

'I'm Patsy Diamond. Why?' asked Patsy, coughing.

'Nice to meet you Patsy. I am your business partner and I have come back to England to claim what is mine.' She reached out her hand to shake Patsy's. A red, lipsticked smile appeared on the woman's face. 'That is right Patsy, I have risen from the dead. For I am Karen Duret.'

ACKNOWLEDGMENTS

Thank you to Boldwood Books and all of the brilliant team and of course my editor, my wing woman, Emily Ruston.

MORE FROM GILLIAN GODDEN

We hope you enjoyed reading *Rough Diamonds*. If you did, please leave a review.

If you'd like to gift a copy, this book is also available as an ebook, digital audio download and audiobook CD.

Sign up to Gillian Godden's mailing list for news, competitions and updates on future books.

http://bit.ly/GillianGoddenNewsletter

Gold Digger, the first in the series, is available now.

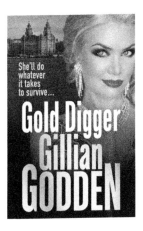

ABOUT THE AUTHOR

Gillian Godden is a Northern-born medical secretary for NHS England. She spent thirty years of her life in the East End of London, hearing stories about the local striptease pubs. Now in Yorkshire, she is an avid reader who lives with her dog, Susie.

Follow Gillian on social media:

 facebook.com/gilliangoddenauthor
twitter.com/GGodden

PEAKY READERS

GANG LOYALTIES. DARK SECRETS.
BLOODY REVENGE.

A READER COMMUNITY FOR
GANGLAND CRIME THRILLER FANS!

DISCOVER PAGE-TURNING NOVELS
FROM YOUR FAVOURITE AUTHORS
AND MEET NEW FRIENDS.

JOIN OUR BOOK CLUB
FACEBOOK GROUP

BIT.LY/PEAKYREADERSFB

SIGN UP TO OUR
NEWSLETTER

BIT.LY/PEAKYREADERSNEWS

Boldwood

Boldwood Books is an award-winning fiction publishing company seeking out the best stories from around the world.

Find out more at www.boldwoodbooks.com

Join our reader community for brilliant books, competitions and offers!

Follow us
@BoldwoodBooks
@BookandTonic

Sign up to our weekly
deals newsletter

https://bit.ly/BoldwoodBNewsletter

Printed in Great Britain
by Amazon

37325357R00185